COLD LIGHT OF DAY

PAUL CAVE

2QT Limited (Publishing)

Third Edition Published 2011
2QT Limited (Publishing)
Burton In Kendal
Cumbria LA6 1NJ
www.2qt.co.uk

Previous edition published
ISBN 978-1-906710-75-0 by Pen Press (2009)

Cover design Hilary Pitt
Images sourced by iStockphoto.com

Printed in Great Britain

A CIP catalogue record for this book is available
from the British Library
ISBN 978-1-908098-49-8

This book is dedicated to my son, Ellis; a brilliant burst of sunshine, which never fails to warm my heart.

Chapter One

The night was ablaze with a dizzying array of neon lights, the blinding white-halogen of headlights, and the bright faces of spirited youngsters.

Josh Sawyer walked among the many night-time revellers with his head bowed and his hands firmly stuffed into his pockets. As he waded through this sea of faces, he pondered over the events, now almost three years ago, which had led him to this moment. He remembered how the day had ended in almost fatal circumstances. What should have been the best day of his life had finished with him fighting for his very survival, bloodied and broken on a surgeon's operating table.

A flash of strobe light exploded beside him. The dazzling whiteness pulsed with the same eagerness as that of a child's heart on Christmas Day. Josh turned towards the pulse and found a window full of illicit promises. Hundreds of pictures or posters pledged that the girls inside were the very best to be found in Chicago. Lots of presents, already unwrapped, offering more mystery and excitement than any unknown gift could.

"We've got everything you're looking for," a voice from a doorway told him.

Josh turned his head towards the speaker. "I'm not looking."

"Sure you are. Everybody's looking for something," the doorman of the strip joint told him.

Josh nodded, "Yeah, I guess that's true. But what I'm looking for isn't inside."

"Maybe not, but who knows, perhaps it'll help you to relax and discover what it is you are looking for?"

Josh turned back to the window and at its pleasures on offer. For a second he was tempted, but then the strobe flashed again in a pulse of pure white light, which was both mesmerising and rhythmic. He squinted and the silent beat drew him in. His eyes became totally fixed as the flashing light hypnotised him. And, standing outside this den of iniquity, he felt himself slip back in time to when he was twenty-one and the world was at his feet.

***

Breakneck Speed. That's what his father had once said. An apt statement, considering Josh Sawyer had been born to run. By the age of just twelve months, Josh had bypassed crawling and toddling, and moved directly to running. He'd found his feet, suddenly, with no prior indication of ability, whilst chasing the family pet – a smelly old terrier named Scratch – in hot pursuit of his recently stolen half-eaten biscuit.

Josh grew up with what seemed like the wind constantly in his sails. He ran everywhere: to school, between lessons – much to his peers' distress, back home from school, around the house – constantly – now able to outrun Scratch with considerable ease. High school came hurtling towards Josh with alarming speed. The **collegiate** circuit had proven the perfect training ground, offering race after race, giving him every opportunity to reach out and embrace his future.

By the time he was twenty-one, he had successfully climbed the ranks to compete in the nation's Olympic qualifiers. He did well too, coming 2nd and making the team as a member of the 400 meters relay squad.

Only providence had other ideas for him.

Just hours after his selection he had been involved in an automobile accident. A drunk driver had crossed the central lane and hit Josh head-on.

He'd almost died in the crash. Emergency surgery had been

required to remove a blood clot from his brain. Then a month of intensive care, recovering from the operation and a shattered tibia had put paid to Josh's Olympic dream.

Even worse had followed for the Sawyer family. His mother had been running her own race – but one that held no winner. Time and illness had been in pursuit of her, a hereditary condition that no female sibling on her side had ever outrun. Breast cancer had taken his mother with callous disregard.

During the long time of Josh's convalescence, his father had sold the family home and moved them into a more practical bungalow. In addition, with the spare money, he had been able to enrol his son onto a Sports Science degree program, in the hope that the possibility of studying would help in his son's recovery from both grief and injury.

***

Josh shook his head to break the hypnotic spell of the strobe light. He turned to the doorman and said, "Maybe another night."

The man's face broke into a colourful smile. "You come back anytime, pal. There are always pleasures to be had day or night. You got the dough, we've got the hoe."

Josh continued along these crowded Chicago streets and headed back towards campus. As he mixed with this bustling nightlife, he walked with gracefulness elegance, although he suffered an almost unnoticeable limp to his left leg. Deep in thought, he was almost on top of her. She appeared from out of the shadows and collided against his shoulder.

"Sorry," she said immediately.

"Sorry," he replied automatically.

He raised his head to see who'd just dragged him out of his thoughts. Standing directly in front of him, hands held high in a show of peace, was a smiling, pretty girl.

"Sorry," she repeated.

"That's okay, my fault," Josh replied.

The girl lowered her arms. "You looked a million miles away," she said in a European accent.

"I was," Josh told her. "Different time, different place," he added. Her strange accent caused him to wonder where she was from, and his face bent itself into a look of puzzlement.

For some reason this made her smile stretch even further across her perfectly formed teeth. For a moment they stood face-to-face as the girl openly studied his features. She gave up the grin but her eyes remained fixed on his face.

He became uncomfortable under the girl's apparent scrutiny, and he surprised himself when he heard his voice ask, "Would you like to get a drink?" With a hopeful raise of his eyebrows, he quickly added, "Maybe?"

Not usually being so direct, he stood, squirming, and felt completely inadequate while he waited for the inevitable refusal, and was very shocked when she answered, "Yes, great! Where?" He broke into a grin of his own which beat hers hands down.

"There's a bar just around this corner," he said. Without another word, he looked in the direction he hoped wasn't the end of the world with not a single bar within a million miles.

***

As they looked for the bar at the end of the world, Josh tried to understand exactly what had just transpired. He was neither an extrovert nor an introvert, just normal. Having bumped into a total stranger he would normally have behaved in a civil and courteous manner then swapped apologies and moved on. Yet, after only being in this girl's presence for little more than a few seconds, he was overcome with a sensation of overwhelming connection, and under no circumstances must he let this girl disappear and be swallowed by the shadows from which she'd come.

Not the romantic type, he did not believe in love at first sight but did understand spontaneous attraction. He could not explain the immediate attraction he felt for this girl, but somehow knew it was mutual. **She was** beautiful, **undoubtedly,** and **he** felt her appeal was on an instinctive, almost animalistic level.

She was tall and slim, almost skinny, but graceful, not gangly. She walked with a gazelle-like elegance, although he sensed that she possessed a hidden catlike strength and was able to pounce at any time. Her hair was long and almost pitch-black. She was pretty, had large oval brown eyes with high arched eyebrows and a finely chiselled nose, which pointed up slightly towards the end. She had the fullest and most sensuous deep red lips, of a kind that Josh had only seen in glossy women's magazines, although he did not detect the slightest hint of lipstick. Hers were natural blood-red lips, which did not close entirely to reveal a shock of white enamel. She had a dusky, almost Mediterranean complexion and flawless skin.

Tonight, she wore a simple dark dress, which fitted her body like silk. It moulded itself around her pert breasts, pulled in around her slim waist, and then flowed out again over her hips. The dress stopped midway over her thighs to reveal her long, graceful legs. She wore simple black-wedged shoes on her feet, which accentuated her slim ankles.

***

They entered the bar and were met by loud music playing from a hidden jukebox. The wail and woe of guitars and keyboards seemed to convey perfectly the singer's apparent broken heart. Josh led the girl over to the bar and asked over the anguish of music, "What would you like to drink?"

She smiled. "A neat Jack Daniel's please, with ice."

Suitably impressed by her choice of drink, he turned to the bar and waited to get the bartender's attention. He caught the guy's eye and ordered two.

While she waited for Josh to receive their drinks, the girl scanned the room, taking in her environment. There were three or four different groups of people standing drinking, and as many sitting in secluded stalls, deep in intoxicated and animated private conversation. She spotted an empty stall, tapped Josh on the arm to get his attention and then pointed at the booth. He nodded, collected their drinks and followed her.

In one fluid motion she took a Jack Daniel's from his hand and slid between seat and table. Josh not so gracefully plopped himself across the seat opposite her. He took a sip of his drink, and then unconsciously grimaced at its sickly-sweet taste.

She noticed his discomfort. "Nice isn't it?" she asked playfully.

"Yeah, but a little too strong," he said sheepishly, embarrassed by his lack of drinking prowess.

They sat in silence for a moment before finally she asked him, "What's your name?" With a tilt of her head, she finished her drink in an easy gulp.

"Josh…Josh Sawyer," he answered, impressed by her drinking panache. He put his drink to one side, in the hope she wouldn't notice. "What's yours? Name, I mean," he asked.

Again the grin appeared as she tilted her head slightly. She leaned over the table, bringing herself closer to him. "Anna Privalova," she whispered surreptitiously. Then, she casually grabbed his drink, sat back, and swallowed it in a single gulp. She looked into his eyes and laughed openly at his awe-inspired silence.

Now laughing too, Josh extended his hand across the table. "Pleased to meet you, Anna Privalova," he said.

"Pleased to meet you, Josh Sawyer," she responded, taking his hand.

They laughed again. And with their hands clasped together a moment of charged electricity passed between them. Josh climbed to his feet, ready to take a step towards the bar. She quickly stood and, with her hands spread out, she stopped him short. "My round," she acknowledged.

"Okay," he replied, retaking his seat. He looked at her outstretched hands. They were the kind of hands that would have looked perfect as they brushed over piano keys, tapping out the finer works of Bach or Beethoven – or, equally, wrapped around his cock. Christ! Where did that come **from**.

As if she'd read his mind, she quickly closed her hands and dropped them to her side. Then, without further comment, she turned and headed for the bar.

She returned a few moments later with another Jack Daniel's in one hand and a glass of beer in the other. The beer was placed in front of Josh, its frothy head slipping slowly down the side of the glass like a small crest of migrating lava.

"Figured you'd like that instead," she said.

"Thanks," he said, relieved.

He picked up the chilled glass, took a long mouthful, sighed with pleasure, and then placed the drink back down. She put her glass beside his and moved over to his side, forcing him to shuffle across. She slid in beside him. A new song started up on the jukebox. This one was slightly louder and, with its faster beat, it drowned out most of the chatter of conversation. She turned to face him and placed her hand on his leg. "I like you, Josh Sawyer."

Unsure of how to react to her directness, he blurted, "Me too," then checked himself and continued, "I mean, I like YOU too."

"Good," she said in simple response.

Raising her drink with her free hand, she emptied the glass, as she lowered it, the ice rattled to the bottom. With two graceful fingers, she reached into the glass and withdrew one of the ice cubes. The ice rose to her mouth, catching the light overhead in a kaleidoscope of colours. She slowly caressed her bottom lip, leaving a glistening wet trail, which now made her lip look even more engorged.

Josh watched as her fingers slid slowly across her full lip. He noticed that although her nails were cut short, she had an unnaturally long nail bed, which gave her fingertips an elongated look. Mesmerized, he watched as her lips parted to reveal her perfectly formed white teeth. Her mouth opened and the near-melted cube was placed gracefully onto her tongue. She closed her mouth and began to suck on the cube. Reducing it to a sliver of cool ice. However, before the ice melted completely, she bit down, crunching it between her teeth.

The sound of breaking ice snapped Josh out of his trancelike state, back to awareness. He looked into Anna's eyes and thought then that she was probably the most attractive girl he had ever seen. Surprisingly self-conscious, he reached for his beer and only just managed to guide it to his mouth. Now aware of how close her hand was resting near his not so dormant member, he tried to cool the situation by asking, "What do you do for a living?"

Her hand moved away from his leg. Instead, she placed it onto her empty glass. "I'm in the professional business," she replied, and looked directly at him, questioningly.

Not exactly sure if she meant professional as in – *prostitute!* – he muttered a weak, "Oh… Right…"

This caused Anna to burst into fits of laughter, which made him look down at his feet, completely at her mercy.

"I know what you think and NO I'm not!" she said, after she'd regained her composure.

He let out a more than obvious sigh, then came back with, "If you were… you know… one of them, that'd be okay," then added, "I guess… "

"I work for a publishing company, freelance, work from home," she said, which was the truth.

"Really?" he replied, impressed.

"Really!" she mimicked.

This time they both laughed.

She dropped her hand to her side but did not replace it onto his thigh, which made Josh feel surprisingly disappointed.

***

Two hours and a lot more *Jack Daniels* and beer later, Josh could not believe he had only known this girl for a little over two hours. Throughout the evening they had covered more topics than he could remember, but Anna had still given little of herself away. She was as mysterious and alluring as any woman he had ever met. She had talked about her work as an editor for a prestigious New York publishing company, and described how she hoped to write her own book one day, but had said little of her past, and had only once briefly mentioned her homeland, Russia.

In response, he had talked about his disappointment with regard to his untimely accident, how he'd then subsequently missed the Olympics and how, in effect, he was now studying for a degree in Sports Science at college.

Late into the night they talked in an easy and relaxed manner, more suited to long-time lovers.

***

Josh felt the effects of his fourth beer on both his head and bladder. He excused himself, squeezed past Anna, and then headed off in search of a washroom. His search took him nearly full circle around the bar before he spotted the familiar signs of *male* and *female* printed on a single door. He entered and was met by a choice of two other doorways: one male, one female. Not being the voyeuristic type, he picked the one with *male* written above. He entered and was immediately assaulted by the two smells that were found in almost every male public toilet throughout the world: stale urine and strong, eye-watering disinfectant.

The room consisted of three urinals, one graffiti-scarred stall and a chipped washbasin. Just above the bowl, there was a misshapen mirror, made from a sheet of metal, which caught the room's reflection in a warped confusion of images.

Josh crossed the room, during which time his reflection was pulled and stretched into macabre shapes, eventually turning him into a bizarre caricature as he stepped up to one of the urinals. He unbuttoned himself then began a steady stream that seemed to go on forever. After he had eventually finished, he shook and buttoned himself back up. He stepped away from the urinal, and caught his strange reflection in the small mirror as he did so. As he drew near, the mirror reshaped his features until they became normal – as if revealing the solution to an elaborate Chinese puzzle.

He had thick, unkempt hair, which had a hint of premature grey throughout, and his salt and pepper locks fell in large curly waves, to his shoulders. His face looked almost too thin, an effect caused by high prominent cheekbones. A straight nose ran down the centre of his face and led to a mouth that comprised of full, almost feminine lips. He was told his best features were his deep blue eyes, intense and always questioning, but which tonight had a slightly glazed and bloodshot look. At six foot, he stood taller than his new friend by only an inch or two. He was square shouldered, lithe and muscular. He wore loose jeans, a faded sports T-shirt and a pair of tatty sneakers.

Using the heels of his hands, he massaged his eyes in an attempt to rub away the bloodshot. He then quickly washed his hands and, after failing to find either a towel or hand drier, he unconsciously wiped them on the back of his jeans. He re-entered the bar area and turned to look in the direction he expected Anna to be sitting, nursing one of her uncountable *Jack Daniel's*.

She'd gone!

Unable to locate her, panic threatened to well up in his chest. Then he spotted her standing by the door, which led onto the main street. She gave him a half-wave and beckoned him over.

"What's up?" he asked worriedly.

"Nothing," she replied, slightly surprised by his concern.

"I thought you were about to leave without me," he said anxiously.

"No chance," she told him. She opened the door and slipped outside gracefully.

Josh followed.

"I thought it was time we *really* got to know each other," she said as she moved up close to gently take his hand.

"You're too much," he told her, relieved and at the same time excited.

"I only live a couple of blocks from here," she explained.

Needing no second invitation, Josh moved away from the bar and was led towards the unknown.

***

The streets were surprisingly empty and eerily quiet for this time of night. Only shadows accompanied them; long spectres of darkness, which reached out from both sides of the street with ghostly arms. Josh and Anna walked with their hands held together and in silence. After a few minutes, Anna came to an abrupt halt, released his hand and then turned to face a near-invisible doorway. The door was sandwiched between an old liquor store and an abandoned convenience market.

Metal shutters that were decorated with the proclamations of bravery or undying love, or simple, raw profanity, hid the contents of the store from the night. The only visible feature on the door before them was a small digital number pad, which glowed dimmest green – almost unnoticeable. The abandoned convenience market offered nothing but the faint stench of alcohol, as if a single collective breath of long gone winos still lingered there.

In a flurry of fingers, Anna quickly punched in a combination of numbers. She was rewarded with a single sharp *click*. The door pushed inward and she disappeared over the threshold and into darkness. Josh waited outside. Expecting an invite. He squinted through the opening in an attempt to penetrate the darkness that lay beyond. Now alone, he felt surprisingly vulnerable. "Anna?" he called. The only answer he got was one of silence. He moved closer to the dark entrance and, with more conviction, he called, "Anna!"

Unexpectedly, hands grabbed at his T-shirt and he was roughly dragged inside. There, invisible, moist lips met him as they pressed against his in a frenzy of passion. His mouth opened, which allowed her to probe deeper with her tongue. The flavour of her sweet breath passed his lips and fixed itself to his eager taste buds. Holding her unseen face, he kissed her and simultaneously breathed in her natural perfume.

She ground her hips against his and felt his erection through the thinness of her dress. Still in darkness, she began to pull him up bare wooden stairs, and not once did she break away from his lips. They reached the top, where she drew away. "I want you," she breathed. Already fully aroused, he pulled her back into his arms and whispered, "I need you, now."

"Wait," she said, as she drew away for a second time. "Let's go inside."

He heard a number of almost inaudible *beeps* and sensed a second door open. With the flick of a switch he was confronted with a scantily furnished studio apartment. Before he had time to take in his surroundings, Anna pulled him inside the room, pushing him over to a king-sized bed.

She pushed him all the way to the edge of the bed, where he fell backwards onto soft, silky sheets.

A surge of fear unexpectedly burst into his mind then, forced into his consciousness by the realisation that he was in the company of a near-total stranger and caught in unfamiliar surroundings. Yet, as she climbed on top of him, all reason abandoned him, replaced instead by lustful need.

She pushed him further towards a wrought-iron headboard. There, she pinned him easily by the wrists. He raised his head to meet hers and, whilst gently biting her top lip, he kissed her full mouth. Her tongue sought his. They came together in a desperate kiss.

Josh pushed himself up on his hands, then raised them, allowing Anna to pull his T-shirt off over his head. She took in his lean and muscular body.

He ran his hand through her thick hair, caressed her face, traced the elegance of her neck and shoulders, and then continued downwards to finish on her firm breast, feeling her hardened nipple through flimsy fabric. She took his free hand

and placed it on her other breast. Her head dropped backward in a cascade of dark hair.

"You're so beautiful," he said, now taking her face between his hands. An elegant finger silenced his words. She removed it from his lips, replacing it by her open mouth. "Make love to me," she whispered in her husky Slavonic accent.

***

He gently pulled her into his arms, feeling her heart pound through her bosom. Affectionately, he began to stroke her damp hair, breathing in the aroma of spent sex.

Josh listened to her rhythmic breathing for a while, then he too closed his eyes, and after a short while he drifted into unconscious bliss. And there, he dreamt about a beautiful but mysterious stranger.

Chapter Two

Newton's Third Law of Motion: Every action has an equal and opposite reaction.

The Lear Jet rocketed its way through the darkened skies. Sucking in air, the two Honeywell TFE731-20 turbofan engines mixed compressed air with fuel, before igniting them both. Hot, burnt gases blew outward through blackened exhausts. The twin engines created thrust, which propelled the aerofoil over high-pressure air. And it was this process that produced sufficient lift to overcome the effects of both gravity and drag.

The aircraft cruised at 25,000 feet as it flew westward to escape the advancing sunrise. With its destination near, it began a slow, gradual descent.

A mixture of passengers filled the privately chartered aircraft. There were twenty in all, comprising of mostly businessmen and women. Sitting in spacious reclining seats, alone or in groups of two, most of the passengers were absorbed by the hypnotic hue of electronic laptops.

At the back of the plane sat a solitary figure. With a keen interest, he checked out his fellow passengers. He was dressed in faded jeans and a light blue cotton shirt, open at the neck to reveal hairless skin. Pointed cowboy boots adorned his feet, scuffed with worn-down heels, and the left one tapped up and down lightly as if the wearer sat listening to a catchy tune. Although he had a pale complexion, he would have been considered handsome, with intense green eyes, finely chiselled features and a mane of dark hair, which accentuated his ashen skin. He had a slim but athletic build and would have stood over six feet tall.

Eyes that were hungry with need came to rest on the form of an attractive businesswoman. She was curled up in her chair and deeply asleep. He smiled, revealing his near-perfect teeth. He stood and walked over to the woman.

One of his emaciated hands rose to open a storage compartment directly above her. After rummaging around inside, silently, so as not to disturb her, he retrieved a leather satchel. He took the bag in one hand and then gently lowered his other hand – palm flat – an inch above her head. "It's time," he whispered. Then, slowly, he made his way back to his seat.

With a flutter of eyelids the woman began to awake. She glanced around, sleepily, searching for the event that had pulled her from her slumber. She found nothing but the usual subdued in-flight activity. A brief frown creased her brow. Then with a yawn, she began to shake away the cobwebs of sleep. Pressure mounted within her groin. She stood. The signs to the washroom directed her to the rear of the aircraft.

He watched as she came towards him. She looked down at him and, in a polite gesture, smiled. He locked eyes with hers and returned a smile, which contained neither warmth nor kindness. She stopped dead but continued to stare into his cold gaze. Her smile slipped, reshaped into a crooked grimace, and her eyes clouded over as if she'd fallen into a sudden trance. She unconsciously nodded, before she mechanically continued towards the washroom.

He waited until he'd heard the washroom door click shut and then, quickly scanning around, he casually stood. Leisurely, he headed to the rear of the plane. Although shut tight the washroom had been left in its disengaged position. He pushed the door open, took one last look backwards, checking his movements had not been noticed – they hadn't, then disappeared inside.

He entered the washroom to find her dazed and confused – the connection having broken temporarily, and she looked suddenly embarrassed by their shared presence in such an intimate location. She laughed nervously, and almost started to question what they were doing here, when he formed a fist and hit her solidly in the stomach. Air exploded from her lungs, and her initial look of bemusement turned to instant agony. She dropped to her knees.

Her attacker grinned maliciously, his canines elongating into sharpened fangs. The hand that had hit out now clutched a handful of the woman's hair. His other hand reached behind him, and the door to the cubicle shut with a gentle click.

The woman gasped for oxygen. Yet, before she could come to her senses, she was roughly pulled to her feet. A burst of adrenaline cleared her mind momentarily, and she bucked and swayed in an attempt to break free. The guy just laughed at her feeble attempts. His mouth opened impossibly wide, his teeth, top and bottom, now two rows of needle-like fangs, dripping with saliva.

Terror drove the woman's fear away. She opened her mouth, a scream ready to burst free. However, a hand clamped itself over her face, and she was rendered silent; her eyes bulging at the sight of what was happening before her.

The guys face appeared to be melting away, his nose and cheek bones cracking and popping as they were seemingly absorbed into the flesh, before his features reformed into something hideous and from the stuff of nightmares. Eyes, red and merciless, bore into the woman.

A sudden gout of liquid pooled onto the floor as her bladder opened. The guy shuffled back slightly, the confined space barely allowing him to. He spun her around effortlessly then. Pushing her face-first against the wall. She whimpered and that caused the vile face behind her to crack open into a horrific smile.

He did unspeakable things to her then, things that no sane being would do, could do, taking both her humanity and spirit.

Finished now, he looked down at her violated form and his vile physiognomy split into a grotesque grin. His needle-like teeth began to retract inside swollen gums, and quickly they began to take on a more humanlike shape. His eyes closed as his face started its transformation back to normal form. Within moments he stood human again. Beads of perspiration dripped from his handsome face. He shook his head and droplets of foul sweat flew from his damp hair.

He moved over to a small washbasin, meticulously washing his hands and face. Satisfied with his cleanliness he then brushed his hair with elongated fingers. He stepped away from the basin and his eyes dropped down to his flaccid penis, bloodied and raw. He grimaced. A small hand-towel hung from a polished bar. He used it to clean himself then replaced his manhood into his jeans and buttoned himself up.

"Thank you, bug," he said.

He left the woman behind, broken and torn, and returned to his seat. Through the small porthole, he saw the dark canvas of night. He smiled, relaxing into his seat, ready to enjoy the remainder of the flight. After a few minutes of silent contemplation, he reached over to retrieve the old satchel. Opening it, he took out a single sheet of folded paper. He delicately unfolded the paper as if it were some long-cherished love letter. Printed on the otherwise blank sheet were a single name and address. He read the name and smiled.

"Soon, bitch. Soon…" he whispered.

Chapter Three

Josh awoke to the sound of padding feet on bare wood. He rubbed his eyes to clear away the fog of sleep, now focusing on a dark shape that wandered around the room. He sat up and felt across the empty bed. Feeling cool sheets at his side, he wondered how long he'd been asleep. "Anna?" he called to the shape. No response came. He searched the room, looking for a clock, but found none. "Anna, what time is it?" he asked.

"Almost dawn!" was the abrupt answer he received from deep shadows.

He sensed a change in her voice and, slightly worried, he stood naked and took a few anxious steps towards her. The shadows formed into substance as Anna stepped out of the darkness. Dressed in simple dark woollen pants and jumper, she appeared suddenly, like a dark apparition. She looked at him, her eyes filled with annoyance, then pushed past and bent down to scoop up his discarded clothes. With anger and irritation clear, she held them out to him. He took his clothes and hopefully asked, "Are we going somewhere?"

"No, Josh, we're not going anywhere," she retorted heatedly. "But you're leaving, NOW!"

Confused by her annoyance, he moved closer. "What happened? What have I done?"

"Just leave," she said, agitated. She moved over to the window and reached out towards a set of black drapes. The dark material parted and she looked out to witness the sky change from an impenetrable black to a dark purple. She turned and then snapped, "GET DRESSED!"

Shocked by her abruptness, he numbly started to pull on his clothes. He found himself one shoe short, so began to search. He looked around and under the bed but was still unable to find it. His search widened.

Becoming increasingly agitated, Anna joined him in his hunt. The shoe was hidden within her discarded evening dress. She picked it up. "Here!" she said, and threw the sneaker. The shoe sailed across the room, hit him square in the chest, then bounced off and landed on the floor.

Infuriated, Josh grabbed the shoe and angrily shouted, "FUCK YOU ANNA!" Barefooted, he turned and headed for the door. A vicelike grip pulled at his arm. He was spun around and his shoes slipped from his hands. Surprised by the movement, he almost fell over his feet. Amazed at her strength and speed, Josh stared at her face, dumbfounded.

She looked at him, her eyes ablaze with anger. "What?" she demanded.

Feeling her painful grip, Josh regained a measure of composure. "I said, FUCK YOU ANNA!" he repeated, but with less conviction.

She stared into his blue eyes. Hurt had replaced his anger. She released her grip, took a step back and then lowered her head, shamed by her unwarranted aggression. "Please leave," she asked in a saddened voice.

Josh felt his emotions for her return. He reached out to touch her cheek. Then with gentle fingers he lifted her head to find her eyes had filled with tears. "Hey, Anna, what is it?" he asked, all anger forgotten, now replaced with concern.

Two huge teardrops welled up before slipping down her face. One stopped at his hand while the other ran towards the corner of her mouth. He wiped her cheek then held her face in his hands and bent slightly. He kissed her gently, tasting the salty tear on her lips. Pulling away, he looked into her bottomless brown eyes, and there he found a deep sadness.

Josh drew her into his protective arms. "Hey, its okay. It'll be okay," he soothed. "Tell me, what's a matter. Maybe I can help?"

She released an immense sob. "Nobody can help."

He held her and waited for her tears to subside. "You can trust me, Anna. I want to help." He squeezed her hands slightly in gentle reassurance.

She stared at his hands then raised her head to look at his handsome and kind face, and almost spoke, but then quickly glanced away and through the gap between parted draperies.

"I don't want your help," she snapped.

He shook his head in defeat. "Okay, Anna, have it your way." He quickly slipped into his sneakers and then allowed himself one last look at her. "Shit, Anna, what the fuck?" he said. Totally confused now, he headed for the door. He stepped into the dark, paused for a brief moment in the hope she would call him back, but when she didn't he disappeared down into shadows.

Anna waited until she heard him leave. Then, with her head held low, she moved to the door and closed it. Her hands fell flat against the wooden frame. She placed her forehead against the cool surface. And, as more teardrops ran down her face, she whispered, "Oh – Josh, I'm so sorry."

***

Josh returned to his deep well of self-pity. Lost within a labyrinth of old buildings, he walked through near-deserted streets with his head bowed and his hands firmly stuffed into his pockets. He trailed aimlessly from street to street, his mind full of confused thoughts, pondering over the events of the night. As he walked these unknown streets and alleyways, a glimmer of first light began to slither upwards from the east, turning the oppressive purple sky to a lighter blue.

A sudden presence pushed at his back. He spun around and was confronted with an empty alleyway. His hands withdrew from his pockets. The night had bled all colours from his surroundings, leaving behind instead a monochrome strip of darkness that was both indistinguishable and hostile. Hard shadows jutted out towards him from every angle. Slowly, his eyes adjusted to the darkness. Midway between the entrance and exit, he found himself enclosed in a narrow passageway, which was comprised of dilapidated and uninhabited buildings. The alleyway was cluttered with piles of cardboard boxes, bins and other discarded refuse.

"Hello...?" he called into the gloom.

He tensed slightly as the only answer he received was one of silence. "Anybody there...?" Now, with a quickening heart, he realised he'd walked into a dangerous part of the neighbourhood. "Shit," he whispered under his breath. He stood perfectly still as he tried to listen for any sounds that might emit from the many hiding places. Silence. He turned slowly and began to walk towards what he hoped led to a populated street.

Fifty yards from the end, two other people entered the darkened alleyway. They headed in his direction. Initially, he breathed a sigh of relief, thankful for another person's presence. He relaxed a little and slowed his pace slightly. After about another twenty yards he began to make out their features.

They were white males. One was much taller than the other and he wore baggy street clothes, with a cap pulled down tight over his skull. Two black pebbles peered out from under the peak of his hat. He had a flat nose and an untidily shaven chin beard. His smaller companion wore similar clothes but had long, greasy blond hair and a slightly gaunt countenance.

Both looked mean as hell.

Anxieties returning, Josh's instincts told him that these two were trouble. His pace slowed almost to a stop and, frantically, he searched the gloom for a potential weapon. In a sick twist of fates, not a single bottle or plank of wood revealed itself. He contemplated turning and running, in the hope that he'd be able to outrun them. He instantly dismissed the idea though, once he'd concluded that there were too many hidden obstacles to navigate. Would his bad leg allow his escape anyway?

They were almost on top of him when the guy with blond hair

asked, "Hey, Buddy, got the time?"

For some reason this made his companion snigger, his face contorting into an even uglier appearance.

Josh eyed the bigger of the two, and in his most forceful voice he said, "NO."

"Shit, the dude ain't got any watch," Blond-Hair chortled.

"Maybe the motherfucker reads the stars," Chin-Beard grunted.

"Fucker will be seeing stars if he doesn't hand over his money," Blond-Hair replied.

"Yeah, where's ya money?"

It became apparent that the situation had rapidly deteriorated. And, with no other alternative, Josh stepped up to the big oaf and said, "Here it is," then threw a wild punch at the guy's face.

Three things happened simultaneously. First, Josh heard a sharp crack and pain snapped at his wrist. Second, Chin-Beard's nose exploded in a mass of red pulp, which caused him to fall heavily on his behind. And finally, Blond-Hair whipped out a long, razor-sharp blade. A shock of white lightning ran from hilt to tip. Josh held his injured hand and looked at the blade. He took a step back to lengthen the distance between him and danger.

"Come on Fucker!" Blond-Hair challenged. The blade waved back and forth, creating a tracer-like effect as the polished steel swept left to right.

Already nursing a broken wrist, Josh decided it was time to get out of there. He resolved to chance a broken leg, rather than a blade in the ribs, and so turned in order to run. He took two strides.

From out of the shadows a bottle appeared and, before Josh could react, it was smashed down hard over his head. Blood poured from numerous lacerations to his head. He dropped onto the alley floor and fell instantly unconscious.

A third assailant appeared then. In one hand he held a shard of glass. He was dressed in similar street clothes – like his friends – grossly overweight, and he possessed a ruddy, cherubic face.

"Bingo!" Cherubic cried, pleased with his direct hit.

"Fuck me Mackie, where've ya been?" Blond-Hair questioned.

"Bastard nearly heard me creeping up. I had to hold back awhile," Mackie/Cherubic replied. The shard of glass fell from oversized fingers. He looked across the alleyway and at his downed accomplice. "What happened to Thad?"

"Sucker got tagged with a haymaker," Blond-Hair retorted.

On the opposite side of the alley, Thad spat out a mouthful of blood and profanities before hauling himself up, mumbling incoherently as he brushed the dust off his jacket.

They turned their backs on Thad and instead stood above Josh, watching as he struggled to regain consciousness. Mackie bent his large frame. He dug his fingers into Josh's jeans and frantically searched through his pockets.

"Hurry…" Blond-Hair said. Nervously, he looked up and down the alleyway. He took a step back, which allowed Mackie to go about his business.

Mackie fished out a handful of bills and loose change. He counted his prize eagerly. "Fuck," he snapped. "Only fifteen dollars and seventy-five cents."

"Shit man," Blond-Hair moaned. A grubby paw rubbed across his waxy face. "Okay asshole, time to die," he said. His grip on the blade tightened. He raised his weapon and took a step towards Josh. However, before his first step was completed, a vicelike grip clamped itself around his head. He heard a single, hollow *snap*. And, suddenly, he found himself facing in the opposite direction. Instantly paralysed, he let the blade slip from his fingers. It landed on the ground with a metallic clang. With a perplexed, dumbfounded look on his face, he slumped to his knees. Now, with his head grotesquely twisted one-hundred and eighty degrees, he toppled backwards, face first, dead.

The clang of the blade caused Mackie and Thad to turn simultaneously. They looked in shocked disbelief at the hideously twitching form of their mutilated friend.

"JESUS CHRIST, MACKIE, WHAT THE HELL?" Thad exclaimed. He retched, and the contents of his stomach fell to the floor.

Mackie pulled a previously concealed pistol from his waistband. His eyes darted left and right as he quickly scanned the alleyway in an attempt to find the unknown enemy. "COME OUT FUCKER!" he yelled into the gloom. He stood with his back pressed to the wall. The gun tracked left and right as he traced the muzzle over the entire area. He found only shadows. He lowered the pistol. Out of the darkness he spotted movement ahead. The gun whipped back as he pulled on the trigger.

The muzzle flashed twice: *BOOM! BOOM!*

Like a small cannon the gun went off in Mackie's hand, shattering the near silence. Within a millisecond the first bullet slammed against the wall opposite in a cloud of fine masonry. A fraction of a second later the second bullet hit a discarded, half-empty gas canister. The canister ruptured and exploded in a flash of light. Molten shrapnel flew in all directions. Windows shattered noisily and debris was blown high into the air. The shockwave rolled across the alley, knocking Thad sideways. He tripped over his friend's body and dropped heavily to the ground. Mackie ducked his huge bulk down, away from the red hot metal.

Once the bright flicker of destruction had petered out, he peered through the smoke to determine if he'd hit anything remotely living. He saw a humanlike shape laid out amongst a pile of burnt garbage. "Bingo!" he chimed. He held the gun at his side and slowly advanced towards the downed figure.

He stepped over Blond-Hair then passed Thad, carefully inching his way closer towards the still figure. He waited until his eyes had readjusted to the shadows before advancing the last few yards.

Finally able to make out vague details, he saw that the body was partially concealed amid scorched trash and foul garbage. It was facedown and rigid. Raising the gun, he began to inch his way closer. Almost on top of the body, he stopped. He bent down and used the muzzle of the gun as an extension to his arm. He flicked away a burnt cardboard box to reveal a torso with one of its upper limbs missing. More junk was removed, and eventually, he uncovered most of the body. He stood back, surprised, his hand running over his face as if to wipe away the unexpected vision before him.

The body comprised of a torso with both legs and a head but only one arm and no feet. The torso and legs were covered in dark combat fatigues, which had numerous holes burnt through them to reveal blackened and scorched skin. The head appeared badly burnt with only a few dark wisps of hair attached. Although badly disfigured, Mackie detected a feminine profile.

"Shit, I've blown some bitch to hell!" he said in disbelief. He laughed, impressed with himself, then he released a huge sigh of relief and lowered the gun. "Hey, Thad, come take a look at this!" With a large stupid grin plastered across his face, he happily kicked the body in the ribs.

Thonk!

His booted foot connected with something hard and hollow. His grin slipped, replaced by confusion. He bent down and hastily turned the body over. A vacant and soulless face looked back at him. "Shit!" he said. The burnt mannequin fell from his fingers. He spun around in time to glimpse a silent apparition stalk Thad. "LOOK OUT!" Mackie screamed. He let loose with the cannon, aiming wildly, firing off three indiscriminate shots in rapid succession.

Within a split second and, before the first bullet had been ejected from the muzzle of the gun, the phantom silhouette covered vast ground. It struck out at Thad in a savage frenzy of teeth and nails. A grotesque claw raked across Thad's throat, shredding flesh into a bloody pulp. Thick crimson was injected into the air. Thad clamped both his hands to his ravaged neck in an attempt to hold in his life's fluid.

Horrified at what he was witnessing, Mackie clamped his other hand around the grip of the gun. He steadied his hands and homed in on the monstrous shape. "DIE FUCKER!" he screamed, pulling on the trigger. The gun jumped in his hands with the power of the recoil. Thad took one last breath and, as he slumped backwards, he caught the impact of the bullet, inadvertently saving his attacker from its full force. The bullet entered the top of his head, exploded through his skull, turning his brain into pulp, before it exited via his face. His jaw and lower face disintegrated in a shower of gore. The bullet continued onwards, slamming into the dark apparition. The power of the impact threw the attacker back against the wall.

Mackie moved closer. Fear in check, and newfound resolve at the fore. His attacker lay crumpled against the wall. Shrouded in dark clothes and black sneakers, the body was almost totally hidden by the shadows that surrounded it. Long hair fell forwards over the deadly foe's face. Its features remained hidden behind a veil of dark strands.

Mackie leaned over and slowly prodded at its head with the muzzle of the gun. He got no reaction. He prodded again, harder. Nothing. Then, brushing away a handful of hair, he revealed a vision from hell.

The face was lupine but effeminate. It had a swollen muzzle and a wide, flat nose. Its eyes were fixed in deep sockets and closed. The forehead comprised of grotesquely gnarled ridges, which sloped back, giving way to a shock of black hair. Protruding through its dark strands were two elongated and pointed ears, which sat low-down along the jaw-line.

"Bitch, what the fuck are you?" Mackie breathed.

All of a sudden, its eyelids sprang open to reveal two hate-filled orbs. A nightmare of a muzzle split open to expose sharp canines and a baleful hiss escaped from between bloodied fangs. Mackie snatched his hand away. He jumped away from the beast and brought the gun back up. In a shout of hysterical bravado, he cried, "EAT THIS, BITCH!"

He pulled the trigger.

Click!

The hammer fell on an empty chamber.

In a quick, fluid motion, the beast reached out. It grabbed the discarded blade and, with the power of a freight train, it sprang up, ramming the razor-sharp steel through Mackie's chin. The blade sliced through his lower jaw, skewered his tongue, and then passed up through his palate. The nasal cavity shattered and the blade eventually stopped three inches inside his cerebrum. Unable to stay conscious, Mackie's eyes rolled slowly into the back of his skull.

Holding the entire weight of Mackie's bulk with the blade's grip, the beast leaned into his dead face. And, in hideous mockery, it spat, "Bingo." Then it effortlessly tossed his slumped form across the alleyway.

The beast turned its misshapen head to look up at the rapidly lightening sky, releasing a slight whimper of fear, scared by what it found there.

Josh was found under a pile of debris and quickly dragged into the deeper shadows. The beast gently brushed a clump of bloodied hair away from his eyes. In a strangely distorted but tender voice, it called, "…Josh …Josh…"

He heard a faint whisper and struggled to drag himself out of a deep abyss.

"…Josh …Josh … "

"Anna?" he asked in an almost inaudible whisper.

"Hey, its okay, you'll be okay," the voice replied.

Unable to open his eyes, he reached out and felt for a hand. He found a gnarled talon, which caused him to snatch his hand back. Forcing one eye open, he saw a hideous visage swim into focus. He tried to pull away. His movements triggered an intense bout of nausea, which almost made him vomit. He decided that he must have succumbed to a severe concussion or delirium, or both, so laid his head down, slipping back into the dark abyss.

"Anna, your face?" he managed to whisper before the darkness consumed him.

The beast checked for the steady rise and fall of his chest. It watched for a second as his chest moved gently up and down. Then, with one last concerned look at his bloodied but handsome face, it turned west, eager to escape the first rays of daylight.

Chapter Four

Using thick, greasy fingers, Harry Balooga stuffed the remainder of his pastrami sandwich into his gaping mouth. He took almost half the sandwich in a single bite and chewed eagerly. A grunt of satisfaction escaped from his greasy lips, followed by a dollop of mustard. The mustard dribbled down his ample chin, hung for a second, and then dropped onto his paisley tie.

"Shit," he said, through a mouthful of chewed food.

One of his cumbersome thumbs dropped to his tie as he tried to wipe away the yellow drop but he only succeeded in spreading the stain further. Now with one hand covered in mustard and the other holding onto the half-eaten sandwich, he held both his greasy hands up in the air, looking desperately around the office for urgent assistance. Before anyone had chance to come to his rescue, the phone on top of his cluttered desk rang with a series of urgent bells.

"Shit," he repeated.

He looked around his desk for a suitable napkin. His eyes came to rest on a partially processed crime-report. Hastily he wiped his hands clean. Then he snatched up the handset and irritably barked, "Balooga, Homicide."

"Harry?" asked the voice on the other end.

"Yeah," Balooga answered, already tired, although it was only 8AM and he'd been at his desk less than half an hour.

"Harry, its Marty Richmond. How's it going, you miserable old goat?" asked the voice teasingly.

Balooga's eyes lit up with genuine affection at the sound of his old friend's voice. "Hey – Marty!"

"How are Esther and the kids?" Marty Richmond asked.

"Expensive!" Balooga replied.

Harry Balooga and Marty Richmond had become instant friends when they'd met at the police academy during their time as fresh-faced police cadets, way back in the late 70s. Although from very different backgrounds, they had been surprised at how quickly they had bonded.

Marty, the only son of a successful district attorney, and a physician, had applied to the academy in blatant rebellion against his overly strict parents. Both had expected him to pursue a career in either law or medicine, and Marty had taken great pleasure in constantly reminding them that policing was indeed a career in law. Just not the highflying lawyer's profile they had anticipated.

Harry, on the other hand, had taken great pride in following in his father's footsteps. After he had graduated from college, he'd immediately applied to the academy in the hope that one day he, like his father, would rise to detective.

Marty got down to business. "Listen, Harry, I need a personal favour."

The words 'personal' and 'favour' turned Balooga's feeling of affection to one of dread. "Okay, go ahead," he said with trepidation.

"Harry, I need you on a case right away," Marty said. "We've got a problem down in the Hispanic borough. Three dead. And Harry, they're all white."

"Jesus!" Balooga replied, the implications apparent. "Gang-related?" he asked, and hoped no rival white gang would be stupid enough to wander into Spanish quarters, triggering a full-scale gang war that would invariably lead to a lot of dangerous policing.

"Not sure, could be, but more likely three innocent fools wandered into the wrong part of town," Marty replied. "Either way, it's going to be trouble for us."

"Okay, send me the files. I'll get right onto it."

"I can do better than files," Marty told Balooga. "If you hurry, you'll make it to the crime scene before anything is removed."

"What?"

"They were murdered this morning, before dawn. Frank Applegate's already there," Marty said, referring to Balooga's immediate supervisor.

"Shit!" Balooga exclaimed, unable to believe he was only just hearing this. "Where?" he asked, and shook his head.

While he listened to his friend, he quickly scribbled down the location on a notepad. He tore the top sheet from the pad and stuffed the page inside his shirt pocket. He offered his old friend a hasty goodbye before dropping the handset in its cradle.

Pulling open a drawer, he gathered his police shield and a leather holster that carried his Smith & Wesson snub nose .38. He strapped the holster on, and then leaned over the desk to retrieve his jacket from the back of his chair. Then, in a rush, he headed out of the department.

***

Balooga sped through the streets of Chicago, with his foot down and the police siren wailing noisily above. The Sedan tore around streets, from lane to lane, with scant regard for other vehicles, which were desperately parting in its wake.

Finally clearing the morning rush, the detective had time to ponder over these recent events. Perplexed as to how Marty Richmond had received the information about these murders so early, he wondered how serious the backlash to the three deaths might become. He checked for a familiar street name or structure. The sign for Halsted Street appeared before him. Making a sharp turn left, he accelerated away. He eased off the gas pedal as he once again began to mix with a heavier flow of traffic.

He cursed the day Captain Frank Applegate had been born. Since Applegate had taken over as head of Homicide,

Balooga's professional life had become increasingly unbearable. Sharing an instant dislike for each other, they had entered into a long drawn-out battle of wills; one which Balooga seemed to be progressively losing. What had started out as just petty differences had now become a mammoth feud of such severity, that Balooga's career was now headed towards ruin. Unable to agree on the most trivial of aspects regarding the methods used for homicide investigations, they had now become rivals.

The Sedan switched to the outside lane and Balooga made a quick turn left as he drove deeper into degradation. Surrounded by rundown buildings on either side, he eventually began to make out the familiar signs of blue and red lights, accompanied by the ever-present crowd of onlookers. Even this early hour had been unable to stop the crowd from forming, and heads twitched and bobbed, in an attempt to get a clearer view. He likened them to a drove of hungry buzzards, and shook his head sadly. He switched the siren off before he brought the Sedan up to the large crowd of bloodthirsty onlookers.

He removed his ID from his shirt pocket and flashed it at a uniformed cop. The cop examined the homicide shield before allowing the detective to pass under the strip of police tape. Balooga drove the last thirty yards, deeper into the Hispanic barrio of Little Village, until three or four parked police vehicles blocked his progress.

He hauled his large frame out of the Sedan, manoeuvred around the parked cars, and then entered a narrow alleyway. About halfway down, he saw the familiar and frantic activity found at most murder scenes. There were about seven or eight people, all busily working the incident.

Balooga walked in and out of shadows, careful to avoid the many piles of refuse. Eventually, he weaved his way up to the throng of people. As he joined the group a tall, impeccably dressed man walked over to stop him short.

"Balooga, what the hell are you doing here?" Captain Frank Applegate demanded, his thin, harsh face turning a deep shade of red.

Although dressed in a smartly tailored and expensive suit, Applegate could not hide the fact that he was grossly underweight – a thin stick of anger and irritation no less. "This is not your case. You're not required here!" he snapped at Balooga.

"Tell that to the Chief of Police, SIR!"

"What?" Applegate looked suitably abashed.

"I've been specifically placed on this case. If you've got a problem, speak to Chief Richmond!" Balooga said, feeling as if he were about to win at least one last round before the fight was over.

Applegate's face turned a dangerous shade of red. He spat, "Indeed I will," and then pulled a sleek-looking cell phone from his jacket. He punched in a combination of numbers and moved a few paces away. Raising the cell to his ear, he began a brief but heated conversation. Towards the end of the exchange he became more compliant, and finished by saying, "Yes sir… Right away… in your office? Now?" By the time he'd pressed END CALL, his face had gone from dark red to a sickly grey.

He returned, eyes on the tarmac, avoiding Balooga's gaze, and simply said, "I'm needed in the city, you're on the case, for now," and then headed off in the direction of his parked car.

Detective Emilio Sanchez moved over with a broad smile on his Hispanic face. He shook hands with Balooga and flipped his dark eyes in the direction of the retreating Applegate. "Asshole," he muttered.

"Major Asshole," Balooga corrected, glad to see at least one affable face.

Sanchez slapped his superior on the back and then quickly led him over to the first covered body. "Let me introduce you to a couple of personal friends of mine," he said, as he bent down. He took hold of a sheet corner and pulled it back to reveal the body underneath.

"Da Dahh!" he said, as if revealing some magic trick.

Having spent the last eighteen plus years in the Homicide Department, Balooga didn't even flinch when confronted with the bloodied and ruined face of a burly white male. Experience immediately told him that a high velocity, large calibre bullet was probably the cause of such extensive trauma to this guy's face. The lower jaw-line had gone, leaving ghastly white teeth jutting down from a squashed nose, and the victim's tongue hung loosely to one side.

Reading his superior's mind, Sanchez asked, "What'd you think. A thirty-eight or forty-four?"

"Probably a forty-four," Balooga answered, thinking the wounds were too severe for anything smaller than a .44. "Has the murder weapon been found yet?" he enquired.

Sanchez surprised his superior. "Yeah, forensics have it. Looks like some old foreign make."

"Really? Where did you find it?" Balooga asked, astounded.

"Over there," Sanchez said, pointing to an open area a few yards away.

"Strange," Balooga muttered, before returning his attention to the corpse. He reached across the body to take a pen from Sanchez's jacket pocket. He turned the ruined head carefully to one side, revealing the entry point. Like a hideous extra eye, the wound blinked back at them, its pupil dark and deep – deeper and more mysterious than any real eye could be.

"Look," Balooga said, with the tip of the pen close to the ghastly hole.

"Ah," Sanchez replied. He recognised the bullet hole but did not see anything unusual.

"The angle," Balooga said, as if it were obvious.

Sanchez shrugged his shoulders. "What?"

"Look," Balooga repeated. He lined up one end of the pen with the entry point and the other with the large exit wound. From one end to the other the pen ran slightly downwards, from the back of the head to the injured lower face and neck.

"Ah… What?" Sanchez asked again.

Balooga looked up towards the heavens. "How tall do you make this guy?"

After quick deliberation, Sanchez said, "About six-two, six-three."

"Exactly," Balooga said. He saw that Sanchez still hadn't clicked on. "Look. He's taller than the average guy – right? So if the bullet travelled downwards then this guy was probably kneeling or bending over."

"Execution!" Sanchez said, pleased with his analysis.

"Maybe," Balooga agreed. Yet, as he leaned closer to the victim, he noticed that there were no powder burns to the scalp. He made a further quick examination around the body. "Maybe he tried to run and slipped before he was shot." He paused, his mind trying to work out certain possibilities. "Has the slug been found yet?"

"Not yet. It may be underneath the body."

"Don't leave until you've found it," Balooga ordered. Then he looked down the body and noticed the extensive amount of dried and congealed blood spattered on the victim's hands. A quick frown appeared on his brow. "Death would have been instantaneous, right?" He didn't wait for an answer. "Show me the other two."

Sanchez dropped the sheet over the corpse. He stood and a wry smile spread across his face. "You're gonna love this one," he said, and led Balooga over to the second body.

Standing over the second body were two people deep in conversation. Balooga knew the first and, extending his hand, he addressed Mary Stapleton, Pathologist and Chief Medical Examiner to the City.

"Doctor Stapleton," he said, and shook the woman's hand.

"Lieutenant," Doctor Stapleton greeted. Her fingers pushed her large framed glasses back up her nose. Standing barely over five feet, the pathologist seemed tiny in comparison to the rest of the group. Yet she was probably the single most important and influential member of the team.

"So you got the call?" Stapleton asked. She offered him a knowing smile, and the plane of her face shifted slightly as her glasses reflected sunlight off their thick lenses.

"Call?" Balooga questioned.

Her smile widened. "From our mutual friend, the Chief of

Police."

"Oh… It was you," Balooga said. Suddenly everything clicked into place. He understood then just how influential Mary Stapleton was. He nodded in silent gratification.

"I only want the *very best* on my team," she told him, with serious conviction.

Although Balooga had never met the other person, he immediately knew what he was. With a huge expensive flash camera hanging from around his neck, Balooga identified him as part of the forensics investigation team. They acknowledged each other's presence, and then both detective and photographer turned together as Doctor Stapleton spoke.

"So Lieutenant, what do you make of this?" she asked.

Balooga looked down for the first time and saw that the white sheet had been pulled away to reveal a mop of greasy hair, neck and shoulders. He squatted next to the corpse to begin his examination. The head was lying face down and appeared to be free of any major gunshot wounds. Again, he used Sanchez's pen, carefully lifting strands of hair, looking for any injuries. He found none. Turning the head gently sideways, he revealed a pair of open eyes, frozen. They stared wide-open, fear captured clearly in them, and they were testament to the horrors that had befallen the victim.

Balooga moved hair away from the collar, but he was unable to detect the nape of the neck where the hairline stopped. Instead, he found stretched, almost torn skin. He pulled the sheet further back and widened his vision. Instantly, he noticed the victim's shirt. Oddly, rather than the usual design of shirt, this one appeared to have buttons that ran down the back. In addition, when Balooga pulled the sheet even further, he revealed a pair of backward jeans and two upwardly pointed feet!

"What the hell?" he said, amazed, and rubbed a meaty paw over his shaven head.

"What do you think was the cause of death, sir?" Sanchez asked in morbid humour, his wry smile returning.

Balooga stood. "Jesus, you'd have to be one strong bastard to break somebody's neck like that!"

"Indeed!" Doctor Stapleton agreed.

Balooga returned his gaze to the body. "Is it humanly possible to do such a thing?"

"If I wasn't standing here, Lieutenant, I'd have said no," Doctor Stapleton answered, as bewildered as the rest of the group.

The Lieutenant felt troubled. "I guess I need to see the last victim," he said. He moved away from the bizarre looking corpse and followed Sanchez to the remaining body. They moved up to a small group of people. All three wore standard issue oversized jumpsuits; they were all part of the forensics team. Sanchez and Balooga drew near. The team appeared to finish their examination and, in a blur of white overalls, they quickly packed up and began to move away.

The last of the three turned and said, "He's all yours," and with a swish of baggy material he joined his colleagues.

As if dropped from a height, the third body was found sprawled on top of a pile of refuse, amid discarded rubbish and old warehouse crates. With its limbs twisted and scattered at odd angles and the head hanging loosely over the edge of a crate, the body had the look of a broken and oversized pot doll. The victim was obese with a babyish and ruddy face.

Balooga found that the face was unscathed, apart from the hilt of a knife that stuck bizarrely out of its fleshy chin. He stood on his tiptoes to take a closer look at the grip of the knife. Apart from being spattered with dry blood, the handgrip looked relatively new. He bent down and discovered that the back of the victim's skull was crushed almost flat. He stood, looked at the wall opposite before returning his gaze to the crumpled body.

"How heavy would you make this guy?" he asked his partner.

Sanchez frowned. "Probably about two-eighty, three hundred pounds. Why?"

"Nothing. It doesn't matter," Balooga answered, puzzled.

He turned to look at the body of the first victim, then returned his gaze to the wall opposite, and shook his head. "Impossible," he muttered, more to himself than to his colleague. "Okay, what about identifications?" he asked, as his eyes fell on the corpse's cherubic face for one last time.

"None as yet. But I'll bet a week's pay we find them in the system," Sanchez answered, referring to the National Database that contained details of all known criminals and felons.

With an electronic jingle, a cell phone bleeped to life. Sanchez reached into his pocket. "Excuse me, Chief," he said, and took the call.

Having seen enough death for one day, Balooga turned and found himself a clearing amid the bloodbath. Standing with his back away from the carnage, the detective began to piece together the evidence. He stood motionless for a while as his brain tried to compute and organise the incredible images that surrounded him. The wind stirred slightly, blowing speckles of dark dust over the tips of his shoes. He thought about wiping them onto the backs of his pants before spotting a couple of piles of ash. He bent closer and used two fingers to take a sample from the first pile, then raised it to the sunlight. This dark cinder had a high density and a soot-like texture about it, not unlike the ash generated from a burning cigarette. He rubbed his fingers together, and then watched as the fine particles gently drifted away in the slight breeze. His fingertips had been left with black smudges on both ends. He wiped them on the back of his pants and, intrigued now by the origin of the cinders, he began to follow the trail of equally spaced piles of soot.

He traced them all the way to the alley wall where, strangely, he found an even larger pile. Perplexed, he looked around the crime scene in search of answers, but didn't find anything that could be responsible for the dark soot. He almost turned his attention away before spotting a similar dark stain splattered on the surface of the wall. Almost immediately, he found a squashed, flattened bullet embedded in the brickwork.

Using Sanchez's pen, ever so carefully, he began to work the bullet free, catching it in the palm of his hand as it dropped out.

"Here!" he said, getting the attention of Sanchez and one of the forensics team.

"What is it?" Sanchez enquired, as he rejoined his partner.

Balooga raised his palm up for Sanchez to see. "Our missing forty-four."

The forensics examiner took the bullet from the detective's palm, quickly dropping it inside the plastic bag. "I'll have this sent to ballistics right way, sir," he said. The bag was sealed shut and the examiner quickly scribbled a reference number onto it, then dropping it into a plastic container, he turned to move away.

"Wait!" Balooga called.

The examiner halted.

"Could you get a sample of that," Balooga asked, and pointed to the dark stain on the wall. Then he lowered his finger, and added, "And this," indicating the largest pile of ash.

"Okay," the examiner said. He took out his equipment and began to collect further evidence. Both detectives moved away from the examiner.

Sanchez said, "One last thing," and proceeded to walk towards the other end of the alleyway. Balooga followed him and was led up to a heap of smouldering refuse. On top of the charred rubbish was a burnt, limbless body. Balooga turned away from the misshapen mannequin and looked at Sanchez with expectation.

The Hispanic's eyebrows rose. With a shrug of his shoulders, he said, "Joan of Arc?"

Before they could speculate on the cause of the fire, a short siren sounded, signalling the arrival of the coroner's ambulance. They both looked down the alley as the coroner attempted to navigate around the many obstructions. Once or twice the wagon became trapped by larger debris, but somehow the driver managed to free himself and continue towards them.

Balooga said, "He'll never make it."

"He will, if he can handle that vehicle as well as the paramedics did," Sanchez disagreed, as he watched the wagon weave left to right.

Balooga turned with a puzzled look on his face. "What

paramedics?"

"The paramedics that took the guy to St Andrews," Sanchez explained.

"What guy?" Balooga asked curiously.

"The survivor," Sanchez said, and immediately realised he should have mentioned this earlier.

The large detective spun on his heels and quickly headed towards the parked Sedan. "CHRIST, SANCHEZ, COME ON!" Balooga snapped.

Cringing now, Sanchez followed his superior away from the crime scene and towards St Andrews Emergency Hospital.

Chapter Five

The wail of distant sirens stirred Josh from his troubled slumber. Feeling slightly nauseous, he opened his eyes and waited until the unfamiliar room swam into focus. He found himself in a hospital bed and panic almost took over. How the hell had he gotten here? Then, as he began to remember the events that had taken place earlier, he cautiously reached up to place a hand on his head. He felt firmly wrapped material around his head, and he wondered if the tight bandage was responsible for the unbelievable pressure to his skull. He probed further and discovered, much to his dismay, that his hair had been shaved so short he could almost feel his scalp underneath. His hand flopped feebly onto his chest.

He remembered the confrontation he'd had with the two street punks and how, after decking one of them, he had turned to flee. The only real recollection he had after that was a single moment of severe pain. He strained to recollect the events that followed, vaguely remembering the terrible nightmare he'd had whilst fighting to regain consciousness. The nightmare had started with a bright flash and the smell of burnt sulphur in the air. Then, after a brief silence, the quiet had been shattered by numerous gunshots, followed by shouts and cries, then again, silence.

The dream moved off on a tangent then, and Josh had unexpectedly been in the arms of some hideous beast. Peculiarly, the beast had known his name, and its face was vaguely similar to that of Anna's. He shivered involuntary as he thought about how real the malformed face had seemed, and how the creature had reached out to touch him with its deformed hand. He slipped into a deep, dark place after that and had not awoken again until he'd felt hands gently lifting him up and voices calmly reassuring him that he would be all right, and that he was in good care. Then he had succumbed once again to the dark abyss, and had been unconscious until now.

He remembered how he had stormed out of Anna's apartment after their argument, and his heart quivered at the thought of her sad but beautiful face. As he lay in this strange room, he was surprised by how deep his feelings had become towards this mysterious girl, and he wondered now if he would ever see her again. He turned his head slightly to one side, peering out towards an open window, hoping she was out there somewhere, her thoughts with him.

His gaze shifted away from the bright glare that streamed through the window and, gingerly, he turned his head in the opposite direction and in time to see a nurse enter.

"Hey, you're awake," the pretty young nurse said. She moved over to one side of the bed to place a plastic beaker on the bedside cabinet. "You don't look too pretty, but you'll survive," she said.

"Thanks," Josh replied, not sure if he should be relieved or insulted. He eyed the bluish fluid in the plastic beaker with trepidation. "What's that for?" he asked apprehensively.

"Don't worry. It tastes better than it looks, and it'll help with the pain," she replied reassuringly. She put the beaker down on a side table, and then reached across him, pressing a button to activate a mechanism beneath the cot, which began to raise the upper half of the bed, and push Josh's head closer to her ample cleavage.

"Don't get any wise ideas," she told him. A playful grin bent her lips. She brought him up to a forty-five degree angle then took the beaker and handed it to him.

Josh reached out with his right hand, to accept the drink. He stopped short when he noticed the hand encased in fresh white plaster. "Shit," he mumbled, then reached over with his left hand and took the blue cocktail. After eyeing the dark liquid for a second, he raised the beaker. "Salute!" he said, and swallowed the medicine in one quick gulp. Its bitter taste caused him to grimace. He handed the empty cup back to the nurse and watched as she replaced it on to the bedside cabinet.

She moved to the foot of the bed, picked up a chart, updated his details then replaced it. Before she left the room, she stopped and asked, "Is there anyone you'd like us to call?"

Josh lay in silence for a moment, testing his bones and muscles. He concluded he was not in any immediate danger, and therefore decided not to worry his father unnecessarily.

"No – I'm fine, thanks."

"Okay, I'll inform the Doctor you're awake," she said, then disappeared.

Alone again and now sitting upright, Josh looked around the room and took in his new environment. The room was bare with minimal decoration and little furniture. A single straight-backed chair stood to the left of his bed, intended to be used by some worried and pampering relative no doubt. Most of the left wall comprised of a large window, which opened outwards towards the sunlit day. Thin drapes, which were open, allowed most of the sunlight to filter through. In the middle of the windowsill sat an empty hand-painted vase in need of flowers.

The opposing wall consisted of nothing but lightly coloured paper. A doorway had been cut into the wall, and Josh suspected that this led to the washroom, although from this angle he could only make out more of the bland wallpaper. The main door and an inexpensive looking closet were over on the right side of the room. The closet didn't have a door and he could see bare, wire hangers inside.

Josh pulled the bed sheet away to find that he had been stripped down to just his boxer shorts. He dropped the sheet and scanned around the room, trying to locate his clothes and sneakers. Unable to find them, he carefully leaned over to his right and opened a small bedside cabinet. Inside he found a collection of old newspapers and yellowing magazine editorials. He closed the door, lay back, and gave up his search for now.

Feeling weary now, he closed his eyes and began to doze. However, before he had time to fall into a deep sleep, he was rudely awakened by the commotion of raised voices coming from directly outside. He had just enough time to pull up the sheet to cover his bare chest before three men barged through the door. The one who made the most noise wore a clean lab jacket, pressed pants and polished shoes. Hanging round his thin neck was a metallic stethoscope. The other two appeared to be together and were both unfazed by the doctor's apparent outrage.

One of the two was large with closely cropped hair and a round full face. He wore a rumpled suit, which had seen better days, and a stained paisley tie. His colleague was considerably shorter with a dark complexion and happy brown eyes. He too wore a worn suit and a faded tie. Both had *cop* written all over them.

The larger of the two moved away from the agitated doctor, and towards the bed. He pulled his ID from his shirt pocket. "I'm Lieutenant Balooga and this is Detective Sanchez," he said with a flash of polished metal. "We need to ask you a few questions."

"Detective, please," the doctor said, exasperated. He moved over to the bedside in an attempt to protect his patient. "Mister Sawyer has only just awakened and is in need of treatment."

The large officer took a step back to allow the physician to begin his examination.

The doctor bent over Josh, then removed an ophthalmoscope from his lab jacket. With delicate fingers he turned the instrument on. A narrow beam of light shone from one end. Alternately, the doctor examined both his patient's eyes. Both pupils reacted to the bright light. "Good, good," he said. He moved his inspection higher and checked the clean bandage that was wrapped around Josh's head. Satisfied with the dressing, he turned his attention towards a deep laceration just above the left eyebrow. "You're a lucky young man. Had the glass been an inch lower, you'd now be lying in ophthalmology," the doctor explained. A tendon hammer was produced as the doctor began to test Josh's reflexes.

Half-naked, Josh began to feel increasingly uneasy and exposed as the two detectives watched in curious silence. And, as the doctor prodded his various nerve endings, he twitched and bucked uncontrollably.

The doctor took a step back, much to his patient's relief, his examination now complete. He updated the chart at the foot of the bed before turning his attention to the two detectives. "Okay, I'll be back in fifteen minutes. I expect that to be plenty of time for your questions. Please remember that Mister Sawyer may be suffering from a slight concussion and shouldn't be tired unnecessarily." Then in a flash of starched material he left the room, leaving Josh at the mercy of the two strangers.

Balooga pulled the straight-backed chair over to the bedside and unceremoniously parked his bulk down. The chair emitted a few painful high-pitched squeals before it settled under his weight. Standing at the door, Sanchez pulled out a small notepad and pen. He flipped open the pad and began to jot down some apparently important provisional details.

"So, why'd you kill three guys last night?" Balooga asked, straight down to business.

"What?" Josh blurted, shocked by the detective's unbelievable question. "What three guys?"

"The three guys lying dead in an alleyway, in Little Village," Balooga said.

"Hey, wait. I had nothing to do with any murders!" Josh said defensively. He looked up towards the Hispanic detective for help, but unsurprisingly he got none.

"If you didn't kill them, who did?" Balooga demanded. "Kill who?" Josh asked, confused.

"The three guys left in the alleyway, out in the Hispanic barrio."

Now, Josh understood exactly whom the detective meant. "Wait, hang on a minute! Those assholes tried to kill me, not the other way around."

"Really," Balooga said, "so tell me, what were four white guys doing wondering around in Little Village in the middle of the night?"

"Probably looking to score some drugs," Sanchez quipped from the back.

Jesus! Bad cop, BAD cop, Josh thought, unnerved. "Listen, I don't touch that shit. I got lost and then these two mean fuckers appeared from nowhere and started giving me hell. Look, I'd had a few beers in a bar, got lost and was then attacked by some punks, okay?"

"Bar? What bar?" Balooga inquired.

After a pause, Josh said, "I'm not sure which bar." He turned towards the window in the hope that his deceit would go unmissed.

"Not sure which bar?" Sanchez repeated, unconvinced.

"You're lying," Balooga told him.

With a heavy sigh, Josh reluctantly said, "Okay, I met this girl and we went for a few drinks, then we left and I got lost." Again, he looked out of the window, but this time he felt guilty and regretful for having brought Anna into this.

Balooga sensed the kid was about to reveal something of great importance so he lowered his tone. "What girl?"

"Some girl I met on the street. I don't know her name."

"This girl – did you meet her or pick her up?" Sanchez asked with his gaze still fixed on his notepad.

"Jesus, man! You think I'm a curb crawler as well as a murderer?"

Sanchez finally pulled his eyes away from the notepad. "Strange you don't know her name, though, isn't it?"

"Listen, we bumped into each other and went for a beer, it was a spontaneous thing."

"So you left this bar with some girl and went where?" Balooga asked.

"I can't say."

"Can't or won't?"

"I'm not sure where we went after that," Josh lied, again.

"Why, were you drunk?" Sanchez asked from across the room.

"Yeah, maybe you bumped into these guys and in a drunken rage killed them all!" Balooga told Josh seriously.

Infuriated by the injustice of the situation, Josh snapped, "Yeah, man, you got me. After raping and killing, then burying the girl, I went out and found me three pussies to kill. After that, I had me a shit load of crystal meth and then must have slaughtered at least another ten Homies. Guess you've caught yourself a regular Hannibal Lecter!"

Stunned by the unexpected outburst, Balooga and Sanchez became momentarily silent, allowing Josh to regain his composure.

"Look, I may have been stupid and wandered into the wrong part of town, but other than decking one of those guys, I honestly don't know what happened."

Balooga read the sincerity on the kid's face. He decided on a new angle. "Relax, son. I *do* believe you didn't have anything to do with the actual murders, but you must have seen something?"

The hideous visage of the beast unexpectedly flashed across Josh's mind. He shuddered involuntarily, the clarity of the image making him doubt his own comprehension. Was the beast only a vision created by his confused and disorientated mind, or, something far more menacing? To believe something so despicable could be real must surely be proof of severe cerebral injury. He shook his head in an attempt to clear his mind of the terrible phantom contained within, but only succeeded in manifesting a grotesque combination of Anna and the beast. "NO!" he cried.

"Christ, kid. Are you alright?" Balooga asked.

"Yeah, yeah," Josh replied weakly.

"Take it easy now, just tell us what you can remember," Balooga said, regaining the initiative.

Josh took a minute to clear his head. "Okay, I met this girl. I don't know her name. We had a few drinks at a bar just off 43rd and West Street. I'm not sure of its name but if you head down 43rd it's probably the first bar you hit. I had a few too many drinks and then she took me back to her place, and I spent the night. I'm not sure of the address but it wasn't far from the bar we were in. All I remember is that her apartment was on a mainly deserted street. I think there may have been a liquor store nearby. Anyway, I left near dawn and got lost, then stumbled into two of your guys. I didn't see the third guy but I think he's the one who tagged me with a bottle." He paused and pointed to his bandaged head for emphasis, then continued, "I think they intended on mugging me but someone or… some*thing*… must have interrupted them."

"And you didn't see who?" Balooga asked.

Suddenly tired, Josh said, "I was unconscious at the time."

"What's this girl look like?" the detective asked.

Anna's beautiful, dusky face surfaced in Josh's mind. Again, he turned to look out of the window. "She's about five-foot-six with average looks and short mousy-coloured hair."

"So, you remember the girl then being hit with something and falling to the floor, and then what?"

"And then I woke up here," Josh finished, leaning back in the pillows, exhausted. And, unwilling to give any more information, he fell silent.

Balooga looked at his partner. They nodded in silent agreement. The large detective stood and joined his partner over by the door.

"That's enough for now. You get some rest and I'll return later, after I've checked out your story," he said.

"Thank you for your cooperation," Sanchez added. Then together, they withdrew and disappeared almost as abruptly as they'd entered.

Now alone, Josh tried to turn his thoughts away from the disturbing images that his mind seemed intent on conjuring up. He closed his eyes and, after what seemed like an eternity, gradually fell into a light but troubled sleep.

***

"He's hiding something," Balooga told Sanchez as they headed back towards the parked Sedan.

"Yeah, but what?" Sanchez asked. He quickly flipped through his notepad. He found what he was looking for. "According to my notes, Dispatch said the call notifying us about the incident came from an anonymous caller. And guess what? A female made the call from a payphone off 42nd."

"Really?" Balooga enquired, eyebrows raised. "That's at least a mile further west from the crime scene."

"Yeah and only one block away from our bar and the mysterious woman," Sanchez finished.

"So what do you think?"

"This woman is more involved than our friend says," the young detective said.

"A girlfriend he wants to protect, maybe? She could have shot the guy with no face and then he did the other two. But it doesn't feel right. Maybe he *did* pick her up, refused to pay and our three friends on the way to the morgue were her pimps or something. Yeah, maybe he's too ashamed to admit he picked her up. He's older than the average student. Perhaps he's already involved with someone and has a lot to lose?"

"Like his scholarship?" Sanchez voiced.

"Exactly," Balooga agreed. "Maybe our friend's meal-ticket is about to run out."

"So you think he did it?"

"He definitely did something, but what?"

"I'm not sure," Sanchez said. "Plus, where is the girl? And who's this other woman who called 9-1-1? Are they the same person?"

"I don't know, but let's find out," Balooga said gleefully.

They reached the Sedan parked at an awkward angle outside. Balooga inserted his key, unlocking the driver's side. He turned to face his partner. "Okay, I'm gonna check out this bar and see if I can trace our female friend. In the meantime you head back to Homicide and start chasing up on forensics, and wait for the report from the coroner."

Balooga heaved his bulk inside the Sedan, turned the ignition and started the engine. He slammed the door shut and wound the window down, popping his head out. "Oh – yeah, one last thing. Keep that asshole Applegate off my back!" Balooga threw the Sedan into gear, and, with a screech of rubber, the car pulled away.

"Shit!" Sanchez croaked, coughing back smoke, watching as his ride disappeared from view. Stranded on the kerbside, he removed his jacket and threw it over his shoulder. Then, with a heavy sigh, he began the long trip back to the precinct.

Chapter Six

Dense smog hung heavily above the city skyline, the mid-morning traffic turning the sky into an oppressive yellow haze. Beyond the caustic fog, the sun burnt with hot intensity and, within the next hour, it would succeed in reducing the unwanted mist into nothing more than the occasional white wisp, leaving behind instead a bright blue magnificence.

Two crystalline eyes, burning with intense fear, blinked. From behind the abandoned dumpster, a shadow formed then hastily moved around to the front of the rusty garbage container. The figure took a quick, anxious look upwards, and its face twisted instantly into a mask of agony. Moving away from the safety of the shadows, the dark apparition made its way towards the busy sidewalk, mixing easily with the city's inhabitants, making its way further westward.

Within the safety of the shadows, cast down by the towering office blocks, the figure moved quickly, staying close to the walls of the surrounding buildings. With the sun threatening to break through, fear pushed the figure onwards with added urgency. Bright slivers of light cut towards the ground, and the bustling commercial part of the city gave way to quieter, less prosperous streets and avenues.

The dark apparition turned in to a deserted avenue, but kept the sun safely hidden from its back by a row of empty storefronts. It stopped abruptly, and turned to face a near-unnoticeable doorway. Situated across the road, the door stood between an abandoned convenience market and a liquor store. Graffiti scarred shutters hid the store's contents behind a montage of profanity and street art. Although the only obstacle that separated the figure from the doorway was about twenty feet of hot asphalt, it remained stationary, waiting. The shadows in which it stood began to recede, melting away into the brickwork of the surrounding buildings.

Anna took a final deep breath, held it in her lungs, and then stepped out into the glare of the sun. Pain exploded against her back and she almost collapsed to the ground. She fought to remain upright, staggering towards the doorway, each step almost impossible to finish. Midway across, she pulled the dark material of her pullover up, over her head in a desperate attempt to protect her face and neck. Instantly though, the hand that held the material began to burn and blister as if touched by vicious flames.

With one desperate lunge forwards, she reached the doorway and collapsed to her knees, allowing the breath to explode from tight lungs. She reached up with a scorched hand and punched in a combination of numbers into a small keypad. Hitting the last digit, her hand burst into flames. Then, with a sharp *click*, the door swung open and she toppled over into the safety of the dark threshold.

Time passed and the sun eventually reached its highest point in the clear blue sky, reducing shadows to nothing more than a hint of black soulless space.

***

Anna crossed the apartment in darkness, gliding soundlessly, switching on two table lamps as she went. The weak lamps offered a minimal amount of illumination, giving the room only slight definition. A dark object, found in the corner of the room, pulled at her attention. The sheets from the bed had gathered at its foot in a rumpled mess, and her evening dress lay in a crumpled heap on the polished floor. She breathed deeply, trying to detect a trace of the man she'd spent the night with. Just hint of his passing lingered, which caused an unexpected ache to spread from the pit of her stomach.

Would she see him again?

Probably not, she thought, with a heavy sigh.

She pushed the memories of Josh to one side, focusing instead on more urgent matters. Moving over to a drawer, she opened it to take out a number of official looking documents. With papers in hand, she returned to a half-filled case, opened out on her bed. The documents disappeared inside with the rest of her belongings. Then, she shut the case, locking her personal effects safely inside. She picked up the suitcase, carried it over to a narrow window at the rear of the apartment and left it there. Her immediate task done, she returned to the bed and sat on the edge to wait for the intense pain in her hand to abate. Sitting there she began to gather her thoughts.

They would come, they always did.

She knew this without any doubt. She felt it instinctively and did not for a single second question her intuition. It was not the first time she'd had to flee and possibly not the last. She was proficient at disappearing without a trace, so this was not new to her. The idea of her immediate escape did not worry her either, although for some reason her gut quivered with nerves. Surprisingly, it was the thought of the man she'd shared her bed with the night before that made her stomach flutter with butterflies. It had been a long time since she'd shared her bed with a man she'd felt close to and uncountable years since she'd felt any real fondness toward a man. So what were these affections she held now?

After they'd made love, she had fallen into an unexpected deep sleep and had not awakened until almost dawn. Had she fallen asleep cradled in his arms because she had felt protected, safe even? Maybe, she conceded, surprised by her own vulnerability. What had she seen in him anyway for her to choose him over all other possible lovers? Although he'd carried himself with grace and elegance, she had instantly detected the slight limp hindering his left leg. This would normally have been a sign of weakness or infirmity to her. Nevertheless, she had felt instantly drawn to his aura of self-contained inner strength and passion. Although she had spotted all these traits at once, it had been something else that had lured her to this handsome stranger.

Something shared.

Loneliness.

Neither sex nor passion, nor even lustful need had drawn them together, but simple loneliness. Both had been desperate to feel another person's warmth and affection, and their souls had been drawn together, sure and inescapable, like the sun is drawn to the distant horizon.

She'd had countless lovers throughout the ages, but none for an eternity and, having spent aeons alone, she had embraced his ardent need. Although she had felt a desperate compulsion to share more than just her body with him, she had been compelled to drive him away, for he must not discover *what* she was. So then, why had she followed him across the city when daylight had been only moments away? She had followed him from rooftop to rooftop as he had wandered alone, not wanting to lose sight of his handsome face. Then, unexpectedly, the three punks had attacked him and she had flown into a bloodthirsty rage, intent on the total destruction of his assailants. Caught up in the bloody carnage, she had not realised how close to sunrise it had become.

She remembered how, after she'd checked on his unconscious form, she had fled westward towards home and safety. But when she'd reached the corner of 42nd, she'd panicked, worried by the severity of his wounds, and phoned 911. Kept on hold for precious seconds, she had finally been trapped by the sunrise.

Now sitting on the edge of the bed, Anna gently pressed her side and felt the tender area where the bullet had hit her. Even though it had only been a matter of hours since she'd been shot, the wound had almost sealed itself shut, with the skin that surrounded the entry and exit points already knitted together. The relentless pain she felt came from her left hand that, although heavily bandaged, seeped yellowish sticky fluid, staining the white material. Although the gunshot wound would heal at an accelerated rate, the burns to her hand would take much longer and remain painful for some time to come.

She stood and moved over to a desktop, where she sat to face a state-of-the-art computer system. She hit the power switch and waited for the software to boot up. A cursor appeared and using the mouse, Anna guided the arrow across the screen. She accessed an encrypted file and was asked to enter a password before she could proceed further. The password was comprised of eight digits. She tapped on the keyboard and entered the name *Carl_Dua,* and was rewarded with a new list of file names. The cursor opened a file named *Plogojowitz,* and automatically the computer began to download numerous account numbers and banking data. Anna took a pen, pad from a desk drawer, and began to jot down long strings of numbers and information. In a flurry of fingers, she transferred money and assets from banks found inland to new, untraceable accounts overseas.

After she'd spent the better part of an hour moving her money from bank to bank, she eventually clicked on an icon in the shape of a crucifix. The screen went blank and then flashed to life with a message that scrolled across the centre of the screen. The message read: *'Fluckinger's report to be deleted by whom?'* This time she typed in the name *Arnod Paole,* and received the message: *One minute until systems shutdown.* A small, animated clock appeared on screen, counting down the seconds. She waited patiently for the count to reach zero, and absentmindedly rewrote the name *Carl_Dua* onto the sheet that contained her account numbers. She looked at the seven-lettered name and her face broke into a wistful smile. Then, as she struck the pen across the name, she whispered, "How long have you been dust, my old adversary?"

The count hit zero and with a pop the computer burst into flames. Acrid smoke escaped from the vents in the case, and within minutes the internal circuitry – including the hard-drive and its secrets – had been reduced to useless lumps of molten plastic and metal. She tore the top few pages from the pad and touched them to blue flames. The pages caught easily. She dropped them onto the desk. Seconds later, the paper had turned to a small pile of cinders.

She sensed something and as she turned away from the smouldering computer, she heard the squeal of brakes.

They'd arrived, and earlier than expected.

Chapter Seven

The Sedan came to an abrupt halt. Balooga parked the Sedan hastily at the kerbside. He heaved his bulk up and out of the car. The mid-afternoon sun had cooked the surface of the road, heat shimmering upwards in great rolling waves, turning the asphalt into a spongy black tar. The detective's first breath was one of acrid fumes. He sucked his second through gritted teeth. Slamming the door shut, he looked across the street and towards an ancient looking Chinese guy who was busy raising the metal shutters to a liquor store. The lieutenant crossed the street quickly, looking up as he went, noticing a number of large blacked-out windows directly above the store. Underneath his feet, the road felt soft enough to leave behind the prints of his passing.

Earlier, he'd found the bar that Sawyer and the girl had visited. He'd questioned the bar staff, and had quickly made a positive ID on Josh, but not the girl. A middle-aged bartender had remembered the couple due to the amount of *Jack Daniel's* the girl had managed to down, and remain standing. Although the description the barman gave matched that of Josh, he said the girl was tall, almost as tall as the guy she'd been drinking with, had long dark hair, and was striking to look at. Not surprised by the difference in descriptions, Balooga was sure that this *was* the girl Josh Sawyer had spent the night with. After his inquiries, he'd cruised along the adjoining streets and avenues until he found this liquor store.

Balooga caught the Chinese guy's attention and flipped his police badge in the man's wrinkled face. "I'm looking for a girl," he said.

The heavily lined face split into a grin and his open mouth revealed whittled down yellow teeth. In a thick Cantonese accent, the man said, "Yes… I… know… girl."

"Do any girls live around here?" Balooga asked the old man.

"Yes… girl…" the man said, with a clap of his hands.

Balooga looked at the man's eyes and saw little, if any, real comprehension. "Do-any-girls-live-near-here?" the detective asked as clearly as he could. He pointed to the ground for emphasis.

The man nodded. "Girl… here… yes," he said, and then hopped from one foot to the other. "Girl… my… friend."

"I'm-looking-for-a-young-girl."

"Youunnng… Giirrrrrl!" A mischievous eye winked back at the detective. "Girl… comes… twice-a-week and… buy groceries… and pick-up… males."

"Males?"

"Yes, yes… Have a lot… of… male!" The old man offered the detective another wink. "She… has males… twice-a-week… sometime three… or four!"

Balooga listened to the guy and recalled that Sawyer had said he'd stayed the night even though they'd only just met. Perhaps the kid was telling the truth after all and that he'd simply stumbled upon a woman who was highly promiscuous. "Lots-of-males?" he asked.

"Yes… different… one… every day."

"Christ," Balooga mused, wondering what had happened to the morals of his generation.

"No Christ… live… here." the little man muttered with a shake of his ancient head.

"Okay-where-do-girls-live?" the detective asked as clearly as possible.

"Here! Here!" the little man said, and jumped up and down excitedly.

Wanting an answer and, before the little man died of a self-induced heart attack, Balooga asked, "Where?"

"Here! Here!" the man said. One of his gnarled hands pointed up towards the blacked-out windows above his shop. Balooga followed the bent fingers and was directed to the black drapes that covered all the windows above. He dropped his eyes and spotted a previously unnoticed door to the left. He moved over to examine the thick wooden door and spotted a small keypad.

"Girl-live-here?" he asked.

"Yes… yes…" the old man said, and clapped his hands enthusiastically.

"Thanks," Balooga said.

The Chinese guy turned his back on the big detective and shuffled over to another shuttered window. And, as he began to lift the shutter, he mumbled, "Giirrrl… Male…" followed by a devilishly long chuckle.

Balooga looked down at the small display at the top of the keypad. Four horizontal dashes waited to be replaced with a correct sequence of numbers. There were ten keys to choose from, and they numbered from 0 to 9. He stood with his hands on hips and wondered how many hundreds, if not thousands, of four coded entries there must be out of the possible ten digits available. Inquisitively, he reached out and punched in a totally random sequence, and almost jumped out of his ample skin when the keypad emitted a short, sharp *click*. The door opened inwards slightly. A slice of oppressive blackness dared him to enter.

He pushed the door further back and peered into the darkness. Only the faint outline of a stairway could be seen. He pushed the door all the way back to allow as much light as possible to filter through. A short flight of steps led upward towards a bare landing. At the top, faint light shone from a half-open doorway. Not wanting to lose the initiative, he decided to enter. He took one final look behind at the safety of the bright, sunny street and then quietly slipped inside. The bulge of his holster offered much needed reassurance.

He began his ascent. His feet made hollow thumping noises on the bare wooden stairs. He guessed his arrival had become more than audible, so he called up to identify himself.

"This is Lieutenant Balooga from downtown. I'm here to investigate three recent murders. I'd like to ask you a few questions."

No response came. He called out, "I'm coming up." He reached the top step with two long strides and turned to face in the direction of the light. The half-opened door beckoned. He rapped on it twice.

Silence.

"Hello, anybody home?" he shouted through the crack.

Again, silence.

He pushed the door open, crossed the threshold and entered.

Two weak lamps illuminated a room. He found himself standing in a large, scantily furnished studio apartment. Immediately to his left there was a king-sized bed and to his right he saw a work-desk that supported a serious amount of computer hardware. As he drew nearer to the desk, he was assaulted by a strong acrid odour that stung the inside of his nasal passages. He dropped his hand over the computer, touched the plastic case and then snapped his hand back, surprised by the heat that radiated from it. A quick examination revealed the plastic to be melted and blackened, and at the centre the plastic had melted away entirely to reveal charred and burnt electronic circuitry. To the side of the burnt-out computer sat one of the electric lamps, which cast its weak light outwards.

He searched for any other signs of fire or damage. Finding none, he moved away and progressed deeper inside the apartment. The centre of the room consisted of little more than a square table accompanied by a single wooden chair. On top of the table was another lamp that offered barely enough light to illuminate a four-foot radius. Unexpectedly, he sensed a presence behind him. He spun around and was confronted by a silhouetted figure at the doorway. A switch clicked off and, as the two lamps went out, the room was thrown into total darkness.

Chapter Eight

Josh swung his legs over the edge of the bed. He stood and cautiously walked to what he hoped was the bathroom. He wavered slightly as he shuffled over to the open doorway. Relieved to find a small washbasin and lavatory, he moved over to the toilet and pulled his shorts to one side. A small window opened out just above the toilet, and the faint clash of guitars found its way inside, coming from some distant workman's radio. It was a familiar song: the same one that had met both Josh and Anna as they'd entered the bar the night previous. A heavy sigh of regret leaked out from between his lips. Was Anna out there, somewhere, carrying the same burden of grief as he?

As he began to empty his bladder, the room began to spin. He closed his eyes and waited for the merry-go-round to stop. With his bladder emptied, he stood back and looked down into the bowl, noticing that the water had turned to a peculiar shade.

"Jesus. . . " he mumbled, wondering what the hell kind of medication he'd been put on.

His hand dropped over the handle and the discoloured water flushed away. He moved over to the washbasin and almost jumped at the reflection in the mirror. He saw a pale face looking back at him with deeply set bloodshot eyes. Just above the left eye a particularly nasty cut ran parallel to, an inch above, the eyebrow itself. The cut was closed by six coarse stitches. His head was wrapped in clean bandages and where they stopped, he could see short bristles of hair poking out.

He reached up to run his fingertips along the skin of his stubbly jaw-line. They made a prickling noise as they rubbed against the rough surface.

He turned away from the mirror and re-entered the main room. Still clothed in only his boxer shorts he moved over to the main door. Not wanting to alarm anyone with his near-nakedness, he pushed the door open an inch or two. Through the crack, he saw a clean-whitewashed wall opposite and a blue and white tiled floor. The floor was polished to such an extreme, the fluorescent tubes above cast large slivers of white lightning across its surface.

Josh shifted his position to the left slightly. He gasped at the sight of a uniformed police guard. Sitting in a chair, the officer appeared engrossed in the magazine he had rested on his lap. He looked barely out of his teens, with a clear, unlined face and ruddy cheeks. As if he had sensed Josh's presence, the officer looked up. He dropped his magazine immediately and stood. Mustering up as much authority as possible, he said, "Inside!"

Infuriated by being under guard, Josh opened the door wider. "I'm going for a walk," he announced, and stepped out of his room in just his under-shorts.

The guard reached for his pistol. "INSIDE NOW, OR ELSE!"

"Or else what?" Josh demanded, defiantly.

"Or else, I'll shoot you down for trying to escape," the guard told him seriously. He unclipped the fastener that held his gun secure in its holster.

Josh understood this kid was all business, so decided to do as he was told. Yet, unable to contain his rebelliousness, he flipped the officer a stiff salute before about-turning and disappearing back inside.

Chapter Nine

Balooga heard a second click and the apartment went from near-darkness to bright lights. He shielded his eyes from the glare of overhead lights, squinting, trying to make out the newcomer. His eyes readjusted and the detective was able to make out the person standing halfway inside the apartment. It was an attractive young woman. And it took only a second for the detective's analytical brain to match the woman stood before him to the same one given by the middle-aged barman.

"It's okay, I'm a detective from downtown," he said reassuringly.

"Hello, Detective," Anna said.

"Your door was open," he lied, reaching for his identification.

She closed the door and moved deeper inside the apartment. Balooga flipped his badge at her. She looked up briefly, waved her hand towards him dismissively, before continuing towards the table and chair. She pulled the chair back and then gracefully slipped behind the table and sat. Balooga was left over by the window. Feeling slightly awkward at the girl's overly relaxed manner, he moved over to stand on the opposite side of the table.

"Do you know a Josh Sawyer?" he asked.

She looked up and made eye contact for the first time, paused for a moment, then said, "Josh, yes I know him. Why?"

He detected a hint of Eastern Europe in her accent. "Because he was involved in an incident last night," he replied.

"Is he alright?" she asked.

Although her posture seemed relaxed, Balooga sensed that

a slight amount of anxiety had crept into her voice. "Not too good, I'm afraid."

"Is he badly injured?" she asked, her words masked with concern.

"Injured?" the detective asked.

"You said he was in an accident."

Balooga frowned. "I said he was in an incident."

"Oh," she said, and looked at the detective reproachfully. "I thought you said accident," she added, now upright and seemingly fully alert.

"As it happens, he was injured slightly but at this moment that's the least of his worries," he explained, pulling on his shirt collar. With the closed curtains, the room seemed to hold heat and tension in equal measure. "It's so hot in here," he said, releasing the knot of his tie slightly.

"Where is he?" Anna asked him.

"Don't worry, we've got him under guard at St Andrews," he told her.

"Detective, is Josh hurt or not?" she asked, agitation now clearly present in her voice.

He undid the top button to his shirt, then said, "He's fine, fine. He's got a couple of stitches and a slight concussion, that's all."

"What happened?" she asked, noticeably relieved by Balooga's diagnosis.

"I was hoping you could tell me. Miss?"

Her chin lifted with pride, a subconscious act, so powerful that Balooga almost took an unexpected step back. "My name is Anna Privalova," she announced.

"Privalova," Balooga echoed.

"It's Russian," she said, with some defiance.

"Russian," he repeated.

"Detective, how can I help you?"

"Okay, Miss Privalova, I need to know exactly what happened last night when you were with Mister Sawyer."

She paused for a second. "We met last night near a bar, hit it off and went for a few drinks. Then we both came back here and he spent the night."

"And then what?"

"And then Detective, we fucked!"

"Oh!" he said, momentarily embarrassed by the young woman's frankness. He remembered the Chinese guy's comment about her going to the store to pick up males, and he became notably embarrassed by his old-fashioned attitude towards sex. He cleared his throat, "After... that, then what happened?"

"Nothing. He left shortly before sunrise," she told him.

"So after he left, you didn't see him again?"

"Correct."

The heat trapped inside the apartment began to make beads of sweat pop up on the detective's skin. With one meaty hand he began to fan his damp face. "It's so hot in here. Could I have a glass of water?"

She flashed him a brief but humourless smile. "Yes, Detective, I'll be right back." She moved away from the table to disappear through an adjourning doorway.

The detective was left alone. He heard a cabinet open followed by the clatter of glass. Moments later a faucet began to run.

He scanned quickly around the apartment, looking for anything that might help him with this investigation. He saw nothing out of the ordinary until his gaze rested on the damaged computer system. Directly underneath the desk lay a small piece of white material. He bent and picked up what appeared to be a piece of burnt paper. The paper was flame damaged down to about two inches square and all that remained was one corner. Fine blue lines ran horizontally, spaced equally apart. Standard writing paper from a notepad, Balooga deduced. Written on two of these lines were the remains of some unknown data. What immediately caught Balooga's attention was a name, written at the bottom of the paper. The name was scrawled in large, neat print, but for some reason it had been struck-out. The single word caused an inexplicable shiver to run up the length of his spine. He heard the faucet stop, and the piece of paper disappeared quickly inside his pocket.

Anna reappeared with a tall glass of water in her hand.

"Thanks," he said, taking the chilled drink. He took a long mouthful from his glass.

"Now, Detective, you've told me Josh was involved in something. What?"

"He was involved in some sort of dispute that led to a couple of deaths," he answered, and placed the glass on the table.

"Deaths? How? Where?"

"A few miles from here."

"And you think Josh was responsible for these deaths."

"In truth – no," Balooga replied.

"Then who do you think *was* responsible?"

"It's too early to say, but I'm sure Sawyer does know who."

"So why not ask him?" she said.

"I have, but unfortunately he doesn't remember all the events of last night."

"But he does remember me and you think I was involved, yes?" she asked.

"Were you?"

She grinned slightly before saying, "I don't know, Detective. Was I?"

"Do you own a gun Miss Privalova?" he asked, abruptly.

"Is that an inquiry or a question, Detective?"

"Does it matter?"

"It does unless you've got a warrant. It is illegal to enter someone's property without one, and I could ask you to leave right now," she warned him.

He knew she was right and that he'd lost all legal initiative. His hands spread in submission. "You're absolutely right. I'm not saying you had anything to do with these murders, but I need to establish why Mister Sawyer was in the wrong part of town in the early hours of this morning."

"As I said, he left a little before dawn, and after that I don't know," she replied.

"Before dawn? That would be at about 6:30AM?"

"If that's just before daybreak, then yes."

"So he left when, exactly?"

"About a half-hour before sunrise."

"And he didn't say where he was headed?"

"Listen, Detective, we had a few drinks and then good sex. I didn't want to know anything more," she told him.

Again, the detective felt uncomfortable with the girl's openness about lovemaking, and he fidgeted awkwardly until his voice returned, "Ah… did he say if he was going to meet someone or if he was headed anywhere in particular?"

"No and no. He just left and that was it."

"Was he with anyone when you first met him?"

"No, he was on his own."

"Did he say where he was headed before you met him?"

"As I've said, I didn't meet him. We just bumped into each other."

"…It was a spontaneous thing." Balooga finished for her.

"Yeah, that's right," she agreed.

The detective became frustrated with the lack of information. He gave a heavy sigh before looking down at his scuffed brown shoes. The shoes offered him little or no inspiration, so he raised his eyes, and for the first time he glanced at the tightly wrapped material that covered her hand. "Your hand?" he inquired, wondering if it was a recent injury, maybe from a sharp knife, a particular knife buried deep into a victim's head?

She raised her bandaged hand protectively to her chest, then covered it with her other hand. "I burnt it," she said, and looked over towards the computer system. He followed her gaze to the scorched plastic case. "What happened?" he asked.

"I spilt a drink," she told him, and gently rubbed her hand through the white material.

"Oh… right," he mumbled, and guessed now that the burnt paper must have happened accidentally, not some cover-up. "So after Sawyer left, did you go anywhere?" then, he spread his hands and added, "I'm only inquiring."

"No. As I said it was nearly daybreak and I don't go out much in the day." She smiled knowingly, as if she had just shared something of significance. "Listen, Detective, it's late. I've been up all night and working most of the morning. I need some rest. What else can I tell you?"

He knew he'd exhausted his line of questioning, and to continue would be close to police harassment. She was in her rights to ask him to leave if he pursued this unsolicited interrogation any further. Reluctantly he said, "No, but I'd like to ask you some more questions at a later date. Can I find you here?"

Her grin returned. "Yes, Detective, I'll be here if you need me."

"Good, then I'll leave you to rest," he said, and made his way to the doorway.

Anna moved around the table to follow him. Balooga crossed the threshold and was instantly swallowed by the shadows. As he descended the first few steps in near-darkness, he heard a brief click and the outer door opened, allowing a beam of sunlight to filter through. Bright sunlight bathed the lower half of the stairway. He'd reached about halfway down, his legs awash with the golden light, before he sensed her directly behind him. He spun around and his feet almost went from under him.

She was standing in darkness at the top of the stairway. "Careful, Detective," she said from the shadows.

Balooga surprised himself with a short nervous laugh. After he'd regained his balance, and his composure, he reached inside his jacket and withdrew a small business card. "Please get in touch if you think of anything that may help Sawyer or myself," he said. Extending his arm, he held the card up towards her. The letters on the card flashed with brilliant golden light, throwing bright slivers of fire onto the stairway wall.

Hesitantly, Anna descended but stopped short. After an uncomfortably long pause, Balooga finally took a step upwards, plunging his hand into darkness. She snatched the card from his grasp and then stepped back before returning to shadows.

He turned his back on her, ready to descend the last few steps. For a second he had the strange sensation of being in mortal danger, but then, as he stepped outside, the inexplicable fear evaporated as the mid-afternoon sun instantly burnt it away.

Chapter Ten

Detective Emilio Sanchez pushed his way through the heavy plastic doors, leaving behind him the stench of sterilisation as he made his way out of the city morgue. Held in one of his hands was a clear bag, containing the large knife that had been left embedded in one of the murder victims. The powdered swirls and loops of fingerprints stained the handle – the forensics team's signature, and the blade carried with it a red tinge – the aftermath of a terrible force now spent.

"Detective."

He turned, halfway outside, the scent of clean air close enough to brush past his nose, and spotted the short figure of Mary Stapleton. The Medical Examiner was standing outside her office, dressed in surgery greens, which had large blotches of red spattered over them. Balanced precariously towards the end of her nose was a pair of spectacles with thick convex lenses, which gave her eyes an oddly magnified look.

"Doctor Stapleton," Sanchez said, as he joined her by the office door.

"You got the knife?" she asked.

"Yeah," he answered, raising it up to eye level.

"Good," she said.

Sanchez lowered his prize. "With a bit of luck, forensics should come up with a set of prints."

"Good," she repeated, then turned her attention away from the knife and entered her office. "Detective, come in, I'd like to share my initial findings from the first two autopsies."

Surprised by the speed with which the post-mortems had been carried out, Sanchez quickly followed her into the office.

"Sit, sit," Doctor Stapleton told him.

Sanchez placed the knife on her desk as he pulled the chair out and made himself comfortable on it.

The doctor undid a fastener to the back of her gown and removed the blood-splattered surgery scrubs. She hung the garment on a coat stand then sat down, opposite Sanchez.

"Well, a very interesting case we have here," she said.

"Indeed," Sanchez agreed. He took out his notepad and pen.

Stapleton pulled open a desk drawer, took out two green folders and placed them on the table. She separated them, took the one on the left and then opened it. "Okay," she began, "our first victim is aged between twenty-eight and thirty-five years. Stands at about five-ten. He's Caucasian and weighs about two-hundred and eighty pounds. Quite a large fellow, wouldn't you say?" She paused to readjust her glasses. "Does he have a name?"

Working overtime, Sanchez's pen tried to jot down the pathologist's findings. "Forensics will be running all their prints now, so hopefully we'll have their IDs anytime soon."

"Good," she said. "He's got numerous puncture wounds on both arms, mainly around the brachial veins. I'd say he was a regular user of morphine, although we'll have to wait for the report from toxicology to confirm it."

"Heroin?" Sanchez asked.

"Maybe?" Stapleton responded with a slight nod. "Now, the best part: the cause of death." She pointed at the bloodied knife. "Surprisingly, that wasn't the actual cause of death."

"Really?" Sanchez asked, shocked.

"Yeah. The blade split his mandible in half then sliced through his tongue, palate and nasal cavity, before eventually stopping embedded in his cerebrum. However, this would have only rendered him unconscious or, at worst, lobotomised. In time, the bleeding would have possibly resulted in a lethal clot to his brain, which may have eventually killed him. What actually did kill him though was a fatal blow to the back of his head."

"The back of the head?" Sanchez echoed, with morbid fascination.

"Correct," she said. "A blow so hard it crushed the back of his cranium almost flat, which resulted in an appalling injury to the cerebral cortex. Death would have been instantaneous."

"Jeez… " Sanchez said, and suppressed a shudder. "Could he have been hit with a bat or pole?"

"No, I don't think he was hit with that kind of an implement. The flattened area of the cranium is too large. Almost all of the back of his skull is depressed. I would say either the injury was caused by a high fall, or he was pushed against something solid by someone possessing immense strength."

Surprised by her final comment, Sanchez asked, "Someone?"

"This may help you to understand," she said, swapping the file. Opening the second file, she began her description of the next post-mortem. "White male, approximately twenty to twenty-seven years old, stands at about five-nine and weighs one-hundred and forty pounds. No sign of drug abuse, although, again, we're waiting for lab reports. Cause of death is simple: his head was twisted almost one-hundred-and-eighty degrees backwards!"

This time Sanchez was unable to suppress a brief shudder as he remembered the bizarre-looking body found on the alleyway floor.

"What worries me, Detective, is that I found specific bruising on both sides of the victim's face. Bruises consistent with that of a human hand. Whoever killed our victim must have held his face with both hands tight enough to leave abrasions and then snapped his neck with an effortless twist."

"Is that possible?" Sanchez quizzed the pathologist.

"Ordinarily I would say yes. The vertebra isn't a particularly strong bone, and if you were to twist it at an angle and were relatively strong then you could quite easily break it. What makes this particular case hard to believe is that the head had been turned completely around. To achieve this, one would have to be strong enough to not only break bone but also be able to rip and tear the sternomastiod and trapezius muscles." She gestured towards her neck, as if for emphasis. "The neck was twisted with such violence the victim's carotid artery was ripped almost in half!"

"Jesus!" Sanchez cursed.

Placing the second file down next to the first, Stapleton looked up at Sanchez. She squinted through her thick lenses and asked, "So, who should we be looking for?"

"Good question," he commented. He remembered Josh Sawyer's crazy comment about Hannibal Lecter, who would now seem like an almost plausible suspect. Unable to come up with any real sane answer, he instead asked, "Does it get any worse with the third victim?"

"Unfortunately, I won't be able to do the last autopsy until late this afternoon," she told him. She took a single sheet from each of the open files and handed them to him. "Here, these are my provisional findings. I hope they help you with your case."

"Thanks," he said, carefully folding the sheets before tucking them safely into his jacket.

Doctor Stapleton stood and quickly replaced the files in her desk. She extended her arm. "Well I'm very busy, so I must leave you now." After a quick shake of his hand, she took her green surgical gown and exited her office, leaving a bewildered Emilio Sanchez sitting alone.

***

After inserting a quarter into the payphone, Balooga punched in a cell phone number. He waited to be connected. Standing at the roadside, he turned his back on the constant buffeting of passing traffic. The connection made and an electronic ringing tone sounded.

"Detective Sanchez – Homicide," the Hispanic detective said, in a flat and digitised monotone voice.

"Sanchez, it's me, Balooga. Guess where I'm calling from?"

he quizzed his partner.

"By the sound of passing traffic, I'd say from Interstate 94."

"Close. I'm on 42nd. I'm calling from the payphone our mystery woman used earlier this morning."

"Have you managed to track her down yet?"

"Yeah, but she said Sawyer left her apartment just before dawn, and after that, she knows nothing. Listen, I've got an idea, where are you now?"

"I'm just about to leave the city morgue and head down to forensics." Sanchez said.

Balooga shoved another quarter in the payphone. "Forget forensics for now. I want you back at the precinct as quick as possible. I've got a hunch."

"What is it?"

"Listen, I'll explain later, just make your way to the precinct, ASAP."

"I'm on my way," Sanchez said, then hung up.

Balooga dropped the handset and returned to his parked car. He made his way across town, a grin spreading across his face. "Yes, my Russian beauty, I think you did indeed go out."

***

"Hey, Chief!" Sanchez acknowledged, as Balooga entered the Department.

The large detective slipped out of his jacket, revealing two dark stains underneath his arms. He threw the jacket onto the back of his chair and then seated his bulk down behind his desk. He produced a tape cassette from out of his shirt pocket, and then began to rifle through his desk until he'd managed to find what he was looking for. "Ah, here you are," he said, as he withdrew a bulky old tape-recorder.

"Christ, Chief. Not Dean Martin," Sanchez joked, referring to Balooga's favourite crooner.

"Something a little more interesting," Balooga replied, as he dusted off the recorder. He placed the tape deck on his desk and hit one of the chunky buttons. The lid flipped open. He slipped the cassette inside and pushed the lid down, then he hit the PLAY button.

"Got this from Dispatch," Balooga explained to his partner.

Sanchez sat on the end of Balooga's desk as the tape began to play.

A high-pitched squeal sounded before a female voice said, "911, which service please?" Instantly, another female followed, saying, "Police." A short pause, then a recorded message repeatedly played: "Please hold the line…" The message droned on for a minute or two before the connection was finally made, and a male voice said: "Police, state your emergency."

"Three dead and one injured. Send police and paramedics to the east-side of 29th and 3rd, turn left after Ellpasso's Bar and you'll find them," the female voice said hurriedly.

"Calm down, Miss. What's your name?" the dispatcher asked.

"There's no time, just do as I've asked," the woman said anxiously.

"Miss, calm down, everything's going to be okay. Just tell me your name?" asked the dispatcher in a calm and relaxed manner. A brief pause followed before the police dispatcher asked, "Miss, are you still there? Hello… Miss?"

Balooga hit the STOP button and ended the recording.

"Okay, so tell me, who is she?" Sanchez asked.

"Listen," Balooga said, rewinding the tape. After a couple of attempts, he found the point he was looking for and eventually reran the tape.

"What, what is it?" Sanchez asked, missing the point.

"Her voice, listen to her voice," Balooga advised.

For the third time, the woman gave her hurried message to the dispatcher.

"So, she's in a hurry. So what?" the young detective asked.

Balooga shook his head. "Don't listen to what she says. Listen to how she says it, her accent!"

For the fourth time, the recorded message was played.

"I've got it! She's French!" Sanchez said in triumph.

"Christ!" Balooga uttered, throwing his hands up to his face.

"What, she's not French?" Sanchez moaned, disappointed.

"No detective, she's not French, she's Russian!" Balooga told him, exasperated.

"Oh, okay – so she sounds Russian," Sanchez said, with a shrug of his shoulders.

"Yeah. *She* sounds Russian and guess what Sawyer's lady friend is called?" Balooga asked.

Sanchez shrugged his shoulders for a second time. "Anna Kournikova?"

"Close. It's Anna Privalova."

"Privawhat?" Sanchez asked.

"Privalova," Balooga repeated. "And she's also Russian."

"So this Priv-a-lova is the girl Sawyer spent the night with, and she told you he left before dawn and she didn't see him again. Yet, that's her on the tape?" Sanchez said.

"Correct," Balooga confirmed. He pulled a piece of paper from his pocket. "Anna Privalova said Sawyer left at about 6AM and after that she didn't go out. But the call was made at six twenty-eight."

"So she's lying!" Sanchez said excitedly.

"Not only is she lying, but so is Sawyer," Balooga told him, snatching up his jacket. "Listen, you chase up forensics. I'm gonna revisit our number one suspect." He took the cassette out of the recorder and then headed towards the door.

Once his superior had left the Department, Sanchez withdrew the autopsy reports. Remembering Doctor Stapleton's unbelievable findings, he rushed after Balooga, and yelled, "But Chief, wait! What about HANNIBAL LECTER?"

Chapter Eleven

Apart from a single visit made by an old, irritable nurse, Josh had spent the best part of the day alone. Unable to leave his room, due to the armed guard outside, he had spent the last few hours trying to make sense of the startling events which had recently encroached on his otherwise simple life. Surprised by the speed and intensity of his emotions towards Anna, he wondered if she herself harboured any affection for him. Surely not, he thought, knowing it must take more than just one night's passion to induce such emotions. But then why, after all the events that had followed, could he not stop thinking about her beautiful face?

After he had awakened in her apartment, he had been shocked and hurt by her cold demeanour. Although she had seemed angry and hostile towards him, he had also felt a conflict of emotions from within: desperation perhaps? Not the desperate need for him to leave as he had first thought, but something else. He had felt she had wanted – no, needed to share something with him, but what?

Now sitting upright in the hospital bed, he recalled the events that had taken place in the darkened alleyway. He recollected how the two punks had attempted to mug him, and how he'd hit one and turned to flee.

Then what?

Then the strangely vivid and fantastic nightmare, a dream so **clear**, he wondered if perhaps part of it had been real. Not the part when he was confronted with the hideous beast, although there was somebody else in the alleyway with him. He remembered his name being called then a hand gently caressing him as he'd regained consciousness. Although it didn't make sense, Josh could not dismiss the fact that the voice he'd heard *did* belong to Anna. With her slightly exotic Slavonic accent, her voice was unmistakable. What disturbed him was the undeniable fact that someone must have come to his aid, and in doing so, killed his attackers. Could Anna be so virulent? In this day and age it would not have come as a surprise to find a young, single woman carrying a weapon. So had Anna followed him and then somehow overpowered his assailants?

Could she be capable of such an atrocity?

Josh suffered with his own confused thoughts until the door swung open with a bang. He looked over towards the doorway and his heart sank as the big detective reappeared.

"Shit," he mumbled, seeing the hostility on the detective's face.

"Hello again Mister Sawyer," Balooga said.

Unable to find his voice, Josh managed a weak nod.

In almost a rerun of their previous encounter, Balooga seated himself on the bedside chair next to Josh.

"Well things *have* become interesting since we last spoke," Balooga said. "Now, do you know a Miss Anna Privalova?"

Momentarily shocked by the use of Anna's name, Josh fell silent, unable to give an answer.

"Mister Sawyer, do you know Anna Privalova?" Balooga repeated.

"Yeah," Josh muttered, finally finding his voice.

"Good, now that's a start," Balooga said, "and is she the girl you spent last night with?"

"Yeah," Josh told the detective reluctantly.

"Oh, it seems like your memory has finally returned," Balooga mocked. "So is there anything more you can tell us about Anna Privalova?"

"No," Josh replied, not wanting to betray her.

"Oh, come on now, Mister Sawyer, you must know something.

I mean, you did spend the *entire* night together!"

"Just get to your point detective," Josh said, unwilling to play games.

"My point is, you did indeed see or at least speak to Anna Privalova after you left her apartment."

"I've told you, I left her in the early hours, and that's the last time I saw or spoke to her," Josh said, and he desperately wanted to believe this.

"Is that so?"

"For the final time – YES," Josh replied.

"In that case, how do you account for this?" Balooga asked. He produced something from his pocket.

Josh found a tape clasped between one of Balooga's big meaty hands. "What's that?"

"This is the recorded call taken from 911. It's the call that led us to you and our three friends lying in the morgue. And guess whose voice is on it?" He waved the tape about as if it was some kind of trophy.

Josh's heart sank, as he understood whose voice must be on the tape. "How?" he muttered, with genuine bewilderment.

"What? How did she get on the tape or how did she phone in your rescue?"

"Both," Josh said. A wave of overwhelming dread washed over him. Did Anna really have something to do with his assailants' deaths?

"The simple truth is – you didn't leave her apartment alone, DID YOU, MISTER SAWYER?" Balooga snapped.

"Yes – No. I'm not sure," Josh mumbled, his mind in freefall.

"Which one is it, yes or no?" Balooga pushed.

Josh pressed both his hands to his head, as if trying to hold in his sanity. "I don't know, I just don't know."

"Think! You must know something."

Slowly, Josh regained his composure. He took a deep breath and said, "There was someone else in that alleyway, but who, I just don't know." And for once, he looked directly into the detective's eyes. "I didn't kill those guys and neither did Anna. I can assure you of that."

"SO WHO DID?" Balooga barked.

"CHRIST! I don't know, you're the detective, you tell me," Josh snapped back.

"Okay, I'll tell you what I think," Balooga began. "I think you and Anna Privalova went to that alleyway to buy drugs. Maybe there's a shortage on campus and you decided you could make a little money selling shit to your college friends. You got to the alley and then decided you weren't going to pay for them, and then got in a fight. What I think, Mister Sawyer is that you *and* Anna Privalova murdered all three, together!"

"You're crazy. If we killed them for drugs, then where the hell are they?" Josh countered.

"I suspect that Anna Privalova has them."

Josh shook his head in disbelief. "If you don't believe me then speak to Anna."

"I already have!" Balooga said, surprising Josh.

"What?"

"I've already questioned Miss Privalova, and she said exactly the same as you. So that makes you both liars!"

Josh found it difficult to breathe. He felt as if the walls of the room were slowly closing in on him, in an attempt to squeeze out the truth, but what truth? The truth that Anna really was in that alleyway with him, and that somehow she did indeed come to his aid, and in doing so killed all three of his assailants? Yes, Josh thought, finally accepting the unbelievable.

Balooga read the sudden realisation on the young man's face. "Talk to me. I'm the only one who can get you out of this mess."

Confronted with this unwanted revelation, Josh remained silent.

"Okay, Mister Sawyer, I'll play it your way," Balooga said. The detective stood and moved over to the door. He took a last look at Josh. "I suggest you get yourself an attorney, because by tonight I'll have both you and Anna Privalova in custody!"

Chapter Twelve

With the last rays of sunshine filtering into his assigned prison, Josh continued to pace up and down, the onset of panic about ready to choke him senseless. Trapped in this hospital room, he anxiously looked around for a way out. For the third time in the last hour he moved over to the open window and contemplated the jump down to ground. He dismissed the idea as suicidal, and instead crept up to the door. Gently, he pushed it open and peered out to find the uniformed guard still sat opposite. He closed the door and returned to the window.

Although it was early evening with only a half-hour of daylight remaining, the sun's rays still carried a considerable amount of heat, warming his worried face.

He looked around the room in the hope that something would materialise to aid him in his escape. But he found nothing. He gave up his search and returned to the bed. Lying down in silent defeat, he folded his hands behind his head and looked up at the cracks in the ceiling. He closed his eyes and began to recap on Balooga's earlier comments.

The detective had warned Josh that he was heading directly for the courts to obtain a warrant for both his and Anna's arrest. Allowed at least one phone call, Josh had insisted on contacting his father. Unable to leave the room in only his under-shorts, he had eventually been supplied with a pair of baggy brown pants, a faded shirt two sizes too big, and a pair of tatty black shoes. All had been supplied from lost and found. His own bloodied clothes were waiting for the trip down town and were sealed in a plastic bag and stored within a safe locker somewhere inside St Andrews.

Dressed in his new, not so refined clothes, Josh had then been marched to a payphone, where he had attempted to call his father. He'd waited and listened to the continuous ringing for what seemed like an eternity. Eventually, he'd hung up. And, not knowing whom else to phone, he had simply turned around and returned to his newly appointed cell. Before he'd left for the courts, Balooga had reassured Josh that a State Attorney would be appointed on his behalf, if so required.

Unable to relax, Josh sat up. He returned to the window before looking out and down at the ground below. He found that nobody had kindly left a mattress or a pile of boxes for him to land on.

He leaned out of the window, as far as he could, and scanned the surrounding brickwork. His hands ran along the gritty surface, but he was unable to find any viable grooves or ledges to grip onto. As he leaned forward, his stomach pushed the vase situated there towards the edge of the windowsill. He pulled himself back into the room. But, as he did so, he caught the vase with his elbow. To his horror it wobbled backwards and forwards before gaining sufficient momentum for it to topple outwards. In a dive through the window, Josh threw himself forwards and heroically caught the vase, saving it from near-certain destruction. He hung precariously half in and half out. Slowly, he eased his way back inside the room. And, with shaking hands, he replaced the ceramic pot back in the middle of the windowsill.

"Jesus!" he cursed, and held his breath. He turned, waiting for the door to fly open, expecting the uniformed guard to come in guns blazing and shoot him dead for attempting to escape Spider-Man-style. The door remained shut and Josh expelled a breath and relaxed, a little. He turned his attention away from the window and returned to the safety of the bed. He sat down on the edge. There, he contemplated his next move.

Less than five feet above his head, the cream-coloured plastic smoke detector began its daily systems check. First, it checked for its expected permanent supply of about 110 volts. The supply voltage tested correct, so the detector connected automatically to the rest of the sensors throughout this floor. It ran an interconnection test to make sure the rest of the alarms operated in parallel to each other. Satisfied, it transferred to battery backup and stayed this way until the electronic circuitry timed out. Then finally, the system reconnected to the mains supply before resetting to detector mode. An electronic beep sounded as it returned to standby.

The noise caused Josh to look up. For the first time he noticed the smoke detector. And instantly he knew that this was an important discovery. He jumped to his feet, his heartbeat quickening, and stood on his tiptoes to examine the plastic case. A single red light blinked back. The only other distinguishable mark to be found was a small vent, which hid the complicated circuitry behind. Josh sat back down and waited for his thoughts to catch up.

After only a few minutes of contemplation, a slight smile bent Josh's lips upwards. He stood then, ready to begin his escape.

***

Imprisoned by the walls, Anna stood and waited, increasingly anxious for her escape. She moved away from the bed and crossed the apartment, then reached out towards the closed drapes. She sensed the sunlight beyond. Unable to move any closer, she waited.

Soon now the sun would retreat, bringing in its place darkness and freedom. She stood silent, pensive for a moment and her thoughts turned towards the man she had met earlier, Josh. She felt a surprising pang of pity, sad to leave now after having spent only the briefest of time with him, sure in the knowledge that something special may have come to them. But cold, hard truth wrapped its brutal hand around her heart, squeezing all sentiment out, leaving her empty and hollow. Now was not the time to get involved. She sighed heavily. Turned away from the window. Leaving both want and anticipation behind her.

Outside, shadows began to stretch and lengthen. The sun swelled into a heavy red ball, slipping quickly towards the distant horizon. Younger, more animated people, ready to experience the pleasures that evening had to offer, had replaced most of the dwindling commuters, making the return trip home.

It was only minutes until dusk.

***

Only fifteen or twenty minutes of daylight remained. Acting quickly now, Josh brought his plan into operation. He moved over to the bedside cabinet and retrieved one of the old yellowing magazines. He snatched up the plastic beaker and hurriedly carried it to the window. And, for once, he did not contemplate jumping out. He flipped open the magazine and leafed through it, trying to find a suitable picture. Nearly all of the pages contained either a slim and attractive model or an advertisement for some life-enhancing beauty product. He saw a suitable picture flick past, and paging back he found an article on breast re-sculpturing.

The article covered two pages and comprised mostly of women's breasts. One of the pictures showed an attractive woman, slim with long brown hair, who was no older than thirty. She stood dressed in only her panties. Although she retained a fair amount of youthfulness, her breasts were very large, but extremely flat, and they hung almost to the point of her waist. Her pale, nearly white skin was lined with deep stretch marks that ran from her clavicle down to her circular nipples.

"She's the one," he said.

He opened the magazine out, over the windowsill, and took the beaker. Using the tail of his shirt, he wiped the bluish liquid clear from the inside of the glass. He turned the beaker over and wiped the bottom clear of any dust. His head tilted towards the dwindling sun as he let the last rays of sunshine wash across his face.

"Okay, here goes nothing," he said.

He took the beaker and held it at arm's length, focussing the reflected sunlight on the picture of the woman. He readjusted the distance between the magazine and his hand, and used the bottom of the plastic beaker as a makeshift magnifying glass. Eventually, after a couple of attempts, he managed to reduce the sunlight to a small, intensely bright spot of heat. Within a couple of seconds the centre of the heated dot began to discolour. It turned from a bright white to a dark brown and then finally to black. The centre of the black spot began to burn, releasing tiny wisps of grey smoke.

Excited by the prospect of his escape, Josh began to tremble, inadvertently moving the magnified rays away from the central spot. With the intense heat lost, the spot failed to ignite fully and, after only a brief life of red embers, it quickly died. A few painfully weak plumes of smoke escaped as the spot expired.

Frantically, Josh cupped the beaker over the smoke in a vain attempt to catch it. The smoke rose to the top of the beaker and formed a thin cloud, filling the top quarter of the cup only. He moved over to the middle of the room. He was about to raise the beaker to the detector when the door swung open and the uniformed guard peered in. Without thinking, Josh turned the beaker upwards and inhaled the smoke hastily into the back of his throat. He looked at the guard with his mouth clamped shut, not daring to breathe out. He raised the glass in a mock toast.

"Asshole!" the young guard said, unimpressed by this prisoner's false bravado. "Better get fit and strong," he added, misunderstanding his prisoner had just taken a shot of medicine. "You'll need to be, if you're gonna fight off all those big butch pussies once you get to the pen."

Turning a slight shade of red, with the acrid smoke burning his throat, Josh spun round, bent slightly, and simulated taking it up the butt.

"Asshole," the guard repeated, before retreating through the doorway.

Josh held the smoke in his lungs for a few more seconds, before finally releasing his breath, expelling a faint grey cloud. He took in a huge lung-full of clean air and returned to his present healthy colour, of ghostly white. He went back to the window to retrieve the magazine, and again extended his arm outwards towards the sun.

My God, the sun!

In the last minute the sun had moved sufficiently westwards to be partially obscured by one of the city's towering office blocks. In minutes it would disappear entirely and take any hope of escape with it.

With urgency, Josh repositioned the beaker and began the process for a second time. Once again he focused the light into a small intense white dot. Without the full magnitude of the sun, the dot struggled to ignite the paper. "C'mon, bitch. Burn!" Josh urged, as the white of the woman's breasts finally began to darken.

After an eternity the paper caught and began to smoulder. The edges of the circular hole started to burn, and this time it generated a thicker and more copious amount of smoke. Not wanting to actually burn down the hospital, he simultaneously blew out the small flames and caught the resultant smoke inside the beaker. Then, the sun finally succumbed to time, disappearing behind the city skyline.

He trapped the grey smoke by cupping the bottom of the beaker, and using his elbow he pushed the magazine out of the window, losing half of the evidence. Then cautiously he moved towards the detector. He paused momentarily and waited, half expecting the guard to appear, when he didn't, Josh raised his hands and offered the beaker up to the detector.

Instantly, a sharp piercing bell began to ring, which signalled an evacuation throughout the whole of the third floor.

Josh threw himself backwards and landed flat onto the hospital bed just as the door swung open.

"STAY HERE!" the guard commanded with a look of panic on his face. Before Josh had time to respond, the guard disappeared back through the doorway.

Josh wasted no time. He jumped to his feet and reached the door before it had time to swing shut. He pulled the door inward and held his breath as he peered out through the gap. He saw nothing but a clear pathway that led straight to the emergency stairwell. He looked in the opposite direction and had just enough time to see the guard hastily disappear around the corner of the corridor. He stepped out of the room.

The corridor began to fill with anxious-looking staff and a few able patients wearing hospital gowns. They stood around, looking at each other, nobody sure what to do.

Swiftly, Josh ran to the emergency stairwell and opened the door. He shouted, "THE FIRE'S THIS WAY. EVERYBODY BACK THAT–A–WAY!"

Now faced with real danger, the crowd hastily began to move away from the stairwell and towards the opposite end of the corridor, directly into the path of the returning guard. The guard spotted Josh and reached for his sidearm. The force of the crowd pushed him backwards and away from the fugitive, before he had time to draw his weapon. With a brief wave goodbye, Josh turned his back on the mobbed guard.

Then, as if the hounds of Hell themselves were snapping at his heels, he quickly disappeared down the stairwell, making good his escape.

Chapter Thirteen

"This is bullshit," Detective John Holloway told his partner.

From across the passenger seat and, having just heard the same words repeated for the fifth time in as many minutes, Ed Newbury gave a heavy sigh. Almost twice Holloway's age, Ed Newbury had little more than eight months left before retirement. Normally patient and diligent, his irksome younger partner had begun to agitate him.

"This is bullshit," Holloway told his partner, again.

"The Chief said to wait, so we'll wait," Newbury explained.

Holloway leaned forward and looked up at the blackened windows. Gripping the steering wheel of their unmarked police car, he pushed himself back in his seat and squirmed about in an attempt to restore the circulation into his numbed-up ass.

"This is—"

"Bullshit," Newbury interjected.

"You got that right," Holloway agreed, missing the bitterness directed at him. "They're both as guilty as hell," he said, and scanned the empty street.

Newbury and Holloway had now spent the last three hours parked at the kerbside, watching for any movements from above. Cramped-up inside the tight confinements of the car, they were both heading quickly towards the point of extreme boredom. So far, only shadows had revealed themselves; deep patches of darkness, capable of hiding any number of unexpected nightmares.

Holloway looked at his watch. "How much longer is Balooga gonna be?"

"The courts closed at seven, so he'll be here any minute," Newbury answered.

"She could've escaped by then."

"Escaped? Escaped to where?" Newbury asked. "There's no way out, apart from the front."

On their arrival, they had checked out the back. They found only one small window at a height of about twenty feet and no fire escape near. Both agreed that the only way out would be by the front of the building. Confident that the back held no escape, they had decided to wait out front, together.

"What if she leaves?" Holloway asked.

"Then we tail her," the older cop said. "Applegate said we're to do this one by the book. So we wait until Balooga brings the warrant for arrest. Okay?"

"I just think this is bullshit," Holloway mumbled, finally feeling the reprimand.

Both fell silent as they continued to survey the darkened street. After only a few minutes, they spotted a silhouette turn into the street. The dark apparition paused momentarily, before continuing towards the two detectives, stopping less than twenty feet away. Both detectives slid down in their seats. The silhouette moved closer to the doorway, stood there for only a few seconds, and then disappeared inside.

Newbury placed a hand on his partner's arm. "We wait… "

***

The silhouette moved slowly upward, an extension to the shadows, and reached the top of the stairway. Josh pushed open the door and slipped silently inside. The large room was almost pitch-black with only a minimum amount of light filtering through the small open window found at the rear of the apartment.

"Anna?" he whispered.

No response.

"Anna, it's me," he said, louder this time, risking detection. His voice echoed back to him, twisted and warped. He moved deeper into the apartment. A strong smell of chemicals wafted over, making him feel slightly light-headed and nauseous.

What the hell was he doing here? Stupid. Yes. Yet something had drawn him here, something that had urged him to warn Anna of the impending situation.

"Anna?"

The apartment was as dead as a tomb.

He moved across the apartment in the near-darkness, blindly, fumbling his way towards the centre of the room. His thigh bumped against something solid. He remembered a table being there, and reached out, intent on finding the lamp. His hand closed around something cold and skeletal. Bones shifted slightly and the lamp clicked on.

"Quiet... " a voice warned.

Surprised by the unexpected voice, Josh stumbled backward, almost losing his balance. The weak light threw a deep shadow across the speaker's face. The shape shifted slightly to reveal a pale countenance framed by black hair. A skeletal finger rose to its grey lips. "We're being watched." The face split into a dreadful leer, revealing perfectly formed white teeth.

"Where's Anna?" Josh asked with worry.

"Now that's a *very* interesting question," the stranger said. He moved around the table to stand directly in front of Josh.

Josh shivered involuntarily. Standing slightly taller than Josh and of similar build, the newcomer wore a light blue shirt, which was open at the neck to reveal pale, hairless skin. The bottom of his shirt was tucked tightly inside a pair of faded denim jeans and, as he took a step closer, his cowboy boots thumped hollowly on the wooden floor. He halved the distance. Then reached out.

Josh drew away from the slim ghost, stepping to the centre of the room. Although physically they were equally matched, he sensed that this opponent possessed immense strength.

"Bug, where are you going?" the guy asked. His face split into an unnaturally wide grin.

"Listen, I'm just looking for Anna," Josh said defensively.

"Ah – yes, the elusive Anna."

Josh backed up alongside the king-sized bed. Something deep within those green eyes struck terror into Josh's heart. As he stared into those terrible green orbs, he felt his strength ebb away, and within seconds he'd been rendered powerless. Then, unexpectedly, the pressure to his wounded head evaporated, to be replaced instead by invisible, icy talons. He shook his head in an attempt to free the cold grasp, but they held steady, before probing deeper into his open consciousness. All strength lost, he slumped backward onto the bed where he sat limp and lifeless like a stringless puppet.

The guy reached out to place his hand an inch from Josh's head. "Good, let me see," he commanded.

After a couple of seconds, his eyes began to turn a fierce red. Thrusting his hand forward, he touched Josh's bandaged forehead and, with a look of pure determination, he cried, "I said, OPEN UP!"

His body began to shake uncontrollably, as if a thousand volts had been applied to his limbs, making him buck and sway. Within seconds, the look of determination slipped away completely, replaced now by one of desperation.

Josh felt the icy talons slice deeper into his very soul. Frozen bolts of pain cut through his entire body. Then, just as he was about to pass out from the pain, the agony stopped as the talons unexpectedly withdrew. The guy growled with anger. He released Josh from his invisible grip, stumbling back as if struck by some unseen force.

"Your brain is useless, bug. I can't read a damned thing!"

The last slivers of pain oozed away. Josh looked up and saw that the guy had almost doubled over with his own pain. He jumped to unsteady feet. In an attempt to escape he staggered towards the landing. He reached the doorway, making good his escape, before the room turned into a sudden blur. He flew through the air, crashing heavily against the wall opposite, the air exploding from his lungs.

"I haven't said it's time to leave yet, bug," the guy said from the doorway.

Already battered and bruised, from his encounter with the street punks, Josh tried to stand in a vain attempt to protect himself. His vision swam out of focus as he stood. He leaned back against the wall and prepared himself for another onslaught.

"WHERE IS SHE?" the guy screamed.

"Here she is," Josh replied, flipping him the bird. In the blink of an eye, the pale face appeared in front of him.

"Time for bug to die!"

An elongated hand reached out. Josh felt himself gripped by the throat. He was lifted off his feet and pinned against the wall with effortless strength. The vicelike grip began to squeeze the life out of him, his vision clouding over, drawing him towards unconsciousness with startling speed. Just before the veil of darkness fell completely, he heard muffled shouts coming from a great distance. And, as he was about to lose all consciousness, he spotted two figures by the open doorway.

***

"FREEZE!" Holloway screamed, with the riot shotgun raised high.

"Don't do anything you may regret," Newbury ordered.

The stranger turned and looked in the detectives' direction. "Regret?" he asked, as if not fully comprehending.

"Just keep cool," Newbury said.

"We'll play later," the guy said, dropping Josh to the floor. He clapped his hands like an excited child. "Bugs with toys! Toys go Bang! Bang!"

Christ! This fucker's flying on PCP, just look at his eyes, Holloway thought.

"Okay, now step away from the suspect," Newbury ordered.

The guy stepped away from Josh and walked slowly towards the armed detectives. He held his hands out, pressed together at the wrists. "Okay, Officer, take me in."

"Easy! Take it easy!" Newbury told him.

The guy jumped unexpectedly in Holloway's direction.

With a boom of thunder the riot shotgun fired.

The pale ghost staggered back. He held his hands to his chest and, with his head slumped forward, he dropped to one knee.

The cordite–filled air cleared. Newbury heard the guy giggle like a lunatic.

"Missed me!" the crazed face told him, with a hideous grin stretched across its mouth. The guy stood to his full height. His hands moved away from his chest to reveal a clean and unscathed shirt and chest. "Silly bug missed."

"Listen, man, backup is on its way, there's nowhere to go," the older detective said, with his gun outstretched.

"Backup! Backup!" the insane stranger chanted, waving his hands in the air like some demented preacher. He took a few steps back, moving away from the detective and shortening the distance to Josh.

Then, even after almost thirty years as a street cop, Newbury made a fatal mistake. Following the lunatic, he stepped directly into Holloway's line–of–fire.

"Step away from the suspect, NOW!" Newbury commanded.

"UH–OH, bug fell for trap," the guy giggled.

"DO IT NOW!" Newbury shouted.

"Stupid little bug, you're already dead!"

"What?" Newbury asked, and his sidearm wavered slightly. He heard the shotgun lock and load from behind him. Newbury grasped that the intruder was heading towards the open window found at the back of the apartment. "Cover the window!" he called to Holloway. No movement or sound or recognition came from behind. "Holloway?" He turned until he could make out the vague outline of his younger partner. "Are you okay?" he asked.

Silence.

Risking a longer look, Newbury turned to Holloway and found that the younger cop had the riot gun up to his shoulder and had it pointed directly at him!

"Holloway, what the fuck are you doing?" the older cop
gasped.

Pull the trigger – Holloway heard from inside his head.

NO! – Holloway tried to cry, but nothing escaped from his lips.

If you don't kill him, he'll shoot you dead. Now pull the fucking trigger!
– the voice ordered him.

I can't!

Yes you can, just squeeze the trigger.

But, he's my partner!

*FUCK HIM! If you don't shoot, he's gonna blow your fuckin' bug brains
all over the place.*

He is?

Look at him! Why's he got that fuckin' huge piece pointed at your face?

I don't know, why?

Because he wants to KILL YOU!

He does?

YES!

OH FUCK…

BOOM!

CRACK!

The buckshot hit Newbury, hundreds of supersonic pellets,
ripping through his upper chest and throat, knocking him
backwards with violent disregard. Lead pellets tore their way
through skin, muscle and bone. His head flew upwards, spun
away from his body, somersaulting twice, before landing on the
floor with a wet slap. His headless body danced a short jig before
it toppled over onto the bloodied floor.

The recoil of the shotgun threw Holloway's arms sideways,
which spun him completely around. Instead of going wide, the
shot fired from the convulsing, headless Newbury, hit him flush
in the face. In a spray of gore, the bullet blew his brains out,
through the open doorway and onto the wall opposite.

"OOPS!" the stranger said mischievously.

Ears ringing from the gunshots, Josh raised his head and
witnessed the carnage before him. He smelt the thick coppery
stench of blood and guts. He lost the contents of his stomach.

He fell against the wall then, spent. The apartment had fallen silent. In the distance a continuous wail of sirens began to grow in volume.

The guy turned with a pleased look on his face. He spotted Josh propped up against the wall of the apartment.

Josh blinked and the maniac stood before him. He was grabbed by the front of his shirt.

"Where were we? Oh yes, I was going to kill you!" the guy said gleefully.

"Just do it!" Josh said defiantly.

He closed his eyes.

While he waited for the fatal blow, he heard the wail of sirens grow louder. You're too late, Balooga, he thought, almost amused. A sharp crack sounded. He heard a second crack, followed by a high-pitched squeal.

Holding Josh against the wall with one hand, the guy placed a bony finger to his lips. After a few seconds of silence, the high-pitched crackle started again but this time a distant metallic voice followed.

"This is patrol 53 headed northbound. We have a positive, I repeat a positive ID on the female suspect wanted for the Little Village slayings. She's headed north along 33rd. She's on foot. Do you want her picking up? Over."

A short bout of static ensued before a louder voice replied. "Negative, I repeat that's a negative, just keep her in sight. Over."

Holloway's walkie-talkie fell momentarily silent before it crackled back to life.

"Sir, we think she may be headed towards the airport. Over."

"Do NOT pick her up! Notify airport security. If she tries to board an aircraft, then we retain her. Over."

"Anna…" Josh whispered, understanding at once that the conversation regarded her.

"Quiet, bug," the guy told him.

The metallic voice sprung back to life. "This is Lieutenant Balooga, requesting immediate backup. I'm in pursuit of the male fugitive. I'm headed towards 42nd and 3rd. Please acknowledge.

Over."

"This is patrol 27, acknowledging request and assisting. ETA three minutes, over."

The siren grew louder, reaching its maximum. Blue and red lights flashed along the inside walls as they were reflected into the apartment. A colourful troop of dancing apparitions spun crazily around the room with devilish delight.

"Well, you and the bitch have been bad bugs, haven't you?" the guy said, and for the first time he broke into a genuine smile. "Maybe I should let you live?" He released his grip and let Josh slump to the floor. They heard the screech of tyres as a car pulled up outside. The guy took one last look at Josh. "If you see that bitch before I do, tell her Jonus has risen from the dead!"

***

Balooga hit the brakes, bringing the Sedan to an abrupt halt. He withdrew his Smith & Wesson snub nose and then climbed hastily out of the car. The dark doorway dared him to enter.

"Shit, I told you to wait," he breathed, spotting the abandoned police car.

A mighty clap of thunder sounded from above, followed by a shower of debris that rained down over the street, covering Balooga with small stinging shards of glass and wooden splinters. He ducked down instinctively but still had time to see a large blur fly overhead. He heard a hollow, metallic boom from the direction of his abandoned car, followed by crazed laughter, which quickly trailed away into the night.

"What the hell?" he said.

With his pistol in a shooter's stance, he traced the gun across the length of the darkened street. The flashing lights of the Sedan threw multicoloured phantoms across the walls of the surrounding buildings, giving Balooga the sensation of being trapped within a huge spinning-top. With his arms outstretched, he moved over to the stationary vehicle.

He kept his eyes on the street until he had reached the Sedan.

He placed his hand on the warm surface of the hood and traced two indentations. The depressions looked as if a pair of feet had made them. "What the hell?" He looked up to find the window above had been completely shattered.

Now fearful for his two colleagues, he quickly returned to the dark entrance.

He took one final deep breath, and then entered.

***

Josh plunged down the stairwell, recklessly, eager to get out, taking the steps two at a time. He neared the bottom. His exit was unexpectedly blocked. Moving with too much momentum, he crashed against the dark obstruction. Both collapsed into the street in a windmill of arms and legs.

Josh landed heavily on the sidewalk, his teeth clicking painfully together. He sat up and shook his head. Directly in front of him was a dark metallic handgun. He reached out and took the weapon.

"STOP!" Balooga's worried face hovered in the darkness like a pale moon.

"It wasn't me," Josh told the detective.

"Stay calm, son," Balooga cautioned.

"You don't understand. I didn't kill them."

"I believe you son. Now take it easy and hand over the gun."

"The ghost did it!" Josh said, with an edge of hysteria to his voice.

Balooga looked in the kid's eyes and saw they had the wild look of shock about them.

"I believe you, I really do. But if I'm gonna help you, you need to give me the gun."

"What if he comes back?" Josh blurted nervously.

"If who comes back?"

"The pale guy with the eyes!"

"I don't know who you're talking about," Balooga said, taking a step closer to Josh and the gun.

"… The guy…" Josh stuttered uncontrollably.

"Son, I don't know who you mean."

"You didn't see him?"

"See who?"

"The guy who jumped out of the fucking window!" Josh snapped. He nodded in the direction of the apartment. "The guy who killed *them*!"

With sickening certainty, Balooga knew that the kid was not talking about the three street punks. "My God, what have you done?"

"I told you, it wasn't me," Josh said.

"Who's up there?" Balooga demanded.

"The cops, man! The dead COPS!"

"Oh – Christ," Balooga breathed.

Josh moved away from the kerbside and reached the Sedan. With the gun trained on the detective, he quickly examined the steering column. Keys hung from the ignition. He opened the door.

"Sawyer, what the hell are you doing?"

"If he finds her first, he'll kill her," Josh told him, climbing inside the vehicle. The side window cranked down and Josh levelled the pistol at the detective as he advanced forwards.

Balooga stopped in his tracks. "You're only making it worse for yourself," he warned.

"Worse? It's way beyond worse."

After a brief struggle to start the Sedan – due to his plastered right hand – Josh eventually turned the engine over. He threw the car into gear and then pressed down on the accelerator. The vehicle jumped forward and, with the engine screaming, it disappeared deep into the night.

Chapter Fourteen

The airport terminal was extremely busy at this time of night. Queues that seemed to stretch for miles ran from one side of the terminal to the next; hundreds of holidaymakers saddled with baggage or children, or both, anxiously waiting to board their flights, ready to begin long awaited vacations with the same eagerness as released prisoners, they themselves freed, temporarily, from the humdrum monotony of a life that was both ritual and repetitive.

The young girl looked up from her desk. "Cash or MasterCard?"

"Cash," replied the woman stood opposite.

"That'll be one-hundred-and-sixty-five dollars, please," the girl said.

The woman, a shorthaired blonde, withdrew a large bundle of green bills. She counted out a handful of money and handed it to the check-in attendant.

"Thank you, Miss," the attendant said. She checked for the correct amount before handing over a flight ticket and boarding-pass. "They'll be boarding at gate six in about fifteen minutes," she explained.

"Thank you," Anna said, taking her ticket.

"How much luggage will you be taking with you?" asked the attendant.

"Just this," Anna answered, holding up a medium-sized case.

"I'm afraid that's too large to class as hand luggage. It'll have to be stored in the cargo hold."

"That's okay," she replied.

Anna lifted her case onto a short conveyor at the side of the check-in desk, stood back and watched as it disappeared through a small passageway. Turning away from the desk, she took a step away.

"Miss, wait!"

Anna turned to find the girl holding something outwards.

"Better not forget this," the girl said, handing over her passport.

"Thanks," Anna said.

"Oh dear," the attendant commented, noticing Anna's heavily bandaged hand.

"I burnt it," she said, in simple explanation.

Anna stepped away from the desk and mixed in with the steady throng of early evening commuters. With a casual ease that was both practised and preformed, she walked through the departures terminal. She found gate six and, seeing a number of other passengers waiting, she took a seat.

She sat and watched as the security guards patrolled around the different check-in desks and main entrances. There were also three or four uniformed cops mixed in with the crowd and they were all paying particular attention to young, single, dark-haired women. She looked down and allowed herself a brief smile. Her trip to the restroom and quick change from brunette to blonde had thrown her would-be trackers off the scent.

Fifteen minutes passed before the passengers began to board. She stood and joined the queue at the boarding gate.

"Anna!"

Her heart jumped.

"Anna, it's me."

She turned to discover a battered and bedraggled tramp standing there, looking at her. The tramp wore oversized clothes and a skew-whiff bandage on his head.

"Sorry, you must have mistaken me for someone else," she said.

The tramp took a step closer, then reached out with his hand. "It's me – Josh."

She recognized him immediately and took his hands. "My God, look at you."

"I'd rather not," Josh joked, trying to find humour in this never-ending nightmare.

Anna looked at his desperate face. She felt a rush of affection towards him. "Are you alright?" she asked with genuine concern.

"I've had better days."

She stared into his blue eyes and for a moment forgot the gravity of their situation. She squeezed his hands with tenderness and then gently embraced him. A soft kiss brushed his lips.

"I've got to go," she whispered.

"Go? Go where?"

"Away from here."

"Anna, I'm in trouble. I need your help."

"I can't help you," she said, and anxiously looked at the dwindling queue.

"You can't just leave!"

"Josh, I can't get involved," she said quietly.

"You already are," he said.

"I don't know what you're talking about."

"I know it was you."

After a slight pause, she asked, "Me what?"

"Last night, in the alleyway."

"I don't know what you're talking about."

"You saved my life," he told her, with both appreciation and sorrow. "Anna, I saw you!"

"You saw nothing!" she barked, and took a step away.

He pulled her back. "Anna, I SAW YOU."

Not understanding the significance of what he was saying, she snapped, "Then you're lucky to be alive!"

Josh brushed off her confused anger. "You don't understand. I saw you and I don't care."

"What?" she asked, bewildered.

"YOU – IT, in the alleyway."

Speechless, she looked at him.

"Don't leave, we can work it out," he told her imploringly.

"I–I'm sorry, I've got to go." She turned her back on him and moved over to the boarding entrance. The male attendant took her pass. She turned to say, "Goodbye, Josh."

"He'll find you," he called to her.

Ignoring him, she moved to the back of the boarding line, paused for a second, confusion and uncertainty holding her there, before continuing along the tight passageway with the rest of the passengers.

"Anna, Jonus has come back from the dead!"

Her heart stopped. She turned slowly, with an uncharacteristic look of fear on her face. Without knowing it, she took a few faltering steps towards him and finished back at the boarding desk. "What did you say?"

"I said – Jonus has come back from the dead," Josh repeated, joining her at the entrance.

"My God… " she whispered.

"Anna, what's going on?"

His question went unheard. "He's dead," she said.

"Listen to me, this Jonus, he's here – in the city, tonight!"

"He can't be. I killed him."

"What?"

"He's dead, don't you understand!"

"He was at your apartment, less than an hour ago!"

"How?" she asked, stunned.

"Miss, boarding time is over, you need to leave," the attendant explained.

"In a minute!" Josh snapped in the guy's direction. He took her by the arm. "I don't know who he is or what's going on, but we need to leave, right now!"

Anna trembled uncontrollably. She looked into his eyes and said, "But he's dead." Her eyes swam with confusion and fear, and Josh understood immediately that she'd slipped into some kind of temporary shock. He pulled her away from the passageway. "We've got to get out of here," he urged.

"Miss, what about your flight?" the attendant called.

"Fuck it!" Josh told him.

Pulled along, Anna followed Josh across the busy terminal, heading towards one of the exits. She regained her senses and brought him to an abrupt halt.

"Wait," she said, "security will be looking for us. They've got all the exits covered."

She scanned the terminal and spotted a utility entrance off to one side. "This way," she instructed, pulling him away from the main exits.

They hastily weaved their way through the crowd of people.

Two uniformed cops spotted them. One of the cops checked a photo-fit he held in his hands. He squinted, then his eyes widened as he matched Josh to the picture. "Hey – you. Stop!"

Without hesitation, Josh and Anna continued to move to the access doorway. They made it to the door, where Josh tried the handle.

"It's locked!" he snapped.

"Stand back!" she ordered.

Anna placed the flat of her hand onto the wooden surface and effortlessly pushed the door open. With a brief crack, the framework splintered and broke, and as one they fell into the room. They found themselves inside a large storage area. Numerous crates and boxes of cargo were piled up towards a high ceiling. Formed into long, equally spaced rows and columns, the containers disappeared in every direction, creating a maze of wooden passageways and tunnels.

"Which way?" Josh asked.

"This way!" Anna said. She dragged him through the maze as they ran between the makeshift passages, looking for a way out.

"Over here!" someone shouted.

They pulled each other along and quickly lost themselves within the wooden labyrinth. Suddenly, they ran up against a dead end.

"Where to now?" Josh asked, pain written across his face. His old leg injury throbbed like hell.

Anna spotted an open skylight. "Upwards."

"What?"

"We go up," she said, and pointed at the open vent.

Josh rubbed his left leg. "My leg, I don't think I ca… "

He felt powerful hands grip his waist and he was hauled unceremoniously onto the nearest crate. "Come on," Anna said, pulling him onto the next crate. Without caution they climbed towards the skylight. They reached the highest box and then crawled over to the opening. Anna pushed the window fully open. "Follow me," she ordered.

She clambered through the hole. Josh grabbed the edge of the window. Hindered by his right arm, he struggled to find sufficient purchase with his left hand and right elbow. Before he had time to pull himself through, a bullet sang off a metal strut, directly in front of him. He instinctively jumped back, lost his grip and fell onto the wooden crate.

"Hold it right there!"

Josh crawled on his front to peer over the edge of the large container. A uniformed cop stood directly beneath him. With a large revolver aimed in his direction, Josh had just enough time to duck his head back before another bullet ripped into the crate, sending needle-like splinters in all directions. He rolled to his right to take refuge behind a smaller wooden box.

"You won't get away!" the cop yelled.

Trapped now, Josh crouched behind the box. He leaned against the crate in an attempt to gain additional cover. His shoulder connected against it, and the box unexpectedly slid forwards. With a push, he found it empty, easy to move. He made a calculation of the cop's position and then hurled the crate over the edge. As it crashed downward, tumbling madly, he dived for the skylight. Not daring to look back, he hauled himself quickly through the hole and to safety. Anna was already halfway across the roof. He hurried towards her.

"We need to find a way down," she told him once he'd joined her. They reached the edge of the roof, peering over to find a twenty-five-foot drop onto hard asphalt.

"It's too high, you'll never make it," she said, making him feel inadequate.

"Can't you just hold me?" Josh asked crazily.

"I'm not superwoman!" she told him seriously.

They looked at each other and realised how absurd they must have sounded. Then they burst into laughter and some of the tension was relieved.

"C'mon," she said.

Anna started to walk around the edge of the roof. Josh followed behind her, staying well clear of the side. They traversed quickly along the rooftop. Then, the unexpected sound of metal against metal began to sound out. The darkness parted and a gun appeared, frighteningly close, directly in front of them. Next, a head came into view, and slowly a dark shape began to haul itself awkwardly up onto the roof. Reaching for the last rung, the police officer's gun caught the side of the access ladder, and another metallic sound rang out.

Panicking, Josh pulled Balooga's firearm from his waistband.

A glint of metal caught Anna's eye. She watched in startled amazement as Josh instinctively trained the weapon towards the officer.

"No!" she cried, swiping the gun out of his hand. With a flash of gunmetal the weapon spun into the night, disappearing instantly, taking with it any chance of irrevocable violence.

A moment of sickening clarity forced Josh to question what he'd been about to do. Hot bile clawed its way to the back of his throat. The night spun, light-headedness threatening to drop him over the side of the building.

"Back!" Anna warned, pulling him to his senses.

Fleeing in the opposite direction, they reached the corner, just in time to see a fully loaded baggage cart drive past.

Anna grabbed his hand. "Are you ready?"

"What? No. Wait!" Josh protested, horrified at what she was about to do.

"Too late!" she responded, and stepped out over the edge.

With Josh screaming, they jumped the twenty-five feet through the air – two dark brushstrokes caught against the canvass of night – and landed safely on the soft luggage. The cart headed for a stationary aircraft, taking them away from danger. They stayed hidden amongst the baggage until the cart reached the plane. Then, jumping clear, they headed away from the aircraft and towards the dark runway.

"Wait, where are we going?" Josh asked.

"Beats me!" she said, but didn't stop.

Josh struggled to keep up but, not wanting to lose sight of her, he pushed himself on, ignoring the pain in his leg. He eventually caught up with her, as she was just about to step onto the black runway.

"Wait," he breathed.

She turned to face him and found he was bent over with pain. She walked back. He leaned against her, breathless, waiting for his strength to return. They stood and held each other tightly. The lights of the runway behind them cast one dark and intertwined shadow.

After a couple of minutes, he stood straight – the cruel talons of pain finally withdrawing. He looked into her eyes and smiled sheepishly. "Never a dull moment, hey?"

She fought the urge to grin, but eventually a genuine smile surfaced on her beautiful face. "You're a real asshole, you know," she told him.

"So everybody keeps telling me," he agreed.

She shook her head. "Oh boy, do I pick 'em!"

The stiffness in his leg lessened. He checked the length of the runway and found it clear. "C'mon, let's get the hell out of here."

Like two fleeting ghosts, they crossed the dark runway before disappearing deep into the night.

Not long after they'd disappeared, a roar of engines signalled an aircraft approaching takeoff. Taxiing onto the dark surface, the plane straightened out and took position on the smooth airstrip. It stood momentarily still before roaring down the runway, gaining speed with every second. And, just before it ran out of blacktop, it took effortlessly to the skies. Like a sleek jet-black raven, it climbed quickly towards the night sky and was eventually swallowed by dark clouds. The aircraft cut its way through the darkness, carrying all but one of its passengers, intent on delivering its cargo well before daybreak arrived.

Chapter Fifteen

A dark festering reality could be found here. A collection of rundown storefronts had become the rotten façade of this place. It was a far cry from the more prosperous commercial enterprises to be found further up town, towards the main part of the city.

Which was surprising considering that sex was the main commodity on sale both here and there. Only difference being – here, there was no attempt at hiding the immorality of such a transaction.

Girls stood around in small gatherings, faces drawn and hollowed-out by years of abuse. Drugs had taken their freedom, totally, a dependency for the needle, and a lifetime of neglect, both spiritually and physically, had robbed them of life. The girls looked more like the undead than a group of twenty somethings.

Jonus had come to the right place then.

Lust for carnal pleasures had not brought him here, however. He had had his fix of that earlier. Now, he was here looking for something else entirely – the pleasures of the mortal soul.

By now he should have been bathing in the blood of his mortal nemesis – the hateful Anna. She was what had originally driven him here, to Chicago. Driven him with a demented single-mindedness that was not unfamiliar to the patrons that inhabited this dreadful place.

It was revenge that fuelled his need though, not the dirty barrel of a hypodermic needle. Anna had betrayed him, a long time ago. When they had ridden the night together, taking the souls of men at their pleasure.

She had stolen something from him. Something he was here to get back.

One of the women approached Jonus, pulling him away from his thoughts. She was tall, emaciated, and stumbled on weak limbs. One of the living dead, Jonus had no use of such a thing. He simply waved her away, before stepping towards another solitary figure.

The girl was slightly younger than the rest. And her features had not, as yet, fallen foul to the ravages of drug abuse. Maybe, thought Jonus, something other than the need to get high had brought this girl here.

Once he neared her – his mind began to tune into some of her thoughts. She was nervous, this being only her second week on the streets. Jonus probed deeper. A young man came to mind, full of false bravado and bluster, her partner, a school dropout with only a low double-digit IQ, and a quick temper to match. The crying of a baby filled Jonus's head with a deafening wail. The next picture to flash before his eyes was the hothead leaving with a single bag packed and an undisclosed destination in mind.

Jonus looked down at the girl before him. What made her different to all the rest? Hope. That was it. She was here trying to make a better life for herself and her young child.

Jonus almost laughed out loud at the absurdity of that. What did she really hope to achieve? Would a knight in shining armour take her from these dark streets? And in doing so, save her and her bastard child from a life of misery and ruin?

Maybe.

Anything was possible.

Only thing was, this girl had now chanced upon Jonus. And he wasn't the type for happy endings. No, he hadn't come here looking for redemption. Quite the opposite, he was here to feed the forbidden hunger that coursed throughout his veins. Jonus reached out, using one of his bony fingers to tilt her head up slightly.

She tried to smile, bending her lips more into a crooked

grimace. He was a paying customer after all. And at least nicer looking than most. Her heart beat a little faster. Maybe it wouldn't be quite as bad this time. Not like the first time. That had not only been physically painful but also agonising to her soul.

Jonus read all these thoughts and concerns in curious silence. Silly little bug didn't know anything. What did she know about pain and suffering? He felt anger then. How dare this pathetic bug before him have any self-pity?

He took her hand, smiling slightly, pulling her away from the main body of prostitutes gathered there.

He would take her somewhere quieter.

And dark.

And there, he would show her what suffering was.

What real pain the soul could endure.

Chapter Sixteen

Josh crossed the small room. He peered out from between thin drapes and found a dark and empty parking lot outside. The night pushed heavily against the window, which was both oppressive and disquieting. Normally able to enjoy the late hours and their uncertainties, Josh felt surprisingly unnerved by the deep shadows and gloom. Any number of unwanted nightmares could be lurking there, including Jonus.

"Relax," Anna told him.

"Yeah, right," Josh said, "we've only got some immortal flesh-eating lunatic trying to kill us."

"Trying to kill me," Anna corrected.

"Yeah, right."

"Listen, we're safe, for now. Nobody knows we're here," she reassured him.

"What about Jonus? He can read minds, right?"

"Yes, but only ones in close proximity," she said. "We'd be pretty unlucky if he just happened to pass. And anyway you told me he said… what was it again?"

"That my brain was useless," he finished for her.

Unable to suppress a grin, she remarked, "See – *your* brain's shit, and I learned to hide my thoughts years ago."

"Thanks," Josh said miserably.

Anna sat cross-legged on a cheap plastic chair, "And if all else fails, we've always got our disguises," she added, and tossed him a blond hairpiece.

He caught the wig and ran his fingers through its coarse manufactured fibres. He raised his eyes and, even though he was breaking apart inside with worry, he gently placed the wig over his bruised and shaven head. He picked up a ridiculous pair of black-rimmed glasses – which Anna had bought for him and made him wear before they had checked into the motel – and slipped them on over his nose. Strumming his fingers against the strings of an imaginary guitar, he said, "Wayne's world, party on!"

She looked at him as if he was the most insane person she had ever met and then burst into fits of laughter. He laughed at his own pathetic joke but held his bruised ribs. Anna stretched her legs out and stood, then joined him on the bed.

"Are you okay?" she asked, with genuine concern.

"Yeah, just a little tender."

She reached out with elegant fingers. Avoiding his facial injuries, she removed the wig and glasses. He tensed slightly as her fingertips brushed delicately across his skin. She moved closer. With exaggerated care, she traced the line of coarse stitches that ran above his left eyebrow. Josh closed his eyes, a sigh of pleasure leaving his lips.

Immediately after they'd fled the airport, they had found a deserted back street. With the moonlight as their only light source, Anna had carefully unwound the white bandage. Aware that the dressing would draw too much attention, she had tossed it inside a nearby trashcan. Then they had slipped into the steady throng of night-time people and had slowly made their way out of town. Anna had made a short stop at a late-night convenience store to buy some supplies – glasses included – and then they had found this quiet motel.

She had carefully tucked the blond wig down inside her dress and arranged it in such a way as to make her look pregnant. Then she'd taken a soft knitted cap and had carefully pulled it over Josh's bruised and shaven head. With a pair of steel scissors, she'd cut off an inch of her own hair and tucked the dark snippets under the rim of the cap to give Josh the illusion of hair. Then, to his dismay, she had made him wear the magnifying spectacles. She'd carefully arranged the thick black frames, crookedly, and had managed to conceal the laceration above his eyebrow. Her own long hair had been rearranged into a tightly woven bun, which had to Josh's amazement, aged her by ten years. Then they had walked boldly into the reception of the motel and played the 'nerds from out of town'. Five minutes and thirty dollars later they were sitting in the small motel room.

At first, they'd sat in silence, eating cold sandwiches and drinking warm Coors. Then, as Josh started on his second beer, Anna had begun to talk. She had told him an amazing tale about how she and Jonus had once rode together, comrades in arms no less, in a time when the world was still an infant. She had explained how they'd once fought together in an attempt to overthrow the brutal rule of a shape-shifter named, Ragnar – an old adversary that possessed similar powers to theirs: the ability to change into a more powerful being, and the extraordinary capacity to survive daylight.

Her tale had taken many twists and turns, captivating Josh with its fantastic account, and rendering him mostly silent, until she had drawn this magnificent story to its dramatic conclusion: A conclusion that saw her taking the heart of the shape-shifter herself.

She finished her story with a startling finale about how she'd foiled Jonus' attempts to kill her, and thus take her newfound ability to walk in daylight.

Only, Anna had not taken all of Ragnar's ability – with the balance of the essence locked away inside her old adversary, Jonus. All he had to do was piece the two together. And this was why he had tracked her throughout the ages, in an attempt to claim a legacy that he believed was rightfully his.

"Does it hurt?" she asked Josh now, as her fingers withdrew from his bruised face.

He raised his fingers to gently prod at the lump on his scalp. A bolt of pain tore across his skull, bringing water to his eyes. "A little," he said, being brave. He looked down at her bandaged hand and asked, "Does yours hurt?"

"A little," she said, and smiled.

"Really? Because mine hurts like hell," he admitted, raising his own plastered hand.

"That's because you hit like a sissy," she laughed.

"You're all heart," he said, then grasped the significance of his comment. "Listen," he said, now serious, "whatever happens from here onwards, I'm not going to leave you."

"I know," she said, and she did.

"This Jonus, he's not gonna to stop, is he?"

"Not until he takes my heart."

"Don't say that," Josh said mournfully.

"Well, it's the truth."

"But he's making a mistake. You can't survive daylight, can you?"

"No," she replied with a slight shake of her head.

"So, we tell him."

"And you think he'll believe us?" she asked, with raised eyebrows.

He shrugged his shoulders. "Okay, not a good idea. I am trying my best."

"I know," she said. "And I know it's difficult for you to understand."

"I just don't get it. This Ragnar guy, he could survive daylight, right? But you can't?"

"Evidently not," she agreed, and raised her dressed hand.

"But why not?"

"Because," she said, "I don't think I'm fully compatible."

"What?"

"My soul, Ragnar's soul – they weren't totally compatible."

"Shit. Not this soul thing again," Josh moaned miserably.

She remembered how easily Josh had accepted her story, sitting silent and thoughtful as she had told him about the battle of ages past. During her long narrative, he had sat nodding or mostly silent. Yet, as she started to explain the transferability of the soul, he became hostile and irritated. He'd snatched up another can and sipped it in silence, impassive, remaining in his private thoughts, mulling over some uncertainty. Eventually, he had simply told her to continue.

"Why do you find it so difficult to comprehend?" she asked him now.

"Anna, I've been pretty open-minded about this whole thing, but to think one person can steal another person's soul… it's ridiculous."

"Why?"

"Because it just is, that's why."

"Why?"

"Because… because, I don't even believe a person has a soul," he lied. "And even if they do, it wouldn't just be found in someone's heart."

"Not all of it is in the heart," she explained, which made him sulk even more.

"Christ," he cursed.

"Listen to me. Have you ever loved someone?"

"Yeah – of course."

"And the love you felt for them, where did it come from?"

"What?"

"Your love. Where do you feel it?"

"Nowhere – everywhere? I don't know?"

"Come on Josh, be honest with yourself."

"Okay, HERE!" he said, and pointed to his chest.

"You mean here," she corrected, placing her hand over his heart.

"Yes," he admitted.

She slid across the bed to bring their faces only inches apart. She looked at him with deep, caring eyes. "And when your mother died, where did it hurt most?"

Tears welled up in his eyes. In a quiet whisper, he said, "Here," and placed his hand over hers.

"Hey, it's okay… it's alright," she soothed.

"But don't you understand. If what you say is true, then someone could have stolen *her* soul," he sobbed.

"Josh, no – no," she said, and shook her head. "Your mother died of natural causes, not by one of my…" She cut her sentence short, ashamed.

They both sat in silence with their heads hung low.

"How did you know? About my mother?" he finally asked.

"I felt your sadness, last night when we met."

"And you think wherever she is now, she's… safe?"

"Yes, I do."

He sat silent for a moment, before coming to some conclusion. "So tell me, why do you think you're not compatible?" he asked with a sigh.

"It's not easy to explain," she said.

"Try."

"Okay, imagine only the essence of the soul is contained in the heart, the core. But surrounding the core you have a residual spirit. For example, when you get butterflies in your stomach or dizzy with giddiness, well that's the residual soul reacting and responding to your emotional state. Whereas the essence of the soul reacts and responds to your physical state."

"Okay."

"Then to take another's ability, you need their entire soul. Not just the core, but the residual soul as well."

"And where is that?"

"In their life's fluid," she said.

"And what is that?"

"Their blood!"

"Christ!" Josh moaned, and stood. "You really are insane."

"Think about it. Scientists have only just recently learnt how to map living DNA. So maybe one day someone will also learn how to map spiritual DNA too."

"Really?" Josh mumbled, unimpressed.

"Yes, really."

"But people have blood transfusions all the time, and they don't unexplainably become someone else," he said, pleased with himself.

"I'm not talking about becoming someone else, not as a whole.

Just taking on certain characteristics.”

“Still, when I had surgery after my accident three years ago, I didn’t wake up speaking a different language or feeling the urge to wear a skirt,” he said, and a slight smirk bent his lips.

“But that’s because *you* cannot convert the information,” she responded, meaning the human race as a whole.

“But what about heart transplants?”

“What about them?”

“Well, people who have heart transplants – they lose their ‘cores’ and have most of their blood replaced,” he said triumphantly.

“Yes, and most die within a couple of years,” she commented.

“Not all.”

“No, Josh, not all – but most.”

He stood and looked at her and tried to think up some other argument. Finding none, he said, “Okay, you win – for now.”

“Good.”

“But I still don’t understand why you’re not compatible.”

“Because I don’t have all the information from the residual spirit,” she said. Then, seeing his blank face, she tried to explain. “Imagine the core as a locked door and the ‘gift’ is on the other side, and to access the gift all you need to do is use a key and open the door. But without the key, no matter how hard you try, it’s impossible to break open.”

“Okay,”

“Then for me to use the gift all I need is the key.”

“But wouldn’t there have been… ” – he paused – “... blood in the heart, you know when you?”

“Yes,” she interjected quickly, making it easier for him.

“So you must have the key?”

“Not all of it,” she said. “Remember the keypad at my apartment?”

“Yes.”

“Then this key – it’s not mechanical, but numerical, and I’ve only got the first two digits. And instead of a four-digit code, we’re talking about an infinite string of numbers to choose from.”

"So it's hopeless. Ragnar must be dust by now," Josh moaned.

"That doesn't matter, because he no longer holds the key," Anna told him.

"So who does?"

"The one person I thought I'd never see again."

"Who?"

"JONUS."

"Fuck! Anna, you can't be serious?"

"That's why he's here, because he knows he's got the key and I've got the gift locked inside of me," she explained. "That's why I must confront him again."

"Wait a minute. Hold on. He's after us, not the other way around. I'm in no rush to meet him again."

"Nor am I – yet," she told him.

"So what do we do?"

"We avoid him – for now."

"But he found you, remember?"

"Yes, but not by some sixth sense. I must have made a mistake and led him to me, left a clue somewhere; something only he would notice – but what?"

"It doesn't matter; let's just keep one step ahead of him from now onwards," Josh told her.

"But I've been stupid, or lazy, and led him right to me. But how?" she said, annoyed with herself.

Josh returned to the bed and sat beside her. "Don't feel too bad about it. You thought he was dead, remember," he soothed. He wrapped his arm around her.

"You're amazing, you know," she told him.

"Me? Why? I haven't done anything."

"Well you've probably just had the worst day of your life – all because of me – and it isn't over yet, and still here you are trying to comfort me. You're a real catch, Josh Sawyer."

"Me? I thought I was an asshole."

She raised a finger to his lips, and with a serious shake of her head she silenced him. "No, Josh, I mean it. Thanks."

He moved her finger away to free his lips and, after lowering his head towards hers, he whispered, "It hasn't been all bad."

They kissed, but not with urgency like before. This was the soft, tender kiss of two people who cared deeply about each other. They embraced for a long time before Anna broke away, breathless.

"C'mon, there's much to do," she said, after she'd caught her breath. She stood and moved away from the bed.

"Hey, wait. Where are you going?" Josh asked, with a slight pang to his heart.

"We've no time for this, we need to get out of the city – soon," she said, now businesslike.

"But how?" Josh asked, as one powerful need was replaced by another instinctive one: the need to survive.

"Via track," she said.

"By what?"

"We're taking a train journey – cross country," she announced.

"A what?"

"You know, a big shiny thing that pulls carriages behind it with people inside," she joked, regaining some humour.

"Anna, I know what a locomotive is. I also know you need tickets to ride on one."

"So we'll buy some, stupid."

"With what?"

"Well, money might work," she quipped.

"Oh yeah," he retorted, "forgot to tell you, I've got a big wad of FUCK ALL in my pockets!" He turned out his pockets to show her exactly what he was worth: nothing.

She shook her head, then moved over to her jacket and reached inside a pocket to produce a credit card. "Don't worry, you can owe me," she said, and tossed it over to him.

He caught the object as it spun towards him. Turning it over, he found the words Platinum and MasterCard stencilled across its surface.

"Alright!" he exclaimed. Then his excitement quickly changed to misery. "Won't the cops be watching all the stations and airports?"

"Of course."

"So how the hell do we board?"

"Well, we're not exactly going to board as such. Not in any conventional sense, anyway."

"What do you mean?"

"We'll be 'boarding' slightly later than the rest of the passengers," she elaborated.

"Anna, what the hell have you got planned?"

"A slight detour, that's all."

"Anna!"

"Okay – Okay, we're going to board once the train leaves the station."

"How?"

She used her good hand and formed it into a fist, but left her index and middle finger straight. Then as she pointed her fingers down, she wiggled them forward and backwards in a running motion then moved her hand quickly across open air.

"You've got to be kidding me?"

"Josh, when do I ever kid anyone?" she asked, and a wide smile split her beautiful face.

"But what about my leg?" he asked, and pointed to the stiff limb.

"Just make sure you pack lightly," she told him.

"Pack? This is all I've got," he said, pulling on the oversized second-hand shirt.

"Well then, it's a good thing you're going shopping."

"I'm not going anywhere."

"Yes you are. We need things for our trip."

"Like?"

"Like tickets, for one."

He moved over to the bedside and picked up the handset of a cheap plastic telephone. "Let's just call and reserve two," he suggested.

"Too risky," she said, and joined him at the bedside. "If by chance we are traced to this motel, then the first thing they'll check is the phone records."

"Yeah, you're right," he agreed, setting the handset down.

"I know a cyber-café near here; you can order them online," she said. "Here, I'll give you my pin number. That way you can buy some new clothes and the rest of what we need."

"Which is?"

She walked over to the opposite bedside and picked up a small notepad: the kind found in most hotel rooms, small yellow sheets with a sticky film running along the top that holds the pad together. She opened a desk drawer to look for a pen or pencil. Finding one alongside an old bible, she began to compile a short list. She tore the top sheet from the pad and then handed it over.

Josh took the list, reading through it quickly. "What the hell is this?" he asked, pointing to one item in particular.

Anna didn't bother to look at the item in question. "Just trust me; they'll all come in useful."

"If you say so," he said, and tucked the list into his shirt pocket.

"And clothes. Don't forget to buy some new clothes," she reminded him. "I don't want you looking like a hobo hitching a free ride."

"What about you?" he asked. "Don't you need more clothes?"

"Yeah, you're right. Get me something simple," she advised.

"Like what?"

"Like anything, doesn't matter."

He looked her up and down and a broad grin spread across his bruised but handsome face.

She read his mind – like any woman could – and said, "No, Josh, something practical."

"Hey, trust me," he chimed, and his grin stretched wider.

"One last thing. When you book the tickets, book three: two double and one single berth."

His smile immediately slipped as he discovered he might be travelling alone.

"Don't worry," she said, "we'll be together. It's just a precautionary measure."

"Oh – Okay. So whose name shall I book them under?" he asked.

She pointed to the card. "Mr. Carl Dua."

He turned the card over. Written in raised print were the words: Mr Carl Dua. "Who the hell is that?" he asked.

"It's another long story," she said. "Now go on, before the stores close for the night."

"You sure you don't want to come?" he asked hopefully.

"No, Josh, it's safer if you go alone," she lied.

"Yeah, you're right – they're looking for the two of us."

"Right," she said.

He moved over to the window and peered outside into the dark parking area. It was still deserted so he moved to the door. He turned back towards Anna. "While I'm gone, are you gonna be okay here alone?"

"Josh, I'm a big girl. I can look after myself."

"Yeah – I guess you can," he said, and opened the door.

"Wait."

He turned to find her holding out the dark spectacles and woollen cap.

"Aren't you forgetting something?"

"Shit," he breathed.

He took the disguise and slipped it on. Feeling like a jerk, he asked, "Well, how do I look?"

"Perfect," she said, looking at his oddly magnified eyes.

"Great, now I really do feel like an asshole," he said miserably.

"Perfect."

He returned to the open doorway and took a step out into the darkness. Then he remembered something of importance. He spun around and popped his head back into the room.

"Oh – yeah, where the hell are we going exactly?"

She told Josh about their destination and then waited ten minutes to give him ample time to clear the motel and its surrounding area. Then, she slipped into her jacket and snatched up the keys to the motel, but left her own simple disguise behind, wanting no confusion between herself and her next intended target.

Chapter Seventeen

For the second time in the same day, Harry Balooga found himself in the maelstrom of a chaotic crime scene. Trapped in this assembly of detectives, patrol officers and forensics, he felt strangely detached, as the multitudes of people appeared to rush about him at an insane fast-forward speed. Unable to comprehend the activity around him, he swayed, intoxicated by the night's events. He blew his nose heavily into a tattered tissue, desperately trying to clear the smell of death from his nostrils.

"Hey, Chief," an unusually cheerless voice said.

In his own world of slow motion, Balooga failed to recognise the speaker.

"Hey, Chief," the voice repeated.

Suddenly dragged into real time, Balooga turned towards the newcomer. "Yeah, what is it?" he asked.

"Just checking you're alright," Detective Sanchez said.

"I'm fine," Balooga sighed, with some irritation.

"Chief, it's been a long day, maybe you should go home – get some rest."

"How the hell can I rest with some goddamn cop killer out there?" Balooga moaned.

"He's not going to get very far. We've got every airport, train station *and* bus depot locked down tight."

"What if he hits the freeway?"

"Then Highways will nail him. We're gonna hit this fucker with everything we've got!"

"Christ, Sanchez. What the hell happened here?" Balooga asked, looking up towards the blacked-out windows. "How did this happen?"

"It just went bad, that's all. It wasn't anybody's fault," Sanchez responded, trying to reassure his partner. "Newbury was a seasoned cop. He knew the risks and still went in. He should have waited for backup."

"Try telling that to his wife and kids," Balooga said with dismay.

"Christ," Sanchez moaned.

A weapon appeared in one of Sanchez's hands. "Here – Chief, better keep this safe. One of ours found it at the airport. Handed it in."

Balooga retook his sidearm – the one that Sawyer had taken – and raised the barrel cautiously to his nose.

"Don't worry," Sanchez said, understanding his superior's unease. "No shots were fired."

"Thank God," Balooga sighed, grateful the weapon had not been responsible for more bloodshed.

"What about prints?" he asked.

"It's not reached forensics yet," Sanchez replied. "Thought you'd want it to stay that way, for now?"

The detective nodded with gratitude, then turned his attention back to the gaping hole of the ruined window pane.

Sanchez traced Balooga's line of sight. "What the hell happened there?"

"I don't know, but whatever came through that window was no ordinary man."

"Probably jacked up on PCP or meth, or both," Sanchez remarked.

Balooga simply nodded absentmindedly. He wasn't convinced of that.

A cell phone bleeped to life. The young detective pulled the cell from his jacket pocket. He checked the small illuminated screen. "Shit," he muttered. "Captain Asshole." Raising the cell, he began a brief discussion. And, after only a couple of short replies, Sanchez handed it to his superior.

"Applegate," the young detective mouthed in warning.

"Christ," Balooga cursed.

Sanchez turned his back on the lieutenant, which allowed his superior a little privacy. He walked around the immediate area, careful not to tread on any potential forensics. Taking exaggerated steps, he moved over to Balooga's replacement vehicle. Not dissimilar to the missing Sedan, this car was an old grey Lexus. Sanchez leaned against the hood of the car and waited. He watched Balooga speak, and witnessed a dark cloud descend over the large detective's face. Balooga snapped the cell shut before joining Sanchez at the car. "Here," he said, as he handed the phone back.

"It's bad, right?" Sanchez asked.

"Yeah," Balooga replied.

Sanchez pulled himself away from the hood. He opened the passenger door. "C'mon, let's get it over with."

"No," Balooga disagreed.

"What?"

"I need you here," Balooga said. "Find out as much as you can, then phone me at the precinct."

"But, Chief, we'll handle Applegate together – as a team."

"No," Balooga repeated. "This is gonna get ugly."

"Hey, we're partners. Good or bad – right?"

"Wrong."

"Chief?"

"I'll handle Applegate. You stay here. Work with forensics and see if you can find where Sawyer and Privalova are headed."

"But… "

"Emilio," Balooga said, addressing his partner affectionately, "I need you here – honest. There's no point us both having our asses chewed. Stay here and work the scene."

"Okay," Sanchez finally agreed, feeling both guilt and relief.

"Good," Balooga said.

The large detective moved around the Lexus, opened the driver's door and climbed in. As Balooga started the motor,

Sanchez leant down, bringing himself level with the passenger side window. "If he lays it on too thick, shoot the son-of-a-bitch," he said.

"You've got my word on it," Balooga promised. He threw the car into gear and, with a screech of rubber, the car shot forwards.

The Hispanic detective turned away from the retreating Lexus and headed back towards the open doorway and the carnage above.

***

Balooga made his way across town. He threaded his way through the tightly packed street, weaving effortlessly between the late evening traffic. He saw her then, stood on the street corner, looking directly at him.

"Jesus Christ!" he exclaimed, pulling the car across two lanes of traffic. He ignored the blare of horns as he swung the Lexus to kerbside. He threw open his door and climbed out, reaching for his weapon. He took a step towards her, but she had already disappeared, swallowed by a wave of people.

"POLICE!" he yelled, wading into the sea of faces.

He pushed his way through the crowd, broke clear, and emerged at the entrance to a murky alleyway. He paused momentarily at the dark entrance, then stepped inside the narrow passageway and worked his way into darkness, away from the busy, well-lit sidewalk. The safety catch of his sidearm clicked off. He squinted through the gloom. "This is Lieutenant Balooga. Come out, Miss Privalova," he called.

The harshness of his own voice reverberated around him, throwing his senses off. He waited for the phantom echo to quieten.

Balooga stepped deeper within the shadows, taking care to step over discarded rubbish or other unknown obstacles. At the rear of the alleyway, a brick wall halted his progress. Up against the dead-end, he reached out with his free hand to feel the coarse brickwork. He looked for an exit or open doorway. Neither presented itself. He became instantly aware then of his exposed back, and, spinning around, he glimpsed a shadow materialise from the gloom.

"Hold it right there!" he commanded.

The woman raised her hands in a show of peace. "Easy, Detective, I'm here as a friend. I mean you no harm."

Balooga levelled the gun toward Anna's torso, and then pushed himself away from the wall.

"Easy. Easy," Anna cautioned.

"Keep your fucking hands up," Balooga ordered.

She stood still, hands raised with her palms out.

"Good, now turn around and face the wall." He waved the gun sideways towards an adjacent building.

"Detective, I don't have time for your bullshit," Anna said.

"DO IT!" he barked.

"Okay – okay," she said.

She turned ninety degrees and walked over to the wall. There, she laid her palms flat against the rough surface.

Balooga placed his free hand onto her back and used his foot to kick her legs further apart. He stood back and said, "Okay, now take a step away from the wall."

"Detective, is this really necessary?" she asked, her head turned towards him slightly.

"Face forward!" he ordered.

"Whatever," she mumbled. She followed the detective's instructions and shuffled her legs back.

Moving in close, Balooga pressed the muzzle of his gun against her side, hard. "Don't even breathe," he whispered into her ear. With his free hand, he patted her down, looking for a concealed weapon. He found none, so took a step back.

"Turn around," he said.

She turned to face the open barrel of his gun.

"Now, stay still," he instructed. He fumbled awkwardly for a second before withdrawing a pair of metallic handcuffs.

"Shit, you're kidding, right?" she asked.

"Hands out in front."

"Detective, I found *you*, remember?"

He ignored her. "Just do it."

"Enough of this bullshit," she stated.

He felt a sudden lifting of weight as his gun was pulled from his grasp. Then he heard two distinctive metallic *clicks*, and surprisingly he found himself without a weapon and handcuffed.

"Now, sit down," she said, pointing with the pistol.

"What?" Balooga mumbled, open-mouthed, now staring at his own weapon.

"Over here," she directed, and pointed to a large, open crate.

Dumfounded, he walked over to the crate and sat down. The wooden container bent inward – dangerously low – but managed to hold the detective's weight.

She found a suitable seat herself and sat facing him. "Now that we're comfortable," she began, "let me tell you a thing or two."

"I'm all ears," Balooga responded.

"At my apartment, earlier tonight…"

"Go on."

"Your…" She paused until she'd found the right word. "Your comrades, they died by the hands of another. Not by Josh Sawyer or myself."

"Bullshit!" Balooga spat.

She shook her head in sympathy. "You have no idea what you're up against."

He sensed she meant him no immediate harm, so he relaxed, a little. "Educate me."

"This city has attracted a dark soul. One that may end both our lives before the sun rises," she said seriously.

"What the hell are you talking about? Make sense."

"There is someone here, tonight. This soul, it took your friends and it will take many more if it doesn't get what it's looking for," she explained.

"Which is?" Balooga asked.

"Me."

"You?"

"Yes."

"Why you?" Balooga asked.

"Because I have something it wants."

"Which is?"

"Which is something it cannot have."

"Why?"

She fell silent for a moment, thoughtful, before continuing.

"This thing it wants, I can't give it. And even if I could, what you've seen tonight at my apartment would be just the beginning."

"The beginning of what?"

"The beginning of the end, maybe," she answered.

This time it was his turn to shake his head. "The end of what?"

"This," she declared, and spread her arms outward. "You. Me. Everything."

"You're a bit late for this end-of-the-world crap," Balooga said. "We're already well into the new millennium. And I don't think the Antichrist is about to inherit the world just yet."

"What makes you say that?"

"What?"

"The Antichrist."

The picture of exploding glass, a fleeting shadow and the sound of manic laughter flashed to mind. Instead, Balooga said, "Just a figure of speech, that's all."

Anna felt the detective's deceit. "Yeah – right."

They sat in silence for a moment.

"So, neither you nor Sawyer had anything to do with the deaths tonight, but what about this morning and the three other dead guys?" Balooga asked.

After a slight pause, Anna said, "They were just scum. You should not lose too much sleep over their loss. They had dark souls also, all of them. The city is a safer place with them gone. When you check their IDs, don't be too shocked to find a history of violence and abuse."

"Who are you, some kind of psychic vigilante?"

"Perhaps," she said, and starlight reflected from her

humourless grin.

"Nobody has the right to decide if someone should live or die," he told her.

"Nobody, apart from the legal system, you mean?"

"Meaning?"

"Meaning, the death penalty still stands, even in this country. And what is the penal system if not some regulated vengeance committee?"

"But justice must be served in a semblance of order and fairness. Not just some random killings in a backstreet. You're not competent to make those decisions or judgments."

"Who says so?"

"I do. The law," he replied. "What if you're wrong about a person?"

"I trust in my instincts as unquestionably as you do in your forensic evidence."

"How?"

"By reading their souls," she said.

"You're crazy," Balooga scorned.

She ignored his remark. "Do you believe man is born inherently good or bad, Detective?"

It took him a moment to measure his response. "I've spent many years in the presence of man's worst acts – too many years – but even with what I've seen in this city, I do believe evil is made, not born."

"Explain."

"I can't believe – will not – believe an infant is born with the presence of evil already rooted within its innocent soul, waiting to grow like some immoral and malignant tumour. It comes down to the age-old argument: nature or nurture?"

"And you believe evil is passed down or materialises in an individual who themselves have suffered some sinful cruelty – like when an abused child grows into an abuser in adulthood."

"Yes," Balooga said.

"So you think evil is passed along in a physical sense, not spiritual?"

"I guess so," he agreed.

"Then you believe our three friends in the morgue are just innocents, slain by my poor deranged and tortured mind?"

"No, I'm not saying that," Balooga countered.

As he tried to piece together the jigsaw of his confused thoughts, he raised his shackled hands and ran his palm across his shaven head. "What I'm trying to say is, even if those three dead guys were evil or bad, then it's not our place – as individuals – to pass judgment."

"Maybe you're right," she agreed, "but it's too late for them, now."

"Then that's one thing we both agree on," Balooga stated.

"I guess so," she said, with a nod.

"So tell me, what's this all leading to?"

She looked across the gloom and into his eyes, and then raised the gun towards him. "You, Detective. It's all leading to you." She pulled her sleeve over the grip of the gun, wiping her prints clean, and then strode purposefully towards Balooga, with the weapon aimed directly at his head.

Chapter Eighteen

Sanchez emerged from the vile stench of the apartment. The detective breathed in a deep cleansing breath. He moved away from the dark building and its macabre contents and crossed the street, ducking under the police cordon.

He pushed his way through the line of onlookers then turned into the main street. Not wanting to wait for a ride back to the precinct, he'd decided to walk for a while, the need for a cleaner breath forcing the crisp night air into his lungs. Although he was accustomed to the sight of death, the sight of his own mutilated colleagues, combined with the dizzying stench of some powerful and unknown chemical agent, had unnerved and nauseated him.

Walking amongst this city's busy nightlife, he tried to clear his mind of the images and smells found at the woman's sombre apartment. He crossed the flow of traffic and reached the opposite sidewalk when his cell phone emitted a number of urgent little bleeps. He flipped it open.

"Doctor Stapleton," he acknowledged.
He held a brief conversation with the city's medical examiner, before snapping the cell shut. He looked at the steady stream of traffic and spotted the bright yellow of a city cab. "TAXI!" he shouted, raising his arm. The cabdriver spotted him and pulled the vehicle alongside.

Jumping into the back, Sanchez slammed the door behind him. "City Morgue. And hurry."

"Okay, buddy," the cabdriver said.

The taxi swerved into the midst of moving chrome. Sanchez leaned back against the padded seat. He ran one hand through his slick, black hair, and then frowned.

Although the City Morgue was only two or three miles away, during their brief conversation, Doctor Stapleton's digitised voice had actually travelled many, many miles. First, it had been transmitted to a local booster station where the signal had been multiplied many times over. Then the amplified signal had been zapped to an orbiting satellite somewhere over the northern hemisphere. The satellite had absorbed the information before locating the detective's unique electronic signature, and then it had bounced the information back down into Sanchez's cell phone. Although the doctor's natural analogue resonance had been lost during its amazing journey, one trait remained: fear. Doctor Stapleton had sounded scared. No, not just scared, terrified, Sanchez thought to himself.

Suddenly worried, Sanchez pulled his police ID from his jacket. He slapped the open wallet against the Perspex and shouted, "This is police business, quick as you can."

The cabdriver took one look at the detective's ID. "You got it, pal." His foot pushed down on the gas pedal and the cab launched itself forwards.

Thrown back against his seat by the acceleration, Sanchez gripped an inside handle and held on for dear life.

***

Sanchez looked at his watch. It was already well past 10PM. He passed only the occasional morgue tech or late night cleaner as he walked these near-deserted corridors. He turned into another passageway. Sensing someone behind, he paused. A couple of seconds passed, but nobody appeared. He turned back to look into an empty passage.

"Hello?" he called.

All the offices on this level appeared deserted. Darkness pushed against milky glass panels in an attempt to flood the passageway

136

with impenetrable shadow.

"Hello?" he called again.

Jesus, it's as quiet as a mor… he thought to himself. Then remembering where he was he almost laughed. He reached the doctor's office and rapped gently on the closed door. Silence. He rapped again – harder – and the force pushed the door inwards by an inch.

"Doctor Stapleton," he called, and opened the door wider.

He entered the office. On her desk he noticed a green folder. Bending slightly, he read the cover. He found the name 'John Doe #3' written on the front with today's date printed neatly in one corner. He flipped open the folder.

"Fuck," he breathed, as a bloodied and ruined face stared back at him.

The first page consisted of a large colour photograph, which revealed a huge open wound. With the entire jaw and chin missing, the rest of the face was a mass of ripped skin, raw tissue and bone fragments.

"Hello again," Sanchez whispered, recognising the victim.

He turned the photograph over and began to read the autopsy report. He read about halfway down the second page when a hand grabbed his arm abruptly.

"JESUS… " Sanchez blurted, shocked by the presence. He looked behind him and found Doctor Stapleton standing in the office. "… CHRIST!"

"Detective."

"Doctor Stapleton, I didn't hear you come in," he said, and dropped the open folder.

"Sorry, I didn't expect you so soon."

"You sounded… worried before, so I hurried," he told her.

"Worried?" she echoed.

"When you called."

"I don't think so," she disagreed.

"Oh," Sanchez muttered, puzzled, but he could see that the doctor was unnerved about something. "Doctor, is everything alright?"

"Yes – yes," she said, with a dismissive wave of her hand. "Sit," she instructed, and pointed to a chair.

He seated himself opposite, as she took her seat. "So why'd you call me?" he asked.

"Because of this," she said, pointing to the open folder.

"Go on."

Doctor Stapleton pulled over the open file. She took a quick look outside, cleared her throat and then began. "Okay, this is the final autopsy, outstanding from this morning. As you can see, the cause of death is pretty obvious." She removed the photograph and handed it over to the detective.

No longer shocked by the gruesome close-up, Sanchez took his time to absorb as much detail as possible. The face looked almost unreal with its lower half in tatters and the upper part unscathed. He looked further down to the bloody neck and spotted something he had missed earlier. The skin around the throat looked as if it had been torn open in about three or four different places.

"These marks?" he asked, turning the photo in her direction.

She took another quick and unexpected look towards the dark corridor outside before focusing on the grizzly picture. "Ah… those, they must have been made posthumously," she said, nervously.

"You mean, after the victim died?"

"Yes," she confirmed.

"But how?"

"Possibly by one or two of the city's larger vermin population. Maybe rats or even a stray cat or dog could have mauled him."

"Really," Sanchez remarked, surprised.

"It's not that uncommon for a victim who dies outside to be found this way."

"No, I guess not," he said, a slight frown creasing his brow.

"Anyway," she continued, eager to move on, "as you can see, the victim died from one major gunshot to the back of his head."

"Yeah, Lieutenant Balooga found the slug embedded in the wall."

"Oh, good, that should help with our analysis," she said.

"Doctor, was this guy executed?"

"A very good possibility. The bullet entered the top of the skull, and as you can see, it exited via the lower part of the face. So that would suggest the killer was standing above the victim."

"Or he was kneeling down," Sanchez added. "Anything else?"

"Yes, due to the severity of the wound, death would have been instantaneous."

"Instantaneous?"

"Yes. Why?"

Squinting, Sanchez felt a stab of pain shoot across his forehead. He pinched the bridge of his nose and waited for the pain to subside. It lingered as a sharp piercing sensation that formed the unexpected picture of a knife slicing its way through butter into the detective's mind. After a couple of seconds, the agony dwindled into just a dull throb. And, although Doctor Stapleton witnessed the entire episode, she sat silent, unemotional.

He regained his senses and asked, "I'm sorry, where were we?"

Stapleton seemed to hold her breath momentarily before she finally found her voice. "You questioned the duration it took the victim to die," she reminded him.

"Oh – yes. You said he died instantaneously, right?"

"Yes."

"Good, but what about the blood found on the victim's hands?"

She opened her mouth, but words failed to form. After a long pause, she managed to say, "Must have come from one of the other victims."

"Possibly," Sanchez agreed. "We did assume they were all associates, but that could be wrong."

Sitting opposite the pathologist, Sanchez sensed an invisible connection trying to pull her eyes towards the dark passageway. He twitched in his seat, now uncomfortable in the doctor's presence.

"Okay, what else?" he asked, ready to end this strange meeting.

"Nothing. We're still waiting for further lab reports to come through, such as blood types and toxicology. Other than that, I think that's it."

"Good," he said and stood, eager to get out.

He reached for the office door, but stopped just long enough to take the sheet of data and bid her farewell.

Back in the deserted corridors, he walked with a more purposeful stride. He made his way towards the main entrance and turned into the last corridor. Inexplicably, he felt an irrational fear grip him. His heart pounded in his chest as he hurried toward the exit. He heard footsteps behind him.

Spinning around, he reached for his gun.

The passageway was empty. His hand froze over the butt of his gun. A minute ticked by. No movement came. He let his hand drop away from the holster. Then, realising he had been holding his breath, too, he sucked in a lungful of sterilized air. Another sound emitted from the shadows, but still nothing materialised.

Fuck this!

Sanchez decided he had had enough, broke into a run and bolted for the exit.

***

Doctor Stapleton's hand shook as it returned the folder to its drawer. She heard the door of her office open. She shuddered and turned towards a silhouette. A hand, pale and emaciated, reached out, resting against her shoulder. Her head turned and her mouth twisted itself into a macabre slash. The fingers were fish-belly white, cold and unyielding.

"Please don't hurt me," Doctor Stapleton begged. "I did as you asked."

Jonus laughed in a crackle of cold-bloodied amusement. His other hand pushed the office door shut. The pathologist looked into two merciless eyes and knew instantly that death was about to reveal its biggest secret

Chapter Nineteen

Anna stood, arm outstretched, with the gun pointed towards the big detective. She walked over to him. Before Balooga could open his mouth, Anna surprised him by letting the gun slip from her fingers. It dropped into his lap. He caught the weapon and instinctively turned it towards her.

Anna took one look at the pistol and laughed. "You don't think I'm that stupid, do you?" she asked, opening her hand to revealed six brass shells. They disappeared quickly into one of her pockets.

The detective clicked open the cylindrical loader and found that all six chambers were empty. With difficulty Balooga slipped the redundant weapon back into his jacket. He twisted his tethered hand awkwardly until the weapon slid inside his shoulder holster.

"So tell me, why is this leading to me?" he asked.

"Because you can determine how this goes."

"How what goes?"

"Tonight – between you, me and Josh Sawyer."

"I don't understand."

"Look, you have two choices. One, you pursue us and more innocents will die, or two, you give us a chance to get out of the city, and by doing so we'll lead a greater threat away from you and yours."

"Are you threatening me or trying to buy me?" Balooga asked.

"Neither," she replied. "What I'm trying to do is give you a chance to save lives, not end them."

"But it's too late," he said, and withdrew a set of papers from his jacket.

"What are those?"

"These are the warrants for both yours and Sawyer's arrest."

Anna leaned forward to take the papers. She opened them and saw the official stamp of the Supreme Court and Department of Justice. Scanning further down the document, she read her own name and address, and on another almost identical sheet, she found Josh's name and a Campus address.

"This is just paper. Lose it," she said.

"I can't, it's too late. These warrants are already in the system," he responded. He stood and took the documents back. "Look, come with me to the precinct and we'll work something out."

"Work something out?"

"Listen, Sawyer has already made a statement saying he was attacked, so we'll say it was all in self-defence," Balooga urged.

"Come on, Detective, we both know that wouldn't stand."

He shrugged his large shoulders. "I'm just trying to find a solution, that's all."

"The solution's simple. Give me and Josh the chance to get out of the city tonight, and by the morning we'll be out of the state and out of your jurisdiction."

"And then FBI will be all over you."

"Let me worry about those 'Fucking Bumbling Idiots'," she told him.

"Cute," he said, getting the joke. "Listen, I'm a law enforcer. I can't just let you walk out of here. Plus, you've virtually just confessed to killing three people."

"Okay, we'll compromise."

"Go on."

"If your reports show that the three dead guys were… bad, then you'll look the other way for eighteen hours."

"No chance," he said.

"Then any further bloodshed will be on your hands!"

"Don't threaten me!" he barked.

"It's not a threat – it's a guarantee!" she countered.

Unexpectedly, he grasped at his chest as pain flashed across his face. His expression twisted into a look of agony. Then, doubling over, he dropped to one knee. "… My… heart…" He gasped. "Difficult… to… breathe… "

"Are you alright?" she asked, with genuine concern.

"Just… need to… get… a breath."

"Do you need help?" she asked, as he struggled to suck in air.

"I'm… alright…" he murmured, bent over.

Concerned for the detective, she looked towards the sidewalk and at the steady stream of passers-by. For a moment she stood indecisive. Then, as his desperate wheezing increased, she finally made up her mind. "Wait here. I'll get help," she said, and moved away from him.

"That won't be necessary."

She turned to find Balooga standing straight with a small, dark revolver in his hands. He shook his right leg and the hem of his pants fell over the now empty ankle holster.

"Cute," she remarked, using his idiom.

"Let's start again," he said. A broad smile split his even broader face. With a slight gesture of the gun, Balooga said, "Now, over here."

Standing in the centre of the alleyway and, with the sidewalk behind her, Anna took a step backwards. "What are you going to do? Shoot me?" she asked.

"Don't push me," Balooga cautioned.

"If you miss or the bullet goes through me, then you could hit an innocent bystander," she warned him.

"It's a chance I'm willing to take."

"I don't think so," she said, regaining her awareness. "You may have tricked me once, but not again." She turned and walked away from the detective.

"STOP!" Balooga ordered.

She heard the hammer of the revolver click back. Unsure of his intensions, she stopped.

"Now turn around," he said.

She stood still.

"Miss Privalova – turn around, NOW!"

"Time for your awakening," she stated, in a slightly distorted voice.

"DO IT!" Balooga's voice revealed his trepidation.

She turned and her upper body fell into shadows.

"Now step towards me," he told her.

She took a step forward, her face shrouded in darkness.

"Closer, so I can see you."

She sprang unexpectedly forwards, her arms outstretched, leaping at the detective. Balooga saw wicked talons clawing at his face, and instinctively he squeezed the trigger. A flash of gunpowder illuminated the entire alleyway, which jabbed painfully at Balooga's eyes. In that split second of brightness, though, something hideous and terrifying filled his vision.

The discharge made a surprisingly loud noise within this confined space as the blast clattered and reverberated off the tightly formed walls. Momentarily disorientated, the detective sensed, more than visualised, a body pass over him. Tracing the revolver in a wide arc, he applied pressure to the trigger. Yet, once his senses had returned, he found the dark alleyway behind him deserted.

"Impossible," he said.

He turned his attention to the small crowd of people gathering at the entrance to the alleyway. After taking one last look behind him, he made his way toward the curious mob.

Chapter Twenty

The parking area was deserted. Josh crossed the empty lot and reached his motel room. He knocked on the door, cringing slightly as the noise echoed noisily around him. He scanned around the motel's front. All quiet: no cries of arresting cops, or Jonus suddenly leering out of the darkness. After a few seconds, he heard the lock *click* and the door opened. Anna stood back, allowing him to enter.

"That's it, the lot," Josh announced, shrugging off the backpack. He reached up to slip off his disguise.

"You get everything?" Anna asked.

"Yeah."

"And the tickets?"

"All booked," he said, and reached inside his pocket. He handed over a folded piece of paper.

She opened it. "The Texas Star?"

"Yeah, it leaves tonight at 12:00AM and gets us into LA at 4:30PM – the day after tomorrow." He knew it was an impossible time for Anna, and added, "Sorry, I couldn't get any others at such short notice."

"Don't worry, we'll be getting off well before we get into LA," she told him.

"Don't tell me, we'll be jumping from a moving train?"

"Don't be stupid, why would we do that?" she joked.

"Thought you liked a bit of excitement."

"I do, but after tonight let's try and keep it boring."

"Fine by me."

She took the backpack and began to check its contents. She emptied the pack completely and then quickly repacked, leaving just two small piles, one of which she handed to Josh. Seeing that his pile consisted of mainly new clothes, Josh instantly realised he did not smell too good. "I think I'll take a shower," he decided, surprisingly self-conscious.

"Good idea, but hurry – we need to leave in about forty-five minutes."

Josh disappeared into the bathroom. After a couple of minutes, Anna heard the steady stream of water. She moved to a wooden dresser and dropped her pile of clothes, then removed her jacket to examine her side. Her dress was torn: a small, perfectly rounded hole at the front and a ragged, open tear at the back. A dry crust of blood surrounded the larger tear, which had spread evenly in all directions. She kicked off her shoes and stepped out of her dress. Dressed only in panties, she crossed the room to stand in front of a small mirror.

She raised her arm, inspecting a deep wound in her side. The wound cut a crude line from just below her right breast. From there, it continued across the length of her ribcage, in an upward direction, finishing in a large tear to her armpit. Prodding at the injury caused the mild sensation of pain. As she removed her finger, a small watery rivulet of blood leaked out. Satisfied the injury wasn't too serious, she returned to her crumpled dress and began to pull it over her head.

"What the hell?"

"What?" Anna said, and she quickly pulled the garment down.

"Don't 'what' me," Josh said, annoyed.

"What?" she repeated.

"Anna, don't fuck with me. What was that?"

"Nothing," she said dismissively.

He stepped towards her, dressed only in a bath towel.

"The water's free, you know. You could have taken longer," she told him. Then she noticed he was still dry. "You're not even wet?"

"I was brushing my teeth," he said, and held up a small plastic toothbrush. "I was about to get a razor, but now I want to know what that is." He looked at the ripped material. "Show me."

"It's nothing."

"Anna."

"OKAY!" she snapped, and removed her dress.

He bent to examine the injury. His examination took him towards her back. "Nasty."

"It's nothing," she insisted, holding the dress over her bare breasts, surprised by her own shyness.

"Wait here," he said, and disappeared into the bathroom. He returned with a damp towel.

"Josh, we don't have time for this."

"Then we'll make time," he argued. He placed the damp cloth against the wound, which caused her to catch her breath.

"Sorry," he said. "Does it hurt bad?"

"No," she replied, "but you could have used warm water."

"Sorry."

"That's alright."

He gently dabbed at the wound to clean away the dried blood. "What the hell happened here?" he quizzed, carefully patting the injury dry.

"I was trying to buy us some time," she explained.

"How?"

"By reasoning with Lieutenant Balooga."

"What!" he queried incredulously.

"Calm down," she said, "nothing happened."

"Then what's this?"

"Son-of-a-bitch shot me," she laughed.

"Anna, it's not funny. What happened?"

"Like I said, I was trying to buy us some time."

"I'm listening," he said, then turned his attention back to her side.

"This Balooga, he's smarter than he looks. I figured if I could convince him you didn't kill those two cops, then maybe he would cut us some slack. As you can see, it didn't exactly go as planned."

"No shit."

"Crazy fool wanted us to practically hand ourselves in."

"So what happened?"

"He tricked me, that's what happened."

"And?"

"And nothing. I got the hell out of there and came straight back here."

"He could have followed you," Josh gasped, and quickly moved to the window.

"Relax. He was in no fit state to follow anyone," she said, and grinned, remembering his look of surprise when she'd cuffed him.

"Christ, Anna. You didn't… "

"NO," she interrupted him, "he was just a little otherwise tied up – that's all."

"Honest?"

"Yes, Josh, honest. I'm not some cold-blooded killer, you know."

He looked into her beautiful brown eyes and believed her. "I'm sorry," he said.

"Hey, come here." Anna reached out to him.

He joined her and she took hold of his hand. "Listen, I'm nothing like Jonus. You must believe me."

"I do."

"After tonight, it'll be just him and us. Nobody else will be involved, I promise."

Not sure if he liked the idea of them having to face Jonus alone, Josh only managed to mutter a weak, "Good."

She gave him a smile of reassurance, and then pulled him closer to place a gentle kiss onto his lips. He returned her kiss and felt his groin swell. He broke away from her. "Do we have time for this?"

She dropped her dress to the floor. "We'll make time."

Chapter Twenty-One

Balooga reached his desk. He pulled his shield out of his inner jacket pocket, removed his holster, and the embarrassing handcuffs, and then tossed them into his desk drawer. He sat down with a heavy sigh.

After emerging from the dark passageway, he'd called upon the help of an onlooker. It had taken a while to convince his aide that he *was* indeed a real cop and not some shackled sex fiend. Eventually though, he had been freed. Using the keys from one of his back pockets, the bystander – laughing uncontrollably – had quickly removed the restraints. Sworn to secrecy with the threat of violence, the guy had quickly fled in fear of his life.

Balooga rubbed his wrists, picked up the handset to a phone and dialled a memorized number. He waited to be connected and then had a brief conversation with his wife. After promising her he would be home this side of Christmas, he hung up. He released a colossal yawn and then rubbed the heels of his hands against his bloodshot eyes. Then standing, he made his way to a large jug of coffee. Not even bothering to see if it was warm or not, he poured himself a cupful. He returned to his cluttered desk and had just enough time to raise the cup before a deafening wail sounded.

"BALOOGA!"

He turned to find the thinly built Captain Applegate stood just outside his office. The captain summoned the lieutenant with a bent finger before disappearing back inside his office.

Balooga contemplated on whether or not he should take his gun, but decided that two dead cops were enough for one night. He crossed the office and entered Captain Applegate's office. Inside the small office, he found Applegate, a miserable looking Emilio Sanchez and an impeccably dressed Indian guy. Not an American Indian but a dark-skinned Mahatma Ghandi type: the kind who would have been found sharing borders with Pakistan. He was dressed in an expensive dark-blue suit, stood at about five foot eight and weighed between 150 – 160 pounds. His jet-black hair had been cut into a short side-parting and he had light hazel eyes, which stood out against his dark skin.

The detective and the newcomer made eye contact, and the stranger nodded in Balooga's direction.

"Now, would you like to tell me what the hell's going on?" Applegate asked. His thin, harsh face darkened by two shades of red.

"What the hell's going on?" Balooga repeated irritatingly. Deciding he'd had enough for one day, he knowingly began to stoke the flames of conflict.

"Don't mess with me, Lieutenant," Applegate warned.

"What do you want to know?" Balooga asked. "That within the space of twelve hours, we've found five mutilated bodies, two of which were cops, one being a friend of mine. Or that our two main suspects have disappeared? Or maybe you'd like to know just why the hell someone in their wisdom decided to put an inexperienced cadet in charge of guarding a ruthless killer!"

It had been Applegate's decision to keep Sawyer confined to his hospital bed and not taken immediately into custody. The captain shuffled awkwardly from one foot to the other.

"What I'm interested in is how this fugitive managed to steal an unmarked police car," Applegate said, directing the blame away from himself.

"Son-of-a-bitch pulled a gun on me," Balooga told him.

"What gun?"

"My gun," Balooga said solemnly.

"Jesus, are you telling me that this kid killed two of our finest officers with a police issue weapon?"

"No, he took the gun after he killed them."

"So you're telling me that this crazed kid is running around my city with a deadly weapon? Your weapon!"

"No, he dropped it at the airport," Balooga said.

Applegate turned towards the smartly dress Indian and flicked his eyes upwards in a *'look what I have to put up with'* gesture.

Balooga saw the act. He snapped, "Listen, Captain, if I hadn't spent the best part of the afternoon sitting around in court then none of this would have happened!"

"But we have to follow procedure," Applegate said defensively.

"Yeah, and procedure just gave our two suspects a helping hand," Balooga said, and threw the crumpled warrants onto the captain's desk.

"Listen, I don't make rules. I just follow them."

"Yeah, and maybe if you had the balls to break a few, we wouldn't be in this mess."

Balooga's rebuke momentarily silenced Applegate. However, he quickly regained his composure. "Okay, this is getting us nowhere. What we need to do is figure out our next move."

"That's simple," the Indian said. "We wait."

His accent surprised the detective.

He stuck out a hand and greeted Balooga. "I'm Special Agent Sebastian Fernandez," the Indian announced in a broad English accent. He spoke with a deep northern brogue, similar to that of the movie actor, Sean Bean. Accustomed to surprised looks, Sebastian Fernandez smiled at the detective's stunned look. "I'm here to represent the bureau," he announced.

"The FEDs?" Balooga spat, and released hands.

Fernandez read the hostility on the detective's face. "Don't worry, I'm not here to piss on anyone's shoes. I'm just here to help with your investigation – for now."

"What did you mean, wait?" Sanchez asked, speaking for the first time.

"We sit back and wait for them to come to us – figuratively speaking, that is," Fernandez told him.

"I don't understand," Sanchez said.

"It's simple. They'll make a mistake and lead us right to them."

"And in the meantime?" Balooga asked.

"We work on forensics and accumulate evidence, and make sure we have a watertight case," Fernandez told the small group.

"Doesn't sound like much of a plan," Balooga moaned.

"Trust me," the agent said.

Balooga looked at Applegate and understood that this was already a done deal. Knowing that they needed as much help and resources as they could get, he gave a heavy sigh of resignation, and then nodded towards the agent. "Okay, what do you suggest?"

"For now, we can look through these," Fernandez said, and retrieved a pile of files from the top of Applegate's desk. He split the folders three ways. "These are for our three boys in the freezer."

"The Little Village slayings?" Sanchez asked.

"Yeah, they make for a very interesting read."

Before either Sanchez or Balooga could begin to read the documents, the FBI agent turned to Applegate. "Thanks for your co-operation, Captain. We'll take this outside and deal with it."

The agent and captain bade each other a short farewell. And, after negotiating his way past the two detectives, the agent left the office.

"C'mon," Balooga snapped at Sanchez.

Balooga and Applegate exchanged a brief but hostile glare before the large detective left the office in angry pursuit of the FBI agent.

The younger detective followed his superior, leaving the agitated captain alone in his office. They joined Fernandez at Balooga's cluttered desk. Already sat in Balooga's chair, the agent was engrossed in an open file.

"Two things," Balooga said, getting Fernandez's attention. "Number one, until we have proof that both Sawyer and Privalova are out of the state then this is still my case. And two, even when this isn't my case, that's still my goddamn chair!"

Fernandez closed the file with exaggerated care, stood and took a vacant chair. He pulled the seat over to the desk and seated himself to one side. With a slight hand gesture, he offered the detective his seat.

"Thanks," Balooga muttered, moving his heavy bulk into the chair. He flipped open his folder and saw a familiar face, long and harsh, with high, prominent cheekbones. The face had sunken eyes, and a mean expression. The last time Balooga had seen this face, it had been staring in the wrong direction. Written in large, clearly typed print was the name 'Vincent Monroe'.

"Okay, Mister Monroe, what can you tell us?" Balooga said. He pulled out the photo and began to read out the rap sheet. He read about three lines only before realising that Vincent Monroe had not been your average law-abiding citizen. The script read like a thousand others.

By the time Vincent Monroe was just fifteen, he had already spent the last two/two-and-a-half years in and out of juvenile care. What had started out as minor misdemeanours had soon developed into serious crimes, such as grand theft auto, assault, and aggravated burglary. In addition, at the ripe old age of nineteen he was already serving a twelve-year sentence for rape and battery.

"Nice, real nice," Balooga said. He flipped over a page and continued to read aloud.

Sent to a maximum-security prison out on the state border, Monroe had been incarcerated for eight of his twelve-year sentence. He was released for 'good' behaviour after serving the mandatory two-thirds of his full sentence. On release, he returned to his old neighbourhood and had avoided serious trouble, until now.

Looking at the bottom of the last page, Balooga found a list of known associates, consisting of just two names. "Okay, so who've you got?" he asked Sanchez.

Sanchez opened his file and found a cruel face looking back at him. The face was so mean it was almost a parody. The picture was split in two, on one side a profile and the other a face-on.

A small blackboard with a serial number printed across hung from around his bull neck. Behind the brutish head were equally spaced black lines with numbers stencilled alongside. Sanchez could see that the guy stood well over six feet tall.

"Real pretty," Sanchez remarked, recognizing him as the faceless victim. "Not much of an improvement," the detective told the other two. He held the picture out so both could see. "Okay," Sanchez began, "I'd like to introduce Thad Paterson, aged thirty-two. Born in the small town of Brookville, which is situated alongside the Mississippi River, and was the first son of proud parents: Dennis and Margaret Paterson."

"Christ, a face only a mother could love," Balooga said sarcastically, looking at the mean and unintelligent face.

"Wrong," Sanchez corrected, "apparently, Margaret wasn't all that smitten with young Thad, because she left both him and his father by the time he was seven."

"Poor kid," Balooga commented, now mournful.

Sanchez continued, "It seems poor Thad developed behavioural problems and spent the early part of his life visiting numerous child psychologists. He was diagnosed with an extreme form of schizophrenia by the age of five and put on Haloperidol. The treatment didn't work, and with their son's apparent unnatural growth, the Patersons struggled to cope with Thad. It says here, he became more and more aggressive towards his parents. Margaret Paterson eventually went AWOL."

"Poor kid," Balooga repeated.

"The last thing a neighbour heard Margaret Paterson say was that her child had been born 'evil', and after disappearing she was never seen again," Sanchez said.

"Give me that," Balooga snapped, and took the sheet. He scanned down the report to the point where a neighbour had quoted Mrs Patterson. Apparently, Thad's mother had expressed a fear that her son had been born 'wicked'.

"This can't be right," Balooga said.

Sanchez read from the second to last sheet. "It says here, Thad went downhill after his mother left him. Before long he'd pretty much beat up on most of the local kids, leaving one almost blind. That was Dennis Paterson's cue to institutionalise young Thad."

"So how'd he end up here?" Balooga asked.

"Looks like he turned eighteen and the state had to let him out. As he was no longer under his father's care, the state couldn't hold him any longer."

"And?"

"And now a young man, he works his way from state to state, drifting and working as an occasional farmhand, until he chances upon a particular farm."

With anticipated dread, Balooga said, "Go on... " Somehow he knew this wasn't going to have a happy ending.

"He started working on a farm owned by the Cartwright family. According to these notes, he stayed for almost a year. Then things started to go wrong. Paterson nearly killed another hired hand: broke his jaw and left him in a wheelchair for the rest of the year."

"Why?" Balooga asked.

"Doesn't say. All it does say is that the Cartwrights asked him to leave. Thad didn't like the idea of being rejected twice in his life so he killed them."

"WHAT?" Balooga asked in disbelief.

"Shot the whole family dead."

"Jesus... "

"State Troopers found him in bed, asleep, all cosy with a shotgun by his side. One trooper told his commander-in-charge that the barrels of the gun were so hot they almost glowed."

"Bastard should have fried," Balooga spat, his compassion now forgotten.

"Probably would have if some hotshot lawyer hadn't got him off with an insanity plea. Paterson spent the next eight years in an institute for the criminally insane. Then some wonder drug came out, Clozapine, and good old Thad was deemed fit and sane and released back into the world," Sanchez finished.

"And then what?"

"Nothing. He must have made his way into the city and made

acquaintances with one of these two assholes," Sanchez said, pointing to the other two folders.

"One?" Fernandez asked, interrupting the detectives' discussion.

Sanchez said, "Doctor Stapleton, the medical examiner working the case, she thinks blood found on Paterson's hands probably came from one of the other victims."

Fernandez's dark brow furrowed slightly. "That doesn't fit the profile. According to this, Paterson, Monroe and Bubba Macintyre were real close."

"Bubba Who?" Sanchez and Balooga asked together.

"Bubba Macintyre, a.k.a. Mackie the Weasel," Fernandez said, with a raised eyebrow.

"Who writes this shit?" Balooga asked, pushing the sheet of paper back to Sanchez.

The young detective slipped the paper inside the folder and rested it on top of the desk.

Agent Fernandez sensed two pairs of eyes focused on him. He began a short narrative. "Okay, my turn. Bubba Macintyre: born in 1968 to a wealthy suburban family. Made straight A's throughout his early childhood and finished at Harvard. He enrolled on a degree program in law and politics. Finished the first year top of his class. Played college football – sorry, soccer. The guy was a real jock. But then early on in his second year it seems everything started to go bad."

"Why?" Balooga asked.

"The guy busted his knee playing ball and subsequently became addicted to Fenbufen and started to pile on the pounds. He… "

"Wait – wait," Balooga interjected. "I'm a detective not some goddamn chemist, now what the fuck is Funbufin?"

"F-e-n-b-u-f-e-n," Fernandez enunciated. "It's an anti-inflammatory, used for injuries to joints and rheumatoid arthritis."

"Right – yeah, carry on," Balooga said, with a nod.

"He dropped soccer and almost doubled in weight. It wasn't

long before he dropped his studies too. He retuned home a different man − worse. It wasn't long before he started to mix with a new fraternity, the kind that deal drugs. Guy is very smart though, always kept to the shadows and never got caught doing anything himself. Used his friends' staunch allegiance to keep him out of harm's way. Hence: The Weasel."

"Not smart enough though," Sanchez said.

"Sorry?" Fernandez asked.

"Not smart enough to keep him out of the morgue," Sanchez pointed out.

"Right," the agent agreed.

"But neither Paterson nor Monroe have records relating to drugs," Balooga said.

"New recruits," Fernandez told him. "Narcotics have been keeping tabs on Macintyre. They both appeared on the scene less than twelve months ago. Narcotics never pulled them in because they were waiting to snatch the bigger fish."

"Looks like they've missed their chance," Sanchez said.

"Yeah," Fernandez agreed.

Balooga began to feel troubled.

"What is it, Chief?" Sanchez asked, seeing his partner's concern.

Lost in his own private thoughts, Balooga missed the query. What had Anna Privalova told him? That he would find three tarnished histories. And the guys growing cold downtown were not exactly good citizens. No, they were… scum. That's what she had told him − *they were just scum.* Had she somehow read their souls? Impossible, Balooga thought. Whatever the answer, one thing was clear, the streets were safer tonight with all three gone. He looked up at the clock and found that it was 11:25PM. He began to mentally calculate ahead by eighteen hours, before abruptly shaking his head clear.

"Wait a minute," he snapped. He leaned across the table to pull Sanchez's pad from the detective's pocket. Flipping through the pages, he stopped halfway. "Sawyer is at college, right? And it says here, he too was involved in some sort of accident three years ago. Busted his leg in a car wreck. And guess what? Son-of-a-bitch was a track and field star – well almost. He qualified for the Olympics just before his accident."

"That's right, Chief," Sanchez confirmed.

"So Sawyer and Macintyre could have been working together," Balooga observed. "Supplying drugs on campus?"

"Maybe," Fernandez admitted. "But if so, then how come Narcotics haven't made him?"

"Because this Macintyre was smart, remember. They must have always met in the most unexpected of places," Balooga explained.

"Like Little Village!" Sanchez said.

"Exactly," Balooga agreed.

"Wait, I'm new in town. What's this Little Village?" Fernandez asked.

"It's the Hispanic barrio. Not the place for white boys," Sanchez told him. Then as he looked at his superior's large, white moon-face, he said, "Sorry Chief."

"But this woman, Privalova, where does she fit in?" Fernandez asked.

Unable to share in the woman's confession, Balooga remained quiet.

"Maybe she's the supplier, works for the Russians," Sanchez suggested, referring to the ever-increasing Eastern European crime syndicates.

"You've got a point," Fernandez admitted.

"Yeah, maybe the deal went bad and she and Sawyer whacked all three," Sanchez said excitedly.

"So where is the stash?" the agent asked.

"We didn't find anything at her apartment," Balooga pointed out, rejoining the conversation.

"So that leaves his place," Fernandez said.

"Right," Sanchez agreed.

"So what are we waiting for?" the agent asked, getting to his feet.

"But it's almost midnight," Balooga moaned wearily.

"Everybody will be asleep."

"We're not, so let's go," Fernandez said, and he headed towards Applegate's office.

Balooga stretched his large bulk, then stood and retrieved his holster, cuffs and badge. He looked down at Sanchez and saw the detective rubbing at the sides of his skull.

"Are you alright?"

Through heavy eyelids, Sanchez replied, "Yeah, must be all this excitement."

"C'mon, let's pacify Agent Hard-on for another hour, then we'll get some rest."

The FBI agent returned with the crumpled arrest warrants. "Let's go," he said, heading for the door.

As the two detectives followed the agent, Balooga felt his anxieties lift slightly. Although he was not willing to share his recent encounter with Anna Privalova with the rest of the group, he did believe that they were heading towards the truth.

***

The dark apparition moved away from the window. Jonus backed away from the precinct and then dissolved into the shadows, disappearing like some forgotten memory.

***

Balooga, Sanchez and the FBI agent arrived late at the Bartlett College for Sporting Excellence and Physical Science. On arrival, they immediately rousted a weary warden and then silently followed the irritable old custodian to Josh Sawyer's dormitory.

Like most of the city's colleges, this institution had been built some one hundred years earlier, with huge empty hallways and barren passageways. Making their way through this ancient academy, their footfalls echoed hollowly off the polished stone tiles. They eventually climbed a twisting staircase to enter a more generous quarter. The bare floors were replaced with darkly woven carpets, and a scattering of drab and antique furniture could be found dotted along these bleak corridors at irregular intervals. Although these passageways were forlornly conservative, the three visitors heard a mixture of laughter, music and the sounds of spirited youngsters coming from closed dormitories. Occasionally, the warden banged against a doorway, and with a cry of "QUIET!" he simultaneously silenced the occupant within whilst waking the culprit's immediate neighbours.

They eventually stopped outside one particular doorway and, with the aid of a huge bunch of iron keys, the warden allowed them entry. The two detectives quickly went about their search. From the doorway, Sebastian Fernandez watched the two cops comb their way through the small room. They found nothing but the kid's personal belongings. They concentrated their search on the many files of coursework. If they were hoping to find some indication of illegal activity, it quickly became apparent that they were not going to. Finally, they gave up their search and the three law enforcers vacated the room. The door was sealed shut with a strip of police tape. Silent, frustrated and exhausted, they then made their way back towards Balooga's Lexus. Even Sanchez seemed disheartened by their lack of success.

After Balooga dropped Sanchez home, he felt obligated to ask the FBI agent if he wanted to spend the night at his place. Thankfully, the agent declined and instead gave Balooga directions to a motel. They arranged to meet back at Homicide later that morning. The detective and agent then bade each other a frosty goodnight.

It had gone 12:30AM before Balooga finally climbed into bed.

Chapter Twenty-Two

Two dark shapes ran parallel to the banks of the Chicago River, staying close to one another, drawing away from the bright lights and highly populated area of the city. They remained near the riverbank until the lights and noise dwindled into the distance.

Josh and Anna moved away from the rippling waters and began to make their way towards the city's rail line. Although Anna carried a heavy backpack, she glided effortlessly alongside the twin rails. Running behind and, with an awkward gait, Josh struggled to keep up. They ran in silence for about another half-mile before abruptly stopping. Directly to their right they spotted an abandoned signal-box. They moved behind the building and hid in darkness.

About three-quarters of a mile further up the track, the colossal Amtrak Superliner pulled away from Union Station. One by one, the carriages followed the massive machine. Like some gigantic silver beast the diesel engine pulled its 120 tons of cargo behind it. To begin with the chrome carriages swayed gently from side to side. Then, as the Superliner gained speed and the carriages bucked about, the wheels scraped against the track, releasing a deafening shriek.

"Okay, you ready?" Anna asked an out-of-breath Josh.

"Yeah," he gulped, sucking in air.

She looked down the dark track. In the distance she made out the outline of the advancing train. She tightened the straps to her backpack. "Get ready. We're only gonna get one shot at this.”

“I’m ready,” Josh said, and crunched on another painkiller.

“Hey, go easy on them,” she warned him.

He swallowed the bitter paste. “It was your idea, remember,” he reminded her, with a foolish grin on his face.

“They were supposed to numb the pain in your leg, not your brain, stupid.”

“Don’t worry, I’m good to go,” he said, and stretched the leg in question.

“I hope so.”

The Texas Star neared, revealing the distinctive red, white and blue streak of Amtrak. Like some unwinding serpent, the Superliner slowly weaved its way towards them. Then, startlingly, the engine roared past in a silver blur. The carriages began to flash past in explosions of bright chrome.

“Not yet,” Anna said, as she sensed him tense. “We wait for the last four carriages, remember?”

“I remember.”

They waited and watched as the carriages whipped passed. Then the end of the train moved towards them.

“NOW!” Anna yelled. She sprang up and began to sprint alongside the train.

Josh jumped up intent on following her. He rushed along, struggling to keep his footing on the stones that shifted underneath his feet. He almost slipped and went down, but managed to remain upright. The slipstream of the train threatened to pull him under the massive iron wheels. Terrified he was going to be sucked right under, he backed away. He looked up to see Anna way ahead.

Anna ran parallel to the speeding train. With a deafening roar, the final carriage flashed by. She reached out to grab a hold of a handrail. The train momentarily pulled her off her feet, dragging her through the air. She quickly succumbed to gravity, and, with a mighty push of her feet, she jumped up over the rail and landed on a small iron platform. She looked out into the night to find Josh stumbling along.

"COME ON!" she yelled.

He lifted his head and saw her standing, arm outstretched, urging him on. Ducking his head back down, he pumped his arms out, desperately trying to gain speed. As he pushed himself on he felt the pain in his leg intensify.

"JOSH, FASTER!"

He chanced a brief look up. To his horror, he saw the gap between him and the train widen. He sucked in a lungful of clear, crisp air. Oxygen filled his lungs, and he felt a sudden burst of energy. He found a strength he believed to be long gone and began to reel in the distance.

"THAT'S IT, COME ON!" Anna screamed over the thunderous combination of machine and wind.

He reduced the distance. Just as he was about to collapse with exhaustion, he reached out and grabbed her hand.

"I'VE GOT YOU!" she shouted, relief flashing across her face.

He looked up, allowed himself a brief smile, but then, before he could pull himself up and over the handrail, his foot slipped in a patch of oily grass.

"NO!" Anna screamed, as his fingers slipped away.

He fell in a cartwheel of arms and legs, and landed in a heap. Rolling back onto his feet, he pursued the train, but now, almost at the point of exhaustion, he felt his legs tighten. Hopelessly, he looked towards Anna and watched as her beautiful face rapidly dwindled into darkness.

He slowed to a canter. Beaten.

The last carriage swayed from side to side, screeching out a piercing mockery. Instantly he grasped that the train had actually slowed to negotiate a tight bend. Exploding into action, he sprinted towards Anna with newfound energy. In moments, he had halved the distance. He pushed himself beyond his limits and reached for her outstretched hand.

"JOSH, YOU CAN DO IT!"

He felt the last ounce of his strength drain away, but with one final desperate push he threw himself at her. He sailed through the air and, as if by some miracle, the slipstream grabbed a hold of him and pulled him within her reach. A vicelike grip tightened around his wrist. He found himself on top of her.

They untangled themselves to face each other. Anna smiled at him. Then, unexpectedly, she slapped his face.

"What the?" he said, shocked.

"You scared the shit out of me," she told him, and then equally unexpectedly she threw her arms around him. They embraced, and he felt her body tremble.

"Hey, it's okay," he soothed.

"You promised you wouldn't leave me," she sobbed.

"Hey, I'm right here. I'm not going anywhere," he reassured her.

They stayed clasped together for a long time, swaying back and forth, as the carriage gently rocked them deep into the night.

Chapter Twenty-Three

The fly buzzed around the woman's body in wide, lazy circles. It continued with its pointless revolutions until finally growing weary, eventually landing on the woman's cheek. There it sat, on cold discoloured flesh, and preened its front legs.

A slight draft blew across the basement floor, which momentarily cooled the otherwise warm cellar. As the night breeze caressed the rigid body, the stench of death wafted from its slick pores.

Another insect appeared and this one danced a short jittery ballet before landing on a bent finger. Underneath the polished fingernail, the fly detected rotten flesh.

The first fly finished its cleaning and thus began to investigate this new world. It scuttled first one way and then the next, finishing at the woman's open mouth. Her lips were peeled back to reveal bright white teeth. Almost all of the front teeth were crowned, and where they stopped a sliver of grey gums could be seen. A deep gash cut into her bottom lip, and a rusty patch of crimson stained her ample chin. Nylon pantyhose were tightly wrapped around the woman's throat, tearing skin where the material had been pulled to almost breaking point.

The insect darted away from the open mouth to stop at a swollen eye. Puffy eyelids sealed the orb almost shut, but a small gap revealed a dull and glazed blue underneath.

The fly found little of interest at the eye, so returned to the open mouth. It hopped from her top lip and landed on polished ceramic. Crawling to the end of the tooth, it hung over the gaping entrance. Wings fluttered and the fly hovered over the open mouth. After a moment's pause, it disappeared into darkness. It made its way to the back of her throat and felt for the remnants of heat. The insect worked its way underneath her engorged tongue, and there, it discovered greater warmth. The fly shifted its body as it nestled within the moist cavity.

And, after a few moments, it began to lay the first of many eggs.

Chapter Twenty-Four

The train beat out a constant tattoo, carriages rocking to and fro, and the hypnotic buffeting helped carry most passengers towards the confinements of sleep. A hint of moonlight found its way inside the compartments, a glowing beacon, which guided many safely through the field of dreams and away from the dangers of dark nightmares.

Anna caressed his face with the ends of her fingertips. His brow furrowed slightly, dark images plaguing him from the recesses of his mind. Anna watched him for a moment, wondering what horrors he had encountered whilst in the presence of her old foe, Jonus. With one finger, she gently traced the coarse line above his eye. Eyelids fluttered and Josh awoke.

"Hi sleepyhead," she said.

He raised his head out of her lap and yawned, then stretched his aching body. "Where are we?" he asked. Careful to avoid his head injuries, he scratched at the stubble to his scalp.

She looked out of the window as dark, open fields rushed by. "Almost at the state border."

"Really? How long have I been asleep?"

"An hour, that's all."

"Shit, Anna! You should have woken me."

"Don't worry, everything's fine."

Josh found himself in a reasonably spacious room, furnished with a surprisingly large double-bed, a single straight-backed chair and a small sofa, which had been pushed up against the wall. Adjacent to the exit was a second doorway, which led to a compact washroom containing a small shower cubicle and toilet.

After gaining entry to the rear carriage, Anna had led Josh towards the front of the train. There, they had found a conductor. Anna had explained that her purse had gone missing, convincingly, and the conductor had rushed off to get them replacement key cards to their rooms, before rounding up a posse to find the alleged missing purse.

"What time is it?" Josh asked.

"Just turned two."

Realising that he had not eaten for some considerable time, Josh said, "I'm hungry. Let's get something to eat."

"Wait," she said.

Anna opened the backpack and took out a number of items. The first was a small roll of dark, coarsely woven material. She rolled the material out onto the bed and then turned to the window. After a mental calculation, she took a pair of scissors and began to cut the cloth into a square. Then, taking the dark square, she held it up to the window. Satisfied with its size, she snatched up a reel of tape. She took a couple of minutes to secure the material over the glass of the window. When she had finished, she pulled the curtains shut to hide her handiwork.

Anna said, "Okay. If anyone looks in from the outside they may be curious, but as long as we keep the light on during the day, the room should remain light enough to pass as normal."

"Right," Josh agreed. Now with the loss of its outside view, he found the compartment almost unbearably cramped. "Let's go," he urged, eager to feel space around him. He stepped out into the passageway and cautiously looked left and right.

"Relax," she said, joining him. "We paid, remember?"

"I know," he said, "it's just… I won't feel safe until we're across state."

"And we will be in an hour or so," she told him. "Relax," she repeated, squeezing his hand.

She shut and locked the door, then hung a sign over the doorknob.

It read: 'Do not disturb'.

She turned to him and grinned. "We're newlyweds, remember?"

He nodded, took a few steps down the passageway and then turned. "C'mon then, wife. Why don't you let me buy you a drink?"

He bent his elbow, allowing her to slip her hand through the crook of his arm. Then they walked arm-in-arm towards the centre of the train and its lounge.

They negotiated through about a half dozen narrow sleeping quarters before entering a more open compartment. With the bedrooms lost, this carriage offered a surprising amount of space. Square tables ran in neat rows along both sides of the carriage, and double-seated chairs were secured on either side. Wooden tabletops varnished to an extreme polish gave a mirror-like effect, and the chairs were padded by rich, velvety material. In the centre of the tables stood elaborately moulded glass lights, which flickered with an electronic flame.

At the end of the carriage, they saw a barmaid dressed in a white shirt and bowtie, standing behind a small arc-shaped bar. Directly behind the barmaid, and held upside down in multi-coloured bottles, were rows of liqueurs. And, as the carriage swayed from side to side, the bottles clinked together in alien chatter.

Although two in the morning, the lounge contained about a dozen people, drinking and chatting, oblivious to the world that zoomed past outside.

"C'mon, my round," Josh said. He reached inside his pocket and retrieved a handful of Anna's cash. They made their way over to the small bar area, drawing little or no attention.

Apart from his injuries, Josh looked like any other young man, relaxing and enjoying the trip. He was dressed in simple, casual travel clothes: a pair of new jeans, T-shirt and sneakers. Anna stood by his side, dressed in her own new outfit of a fitted dress, which ran just past her knees, a dark knitted jacket and black wedged shoes. Standing almost as tall as Josh, and with her hair hanging loosely around slim shoulders, she looked stunning. Nevertheless, with most of the patrons either too drunk or tired, or a combination of the two, she went unnoticed.

"Jack Daniel's and a beer, please," Josh asked the barmaid.

Whilst he waited for their drinks, he turned and surveyed the room. Most of the people were either couples or small groups of friends who chatted quietly, conscious of the late hour.

Then, immediately to his left, Josh heard a '*whoop, whoop*' of laughter. He turned towards the noise and saw a middle-aged man with a huge pink cocktail in one hand and a girl's slim hand in the other. The hand that held the exotic drink had thick sausage-like fingers, on which Josh counted three or four hefty, sparkling silver rings. With a deep golden tan, the guy looked as if he'd spent most of his life either bathing in the hot sun or asleep under a cover of ultraviolet lights. To Josh, the guy looked as if he had just escaped from a convention of travelling salesmen. The girl who faced him was about half his age and, apart from the lack of any intelligence, she was quite pretty. She held her hand over her face, trying unsuccessfully to hide her discomfort. The man saw his companion's unease and he whooped again, enjoying her embarrassment.

Josh turned his attention back to the barmaid and paid for their drinks. After a moment's deliberation, they seated themselves at a table directly behind the odd couple. They sat opposite each other and sipped their drinks in silence for a minute or two as they listened to the couple's drunken chatter.

From what they heard, they determined the guy to be a salesman – exactly as Josh had thought – and her, his mistress. The guy seemed to spend most of his time either making lewd comments about his younger partner's immeasurable libido – hence her embarrassment – or trying to convince her that he had indeed finally left his troublesome wife, aka 'The Bitch'.

Josh looked at Anna, shook his head slightly and smiled.

"What is it?" she asked, seeing his amusement.

"It's true what they say."

"What?"

"That there's somebody out there for everyone." He raised his beer to his lips and took a long swig.

She looked over his shoulder at the guy's flabby face and greasy hair, and then turned her attention to the pretty girl who sat opposite. In a slightly disapproving tone, she said, "He's old enough to be her father."

"What?" Josh blurted in surprise, almost covering her in beer.

Not understanding his reaction, she gave him a quizzical look.

"If he's old enough to be her father, then what's that make you?" he asked, his grin stretched wide.

"What do you mean?"

He leaned over the table and in a surreptitious whisper said, "Anna, if he's old enough to be her father, then that makes you old enough to be my… great-great-great-to-infinity grandmother!"

"Really?" she said and smiled, the irony of her own comment now understood.

"Yeah – really," Josh said. He leaned back and took another swig of his beer.

She looked across at the overweight guy opposite and then pulled her jacket to one side. She took Josh's hand and placed it over one of her breasts. "Yeah, but do I feel old?" she asked, and squeezed his hand against the firm tissue.

"Christ, Anna!" Josh blurted, covering them in a layer of Bulgaria's finest.

"Relax," she said, "we're newlyweds."

Josh looked around the carriage to see if the incident had gone unnoticed. Seeing it had, he leaned over and kissed her full on the lips. He gave her breast another quick, unassisted squeeze, before breaking away.

"Careful, don't get too adventurous," she mocked.

"Hey. If it was up to me, I'd do you right here on the table," he said.

Surprised by his out-of-character crudeness, she gasped slightly. "Josh Sawyer, where on earth did you learn such manners?" she asked, mimicking an innocence long forgotten, if ever known.

"It's the company I've been keeping lately," he joked.

"Well, I can't say I totally condone your choice of companionship," she said, with an exaggerated shake of her head. She finished her drink in a single gulp, and then tilted the glass towards Josh's empty bottle. "Same again?"

"Yeah, thanks."

She stood up and headed for the bar; leaving Josh to look out of the window and at the life he was leaving behind.

"Looks like you've got your hands full there, Pal."

Josh turned his attention away from the passing night. He spun in his seat to look at the round face of the middle-aged salesman.

"Sorry?"

"Your friend – she's a real looker," the guy said.

Not sure of his expected response, Josh simply muttered, "Yeah... " With no wish to strike up a conversation, he turned the other way.

Unperturbed by Josh's apparent rudeness, the guy asked, "You kids goin' anywhere special?"

Josh flicked his eyes heavenward. "We're on our honeymoon," he told the man.

"Really?"

Wearily, Josh realised he was having this conversation whether he liked it or not. He gave a heavy sigh. "Yeah, we're headed for Palm Springs."

"On your honeymoon to Palm Springs," the guy said. "Gee, you're a lucky man."

Josh looked over to Anna who was standing by the bar. Although their situation was about as dire as it could get, he could not help but agree. "Yeah, I guess I am," he said, and felt a rush of affection.

"Reminds me when I was younger and I was settin' out in the world with my Honeybell."

"Your Honeybell?" Josh repeated.

"Yeah," he said. "My, was she a doll."

"Was?" Josh asked. He pointed to the previously occupied seat. "Isn't she your…?"

"Hell, no," the guy said. "She's my Trixybell."

Laughing now, Josh relaxed a little. "Looks like you have your hands full."

"Ah, women – don't you just love 'em?" he asked, and his bronzed face beamed.

"Yeah," Josh agreed, and looked towards Anna.

The salesman stuck out a meaty hand, pleased to have found a mutual soul.

"I'm Dan 'Buddy' Perkins – Pleased to meetcha, kid."

Josh took the fleshy hand and found it hot and slick. "Pleased to meet you Dan, I'm Joo… " His name faded out. Josh was uncertain if it was prudent to use his real name or not.

"Hey, call me Buddy. Everyone does, Joe," Buddy Perkins said.

Before Josh could correct the misunderstanding, or work on an alternative, Buddy said, "Say, Joe – looks like you've had a bit of trouble," and indicated his plastered arm and cut brow.

With the combination of painkillers and beer, Josh no longer felt the wrist's dull throb. Although, now that he thought about it, he felt as if his entire body ached like a kicked dog. He raised the plastered arm and said, "I – I'm... a…"

"He's a motorbike racer."

Josh found Anna stood near with two drinks in her hands. "Yeah, he races bikes. Don't you honey?" she said, and looked from Buddy Perkins to Josh.

"Really, and what do you do, my little Tinkerbell?" Buddy asked, once he had noticed her bandaged hand.

"Me," she paused briefly, "I'm his mechanic."

"Mechanic?" Josh blurted.

With her eyes full of mischief, Anna ignored Josh and turned her attention to Buddy Perkins. She said, "Goddamn best mechanic this side of Kansas City. You need somethin' fixin' then I'll come a greasin'."

"Wow. Looks like you've got yourself a real sly fox, Joe," Buddy said, and slapped his huge thigh.

"Yeah – Joe – d'ya think you can handle me?" Anna said, her face beaming.

Josh pinched his leg in the hope that he would wake up and find himself out of Alice's rabbit hole. Yet, apart from the stinging pain to his leg, nothing changed. And sitting there he remained trapped inside this crazy episode of Twin Peaks.

"Say. Are you okay, Joe?" Buddy asked; the confusion on Josh's face was apparent.

"Yeah – yeah," he said. "Long day, that's all."

"We didn't get much sleep last night, newlyweds and all," Anna explained with a wink to Buddy Perkins.

Buddy understood her language. He slapped his thigh again and whooped with laughter.

Anna returned to her seat, reached across the table and squeezed Josh's hand in gentle reassurance.

Josh turned to her and, before she could say it, he grumbled, "Relax, we're newlyweds. Remember?"

She flashed him a huge smile. "I think I'm gonna like you, Joe."

"It's a good job, because if you didn't, I'd throw you off this damn train myself," he told her, and broke into a grin of his own.

Buddy Perkins picked up his large pink cocktail then heaved his bulk up before shuffling over to Josh and Anna's table.

"Don't mind if I join you two lovebirds, do ya?" he asked.

Before either of them could respond, Buddy lowered his weight into the chair opposite Josh.

"Why not?" Josh said, as the guy squeezed in beside Anna.

"Ain't life grand?" Buddy said. He drew a mouthful of the liquid up through the twisting straw. With an audible gulp, he swallowed the drink, and then looked up from the pink mix to scan the carriage. "Where in hell has my little Trixybell gotten to?"

They heard a brief rush of air as someone entered the compartment. "Ah, here she is," Buddy Perkins said, his tanned face splitting into a huge smile.

They turned and watched as Trixybell made her way back through the carriage, the door behind her closed with a quiet release of compressed air. She weaved her way over, staggering slightly; whether this was from the gentle rocking motion or some other intoxicated reason, Josh could not tell. She reached the table where she and Perkins had been. Unable to see him, she stood confused.

"Trixybell," Buddy called to her.

She looked over at the table but remained perplexed, wondering how this small group of strangers had come to know her special name. Then something clicked inside her head and she finally recognised the fat guy with a huge cocktail before him.

"Buddy," she said, like a child addressing a loving parent.

"Come, sit here," Buddy said, and pointed to the empty chair that faced him.

She slid in beside Josh, then took a lock of her hair and sat twiddling it absentmindedly.

"Trixybell, this is Joe and his lovely bride…?"

"Natasha," Anna said, beaming.

Trixybell sensed the group were talking to her. Somehow, she managed to pull her attention away from the secrets of the smooth tabletop. "Hi, Joe. Hi, Na-tash-ya," she said in a thick South-western drawl. She held her hand out in the centre of the table, not sure whom to greet first.

Anna took the young girl's hand. "Pleased to meet you, Trixybell."

Hearing a stranger say her name caused the girl to giggle. She leaned over the table and, as if they were alone, she told Anna, "My real name's Dawn. Only Buddy calls me Trixybell."

"Well, it's still a pleasure to meet you, Dawn," Anna said sincerely.

"Hi, Dawn," Josh said, deciding this girl was not pulling a full carriage load.

The girl looked at Josh's outstretch hand, but before she took it she quickly looked at Buddy Perkins. Buddy gave a slight nod – it's alright, go ahead. "Ell-O, Joe," she said, timidly. Her gaze returned to the tabletop and she fidgeted in awkward discomfort.

Introductions finished, the group sat in silence for a moment or two before Anna asked, "So Buddy, what do you do?"

Suddenly, the conversation turned to Buddy's favourite topic: himself. His brown face split into a huge smile. "Well there pretty, I'm the Executive Salesman for the Sterling and Hardy Silverware Company," he announced proudly.

"Really?" Josh asked, unimpressed.

"I am indeed," he said, "I'm known from state-to-state as the Silver Sheikh."

Buddy raised his hands and looked into his jacket sleeves, mimicking the theatrics of a magician. Then, to the group's amazement, a bright silver business card appeared from nowhere. With a flip of his wrist, he spun the card through the air, from one hand to the other. He held the shiny card out towards Anna. "Buddy Perkins at your service."

The girl at Josh's side squealed with delight and began to clap her hands enthusiastically.

Impressed, barely, Josh offered the guy a brief applause.

Anna took the card. "Why thank you, sir."

"My pleasure," Buddy said.

Anna turned the card in her hand and saw bold letters emblazoned across a background of dazzling silver. Each corner held an image of an ornate-looking table knife. "Thanks," she said, and dropped the card inside her jacket pocket.

Enjoying his audience, Buddy Perkins repeated his trick – much to the excitement of his companion – and handed another magical card to Josh.

"Thanks," Josh said.

"My pleasure, Joe" Buddy beamed.

The card disappeared inside Josh's pocket. He looked up, smiled ruefully at Anna and then gave her a quick – *'sorry about the unwanted guests'* – look.

"So, where are you two headed?" Anna finally asked.

Buddy offered her a brief flash of bright ceramic teeth. "Memphis – Tennessee."

Nothing in Memphis… well, except for the home of the King, Anna thought. "Graceland?" she asked him.

"That's right, my little Tinkerbell, we're going to see the

King."

"The King?" Josh asked, a generation too late.

"He means Elvis, honey," Anna told him.

"Oh, right," Josh said, confusion written across his face.

She saw his bewilderment. "It's his anniversary. Thousands of people will be holding a vigil at his graveside, in a mark of respect."

"Oh, right," Josh repeated, still in the dark.

"That's right, Tinkerbell," Buddy said. "I'm heading to Graceland on my annual pilgrimage. Made this trip every year since the King died. This time though, I've got company." He reached out, a sparkle of silver against dark skin, and affectionately patted Trixybell's hand.

"Guess you really miss him?" Anna commented.

"Yeah, but maybe this year will mark his return," Buddy said, excitedly.

"What d'you mean?" Josh asked.

"Everybody knows he ain't really dead," Buddy elaborated. "He's just away on business."

"Business?"

"Yeah, he's been working as an ambassador for Earth," Buddy stated with total conviction.

"Really?" Josh asked.

"That's right. Saved the planet from total annihilation."

"How?" Josh inquired, and for a brief second he found himself interested.

"Men from outer space were about to zap us into a million atoms, but then the King stepped in and saved us all. He's been working with *them* ever since."

"My God," Josh said in awe; and he wondered if this guy was either the craziest fucker he had ever met, or worse, telling the truth.

Unexpectedly, Buddy slapped his hand down on the table and whooped in amusement. "Had you going there, Joe," he beamed, and his entire body wobbled with laughter.

"Yeah, you got me," Josh said, but thought: any more of that crap and I'll have my two–thousand-year-old friend here rip your fucking throat out!

"Say, why don't I buy you two lovebirds a drink and celebrate your recent wedlock?" Buddy suggested. He'd emphasized the *lock* part. And, before anyone could object, he headed for the bar.

***

For the next hour or so Josh and Anna (Joe and Natasha) pacified their unwelcome guests. During this time, they discovered Buddy Perkins to be a harmless, lively and bright, if somewhat irritating character. His companion sat mostly silent, but on occasion she surprised them with a quirky comment or two.

From Buddy Perkins' ramblings, Josh and Anna discovered that he had recently parted from his wearisome wife, and had embarked upon a new and exciting voyage with his younger lover Trixybell. Trixybell, they learned, had left her life as a waitress and the lavish contents of her trailer-park home behind her in the hope of a better life with this energetic salesman. With Buddy's eagerness to talk about himself, neither Josh nor Anna had needed to elaborate on their own backgrounds or immediate future.

Whilst they sat sipping beer or cocktails, the rest of the lounge began to empty as most of the occupants returned to their sleeping compartments or, for the unlucky few, their seats. Without the faintest suggestion, the train crossed the invisible Illinois border, and, in doing so, it took the two fugitives into Kansas State and out of the jurisdiction of the Chicago Police Department.

***

Josh finished the slightly stale sandwich that the waitress had had whipped up for him. He drained the dregs of his third beer and then, with a heavy yawn, he rubbed at his grainy eyes.

Seeing that Josh was ready to excuse himself, Anna stretched her arms and yawned wearily. "Well, I'm beat. I think it's time me and Joe hit the sack."

"Aye, I've kept you two lovebirds long enough. Maybe we could meet up later tomorrow," – then he noticed the time – "I mean today, and share a few more drinks?" Buddy suggested.

"Yeah, I'd like that," Josh lied.

"Me too." Anna lied as well.

"It's been real swell meeting you, Joe," Buddy said, and with a chubby hand he bade Josh goodnight. He turned to Anna and added, "You too, Tinkerbell."

Buddy took hold of Anna's hand and, proving chivalry was not dead, he raised it to his lips and kissed her fingers.

Unexpected bright colours exploded across Anna's eyes, momentarily blinding her. His lips lingered at her fingertips. She felt a brief but agonising pain rush up her arm and across her shoulder. The pain intensified, choking a short breath of air from her constricted throat. Then… nothing.

Buddy Perkins broke away from her fingertips. He grinned sheepishly and said, "See you two lovebirds later."

"Bye Joe. Bye Na-tash-ya," Dawn mumbled.

"C'mon Trixybell," Buddy said, moving away from the table and a stunned Anna Privalova. The odd couple retreated to their quarters.

Josh walked in the opposite direction, towards their compartment. He reached the automatic door before sensing Anna had not followed him. He turned to find her standing at the table, rigid, looking in the opposite direction.

"Hey, are you okay?" he asked, after returning to her side. She was lost in thought. He took her arm and gently shook her. "Anna, what is it?"

She blinked then regained her senses. "It's nothing."

"I lost you there for a moment. Where were you?"

"Nowhere. It doesn't matter. Let's go to bed," she told him, and turned away from the table.

"At last," he said, following her out of the carriage.

They made their way through the gently buffeting carriages

and toward their quarters. They reached their compartment and Anna opened the locked door with a swipe of the flat key-card. Totally beat, Josh entered the room and collapsed onto the bed. Anna shut the door behind them then flipped the lock. She took the single chair and jammed it up against the handle. Over at the blacked-out window, she checked the tape to make sure that the dark material was held fast. Satisfied with her inspection, she finally joined Josh on the bed.

"Hey," he said sleepily, pulling her into his arms. He kissed her on the cheek before running his hand over her breasts.

"Let's get some sleep," she told him, ending his playfulness.

He managed to stay awake just long enough to feel a slight pang of disappointment. Then fell into a deep sleep.

At his side, Anna lay awake. Hearing his heavy breathing, she leaned across the bed and hit a switch. The room fell into total darkness. She listened to the hypnotic buffeting of the wheels for a while, before finally closing her eyes. Eventually, she drifted off, but only to be plagued by images of tormented and tortured souls.

Chapter Twenty-Five

The three law enforcers entered the high tech forensics department. They made their way towards the back of the cluttered room and found a familiar lab technician.

"Hey, Elliot," Sanchez said.

"Yo, Emilio," the tech responded.

The forensic technologist quickly welcomed the three men to his workspace.

Over six feet tall and with wild but receding curly hair, Elliot Saunders had the look of a young Art Garfunkel about him. Electronic gadgetry and computers took up the majority of his workbench, which flashed black and white pictures across their screens at almost lightning speed.

"So, what have you found?" Balooga asked, straight down to business.

"Okay," the tech said, sensing the detective's eagerness. "I've found two prints from the knife Emilio brought me. One set belongs to this guy." He retrieved a printout and handed a picture to Sanchez. "But so far, AFIS hasn't been able to find the second set."

"AFIS?" Balooga asked.

"Automated Fingerprint Identification System," Fernandez explained.

"Right," Balooga said. He took the printout from Sanchez and looked at the skinny face of Vincent Monroe.

"She's been running all night," the tech said, placing his hand on top of one computer. "But I doubt she'll find anything."

"Why?" Fernandez asked.

"Well, because of this," he said, and clicked on a mouse. He brought one of the flashing screens to a halt. The cursor moved as he activated a file to reveal a screen full of fingerprints. Most of the prints were smeared or partial finds only, but a clear black and white print could be seen in the centre of the screen.

Balooga saw nothing but the expected swirls and loops. "What are we supposed to be looking at?"

Realising the group's expertise lay in another field, the tech began his explanation. He raised his hands to show all three his slim fingers. "Pretty long, right?" he said, and wiggled the lengthy digits in the air. Then he placed his thumb on a small plastic scanner and hit a computer key. The little scanner flashed to life as a line of blue light ran across its glassy surface. Immediately, the computer screen revealed a new, clear picture of the tech's print. He turned his back on the small group and in a flurry of fingers he worked on the image for a couple of minutes. Then he stood back to reveal the outcome.

Now the group saw two prints, side by side. It was obvious that the larger of the two belonged to the forensics technician.

"Okay, so the one on the left is much smaller, maybe it belongs to a child," Fernandez said.

"That one's mine," Saunders corrected, grinning.

"What?" the group said in unison.

"It can't be, look at the size of it," Sanchez said.

"Yeah, that's what I thought," Saunders agreed, "but if you look closer, you can see the print on the right is much narrower than mine due to its elongated shape."

"So what are you saying?" Balooga asked the tech.

"What I'm saying is, that this print belongs to someone with extremely long, but thin fingers. And another thing, I think it maybe a woman's print."

"What?" the group repeated together.

"You can't tell from this image, but I found a small crescent-shaped indent just above the area of the print."

"Which means?" Fernandez asked.

"This," the technician said, and he pulled open a desk drawer. He took out a small wooden block and placed it on top of his bench. The block was split in two parts, with the first part being a simple wooden base and the second consisting of a blue rubber-like substance.

"What's this for?" Sanchez asked, pushing his finger into the blue Plasticine.

"Christ, Sanchez, watch what you're doing," Balooga cautioned.

"Jeez, sorry Chief," Sanchez said, wiping his hand against the back of his pants.

"It's okay, that's exactly what it's made for," the tech explained. "Look." He pushed his finger into the Plasticine and left a clear print. Then, using his pen, he pointed out the slight outline of his nail. "Okay, you can't actually see the indent on the knife handle with your naked eye, but it's there."

"That doesn't explain why you think it's a woman's though," Balooga remarked.

The tech raised the board. Again, he used his pen as an indicator. "The gap between the visible end of this print and the nail's indentation is about one-sixteenth of an inch, but the gap from the print on the knife is almost a quarter of an inch."

"So we're looking for a woman with long hands and sharp nails," Sanchez summarized.

"That'd be my educated guess," Saunders confirmed. "Does it sound like anyone you know?"

"Maybe… " Balooga said, remembering the flash of talons in the alleyway. "Wait a minute." He dug inside his pants and pulled out a small, crumpled piece of paper.

"What's that, Chief?" Sanchez asked.

"Non-admissible," Balooga replied abruptly. "Listen, is there any way you could pull a print off this?" He held the paper fragment out.

The technician took up a pair of tweezers to inspect the small piece of burnt paper. He flipped the fragment over and read the name written in the corner. One eyebrow rose.

"Humour me," Balooga told him.

"Okay," Saunders agreed. "Has anyone else handled this?"

"No, just me," Balooga said.

"Good." He moved over to an elaborate piece of machinery. "I'm gonna run this through the machine and see if Ninhydrin can pull out any prints."

"Nin-hid-rin?" Sanchez asked.

"Yeah, it's a chemical we use to pull latent friction-ridges off objects such as paper, cardboard or other porous surfaces," Saunders explained. "Okay, Detective, I need to run your prints through the computer."

"Yeah, right," Balooga said. He placed his hand over the scanner.

"That won't be necessary," Saunders stated. He reached past Balooga and typed a couple of commands into the computer. The screen flickered with a strobe of white, black and multiracial faces before it stopped to reveal a picture of a younger moustachioed Lieutenant.

"Hey, Chief, I like the… "

"Shut it!" Balooga warned. And right there and then he decided that, no matter what, he would indeed learn the secrets of this microelectronic age.

Saunders clicked on a mouse button and pulled out Balooga's fingerprints. "We're all in here," the tech commented, referring to AFIS. He checked his watch, "Okay, that should just about do it." He returned to the Ninhydrin machine, taking the tweezers with him, and retrieved the piece of paper. Back at his bench he placed the paper onto glass with exaggerated care. Hitting a computer key, he activated the small scanner. He allowed the blue light to sweep across the paper two or three times before turning the fragment over and repeating the process. Then, in a flurry of fingers, he drew up a number of computer-generated prints. He eliminated the prints one by one until only two remained: the original elongated print and a new, crisp and clear one.

"This one belongs to someone other than you," Saunders told

Balooga, pointing to the newer of the two.

"Good. Now, can you place it side by side with the other print?" the big detective asked.

"Yeah, sure. No problem," the tech said; and he did just that.

All four leaned closer towards the computer screen.

"Shit," Sanchez snapped, seeing the prints were not alike.

"Sorry guys, looks like we'll just have to keep looking," Saunders said. He leaned over, ready to switch off the screen.

"Wait," Balooga ordered.

The tech's hand hovered over the power switch. He looked towards the lieutenant.

"The new one – can you elongate it?" Balooga asked, and he pointed to the new fingerprint.

"Yeah, but the original one isn't a smudge, it's a clean print," Saunders explained.

"Please."

With a shrug of his shoulders, Saunders began to modify the image. "Okay, I'm gonna stretch the length but at the same time reduce the width – proportionally." The technician lengthened the new fingerprint to the same size as the original.

Balooga asked, "Now, can you superimpose the new one over the first?"

"Yeah."

They watched the two prints merge; and even with his limited computer knowledge, Balooga saw that they matched.

"I'll be damned," the tech muttered.

"So who's that belong to?" the agent asked Balooga, now excited.

"Not here, I'll explain later," Balooga told him.

"But… "

"No buts. This isn't the place," Balooga insisted, and he placed a reassuring hand on Fernandez's arm.

"I'll play it your way – for now," the agent replied.

"Good," Balooga said, then he saw that the technician was about to click on the SAVE button. "STOP!" The curser stopped over the icon. "Everything you've just done – delete it," the lieutenant ordered.

"But what about the evidence?" Saunders asked.

"That's not part of it, delete it – now."

Saunders turned to the FBI agent. With a nod of approval, Fernandez gestured for him to go ahead. "If you say so," Saunders said, with a shrug of his shoulders. The cursor moved away from SAVE and stopped over DELETE. "You sure about this?"

"Yeah," Fernandez and Balooga said together.

The technician clicked DELETE and the mysterious print disappeared.

"What about the pistol?" Balooga asked. "Did you find any prints on that?"

"Yes," the tech confirmed. "Just one set. They belong to this guy." He handed Balooga another printout, which belonged to Bubba Macintyre.

"Okay, good, but did you find anything belonging to a Thad Paterson?"

"Who?"

"Never mind. What about Josh Sawyer?"

"Who?"

"Christ! What else have you got?" Balooga asked.

"Nothing, as yet. Ballistics are working on the slug you found yesterday, and I'm running a carbon test on a sample of ash the field techs brought in."

"How long will that take?"

"About another two hours."

Balooga looked at his watch and saw that it had just turned 8:35AM. "Okay, we'll be back before lunch." He turned to Fernandez. "Let's go see Doctor Stapleton. See if she can throw any light onto what happened at Anna Privalova's apartment last night."

Together, the agent and lieutenant withdrew from the tech's office, leaving Sanchez behind. Once they were out of earshot, Fernandez said, "I can see you're trying to keep the integrity of this case safe, but what the hell was that all about?"

"This is off the record, right?"

"Yeah."

"That piece of paper – I found it at Anna Privalova's apartment."

"So, we can use it as evidence."

"No, I took it before the warrants had been issued."

"Shit, bad move." He paused, gathering his thoughts. "It's not a total loss, though. We can still cross-check with any of the prints we find at her apartment."

Balooga offered the agent a brief shake of his head. "The apartment's clean."

"What do you mean?"

"She must have used some powerful cleaning solution. The place is cleaner than a nun's crotch."

"Shit," Fernandez snapped. "So that paper is the only forensics evidence to link her prints to the ones found on the knife?"

"Yeah."

"So what else have we got on her?"

"Well, we still have the tape recording from 9-1-1, but without Privalova to do a voice check, it's useless."

Fernandez walked in silence for a minute. "We're still off the record, right?"

"Yeah."

"Who else knows about the paper's origin?"

"Nobody, just the two of us."

"Then we could still include it as evidence?"

"Technically – yes."

"So let's keep it safe. We may need to 'include' it somehow at a later date," the agent said, and his usually stolid face broke into an awkward smile.

"Hey, you're not Internal Affairs, are you?" Balooga asked with suspicion.

Fernandez's face returned to its more accustomed seriousness. "You don't think I got this far playing by the rules, do you?"

"I guess not," Balooga said, and he decided the agent was not all he seemed.

"Now, give me the paper," the agent asked.

"Christ! The paper… " Balooga moaned, remembering that it was still on the scanner.

"Chief, wait!" Sanchez shouted from behind them.

Balooga looked back the way they had come and spotted the young detective heading towards them. With the piece of burnt paper held high by the pair of tweezers, Sanchez said, "You forgot this."

Chapter Twenty-Six

A bright sliver of light found its way inside the basement. The sun moved across the morning sky, and a shard of light crept its way towards the corpse. Unlike the night before the body was a vessel of life. Not with the energy of one spirited individual. Now, the woman's body was a rippling mass of squirming white tissue. And above it, hundreds of flies buzzed noisily as they circled around in a huge blanket of assorted blues and blacks.

Occasionally a small portion of the writhing cloud broke away to descend upon the corpse. There, it feasted on a mixture of putrid flesh and secreted bodily fluids. The heat in the basement increased. Trapped gases built up in the corpse's gut. Eventually the gas exploded from the woman's swollen intestines. And, with an audible belch, the foul vapour escaped from between grey lips in a spray of twisting maggots.

The day lengthened and the sun's rays began to fill the basement's single window. Instinctively now, the winged insects began to mass around the glass barrier in an attempt to follow the light. From the inside, the layer of flies covered the entire window, hiding it from the outside by a shroud of rippling, dark life forms.

To the occasional passer-by, the window went unnoticed as it merged into the dark wall that surrounded it. One or two caught a whiff of something unpleasant and grimaced with disgust as they walked by. However, as they took their next step into cleaner air, they instantly forgot and continued on about their business.

Chapter Twenty-Seven

"Anna, it's me."

She pushed herself into one corner, and then pulled the cover up under her chin. "Okay, come in," she said.

The lock buzzed. Then, as the door opened, a brilliant shard of sunlight filtered through. The golden ray crawled its way across the compartment floor. Just before the bright arc of light reached Anna, she pulled the cover over her head and waited until the door clicked shut before lowering the protective material.

"Where the hell have you been?" she snapped at Josh.

"What?"

"You've been gone ages."

Surprised by her anger, he held up the bag. "I was doing exactly what you told me to do."

"Christ, Josh! How long does it take to cover a couple of goddamn windows?" she barked. She crossed the room in three long strides and with a flick of her wrist she secured the door.

"I'm sorry, but the other two compartments are right at the other end of the train," Josh said.

"And will you lock the door when you enter," she shouted angrily.

"I said I was sorry," Josh said, and placed the bag onto the bed. He moved over to her to lay his hands gently on either side of her waist. "Relax, Anna. Everything's gonna be okay."

"No Josh, everything's not okay," she replied, and dropped onto the bed.

He knelt down between her legs to take her hands. "Hey, I'm not going to let anything happen to us."

She looked down, seeing his grim determination, and placed her hand against his cheek. "I know and I'm sorry. It's just this god-awful room. I feel trapped."

"Don't worry, we're a thousand miles from Chicago and the cops, and even Jonus can't possibly know where we are. Hell, I don't even know where we are!"

His feeble attempt at humour managed to curl her lips by a fraction only. He climbed to his feet, leaned over and placed a soft kiss on her brow. Then he turned his attention to the bag at her side.

Pulling open the drawstrings, he emptied its contents. The remainder of the dark material, scissors and a reel of sticky tape fell out. He reached into his pockets and took out the three key-cards, then placed them on the bed.

"Okay, I've covered the windows in both compartments, so if we need to swap rooms we can move straight away," he said.

"But what about all the windows between here and there?"

"What do you mean?"

"I mean, it's all very well hiding in here, but what if I need to go outside?"

"You won't have to go outside."

"But what if something happens?"

"Relax, nothing is going to happen. Anna, you can't sit here worrying all day."

"Said who?"

"Me. If you don't cheer up then I might have to invite Buddy and Trixybell over," he said, trying to lighten her mood.

Instead of the expected or hoped-for smile, Josh was rewarded with an anxious look.

"You haven't been speaking to him, have you?" Anna asked.

"Yeah – why?"

"When?"

"Just now, on the way back here. I bumped into him in the dining car."

She stood abruptly and looked at him with something unexpected in her eyes. "Josh, I don't want you talking to him," she said fearfully.

"Why? He's alright. I know all this 'Hey, Joe – say, Joe – what do you know, Joe' can be really irritating, but he means no harm."

"Josh, you're not listening to me. I said, I don't want you talking to him, understand?"

"Why?"

"Because… the guy's trouble… maybe dangerous… I don't know, but he's something. I don't trust him."

"Trouble? Dangerous? You're not serious. The guy's just an asshole."

"No, he's something else."

"Such as?"

She sat back on the bed as she tried to gather her thoughts. Her hand rose to her neck and, as if the pain she had felt the night before was still present, she absentmindedly rubbed at her throat. She used her mind's eye to replay the bizarre confusion of images, which she'd witnessed, attempting to make sense of the unexpected visualisation.

During their time spent with Buddy and Trixybell, Anna had begun to relax as they'd started to distance themselves from the recent carnage and troubles of Chicago. She'd enjoyed the quiet early hours of the morning, and had even managed temporarily to put the worrying return of her old foe Jonus to one side. Then, just before they had parted company, she'd been witness to a vision of such clarity that she had almost cried out. She had not seen pictures like a human would, but instead had glimpsed a brief miasma of tortured souls.

Although in years gone by she had herself been guilty of taking the soul of an innocent, it had now been a millennium since she'd last been driven to steal the spirits of the unblemished. For, in this new 'civilised' world, there was an abundance of immorality on which she could feast upon. She had spent a thousand years surviving on the souls of the sinful and had unquestioningly trusted in her judgment to sift out the bad from the good.

Until now!

Shocked by the vision that had rocked her senses, she now sat trembling as the realisation that she may have been responsible for the deaths of countless innocents hit her.

Josh recognized her distress. He sat beside her. With a concerned look on his face, he asked, "Anna, what is it?"

"Oh, Josh, what have I done?" she sobbed uncontrollably.

"Hey, what happened?" he asked, confused by her pain.

Her body shook as great waves of agony poured out. His confusion turned to fear. "You're scaring me. What is it?"

She glanced at him and, with a look of pure anguish written across her face, she sobbed, "I think I've become Jonus. No – I've always been Jonus!"

"What the hell are you talking about?"

"Me, him – we're the same. Don't you understand?"

"No Anna, I don't. You're nothing like him."

"Yes I am. I must be," she wept.

He pulled her into his arms. "Please tell me what's going on."

She gripped onto him tightly, unwilling to let go, and her body quivered as the grief poured out. Finally, she pulled herself from his embrace. Teardrops streamed down her face as she began to talk, "Josh, do you know what I am?"

"Yeah," he said, but too abruptly.

"No, Josh. Do you know what I am?"

"I think so… I'm not sure."

"This is important. What did you see in the alleyway the other night?"

He tried to keep the vision of the beast deeply hidden inside the darker recesses of his mind. He answered, "I don't know. Something. Christ, do we have to go through this?"

"Yes, we do."

He gave a heavy sigh. "Okay, what I saw was something incredible but also terrifying. It was you – but not you, if you understand."

She offered him a slight nod.

He continued, "I remember watching a film when I was a

kid – scared the shit out of me. It was some old silent movie, German I think. Anyway, it was about some horrible-looking guy, his name was… Nosferatu, and he sucked the blood from young women. He was also susceptible to sunlight as you are. In the end, he became so enraptured by one night's feeding that he got caught by the advancing sunrise."

Her teardrops fell with less frequency. "So you think I'm like him?"

"Maybe, I'm not sure. But the strange thing is, although the guy looked like shit, he had a strange sensuality about him."

"So this feeding… he didn't kill them?"

"Not in the normal sense, no. After a while, they became like him. Or was that another film? I'm not sure."

"So you think when I feed, it's the same?"

"I don't know, is it?"

"No, Josh, it's nothing like that. When I feed there is no resurrection or romance involved. For the victim, it's the end!"

"Christ, Anna. Can we leave this alone?" Josh pleaded.

"No we can't. You have to understand this."

"What?"

"That for me to survive, others must die!"

He jumped to his feet and moved away from the bed. "I don't want to hear this."

"But you have to," she insisted, following him.

"Why?"

"Because it's who – *what* – I am." An inner pain flashed across her face.

"So are you telling me you just kill people randomly for your own survival?" he asked, sickened.

She lowered her head, and Josh saw fresh tears drop from her face. He reached out with one hand, but, confused and dismayed, he let it drop back to his side.

"That's just it. Until last night, I thought not. But now, I'm just not sure," she sobbed.

"Why, what happened last night?"

She regained some composure and shuffled back to the bed

with her head hung low and her shoulders slumped. She sat down and expelled a weary breath. Josh pulled the single chair over to the bedside, seated himself and waited for Anna to continue.

"For as long as I can remember, I've taken great care in selecting my… *prey*." She looked up and offered him a weak apology. "I've always been meticulous in choosing the right … candidate," – another brief apology – "and I've used my instincts to save the innocent and slay the wicked."

"So that's good, right?" Josh asked, and a new hope rose from the depths of his soul.

"Yes, but after last night, I'm not sure I have been saving the innocent."

"Why?"

"Because all my instincts and intuition told me Buddy Perkins was nothing more than a sad middle-aged fool."

"And that's all he is," Josh reassured her.

"But that's just it, he's not," she said mournfully.

He leaned forwards, closer to her, and asked, "So what is he?"

"A cold-blooded killer!" she declared, stunning him.

"What!" he asked incredulously.

"He's a killer – Josh, don't you UNDERSTAND?" she bawled at him.

As his mind tried to compute this startling revelation, Josh felt his head spin out of sync and, unable to grasp what she was telling him, he answered, "No, I don't."

She threw her hands up in exasperation and then jumped to her feet. "If I was so utterly wrong about him, then I could be wrong about everyone and everything!"

"I still don't understand?"

She took a deep breath and then said, "Josh, I have lived so long I cannot remember how I came to be. I have seen this world of ours grow from the troublesome adolescent that it was to the generous adult it is now. But even as we stride towards a more benevolent future, there is still one thing that remains: evil. Not the comic book ramblings of some insane maniac, but the human capacity to consciously take one of its own. And I don't mean the crimes of passion or self-defence, but the cold calculating of a sane mind. Just think: how many people in our country alone have killed for their own gain, or lust, or just plain satisfaction? So, I saw this impediment as a malignant but treatable cancer. And to justify my own existence, I embarked upon the cleansing of this living disease."

Stunned by Anna's confession, Josh remained silent.

"So now do you understand?"

"No," Josh said, and he felt like the dumbest person on the planet.

"It's simple. Last night when we were in Buddy's presence, I sensed him to be just a little boy – innocent – trapped within a man's body. His over-eagerness to impress was just an immature way of him saying, 'Please like me'."

"But what about your comment about his friend being only half his age, remember?" Josh asked, trying to find sense in all of this.

"That was before he came and sat next to us. Once he had, it was obvious his affection towards her was genuine – true love – and not some sick sexual fantasy." She paused momentarily and then added, "Well, that's what I believed up until he kissed my hand."

"And then what happened?"

"Something that I've never experienced before."

"What?"

"I saw – no, felt – some sort of conflict or warning trying to get out of his very soul," she explained.

"Christ, not this soul shit again," Josh moaned.

"Josh, the guy scared the hell out of me."

"But why?"

"Because if I was so utterly wrong about the integrity of his spirit, then I could also be wrong about the wickedness of all the other souls that I have taken. And, if that's the case, then I have to question the very code by which I've lived."

"But you instantly knew I wasn't bad or evil or whatever," Josh reminded her.

"But what if I'm wrong, and always have been?" she sobbed.

"Hey, listen. You can't think like that," he soothed, and reached for her hand.

"No," she said, pulling her hand away from his. "I can't bear to see any more."

Josh moved closer. "Anna, all you'll see are my feelings for you, I promise. Now please, take my hand."

She looked into his eyes and read only kindness and honesty. She extended her arm towards him.

"Good – that's it."

As their fingers touched, they felt a prickle of energy pass between them. This power was not malevolent, though, but rather the simple raw force of unquestionable love.

"See. Now tell me, what do you feel?" he asked, placing her hand over his heart and showing her the way.

She resisted briefly, before eventually allowing him to steer her hand towards the very centre of his being. She felt the rhythmic beat of his heart as it tirelessly pumped life's liquid essence through his veins. Then she closed her eyes and allowed herself to be immersed in his spirit. Almost immediately, a rush of overwhelming sensations struck her. The first was a mixture of intense nervousness and exhilaration. She instantly recognised this to be the giddy but frightening emotion called love. Then, as she realised it was directed at her, she smiled. She tilted her head slightly and said, "Yes Josh, me too."

She bathed in his pure, unquestionable warmth for a short time. Eventually, and just before she became intoxicated by him, she drifted away, but immediately her own heart cried out for its return.

She probed deeper into his very soul and was not surprised when she came across a well of pain. Not a physical pain, but the slow, burning anguish of someone who had felt loss. She raised her hand and gently touched his face. "She's in a better place now, and safe," she told him, as she sensed this grief was meant for his mother. She drifted away from this private sorrow, and instead made her way to the very core of his soul.

There, she was struck with a sensation of righteousness. A charge of energy flowed through her body as she soaked within his bright and wonderful spirit. Nonetheless, she occasionally sensed a darker presence. Quickly she moved away, allowing him to guard these secrets. She was not alarmed by these uncertainties, for she was aware that all living beings were born with a darker and more sinister side. Instead, she took comfort in the good and greater part of his soul.

Anna opened her eyes and offered him a warm smile. Then, after kissing him, she said, "Thank you."

"Hey – don't mention it," he replied, relieved to have her back.

"Okay, so my ability is still intact," she said. "But that doesn't help in unravelling the mystery of Buddy Perkins."

"Maybe that's what it's meant to be – a mystery."

"I don't know. It still bothers me."

"Listen. We had had a long day, both of us, right? So maybe you got confused and misread the signals."

"Yeah, maybe you're right," Anna conceded, but not wholly convinced.

"Let's just try and keep our distance from him," Josh suggested, "that way, if he is more than he seems, then it's not our problem. We can't afford to get into any more trouble."

"Good idea."

"Now," he said, and his face went serious. "What the hell are we having for breakfast?"

Chapter Twenty-Eight

Even though the early breakfast rush had ended, the kitchen of the dining car was still a buzz of activity. A dozen hot and sweaty individuals bustled about this tightly spaced compartment, working ardently towards the rapidly advancing lunchtime. For most, the job's rewards were not financial, but rather the simple satisfaction of cooking a meal, which was to be enjoyed, if only for the brief time that it lasted.

Amongst this hive of activity, the head chef stood in the centre of his miniature domain, with his chopping knife in one hand and a fistful of orders in the other. He commanded this vessel with the same conviction as the Commander of a military submarine. He spoke in single-word sentences as he barked quick instructions to his fellow enlistees. "Salad!" – "Oil!" – "Heat!" Were just some of his orders, and, like all good soldiers, the troop followed his every command.

Happy that his ship was running smoothly and on time, the chef turned his attention towards the huge bowl of salad in front of him. He found the salad unfinished so took an onion, and, after peeling the skin with one hand, he laid it on a deeply stained chopping board. Then, in a blur of flesh and steel, he reduced the vegetable to tiny square chunks. With the flat of the blade, he scraped the chopped onion into his other hand and then tossed it into the mix. As they worked, chef and carriage swayed in rhythmic synchronization.

He finished the salad, then picked up the huge bowl, spun

around and dropped it in a nearby sink. Turning on a faucet he began to run cold water into the bowl. He placed the knife to one side. Then, with a single-minded eagerness found only in the truest of artists, he plunged his hands into the bowl and enthusiastically washed the mixed vegetation. Satisfied, he turned the faucet off. Strong wrists tossed the salad. Finished now, he spun around. Just at that moment the carriage lurched violently to one side. His foot veered to the left slightly, landing at an unexpected angle. The heel of his shoe slipped in a spot of grease. His leg shot from under him and instinctively he reached out. The large bowl slipped from his fingers. It clattered to the floor, the mixture of onions, cucumber, lettuce and tomatoes jumping out to disperse in a shower of wet chunks.

Two or three small portions of onion found their way under the collar of a busy assistant. Startled, he leapt forwards in surprise. The flow of oil that he was pouring into a hot griddle pan missed altogether, and landed instead on a burning cooker-ring. The oil ignited with a flash. Flames shot towards the bottle of oil. He jumped back, away from the flames, and released his grip on the bottle. The flames found a wealth of fuel and the oil erupted in a silent flash of fire.

And, with the same cruel conviction as a Molotov cocktail, the resultant explosion covered everything around it in a layer of sizzling hot grease.

***

Anna sat on the bed, fidgeting awkwardly as she waited for Josh to return with their late breakfast. Sitting there she tried not to dwell on a more rapidly growing and forbidden hunger.

She stood and moved over to a small cabinet, opened a drawer and removed one of three outfits. Still dressed in the clothes from last night, she quickly climbed out of them and dropped them to the floor. She pulled on a pair of new, loosely fitted jeans and a T-shirt with 'UCLA' written across the front. Scraping her dark hair back, she used a thin strip of cloth cut from the black material used earlier to tie it into a long ponytail, then scooped up her dirty clothes and quickly packed them inside the half-filled backpack. The key-cards disappeared into her jeans. Then she seated herself back on the edge of the bed and waited for Josh to return. After only a couple of minutes of waiting, she sensed someone arrive at the door.

Thump – Thump – Thump!

Unlike Josh's cautious tap, this knock had an urgent sound about it.

Thump – Thump – Thump!

"HELLO?" a voice called.

Anna jumped to her feet, crossed the room and checked the locking mechanism. She found it secure, so breathed out a sigh of relief.

"HELLO?" the stranger repeated.

Anna stood silent. A couple of seconds passed. Nothing further happened. She placed her ear against the surface of the door. Unexpectedly, she heard a loud buzz. The lock disengaged and the door was pushed in slightly. Anna threw her shoulder forwards to hold the intruder at bay. She heard a muffled cry from the other side and then another series of knocks rapped out.

"Hello? I'm the Assistant Supervisor of Passenger Management. We've got a slight problem up in the dining carriage, and we need everyone to move down into the lounge," the voice said, failing to hide its concern.

"I'm not dressed," Anna told him through the wooden barrier.

"Miss," he said, "there's nothing to worry about, but please get dressed and assemble in the lounge, quick as you can."

She sensed him leave and heard the urgent knock repeated at the next door along. She returned to the bed and quickly slipped her shoes on. Drawers were thrown open and their belongings were tossed roughly into the backpack. While pulling the drawstrings tight she got her first whiff of smoke.

"A slight problem – really?" she said to herself.

A thin layer of grey smoke found its way under the door. From outside, she heard the bustle of activity as passengers hurried by. The commotion outside lasted for only a few fleeting seconds before it fell silent.

She moved over to the door and again placed her ear against it, listening for signs of life. All she heard was the hypnotic buffeting of the wheels of the train, mixed with the rhythmic beat of her heart. As she stood at the door, the fog around her ankles thickened. Slowly, it made its way upwards toward her knees.

Within minutes, the room began to fill with a choking, acrid mist. She pushed as far away from the door as she could, her back pressed against the window. The sun's heat throbbed at her back, full of fiery intent and menace. Trapped now, between two deadly types of fire, and with burning tendrils clawing their way into the back of her throat, she panicked. And, with one choking breath, she screamed, "JOSH, WHERE ARE YOU?"

***

Josh heard her scream and reached their compartment in one long stride.

"ANNA!" he yelled, pounding on the door.

The door opened in an instant and he fell through with a wave of black smoke at his back. He landed heavily on the floor, rolled onto his back and kicked the door shut. For a few precious seconds the black fog remained trapped outside their compartment. Nevertheless, like a lethal exhaust, the gap at the bottom of the door pumped in thick caustic vapour. Josh looked up to find Anna stood in the thick of the smoke. He reached up and pulled her down into cleaner air.

Teardrops cascaded down her face. "What happened?" she asked, coughing smoke clear from her lungs. Before Josh could answer, they felt the compartment judder around them as the train lurched forwards in a sudden increase of speed. "Josh, what's happening?" she cried.

"Goddamn dining car went up like a bomb," he told her, and

wiped away his own smoke-induced tears.

"How?"

"Some sort of explosion, in the kitchen… I don't know. One minute I'm ordering bagels and coffee – and the next, all hell breaks loose," he said, his throat burning with raw pain.

Anna sensed the train had gained even more speed. She gripped his arm. "Why aren't we stopping?"

"The fire's really blazing and the dining carriage is right next to the fuel tanks."

"So?"

"So, some asshole next to me, said he use to be a Fire Marshall and the quickest way to put it out is to choke it with air."

"Is he crazy?" she asked.

"They've opened all the compartment windows between the engine and the fire, in the hope that the slipstream will either blow it out or spread the flames this way and away from the fuel."

"Are they crazy?"

"Anna, I can't breathe," Josh said, and coughed back smoke. He stood and grabbed the straight-backed chair.

"JOSH – NO!" she screamed, seeing his intentions.

The chair slipped from his fingers. Instead, he threw the backpack down next to her and pulled away the bed sheet. He opened the sheet out, covered her with it, and made sure its edges were firmly tucked underneath her body. Then he snatched the chair back up, and, ignoring the pain in his wrist, he launched it through the window. The chair crashed through the window in an explosion of shattered glass, sticky tape and dark material.

A blast of fresh air entered the compartment. Within seconds it cleared the room of the thick choking fog. A light haze of grey mist lingered like rancid breath.

Anna moaned in agony.

"Shit," he snapped. The flow of air made the sheet flap wildly around her head and shoulders.

"It burns. It burns," she whimpered, as the sun's rays scorched her exposed skin.

He smothered her in his arms and held the sheet down at her sides. "We've got to get out of here," he said, over the shriek of the wind.

"Josh – I can't leave."

"Anna, we've got to go – now."

"No, I'll burn. The sun – the sun!"

"If we stay here, we'll both burn! Now come on," he insisted, and dragged her to her feet.

He pulled her up, wrapping his arms around her, holding the cover tight. "I'll look after you, I promise, but we've got to get to another room."

"You go. I'll wait here and take my chances." Her hands rose and she shaped the sheet about her head into a makeshift cowl.

"The hell you will! You're coming with me," he said flatly.

"But I can't let anyone see me like this, and we'll need to pass through the lounge to get to the other side of the train."

"Then we'll find another way," he said, moving up to the door.

"There isn't another way."

Ignoring her, he placed his hand against the wooden surface. The door felt warm but not hot. The flames had yet to reach this far. He ordered her to stand back, and then pulled the door open. Thick smoke filled the compartment in an instant. Black vapour swirled about them like some miniature tornado. Josh reached out blindly to find Anna's hand. He pulled them out of the compartment and into the narrow passageway. Most of the corridor was cloaked in a blanket of dark mist. The smoke churned about them. Bright slivers of sunlight pierced through this living black cloth. Josh timed their progress, careful to avoid the shards of light. Occasionally, Anna had to duck under or step over the burning beams. They reached the automatic door and waited for it to open. There was a quick release of compressed air and the door threatened to open. It released a squeal of protest and held fast. Jammed, the door offered an inch of escape only.

"What's happening?" Anna asked, her face hidden inside the folds of the sheet.

His eyes burnt with hot tears. "I don't know. The door is stuck or something," He gasped.

"Move over."

He stepped aside quickly to allow her access. She reached out with her bandaged hand, careful to avoid the light, and ran her fingers along the border. A slight gap offered itself between the door and its frame. She pushed her fingertips into the crack. "Stand back," she ordered.

Josh took a step back to give her more space to manoeuvre. He watched her fingers disappear into the crack, leaving only her thumb visible. The door squealed in short protest. Anna pushed against it with strength unmatched. It gave way and slid open with a short shriek, allowing both to pass through. They tumbled into the next carriage and quickly reached the second doorway.

"Shit," Josh said, as the next barrier failed to open.

He turned to Anna, and said, "This one's locked t-" His voice caught in his throat as he glimpsed the hideous face, hidden within the folds of her cowl. "My God," he gasped, sickened, as he witnessed the true form of the beast.

She read his disgust and turned her head away.

Shame and guilt hit Josh in equal measure as he watched Anna push herself into a corner in an attempt to hide her features.

"Hey, I'm sorry. Anna, I'm sorry. You took me by surprise, that's all," he told her.

He bent down in front of her and laid his hands gently over the outline of her hand. He squeezed her hand through the impeding cloth. "Anna, I'm sorry."

She heard his words and tilted her head towards him. Through the shadows of the cowl, she asked, "Do you mean that?"

"Yes," he answered, and his heart swelled.

Then, he leaned into the darkness of the hood to kiss something swollen and forbidden. She expelled a pitiful breath, and he felt a woof of warm air pass over his lips.

He broke away from her. "Come on, we've got to go," he said, and helped her to her feet. They turned towards the locked exit. Someone unexpectedly appeared through the window.

"Christ!" Josh exclaimed, another face catching him by

surprise.

In a flap of billowing material, Anna threw herself to the floor in an attempt to remain hidden.

The man's face at the window spoke, but Josh was unable to hear him.

"I CAN'T HEAR YOU," Josh shouted to the guy on the other side.

The guy cupped one hand to his ear.

"I CAN'T… " Josh stopped, understanding it was futile. He pointed to the sealed door, and mouthed, O-P-E-N T-H-E D-O-O-R!

The guy nodded vigorously to acknowledge Josh's request. I-T-S L-O-C-K-E-D, he mouthed back.

W-E-L-L U-N-L-O-C-K T-H-E F-U-C-K-I-N-G T-H-I-N-G!

The guy nodded again, and quickly turned to head off in the other direction. By his dark blue uniform, Josh recognised the man to be an Amtrak employee. He realised the guy had gone for help.

"They're coming. Hold on." He turned, but struggled to see her as the smoke began to rapidly fill the passageway. The haze broke momentarily and he found her pressed into the corner.

Coughing, he reached her. "It won't be long. Help is on its way."

"I've got to go back," she announced.

"What?"

"Josh, I can't let them see me like this."

"Can't you just change back?" he asked.

She shook her head. "It's not that simple. Fear and anxiety impede my control over it. I don't think I've got time to bring it under control. I've got to go back."

"There's no way back," he said. The carriage behind them was a mass of churning black mist.

"Then I'll hide in one of these rooms," she decided, climbing to her feet.

"In a few minutes, you won't be able to breathe," he told her.

Frantically, he looked around the passageway in search of an alternative escape route. "What if you go outside and along the roof?" he asked.

"I can't. The sun."

"Then I'll wrap this tight," he explained, and pulled the sheet securely around her. She reached out to stop him. "Honey, it's okay, I'll stay here," she said, moving to the locked door. She ran her hand around the doorframe but was unable to find a gap large enough for her to grasp.

"What are you doing?" Josh rasped.

"I've got to get you out of here."

"Anna, no," he said and took her hands. "Listen to me. The door is locked. But the guy's gone to get help and he'll be back any minute, so we've got to get you safe."

"But how?" she asked.

"I don't know − but there must be away," he replied, and continued with his search. A window gave him an idea.

"Wait. What if you climb through the window and work your way along to the end of the train, keeping the sun on the opposite side, then you should be able to come back in through the last carriage."

"Through baggage?" she asked, and her hope rose.

"Yeah."

Her hope swelled, but then it quickly burst as she realised that she would be totally exposed to the passengers inside.

"But *they'll* see me," she pointed out.

"Shit!" he snapped, dismayed.

"Wait!" Anna said. "If I can't go along the train, then I'll go under it!"

"What?"

"Help me," she demanded and she squatted next to a floor panel.

Josh noticed that the panel was slightly different to the rest. It had two sunken hinges fixed to one side, and a round opening mechanism on the other. He bent down beside her and watched as she flipped up a circular toggle. She released the mechanism to pull the access open. A blur of speeding earth passed below. And the sound was deafening. Anna pushed the panel towards Josh.

"DON'T LET GO," she cried over the thunderous flow of air.

"I WON'T," he yelled back, struggling to hold the panel open.

"YOU'LL BE AT THE OTHER END?"

"I PROMISE."

Then, before her courage failed her, she dropped through the hole and disappeared underneath. A thick trail of black smoke followed her, before Josh cut off its escape by slamming the access panel shut. His ears popped painfully with the rapid change in pressure. He stood and fell back against the door, coughing out a lungful of acrid smoke. Then, he heard the hiss of released air, and felt a pair of hands roughly grabbing at him.

***

She held on and fought against the cruel and mighty airflow. The huge wheels to her left and right sounded like the constant rumble of thunder as they raced along the track, gaining speed with every second. The carriage above swayed violently from side to side. The wheels jolted and red-hot sparks burst all about her.

Anna screamed in pain and anger as the hot sparks stuck to her arms, stinging her skin like little angry hornets. She struggled to keep hold. Desperately she pulled herself along the undercarriage. Holding on tight with her hands and feet, she inched further along. The bandage on her hand began to impede her progress, so in a frenzy of sharp teeth she ripped it away.

Racing along now, only inches above the ground, Anna continued with her bid for safety.

***

Josh hurried to reach the lounge. He found it packed with

anxious and worried looking passengers. Seeing the soot- and dust-covered newcomer, some of the more decent passengers stopped him in a show of concern. Yet, with no time to spare, he waved them off and continued to weave his way through this packed assembly.

He passed an overly tanned face and heard a familiar voice.

"Say, where've ya been, Joe?"

He didn't break his stride.

"Say, where ya going, Joe?"

He reached the automatic door and was rewarded with a brief hiss as it slid open. As he hurried towards the baggage compartment, he tried to stop the images of Anna being crushed under the train's huge wheels from invading his mind. He quickly passed through the rest of the narrow passageways and eventually reached the baggage compartment. He pushed against the door.

It was locked tight.

He immediately recalled the previous night's illicit entrance, remembering the two heavy-duty locks on the other side of the doorway. Although the locks were easy to disengage from the inside, they would be almost impossible to break from the outside.

"SHIT!" he cried, dismayed at his own stupidity.

He reared back and threw his shoulder against the near-impenetrable barrier.

***

She gained another foot or so before a third void appeared. Anna measured the four or five feet of open space between her carriage and the next. A huge oily connection buckled and squealed as it held the two together. Although the distance between the carriages was not a problem, the bright sunlight that filled the gap was.

Anna lowered her head so that her hair trailed along the surface of the earth, and then pressed her feet against the iron framework. She readied herself. Finally, she breathed in a lungful of scorched air, held it, and then arched her back and sprang towards the next carriage.

Her skin began to burn instantly. Two desperate hands grabbed onto an iron strut, knuckles turning white with effort, hanging on for dear life. Now with her legs trailing behind her, she pulled herself into the shadows. Before she had time to wrap her legs around the metalwork, her shoe caught against one of the sleepers. With an audible *snap*, her anklebone broke in two. She screamed in agony as the combination of broken bones and sunlight assaulted her foot.

Battling against the pain, she somehow managed to pull herself further underneath the train and into the safety of its shadows.

***

He tightened his grip on the handle of the fire extinguisher and used the heavy cylinder as a battering-ram. The canister slammed against the wooden barrier. Josh heard another satisfying crack. He drew the extinguisher back and this time threw his entire body forwards. The wood finally splintered, allowing him access.

He threw the extinguisher to the ground and scrambled across the cluttered compartment. He clambered through this dark, windowless room, tripping over a case. He fell to his knees, but quickly clawed his way back upwards and frantically tore his way towards the rear of the train.

***

Anna pulled herself along the last of the carriages. She felt her strength rapidly drain away. With her shattered foot hanging uselessly behind her, she forced herself onward, ignoring the pain that gripped her entire body. She reached out to grab the last of the framework, and surprisingly, she found herself at the end of the train. With only the guardrail to overcome, her ordeal was almost over. She sensed a rush of raw energy flow through her veins, which gave her body new strength.

Then, unexpectedly, the ground underneath her fell away as the train hurtled over a suspension bridge, the ground was replaced by a vast body of sparkling blue water. Sunlight hit the water and its reflected rays shot upward in an explosion of bright beams. Some of these magnified rays hit Anna and, as they connected with bare flesh, she felt her skin burn and blister. She screamed in agony, dazzled by the sunlight, squeezing her eyes shut. Blinded now, she reached up toward the handrail. She felt a vicelike grip grab at her arm.

Just before she passed out, she heard a voice say, "Hold on baby. I've got you!"

Josh heaved her limp body over the guardrail before dragging her into the safety of the darkened baggage-car.

There, they collapsed together in a limp and lifeless heap.

Chapter Twenty-Nine

Balooga turned to his partner. "Still no sign of the doctor?"

Sanchez flipped his cell phone shut. "Not since last night."

"Christ! That's all we need," the large detective snapped, throwing the Lexus across two lanes of traffic.

"Maybe she's sick?" the FBI agent said from the rear of the car.

"Then why hasn't she phoned in?" Balooga asked.

Sebastian Fernandez offered the lieutenant a brief shrug of his shoulders. "I'm not sure."

"Maybe she's really sick and can't make it to the phone," Sanchez suggested.

"When we finish with forensics, I want you to call in and see if there's been any sign," Balooga told his partner.

The young detective remembered the pathologist's strange mood and the weird sensation of being watched the night before. He offered his superior a quiet, unenthusiastic, "Great … "

"And if she's still missing, I want you to find her address and pay her a visit," Balooga added.

Another unenthusiastic, "Great… "

"Now remind me, what did Elliot Saunders just say?" Balooga asked.

For the second time in as many minutes, Sanchez repeated the technician's anxious phone call. "That there's been a 'development' and for us to get to his lab as soon as possible."

"And that's all he said?" Balooga enquired.

"Yes."

Making their way from ballistics, the three law enforcement officers were heading back towards the forensics department and the excited, if somewhat uneasy-sounding, lab technician.

In Sanchez's lap were three bagged and tagged firearms. Two were small hand pistols, one being the old foreign revolver found at the original crime scene, and the other the standard issue Chief's Special that had belonged to the recently deceased cop, Ed Newbury. The third weapon that lay across the detective's lap was Holloway's lethal riot shotgun. All three were on their way to be logged as evidence concerning the recent Sawyer and Privalova murder spree.

Balooga weaved his way in and out of traffic, recapping the ballistics expert's findings as he did so.

The first thing that had been apparent was the ballistics expert's open delight at having found a working Russian Tula-Tokarev TT-33. He explained animatedly that this Eastern European revolver was a World War II firearm that had been issued to the frontline officers of Stalin's mighty war machine. The weapon fired large calibre shells. Although how the hell the gun had not exploded in the user's hands, due to its poor maintenance, he could not say. The expert then quickly explained that one shot had been fired from the Chief's Special, and the riot shotgun had discharged two shells only. He had then signed over the firearms for evidence. He seemed reluctant and almost sad as he handed over the Tula-Tokarev TT-33. Saying good-bye to the weapon like it was some dear departing friend.

The Lexus pulled into the forensics lot. Balooga hit the brakes and brought the vehicle to a halt. He opened the door, climbed out and walked around to the front of the car.

"Okay, you stay here and watch them," he told Sanchez, pointing to the small arsenal.

"But, Chief," Sanchez moaned, already out of the passenger side.

"No buts, and while you're guarding them, keep trying to reach Stapleton."

"That's alright, you two go ahead," Fernandez said. "I'll stay here. I've got to update the Bureau anyway. Give me the doctor's number and I'll try."

Sanchez quickly gave the agent the medical examiner's number. Then the two detectives left the FBI agent alone as they made their way back into the forensics department. They entered the forensics tech's office.

"Yo, Emilio," Elliot Saunders greeted them.

With no time for pleasantries, Balooga asked, "So what've you got for us?"

The forensic tech's face beamed like a child's on Christmas Day. "Wait," he said, with a raised finger. He pulled on a cord to shut a set of blinds, blocking out the sun. Passing the detectives, he closed the door, then hit the light switch and threw the room into near darkness. They heard the tech fumble about in the dark for a minute before a small light clicked on at the back, which gave the room only slightly better definition. Saunders returned to his workbench, opened a desk drawer and retrieved three pairs of safety goggles.

"What the hell are these for?" Balooga enquired, as the tech handed them out.

The tech silenced the detective with one raised finger. "Trust me."

Balooga and Sanchez slipped the goggles over their heads. They stood at the tech's bench and eagerly waited like a pair of oversized school kids. Now that they were wearing their eye protection, Saunders slipped his own glasses over his large brow and then opened another drawer. He pulled out a small plastic container and gently placed it on his workbench.

"What's that?" Balooga asked.

As if silencing an over-eager ninth-grader, the tech raised his finger and placed it over his lips. "Quiet," he whispered. "We're only gonna get one chance at this."

Balooga remained silent, resigning himself to the eccentricities of the forensics technician.

The tech opened the lid of the plastic container and took

out a small glass slide. The slide trembled slightly while being carefully placed on the small fingerprinting scanner.

"Is that what I think it is?" Balooga asked.

"Yeah," Saunders said with childish wonder, "Okay, are you watching?"

"Yeah," both detectives responded in unison.

"I've modified the scanner to run slightly slower than before, but this is gonna happen real quick – so don't look away." Then he leaned back and hit a computer key.

The machine flickered into life. Unlike earlier though, the blue strip of light paused at one end before it slowly glided across the entire length of the scanner. The light ran along the glass surface, and the small drop of crimson liquid on the slide began to release tiny wisps of smoke. At the point at which the light and liquid connected, the drop of blood exploded in a burst of energy, shattering the glass slide to pieces.

"What… the… hell?" Balooga muttered, as the tiny tendrils of smoke rose towards the ceiling.

"My sentiments exactly," Saunders said, the astonishment from both the detectives' faces was mirrored by his own.

"What the hell just happened?" Balooga asked.

The tech's face split into a wide grin. "Probably the worst case of Xeroderma Pigmentosum ever recorded."

Balooga looked at his partner to see if any of that last comment meant anything to him.

"Don't look at me – I flunked Latin," Sanchez responded with a shrug of his shoulders.

"Say again?" Balooga asked the tech.

"Xeroderma Pigmentosum," Saunders repeated. Seeing two blank faces, he elaborated, "It's a rare genetic disorder, affects about one in every two-hundred-and-fifty thousand people. The victims are unable to repair damage caused by ultraviolet light at DNA level."

"Which means?"

"Which means the wavelengths created by the sun – which includes UV – are lethal."

"Lethal, how?" Balooga asked.

The tech took up an opened journal and began to read, "Xeroderma Pigmentosum, the defect in UV-induced DNA repair mechanisms, which results in the sensitivity of skin to wavelengths of between 280-340 nanometres. Cells are unable to repair sunlight-induced DNA damage, which mainly affects the areas of the face, neck, hands and arms…"

"So who are we looking for – someone with a bad case of sunburn? Sanchez asked.

"I don't think so. Whichever poor soul suffers from such an extreme case would be unwise to go out in the daylight."

"So where did you get that sample from?" Balooga asked.

"The crime scene boys brought it in from the Little Village case. It's a miracle the sample made it as far as here, before… well… that," the tech said, gesturing to the scanner.

"So it could be from one of the victims?" Balooga inquired.

"No, I've run tests and ruled out all three."

"What about the suspect, Sawyer?"

"No."

"Then who?"

"Possibly the same person who our mystery print belongs to?"

A comment Anna Privalova had made the day before sprang to Balooga's mind… *It was nearly daybreak and I don't go out much in the day…*

"Can you determine the age and sex of the person?" he asked.

"I can't give you the person's sex, but I can give you the age," Saunders said.

"I don't understand," Balooga said.

"Okay. We've got a limited supply of this 'unusual' blood, so until I figure out a safe way to handle it, it's staying put. Therefore, the sex will have to remain a mystery for now. Having said that, I managed to take a sample of the resultant carbon taken from the original experiment and I've run it through the mass spectrometer to determine its age."

"And?"

"And, I think you'd better hold on to your panties, ladies,

because the result is astonishing."

"Go on," Balooga said with trepidation.

The forensics technician cleared his throat. He reached inside his lab jacket to retrieve a folded piece of paper. He opened the paper, revealing the printout of a computer-generated line graph. "I've run the test twice already, so I'm pretty sure it's correct. And the results I got from this matched the ones taken from that ash I ran earlier," Saunders explained, waving the paper around.

"Just tell us," Balooga said, sick of the technician's theatrics.

"Ladies and gentlemen, I do believe you're looking for a two-thousand-year-old killer!"

Chapter Thirty

Josh used the key-card and slipped inside the tiny room. He closed the door quietly behind him. The smell of cooked meat and something worse hit him the second he entered. He tried not to breathe too deeply as he moved over to the bed.

"Hey, keep those on," he said, seeing that some of the damp towels had slipped.

"It hurts too much," Anna's weak voice told him.

"I know, but it'll help with the burns," he responded. He bent over and gently replaced the wet cloth over her blistered skin.

"How much longer?" she asked through gritted teeth.

"I'm not sure. They're replacing the last carriage now," he informed her, and brushed a damp strand of hair away from her face.

Naked, except for her underwear, Anna lay under a blanket of wet hand towels, but where her skin was still visible, a combination of cracked skin and leaking pus could be found.

Careful not to aggravate her wounds, Josh replaced another towel. Then he leaned over to kiss her cheek. The intense heat that rose from her limp body made his heart swell with pity. He caressed her cracked lips with his own, then stood and moved over to the window.

Fearful they would draw unwanted attention, Josh had removed the black cloth from the window, and now, with only the thin curtains as protection, the room was bathed in a modest coating of light. Fortunately, the mid afternoon sun had crept around to the other side of the train, taking its more powerful glare with it and allowing Anna this minor relief.

"Where are we?" Anna asked for the third time. Her eyelids closed and she slipped out of consciousness. Then, as she unwittingly moved her body, the resultant pain snapped her awake.

Seeing she had returned from her brief but painful slumber, Josh answered, "Del Rio. They're swapping the damaged carriages for new ones."

"How?" she asked; and briefly she slipped away again.

He moved over to kneel beside her and she opened her eyes. "They brought in a spare train from San Antonio, remember?"

"Oh – yeah," she mumbled weakly.

Unbelievably, the retired Fire Marshall's plan had succeeded. After gaining sufficient speed, the train had created a slipstream powerful enough to 'choke' the fire and halt its progress before the flames had reached the sealed but tightly packed lounge. With damage to just three carriages, the Superliner had been able to limp its way into the next train station. There, emergency paramedics had been waiting at trackside, ready to evacuate the injured and deliver them to a nearby hospital.

Amazingly, only one person had been seriously hurt and he had been whisked away with an accompaniment of red and blue lights. Some of the passengers had quickly disembarked, with the threat of legal action or a vow never to travel with the reckless company again. Most had stayed on board and waited patiently for the Superliner to continue on its course.

After a couple of anxious hours waiting, Josh had eventually found out that replacement carriages would arrive shortly from neighbouring San Antonio. He had been allowed to return to their damaged compartment to collect any surviving belongings. Not wanting to leave Anna for any length of time, he had quickly snatched up their few smoke-tainted possessions and returned to the cramped compartment.

Unlike the deluxe room of earlier, this one was much smaller, with two single bunk beds, one side cabinet, a tiny trash receptacle and a bathroom – which contained toilet and sink only. Even with the top bed folded away, the compartment was still little more than a mobile cell, which made Josh feel utterly depressed and claustrophobic.

The carriage moved slightly. He peeked around the curtains and found that they were moving slowly backward. The carriage stopped with a short squeal of brakes.

"Are we moving?" asked Anna through dry, split lips.

"Not yet, baby. They're attaching the last carriage."

"How much longer?" she mumbled.

"Soon, I promise. Then I'll re-cover the window and everything will be okay," he said, trying to sound cheerful and optimistic.

She sensed his bravado and laughed feebly.

"What is it?" he asked, relieved to hear her laughter, no matter how pitiful.

"You," she answered.

"Me, what?"

"You're the eternal optimist," she replied, before a violent cough erupted from her scorched throat. A bloody dribble of phlegm stained her bottom lip and chin. Josh bent, using his hand to wipe away the dark spot. He placed his other hand across her forehead and felt an impossible heat radiating from within her core. He pulled some of the drier towels away from her skin. Moving into the small washroom, he ran them under cold water. Small pieces of loose, burnt flesh dropped away to block the sink.

He returned with the wet towels to lay them out over her scorched body, then exhausted, he sat on the floor and placed his head beside hers. He closed his heavy eyelids and decided to rest for a while.

***

Josh opened his eyes what seemed only a few moments later, yet the sour taste in his mouth, told him that he had actually been asleep for some time. The next thing he noticed was that they were on the move! Climbing to his feet, he moved to the window and peered out between parted curtains. Vast, never-ending fields of coarse grass rolled by, and in the far distance he spotted giant mountains with peaks shrouded by white mist.

He turned towards the bed. His heart almost stopped when he discovered Anna missing. Instead of her lying before him, all that remained of her was the outline of her body, made up from pieces of shed skin, oily stains and the dry, encrusted towels. With panic filling his chest, he realised the room was extremely bright. He looked back to the window and then traced the sun's rays directly to the bed. Fear gripped his heart like a tightened vice.

He fell to his knees. "ANNA!"

"…Josh… "

Josh heard his name and jumped to his feet. He opened the washroom to find her on the floor, curled in a foetal position.

"Hey – baby," he said, as a flood of relief coursed through his veins.

He knelt beside her and pulled her into his arms. And, forgetting about her injures, he hugged her tightly. He heard a squeal of pain. "Sorry," he said, loosening his grip.

"Easy there comrade," Anna told him, her eyes burning with an intense fever.

"You scared the shit out of me."

"Why?"

"I thought the… remains on the bed… it was…" He struggled to finish his sentence as the possibility pained him too much.

She offered a short laugh at his mistake, but then, seeing he was genuinely upset, she wrapped her arms around him and hugged him tight, ignoring her agony.

"Hey – it's alright – everything's okay," she soothed.

He felt a river of teardrops pour down his cheeks. And, not knowing if they were the tears of joy, relief, sadness or even fatigue, he held her in his arms for some time as he let these confused emotions flood out.

"Are you alright?" Anna asked, once his tears had dried.

"Yeah," he answered sheepishly, embarrassed by his outburst. "Wait here. I'll prepare the room."

With his composure regained, Josh stood and left the tiny washroom. He pulled the square piece of dark material from under the bed, took the reel of tape, and within minutes he had thrown the room into near darkness. Leaning over the bed and its rank contents, he flipped a switch to turn on the overhead light. Josh folded the sheet over on itself to clear away the foul mixture. The dark fluid had leaked through onto the mattress. He flipped it over to reveal a dryer side. Then, taking a clean sheet from the top bunk, he made up the lower one, before taking the soiled blanket and dropping it in the small trash receptacle.

Although the room still carried the slight smell of cooked meat, it no longer held the stench of decay.

He returned to the bathroom and found Anna standing on weak legs. "Hey – easy," he said, as she wobbled backwards dangerously. He took her by the waist to steady her. "What about your ankle?" he asked.

"It's fine, look," she said, and to prove it she flexed her foot.

"Okay, but take it easy."

She smiled at him stupidly.

"I'll follow from behind," he told her.

"Whatever you say, Joe," she joked.

He followed her out of the bathroom and, as she made her way to the bed, he saw a mess of fierce reds and bright pinks. Dotted randomly about her body were numerous blisters, which appeared to throb with their own painful energy. The only unblemished parts of her body were her slim legs, which glistened with a healthy sheen. Even her hair had a wild and frazzled look about it. Nevertheless, as she climbed into bed, Josh could not argue against the fact that she still looked beautiful.

"Is there anything I can get you?" he asked, once she had slipped under the sheet.

"A drink would be nice," she answered.

"Okay. What?"

"A neat Jack Daniel's," she told him, and her face split into a forced smile.

"What?" he asked in disbelief.

Laughing now, she said, "I'm kidding. Just anything with ice."

"Okay, what about a double?" Josh joked.

"Hell, make it a triple!" she smiled, and her face beamed.

"Juice it is then."

"Killjoy," she said.

Josh reached for the door. "You'll be alright while I'm gone?"

She offered him an exaggerated nod. "Now go on, or we'll be in LA already."

"Okay, I'm gone," he said, and with a relieved smile on his face he slipped outside.

The second he was gone, Anna's own smile vanished, replaced instead by a look of absolute torment. She doubled over at the waist, wrapping her arms around her raised legs. She moaned in agony as an internal hunger ripped through her body. It clawed its way inside her body, from cell to cell, as it journeyed towards her fevered mind. She tried desperately to hold onto her senses but knew that, in the end, the hunger would prevail. For this unwanted yearning was infinitely more powerful than any conscious reasoning, and must be satisfied – no matter what.

She closed her eyes and tried to squeeze away the invading red mist. The last threads of her conscious mind began to snap. Now, she realised that Josh would be returning to a terrible danger. Shocked by the speed at which the hunger had consumed her body, she tried to climb out of bed to secure the door. Yet, as she pulled the sheet away, the cravings whispered urgent warnings. She dropped to the floor and clasped her hands over her ears in an attempt to block out these spiteful murmurs. Rolling onto her belly, she crawled towards the door. The hunger pinned her down with its brutal hand, and, there, she squirmed uncontrollably. The remnants of her conscious mind retreated into the dark recesses of her soul. Then, with one final jolt, she succumbed to her true self.

The beast.

***

Josh juggled with the two large glasses of chilled juice. The sway of the train jostled him from side to side and the ice that floated at the top clinked together, sounding his arrival. Making his way through the narrow passageways, he was occasionally stopped by one or two of the passengers and asked if he was okay or told what a lucky escape he'd had. He said he was fine or agreed with their comments, and finally reached his carriage.

"Say, Joe, where've ya been?"

Josh looked up from the drinks to find the overly tanned Buddy Perkins stood directly outside their compartment. His heart missed a beat. His immediate thought was that Buddy Perkins had just emerged from their room. But then, as the salesman swiped a key card across the adjacent door, Josh guessed the guy must be staying in the same carriage.

"Shit," Josh breathed, reluctant to speak to the guy and have him stay so close.

"Say, Joe, why don't I give you a hand?" Buddy offered, moving along the passageway.

"I'm fine," Josh told him. The automatic door hissed and he narrowly avoided becoming a door sandwich.

"Hell, it's no bother," Buddy said, and reached for the large beakers. Before Josh could convince him otherwise, Buddy took both drinks. "Hey, looks like we're practically roomies," Buddy beamed.

"Great," Josh sighed.

"Isn't it?" Buddy agreed, missing the sarcasm.

"Say, why don't you and your lovely bride join me for a drink?"

"I'm sorry, Ann… Natasha doesn't feel too well."

"Gee, pal, what's the matter?" the overweight salesman asked, with genuine concern written across his round face.

"It's just a stomach bug," Josh lied.

"Hey, Joe, maybe I should get a doctor or something?"

"No – no. It's not that bad, honest."

"Okay, Joe, if you say so."

"Well, this is me," Josh said, reaching his doorway. "Thanks for the help," he added, before swiping his key-card and opening the gloomy compartment. He took the drinks from Buddy's hands. Then used an elbow to push the door open. After a hasty goodbye, he disappeared inside.

Josh placed the drinks on the side cabinet and then turned to Anna.

"They had a deal on triples, so I got you two," he said.

The overhead light clicked off and he was roughly pulled onto the bed. He felt Anna's lips at his. His mouth opened and he allowed her to probe with her tongue. Although her lips were dry and cracked, he returned her enthusiasm with added eagerness. Her hands dropped to his side and, with a quick tug, she ripped the T-shirt off his back.

"Hey, what's the rush?" he asked, breathing in cotton dust.

She offered him no explanation, but instead clamped her hands to the sides of his head and returned him to her lips. Deciding she had obviously made a speedy recovery, Josh ran his hand over her chest, squeezing her breast. He felt one of her hands clamp over his own. She released a muffled cry. He broke away to look down at the silhouette of her face.

"Anna, I love you."

She raised herself up onto her elbows. "Fuck me," she growled in a husky voice.

He pushed her down onto the bed, gripping her hands, pinning them above her head. They kissed hard and Josh felt her teeth bite into his bottom lip. Skin split. The small wound leaked fluid and he tasted his own blood.

"Easy," he said.

She ignored him, clamped her lips against the gash and eagerly lapped at the coppery liquid. He allowed her to stay at his lip for a little while longer, until the painful throb became too intense.

"Hey, save some for me," he joked, uneasily, pulling away from her cruel kiss.

She sat up and gripped both his arms, pinning them behind his back. His fractured wrist throbbed with a sickening agony.

"Careful," he warned her, as he tried to free his restrained hands. "Anna, you're hurting me."

She disregarded his plea and continued to hold him tight.

"Anna, I'm serious," he said, struggling in her grasp. "ANNA!" He prised his arms free, then pushed away from her. "What the hell's got into you?"

She sat panting in front of him; and it was then he noticed the face in the shadows belonged to someone – some*thing* – else. He bolted off the bed and hit the light switch.

A hideous combination of Anna and some nightmare creature revealed itself.

"SHIT," Josh cried and stepped back. He fell over his own feet and dropped to the floor.

"Where are you going?" she asked in a warped voice. She climbed out of bed to stand over him.

He looked up and saw long talons hanging dangerously at her sides. Her entire body had swollen with muscle and, rather than her naturally lithe and slim build, she now possessed a solid mass. Two cruel and feverish orbs had replaced her usually deep brown eyes. And as she looked down upon him, he saw that they no longer held any humility or compassion. Instead, they were filled with an intense obsession for something deeply forbidden. Josh crawled towards the doorway, understanding that what stood before him was no longer Anna.

"Where are you going?" she repeated. Her elongated tongue ran slowly across her blood-smeared lips.

"I … left something at the bar," Josh stuttered.

"Something?" she asked. She tilted her deformed head to one side, as if assessing him.

"Yeah, I'll just be a minute," he said, climbing to his feet.

"Then hurry," she told him, her sharp canine teeth exposed.

"Okay," Josh mumbled. He reached for the door handle, and opened the door by an inch or two before turning his back on her.

Thump!

The door slammed shut, his escape cut off. He saw a wicked

talon pressed flat against the surface of the door and turned to find he was trapped between her outstretched arms.

"On second thoughts, why don't you stay here?" she said, with her gruesome face only inches away from his.

Her mouth split open and a ghastly tongue snaked out to lick at his lips. Josh turned his face to one side and the slick tissue missed his mouth, instead sliding with a sickening, slow pace across the length of his cheek.

"Aw! Doesn't boy want to play?" she mocked.

"Anna, please," Josh said, revolted.

"Aw. Anna, please," she mimicked.

She leaned in to sniff around his eyes, ears and neck. And, as she reached the side of his throat, she released an agreeable woof of air. Her eyes swam with desire. "You're hot stuff, whoever you are."

"Anna, stop fooling around," he said, but knew this was not any kind of game. More like, he'd just become game.

She released a furious snarl, picked him up and tossed him effortlessly onto the bed. He landed half on the bed and half against the wall. Air exploded from his lungs. She pounced on top of him, dragging him to the centre of the bed, smothering him with her gruesome, near-naked body.

Josh managed to work one arm free. He reached up towards the blacked-out window, struggling to pull the material free. Anna's face underwent its full transformation then. He heard a sickening pop of bones, and he watched as her mouth exploded outwards into a swollen muzzle. Her elegant nose pulled itself flat against the snout. Two elongated ears sprung from the surface of her dark hair and, as the skin of her brow thickened into gnarled ridges, her transformation became complete.

"Jesus," Josh gasped, as sunken eyes fixed upon him.

Her jaws opened. Sharp teeth struck out in a sudden blur. He managed to twist underneath her. Instead of clamping around his throat, the lethal jaws ripped into the skin of his shoulder. He screamed out in pain. The agony of torn flesh sent urgent messages up to his terrified brain. A burst of adrenaline coursed throughout his body. He felt an explosion of energy flow into his muscles, and he heaved her up, pulling her jaws free from their ghastly bite. He folded his leg under her, kicked out and sent her flying across the room.

He rolled off the bed ready to snatch at black cloth. A powerful hand gripped his leg, pulling him back. His hand closed around nothing but air. Twisting onto his back, he found her hand clamped around his ankle. With effortless strength she dragged him across the floor. Then, releasing her grip, she launched herself at his exposed throat. He threw his arm up to protect himself.

"NO!"

He heard a thunderous pop. Her jaws were clamped around the plaster cast on his arm. She shook her head from side to side and tore away at the white plaster. A layer of chalky dust was thrown into the air. She released his arm and reared back. Her jaws opened impossibly wide as she readied herself for another attack.

"ANNA – PLEASE!" Josh begged.

***

Anna drew away from this hateful figure. With a mixture of sweet blood and bitter powder in her mouth, she tensed, ready to strike. Then, unexpectedly, an unbearable pain ripped through her body. She dropped to the floor before wrapping her arms around her aching stomach. The sweet blood on her tongue turned sour. Tasting nothing now but hot bile, she opened her mouth and heaved out a pool of red liquid. A mixture of blood and stomach acids splattered onto the floor. Anna opened her eyes as Josh reached towards the darkened window.

"NO!" she cried.

His hand paused.

Another wave of nausea hit her. She retched violently to expel a second mouthful of hot blood. Now with her belly clear, she felt her senses return, as if suddenly recovering from

228

an incomprehensible bout of delirium. The terrified face of someone familiar stared back. She blinked and Josh's handsome but fearful face swam into focus.

"Josh?" she said, confused.

She gasped at the bloodied and punctured skin to his shoulder. Climbing to her knees, she reached out with her hand. Only what she held out was a twisted talon. She snatched her hand back, her confusion growing.

"What happened?" she asked.

Her words were spoken through jagged teeth. Her deformed hand rose to her mouth. Strange contours revealed themselves. She pulled away wet fingers to find them smeared with blood. Instantly knowing this blood belonged to Josh, she shuddered at its terrible significance. Her stomach twisted with a different type of agony.

"My God, what have I done?" she groaned, sickened.

Josh climbed to his feet, which caused the wound at his shoulder to ooze dark liquid. He almost lost consciousness and went down. She reached out to help him but he cringed away, which stopped her hand short.

"What have I done?" she moaned, remorsefully.

"What have you done?" Josh snapped. "What have you done? FUCK YOU, ANNA!"

His words hit her hard.

He seized the moment, pushed past her, stopping just long enough to grab the backpack. She went after him, needing to explain, but as he opened the door a shard of light cut a barrier across her path.

"Josh – wait!" she pleaded.

Josh stepped into the safety of the bright passageway. He turned to her and grunted, "FUCK YOU, ANNA!" with just as much conviction.

She watched him disappear into the glare of sunlight. Unable to follow him, she instead cried, "Please, Josh, you don't understand. Come back!"

Chapter Thirty-One

The FBI Agent placed another cardboard box on Balooga's already overcrowded desk.

"How many more of those things are there?" Sanchez asked.

"That's the last one," Fernandez answered.

The agent lifted the lid off the box to pull out a thick stack of computer-printed paper. He split the pile in two, handed over the separated stack to Sanchez, then repeated the process and offered Balooga a second mass of printouts.

"So who've we got now?" Balooga asked, turning his attention away from the book at his side.

"These are all the passengers who travelled via track, from late yesterday evening to early this morning," the agent explained.

"Christ, I thought we'd done those," Balooga groaned. A huge pile of paper cluttered the side of his desk.

"No, they were airport boarding lists, remember?" Fernandez said.

"Oh, yeah," Balooga acknowledged. A phantom list of typed names swam before his eyes. "Okay, but I still think this is a waste of time."

They had spent the last three hours painstakingly working their way through hundreds of computer printouts. They were now down to their last box. Delivered to the FBI agent at his request, the numerous boxes had begun to arrive as soon as they had returned from Balooga's unexpected trip to the city library.

After leaving the forensics department in a cloud of smoke,

the large detective had made a beeline towards city central and its public records. Diving out of the stationary Lexus, Balooga climbed the stone steps up to the institute's wooden doors. Dwarfed by their size, he'd been quickly swallowed by the entrance.

Sanchez and the agent waited in the car, perplexed, until Balooga reappeared some thirty minutes later with a stack of books under his arm. He offered no explanation for his unscheduled stop and had simply restarted the vehicle and headed back towards the precinct. Immediately on arrival, he had parked his heavy bulk behind his desk and eagerly begun to digest the withered archives. Occasionally, he turned his attention away from his books when the agent or Sanchez made an interesting comment or two, and had paid particular attention to Fernandez's comment about Anna Privalova being a ghost.

While the two detectives were visiting Elliot Saunders, Fernandez had called the Bureau to request an update on their two fugitives. The information he received came as a shock. According to the FBI database the mysterious Slavic woman had never paid a dime in tax payments, nor had she been issued with a social security number or credit card. Not even a simple video membership could be pulled from the infinite memory of the database.

After he heard the FBI agent explain this fact, Balooga hit the books with a new-found enthusiasm and could not be prised away, no matter what, until finally coming to some conclusion. Eventually, he closed a large hardbacked book, mysteriously called *Murony of Wallachia,* and placed it on a small pile, which comprised of such books as *Lilith the Babylonian Devil, Transylvanian Superstitions, The Phantom World* and a particular famous novel, written by a guy called Bram Stoker.

Seeing that both Sanchez and the FBI agent were drowning under a sea of paperwork, Balooga had finally turned his attention away from his strange collection of books and begun to work his way through the endless scrolls of printed names and destinations. The detective had originally started with optimism.

However, he had soon slipped into a bleak depression once he concluded the almost total improbability of finding their two fugitives by this method.

He looked at the hundreds of names on the Amtrak passenger manifesto. "This is a waste of time."

"Just keep at it," the agent told him.

"We should be out there tracking them down," Balooga moaned.

"How, with bloodhounds? Fernandez asked.

Hell, that might just work, Balooga thought, because of his recent readings. He knew the agent was right and that they didn't have a single clue as to where the two might be, so he began to scan down the list. He looked for one recognisable name out of this possible endless supply. A few minutes later he spotted something of interest. Two large hands began to reel back the printout. Sanchez and Fernandez watched as the lieutenant's excitement grew.

"What've you got?" Sanchez asked.

"Wait a minute," Balooga mumbled to himself.

He snatched up a pencil and pad and began to jot down some details. After only a moment or two, Balooga turned to Fernandez. "Our piece of paper – you still have it?"

"Yeah," Fernandez replied.

The agent reached into his dark suit and handed Balooga the fragment, relinquishing the now possibly 'admissible' evidence.

The fragment was now safely protected against any unwanted contamination, held within a clear plastic bag.

Balooga took the fragment, turned it over and read the name found printed on it. He placed the paper at the side of his pad and quickly copied the name down. Then he took the datasheet and copied another name directly underneath. With the pencil he began to run short lines from the letters of the top name down to the letters of the second, connecting them together. The name from the paper appeared to be an anagram of the one printed on the manifesto.

"I'll be damned," Balooga said.

"What's that?" Fernandez asked.

"I'm not sure yet," Balooga responded. Then he double-checked his findings. "Okay, this might be a long shot, but take a look at this."

"What?" the agent asked.

Balooga turned the pad over and began to explain his theory. "See how the top name spells out the bottom?"

"Yeah," both said.

He held up the computer printout. "Then look at this. See how the last four digits of these transactions match the partial number found on this piece of paper?"

The circled transactions printed onto the Amtrak manifesto did indeed have the last four digits.

"My God, you're right," Fernandez agreed.

"Coincidence?" Sanchez asked.

"Hell no," Balooga replied.

"Wait a minute," Fernandez said.

Taking his cell phone, the agent punched in a speed-dial number and waited for a couple of seconds until the connection was made. Quickly, he relayed a message to the operator on the other side. "Yeah, that's correct. 9-8-6-7, possibly the last four digits to a credit card," he told the operator. "Okay, but as quickly as you can." He put the cell on Balooga's desk. "It'll take a couple of minutes."

Then, for the next five minutes, the three sat or stood, watching the silent cell, anxiety gnawing at the pit of their stomachs, waiting for it to spring to life. Just before the tension became unbearable, the phone emitted a short electronic bleep. By the second bleep, Fernandez had already snapped it up. "Yeah?" He used Balooga's pad and pencil to jot down a short list of details. And, even though his face remained indifferent, both detectives sensed Fernandez's excitement.

"Got them," Fernandez declared, and a brief smile occupied his face. "The department have just confirmed that that credit card was recently issued to a customer who lived on the same avenue as Anna Privalova."

"But you already checked her name and address and nothing came up," Sanchez reminded him.

"Yeah, we checked *her* name but not the one on the passenger manifesto," Fernandez told him.

"But what about her address?" Sanchez asked.

"It wasn't issued to that address." Fernandez paused for a second, which added to the tension. "But it was issued to the store underneath her apartment."

"No way!" Balooga exclaimed.

Finally he understood the Chinese guy's strange conversation about Anna Privalova's repeat trips to the store to pick up males. He blurted, "Males!"

"What?" both agent and detective asked together.

"The guy who owns the shop, he told me she went there for males."

"And?"

"Don't you see, he meant – mail! LETTERS!"

"Son-of-a-bitch," Sanchez muttered.

"Told you they'd make a mistake," the agent said, and slapped Balooga's shoulder affectionately.

"Good work Chief," Sanchez congratulated.

"Hey, let's not get carried away," Balooga warned. "They may have disembarked already."

"Shit, you're right," Fernandez agreed. "Which train are they travelling on?"

"The Texas Star," Balooga said, reading from the printout.

The agent tore off the sheet with the fugitive's pseudonym on, and then made another phone call, this time to Amtrak travel enquiries. He held a short conversation with one of the rail company's employees.

"Good news," he said. "According to enquiries, our Mr. Carl Dua is still onboard. Apparently there was a slight technical problem with one or two of the carriages, resulting in some of the passengers having to disembark early, which caused a slight delay in the Star's journey. Some of the remaining passengers had to be relocated so an updated list had to be compiled, and after doing a passenger check, they've just confirmed Carl Dua is still present. Plus, the Star isn't scheduled to make its next stop for another three hours, so we can have a welcome committee ready and waiting."

"Ready and waiting where?" Balooga asked.

"Grand Junction, Colorado," Fernandez announced.

Balooga realised they were well out of his jurisdiction. "Shit!"

"Something wrong?" Fernandez enquired.

"Goddamn right there is."

"What?"

"They're out of our hands," Balooga pointed out, referring to the Chicago police department as a whole.

"Okay, that's a problem," Fernandez agreed. Then his face turned surprisingly optimistic. "On the other hand, you're the only person who can identify this Privalova woman. So what are you waiting for? Come on!"

"Come on, where?"

"Hell, Lieutenant, Colorado!"

"You serious?"

"Yeah, I can have us in the air within the hour," the agent answered.

"But what about procedure?" Sanchez asked.

"To hell with procedure," Balooga told him. He'd already gathered up his few belongings.

"Wait a minute," Fernandez said, seeing the large detective take his holster and cuffs. "They'll have to stay. I can only get you on this trip as a consultant or observer."

"But we'll need firepower. This Sawyer guy is a real asshole," Balooga informed him.

"I'll get us all the firepower we need."

Uncomfortable about leaving his own weapon behind, Balooga almost complained, but then feeling a reassuring pressure to his right ankle, he obediently replaced the Smith & Wesson in his top drawer.

"And the ankle holster," Fernandez said.

"How the hell?"

"You didn't object," Fernández replied, and offered him an almost apologetic smile.

"Christ," Balooga moaned. He bent to remove the concealed weapon.

"What about me?" Sanchez asked hopefully.

"I'm sorry, Emilio, I've only room for one."

"Shit."

Seeing his partner's disappointment, Balooga dug into his pocket. "Here," he said, and threw him the keys to the Lexus.

"Alright," Sanchez chimed, pleased at finally having his own ride.

"Now go and find Doctor Stapleton," his superior ordered.

"Shit," Sanchez cursed, his pleasure dying instantly.

Chapter Thirty-Two

Josh cut another strip of sticky tape, then pressed the adhesive to his chest in an attempt to secure the makeshift bandage at his shoulder. Made up from strips of cut pillowcase and sticky tape, the dressing leaked with red fluid. The bulkiness of the dressing made it almost impossible for him to move his right arm, rendering him virtually paralysed on his upper right-hand side. As well as his shoulder, the plaster around his arm was also held together by strips of tape.

He stood, took up his smoke-tainted T-shirt and struggled for a while to pull the garment over his head. He returned the tape to the backpack, then picked up the scissors and dropped them inside the bag. Thinking better of it, he retrieved the sharp cutters and then dropped them into his back pocket. He moved over to the window. Strange lands rushed past: lush green fields with a wall of distant mountains as a backdrop. These mountains were capped with a layer of snow, and beyond their white peaks the sun burnt brightly.

Josh tilted his head back. The clock moulded into the carriage wall above read 5:10PM. Only a couple of hours of sunlight remained. He checked that the door was still locked and the chair he had used to secure it was firmly in place. It was, and a sigh of relief escaped from his lips. Nevertheless, even with this small reassurance, his heart still throbbed with a mixture of fear and desperation. Fear at what Anna could do; desperation at what she had already done.

After escaping from Anna's terrifying attack, Josh had fled to this last remaining room. Here, he barricaded himself in before quickly tending to his wounds. The punctures to his skin had been deep but they had already begun to dry. He'd gently cleaned them before wrapping them up with a wet hand-towel. Feeling faint from the blood loss, he had laid his head on the bed and slept. An hour or two later he had awoken, bathed in a sheen of cold sweat. He spent his entire troubled slumber being chased by some hideous menace.

He returned to the bed and sat. After a few moments in thought, he reached into his pocket to pull out a crumpled timetable. From the list he saw that the official time of arrival at Grand Junction should have been at 5:25PM. Due to their unofficial stop of two hours, they would now arrive at about 7:25PM. He gathered his thoughts and tried to work out a possible escape. If sundown in Chicago was at about 7:30PM, then due to the train's constant travelling in a western direction, they should have crossed at least one time zone, which meant dusk in Colorado would now happen at about 8:30PM Chicago time. That gave him only a few minutes to disembark and escape.

But escape to where?

With only a couple of hundred bucks in his pocket, he knew that without Anna's help, he was fucked.

But what about Anna?

Aware that she had suffered from some kind of delirium, Josh wondered if she had really understood who she was attacking. Because if she hadn't, then why had she suddenly stopped?

He shook his head in an attempt to clear his mind of the terrible images trapped inside his unforgiving memory. Anna's beautiful face rose from the depths of his troubled mind. He stood and returned to the door. He contemplated removing his flimsy barricade, but as he reached out towards the chair, pain erupted across his shoulder, which caused him to stop.

His arm dropped to his side, useless.

He breathed out a heavy sigh and tried to clear away the phantoms that haunted his mind. Briefly, he decided to forget about his plan to disembark at the next station, and instead, wait to see if Anna arrived at his compartment, pleading for forgiveness and willing to lead them to safety. But then his head overruled his heart and he moved away from the door. He returned to the backpack and began to bundle the remainder of his things inside.

Fuck her, he thought sullenly, as the last of his possessions disappeared into the pack. What did she have to offer him anyway? A guaranteed life on the run? Hiding from either the law or worse, Jonus. Because of her, his life had become a constant battle for survival, and even if they did somehow outrun the troubles of Chicago and defeat Jonus, then what? A life of seducing young virgins for Anna's own pleasure? Because if what had happened earlier was something other than a terrible mistake, then everything Anna had said about only taking the wicked and immoral had been nothing but lies. Had she used him as some sort of familiar, requiring his help only long enough for her to escape the deadly sunlight? And once past that difficulty, he was no longer needed?

As his mind played out these thoughts, Josh climbed wearily onto the bed. He lay his confused head on the bare pillow. Then shut his eyes. After what seemed like a long time, he finally succumbed to sleep and its welcome release.

***

Unable to cross the simplest of barriers, Anna moved away from the closed door and the light beyond. She returned to the bed and sat, then ran one hand over her fevered brow.

Slipping in and out of consciousness, she had a brief moment of clarity before another bout of hunger ripped through her body. She slipped back into the abyss of darkness, and as she did so, her face flipped between beauty and beast. She gripped onto the sheet, holding her breath, waiting for the latest unbearable surge to pass. Eventually, her face relaxed its obscene battle, finally settling for a beautiful, if somewhat worn look. Exhausted now, she collapsed to her knees. Her head fell forwards and a shower of foul sweat cascaded from her face. The latest bout of hunger passed. Now delirious, she looked around the room in search of Josh. Panic rose in her chest as she realised he was not here.

"Josh?" she called out.

She climbed to unsteady feet before staggering over to the small washroom. She found it empty but, after catching her reflection in the mirror, she entered the smaller room. Her breath caught in her throat as she saw the dark muddy stain smeared across her lips and chin.

With a trembling hand she raised it to the dry stain. Her fingertips brushed across her face, and dark speckles of blood broke loose to fall into the washbasin. She pulled her hand away to find a couple of the rusty flakes had darkened her fingertips. Her heart pounded in her chest. She raised the crimson flecks to her mouth and her tongue poked out between cracked lips. Not in a seductive or pleasurable way. This time she licked at the mysterious flecks with only trepidation and fear in her heart. Her tongue connected with the blood, which made her mouth drip with saliva. For the briefest of instants, she tasted the sweet essence of life, but then, the blood burned at her tongue as the sweetness turned acidic.

She understood instantly that her body had rejected the clean and uncorrupted life fluid of someone decent. For, over the last thousand years, she had trained her body to deny her of everything that was innocent or righteous. Instead, she could now only feed on the blood of the sinful and depraved.

How had this blood come to be?

She had a brief flash of memory, which involved some hateful intruder. Then her mind cleared, and she could only remember Josh, bloodied and scared as he'd unexpectedly fled their compartment.

But why?

Because of what she had done, she thought, her gut twisting with a dreadful agony. "My God," she moaned, as the full understanding of what she had done hit her. She had attacked Josh whilst under some kind of delirium, brought on by the all-powerful hunger. A hunger accelerated by her burnt and weakened body. And, without warning, her exhausted soul had responded instinctively and driven her into some insane and uncontrollable frenzy. Somehow, Josh had been able to defend himself long enough to survive her initial attack, but not before being seriously injured. The picture of his bloodied shoulder, and worse, his horror towards her, flashed across her mind. She dropped to her knees as a wave of revulsion crashed over her. Another picture forced itself in her mind, but this one was an image created by her imagination. It comprised of Josh lying in his own blood as he bled to death.

"NOOO!" she cried, in a mixture of desperation and anger.

She gripped the washbasin and used it to pull herself up. Retreating from the bathroom, she snatched up the sheet from the bed. She threw the cover over her head and shoulders and then stepped towards the doorway.

Anna decided she must find him, whatever the consequences to herself. She gripped hold of the door handle. Before she could open it, another surge of hunger hit her, and it dropped her to her knees like an obedient servant. She groaned in agony as her face underwent its full transformation. Her eyelids opened and she stared out through blood-hungry eyes.

Clawing her way upwards, she stood at the doorway. Something beyond sent a rush of pleasure through her body. She listened as the door adjacent opened to allow a sinister spirit to enter. Her talons flexed. With all thoughts of Josh now forgotten, she rocked from side to side, and dreamt of the bloodbath to come.

Chapter Thirty-Three

Harry Balooga looked down at the distant wisps of cloud somewhat apprehensively, feeling a sickening wave of vertigo crash over him. He turned away from the window of the aircraft and concentrated instead on the open book in his lap.

"Are you alright?" Fernandez asked, seeing the big guy's unease.

"Yeah – I'm fine," Balooga replied, forcing a smile.

"You look a little pale," the agent said from the seat opposite.

"Just tired, that's all."

"Don't worry; this'll be all over in about… " – he quickly checked his watch – "… just over two hours."

"I hope so," Balooga said.

"I can't wait to see their faces when they see the welcoming committee at Grand Junction."

"What time are they expected?"

"At about eight-thirty."

Balooga looked at his watch and found that it had already turned 7PM. "Shit," he cursed, "we'll never make it."

"Relax. We touch down in Colorado Springs in about fifteen minutes. There, we have a chopper waiting to take us the rest of the way. We'll make it – just."

As if on cue, the plane tilted and began its descent towards a small private airstrip somewhere near Colorado Springs.

"Since leaving forensics, you've been a little preoccupied with those books. What's bugging you?" Fernandez asked.

"It's nothing," Balooga lied.

"C'mon, Lieutenant, level with me."

Stuck between wanting to share his concerns and not wishing to look stupid, Balooga squirmed in his seat.

"Hey, we'll keep it off the record," Fernandez promised.

"Okay," Balooga said, with a spread of his hands. "This is strictly off the record, right?"

"Off the record," Fernandez agreed.

"Where you come from, do they believe in… the paranormal?"

"You mean like magic or the supernatural?" the agent enquired.

"Yeah – I guess," Balooga responded, a little uncomfortable.

"Not really. Why?"

"Oh," Balooga said in surprise. He had expected a country that was steeped in religion and ancient culture to believe in such things.

The detective's mistake was clear. Fernandez offered him a brief smile. "I was born in Yorkshire, England, not my parents' native India."

"Oh, sorry," Balooga said.

"That's alright," the agent told him.

"What about your parents – do they believe in such things?"

"Such things as what?"

"You know – ghosts, demons and such."

"Yeah, I guess."

"So they must have told you stories when you were younger?"

"Yeah."

"What stories?"

Fernandez paused for a moment, his dark brow creasing slightly.

"I remember my father telling me and my brothers about a large creature that hung upside-down from a tree," he began. "It hid in shadows and would hold food or treasures out with its bark-like arms, waiting for hungry or unwitting travellers to pass by. Then, as the travellers tried to take the offerings, it would catch them in its huge wings and devour their souls."

"Really?"

"Yeah, it looked like a giant bat, apparently," Fernandez added.

"Their souls, how did it devour them?" Balooga asked, leaning closer.

An uncomfortable grin spread across Fernandez's face. "By drinking their blood."

"You're joking, right?"

"Hell, no. My mother used to call it the Baital."

"What else?"

"Ah… oh yes, the Rakshasas," Fernandez said.

"The what?"

"The Rakshasas," he repeated. "I think it means 'to destroy' or 'the destroyers'. Anyway, these Rakshasas were creatures that only came out at night, and like the Baital they fed on the blood of humans."

"What else?" Balooga pushed.

"That's it. Now, where is this going?"

"I'm not sure yet," Balooga answered.

"So tell me, what ghost stories did your parents scare *you* with?"

Balooga leaned closer to Fernandez. "Have you ever heard of Murony of Wallachia?"

"No," the agent answered with a shake of his head. "Who the hell is he?"

"Not he – her," Balooga said.

"Go on."

"When I was a boy, my father told me that this Murony was a bloodsucker that used to stalk the woods surrounding the town of Biska in the late seventeen hundreds. She would only be seen in the middle of the night or in the early hours of the morning, mainly just before dawn. He told me that she'd wait around at the edge of the forest and as peasants or livestock passed by she'd snatch them up and carry them deep into the woodlands, then eat their flesh while they still lived."

"Really?" Fernandez asked, goose bumps covering his skin.

"Yeah, she was a real nasty piece of work. Fed on the young and innocent as eagerly as she did on the old and depraved. That's not all. She also had the power to change her shape."

"What?" Fernandez asked, now seemingly absorbed in this chilling tale.

"She was a Shapeshifter," Balooga said with the utmost conviction. "Her normal appearance was that of a human female – a beautiful girl even – but it is said she also had the ability to change at will into the shape of a dog or wolf and run on all fours."

"So what happened? To her, I mean?" Fernandez asked.

"Apparently she just disappeared over one particularly hot summer and was never seen again," Balooga said. "Although there is another story that some say may have happened."

"I'm listening."

"Some say a mysterious and exotic foreigner appeared that summer. He visited the local tavern each evening for almost a whole week before eventually revealing himself to be some sort of hunter. One who could rid the village of its hateful legacy. He said he needed the help of some of the stronger and braver townsfolk to conquer the evil Shapeshifter. So one hot night, he and six brave young men left the safety of the village and set out for the woods. The remaining villagers gathered in the middle of town and stood around a huge blazing fire. As they waited for their brethren to return, some said they heard terrible screams come from the dark woods. Then, just before sunrise, the hunter returned carrying the severed head of a beautiful young woman. Covered in blood himself, he tossed the head onto the fire. Then, without a word or any form of payment, the stranger simply vanished."

"But what about the six men?" the agent asked in a whisper.

"They were found later that day, torn to shreds," Balooga whispered back.

"My God," Fernandez mumbled.

"That's not all."

"Tell me everything."

"The reason some of the villagers decided to stick with the simple tale of her disappearance was because, when the stranger returned to the village, he wasn't exactly covered in blood but more like dripping in great rivers of red liquid, almost as if he'd bathed in the spilt fluid. Fearing word would spread of a greater evil, they'd simply said Murony had just disappeared over the hot summer and never returned."

"What an amazing story," Fernandez remarked.

"What if it's not just a story, but fact?" Balooga asked, surprising the FBI agent.

"Are you serious?"

"It's a possibility, right?"

"Wrong. You know as well as I do that this type of rumour stems from paranoia and our forefathers' inability to explain the then inexplicable. Hell, next you'll be telling me you believe in werewolves and the undead?" Then, seeing Balooga's raised eyebrow, he added, "Christ, Detective, you really are serious?"

Balooga raised his hands. "I'm not saying I believe in all that, it's just not everything can be dismissed as tales of wild imagination."

"Okay, let's say for argument's sake I agree with you. What relevance does this have to our case?"

"Remember how I said Murony was a Shapeshifter?"

"Yes."

"And remember how the print from the knife only matched the print on our piece of paper *after* we'd reshaped it?"

"Christ!"

"Wait. We both know those two prints belong to the same person. So how the hell do you explain that?"

"I don't know, but there must be another explanation," Fernandez said, "instead of this monsters and gargoyles bullshit."

Balooga leaned forward so he was only inches away from the agent's face. With the utmost conviction, he said, "Believe me, Special Agent Fernandez, there is no other explanation, and the reason I know this for sure is because I've seen the beast with my own eyes!"

Chapter Thirty-Four

With the last of the sunlight filtering through his small compartment, Buddy Perkins shuffled his large body to the centre of his bed. In doing so, he relieved the pressure on his tethered wrists. Apart from his dark cotton socks, the salesman lay naked on the bed, and felt both excited and nervous at the thought of things to come. As well as his mixed emotions, he also felt slightly light-headed as the wine in his stomach finally began to take effect, producing a pleasant buzzing sensation in his brain.

His excitement came from the imminently expected pleasures that Trixybell had promised him. He heard her humming softly while she prepared herself in the closed washroom. His nervousness extended from the unknown. It had been her idea to tie him up. Now, he lay completely exposed and at her mercy. For, although he had known his new lover for only a short while, she had already introduced him to the more daring and unusual acts of lovemaking. Having spent years in a sexually suppressed relationship with his recently estranged wife, he now felt like a giddy teenager, ready to experience the opposite sex and their mysteries for the first time.

He closed his eyes and lapped at his fat lips, tasting the fruity wine that lingered. He raised his head and strained to peer over his ample gut. He could just about make out the erect tip of his manhood.

"Ah, women! Don't you just love 'em?" Buddy said, and

dropped his head. He pushed blood into his penis, which made his short length of flesh twitch with excitement. Whooping with joy, he called, "Say, Trixybell, what's keepin' ya?" The only response that came his way was the repetitive humming.

He huffed like a child.

Twisting his head, he saw the tightly wrapped material that secured his wrists. Blood had drained from his chubby fingers, losing their usual tanned colour, leaving them grey and pallid. He pulled at the restraints and noticed that his wrist had now begun to feel quite painful.

"Say, Trixybell – maybe you should loosen my hands a little?" he called towards the closed door.

Buddy's plea went unnoticed.

The beat of his heart quickened, and he decided now that his immediate predicament was not exactly exciting, but worrying.

"Hey, Trixybell! What're ya doing in there?"

Humming.

He pulled at the restraints, harder and a cold sheen of sweat began to cover his generous body.

"What the hell?" he mumbled, as he felt his hands grow numb.

The sun outside slipped behind a mountain peak. Like the dropping of a theatrical curtain, the last rays of light flickered out, which plunged the room into near darkness.

Not wanting to be tied to this bed naked and in the dark, he pulled harder against his restraints. Pulling tighter still, he felt his hands growing suddenly numb.

It was then he became aware that the humming had stopped. An incoherent mumble had begun in its place.

"Hey, Trix… Dawn. Who the hell are you talking to?" Buddy asked the closed door, his anxiety clear.

The mumble stopped.

"At last," Buddy whispered. Finally, he'd gotten her attention. "Listen, Trixybell, maybe we should give this idea a miss?"

Silence.

"What the hell?"

The mumbling returned, but this time it had an added

intensity and urgency about it.

"Christ," Buddy moaned.

The mumbling stopped.

He heard the click of a switch and the thin strip of light under the door went out. The door opened. He sensed someone enter the room. He peered into the darkness and saw a shape standing at the bottom of the bed. The shape stood in silence, looking down at the tethered body before it.

"Trixybell, what the hell have you…?"

Buddy's sentence was choked short as the gloom revealed a vision that almost stopped his heart dead.

Chapter Thirty-Five

With the drop in temperature, most of the dark insects had taken refuge in and around the decomposed body. There, they squirmed about lethargically as a fat and bloated mass. Due to the lack of light and activity, the basement was now shrouded in a dark, quiet ambience.

The quiet was shattered abruptly by a loud crack that came from the basement door. Another crack ripped through the basement, sending dark shapes up in the air. Then a third, and, with a splintering of wood, the inner door flew open to reveal a large silhouette beyond.

Part of the shadow moved and, with a barely audible click, a bright beam of light burst from the dark shape.

"Jesus… " a voice moaned, quickly followed by a heave of its chest.

"Fuck. If ya gonna puke, take it outside," another voice warned.

"I'm fine," the first voice lied, before gagging on its own vomit.

"Get out of here!" the second commanded.

In a shifting of angles, the silhouette split down the middle as half of it returned outside. The remaining half slowly worked its way down the short flight of steps and towards the body that lay swollen and bloated in the centre of the basement.

Officer Janet Lindsey crept down the stairs with exaggerated care as she tried her best not to squash the bugs that squirmed under her boots. She reached the bottom and swept the torchlight across the centre of the basement.

"Sweet Jesus," she groaned through gritted teeth.

Her hand rose and she covered her mouth with a handkerchief. She breathed in a lungful of scented oils, remaining at the foot of the stairs, waiting for the stench of decay to pass. She lowered the handkerchief and was again assaulted by the foul gasses that leaked from the swollen corpse. She clamped the flashlight between her thighs, held her breath and then quickly pulled the handkerchief over her nose and mouth before tying it in a knot at the back of her head. Hidden now behind her makeshift mask, Lindsey gripped the flashlight and stepped closer to the body. The beam played over the corpse to reveal the remains of a middle-aged woman.

The woman was clothed in a tight dress, which had a cheap pattern emblazoned across the front. In places, the dress had burst at its seams, and through these holes, Lindsey spotted sickly coloured skin bulging through. She moved her examination higher and the torchlight revealed a ghastly mask of writhing maggots.

Choking back revulsion, she let the light rest at the woman's neck. She leaned closer to examine the twisted material at the throat. Tied in an intricate knot, a pair of pantyhose had been pulled so tight skin had broken, covering the nylon with a dark patchy stain of dried blood.

Officer Lindsey released a pitiful breath. She decided she had seen enough and so retreated to the bottom of the stairs. With one final look at the sad submission on the floor, she quickly climbed the steps.

She entered the small kitchen to find her colleague at the back door. She turned and headed towards the front of the house.

Entering the hallway, she traced the beam of light towards the stairway above. The passageway was clear. Uncertainty held her there for a second, before a combination of duty and curiosity pulled her upwards. She climbed up and found herself at a half-open doorway. She used the handle of the flashlight to push the door fully open. Then stepped into the room. Light from the streetlamps outside found its way inside, bathing the contents in a yellow murkiness. The patrolwoman made her way into the centre of the room. The weak light outside had barely enough strength to draw angles around the few meagre contents. After a quick inspection, she found it empty except for a few personal belongings. Retreating, she moved her search to the next room. She pushed open another door to find a small washroom.

Empty.

In the next room, she discovered an untidy work-study and, apart from rows of stuffed bookshelves and a desk, it too was empty. She found herself at the end of the landing. The final door beckoned. Before she pushed it open, her instincts told her that something unpleasant lay beyond.

Lindsey held her breath before pushing the door open by an inch or two. She peered inside and saw a huge wooden wardrobe covering most of one wall. She pushed the door fully open and caught **her** breath as another body revealed itself.

This one was stretched out over the bed, totally naked except for a nylon stocking twisted around its neck. The hands had been pulled high above its head. Where they joined the headboard, Lindsey saw that two strips of cloth had securely fastened them. Due to the body's badly bloated and decomposed state, the patrolwoman struggled to make out the victim's sex. However, as she moved over to the edge of the bed, she spotted the shrivelled remains of a penis and testicles.

She stayed at the foot of the bed, the light playing over the tethered form. Dark patches of dried blood, directly underneath the victim's hands, stained the soiled sheet. She let the light remain at the head for only second, but still she got a glimpse of squirming white tissue. Not wanting to contaminate any potential forensic evidence, she carefully backed away from the bed. A sudden presence materialised before her. The bright torchlight picked out a sickly white face.

"Jesus, you scared the shit out of me," Lindsey gasped, her heart pounding in her chest.

"Jeez, sorry," her male partner said.

"Are you okay?" the patrolwoman asked.

"Yeah, just ate too much for lunch, that's all," the guy responded.

"Yeah – right," she said, knowing the truth.

"I guess we should call this in," the patrolman commented.

"Yeah, I guess we should," Lindsey agreed. "Poor bastards. How long do you suppose they've been here?"

"By the look of 'em, I'd say a week – maybe longer."

"Poor bastards," Lindsay repeated, then crossed the threshold.

The patrolman clicked on his own flashlight. "Wait a minute, what the hell is that?" He traced the beam of light across the wall to reveal a scrawl of writing.

"What the hell does that say?" Officer Lindsay asked, struggling to make out the barely legible words. She took a step closer until the words became clear.

"Christ," the patrolwoman exclaimed. "I think we'd better call it in – right now!"

"Yeah – I'm all for that," her partner agreed, as he backed out of the room.

The two patrol-officers quickly descended the stairs, leaving the second corpse and its chilling message alone.

Written in large, childlike letters were the words:

Daddy likes to play…!

Chapter Thirty-Six

Buddy Perkins let loose a tremendous cry. Yet the thunderous noise of the Superliner drowned out his cries for help. The figure above him loomed closer to reveal its hideous face. He tugged at his arms with renewed urgency, ignoring the agony that burned at his wrists. His huge gut quivered with terror. He tried to twist his body to one side in an attempt to keep his legs between him and the monster that stood next to him.

"Wait, please, " Buddy pleaded.

Standing over him, dressed in revealing underwear and high heels, was Trixybell. And, if not for the nylon stocking that had been pulled tightly over her head, and the long blade she held at her side, she would probably have been every male's fantasy.

The stretched nylon pulled her features down and flat, which gave her face the gruesome look of melted wax. She stood in silence over her tethered lover, gently rocking from side to side, as if swaying in time to some privately heard tune. She raised the steel knife up to her ghastly face and, in addition to her swaying, she tapped out the unheard melody by drumming the tip of the knife against the side of her head. The blade cut through her synthetic mask. One of her squashed ears sprang out, which gave her an almost comical look. She pulled the knife away from her face and saw that, as well as nylon, the steel had cut skin. She focused on the small rivulet of blood and watched as it slowly ran down the length of the blade. Grinning, she licked at the red liquid and left a dark smear over the thin membrane that covered her face.

"Trixybell, maybe you should put down the knife," Buddy said, as if addressing a bemused child.

Her vacant eyes poked from under squashed eyebrows, focusing on him for the first time, which made him wish he had not spoken.

The blade swung down to her side. "But Daddy likes to play with knives," she said.

"Oh… shit," Buddy moaned.

She raised her leg and stretched it out over his midriff. He saw that her toenails were painted a bright red. Instead of finishing at her cuticles, the paint had splashed over onto her skin, making the ends of her toes look as if they had been dipped in blood. She climbed over the bed and straddled him. The blade fell over his gut.

"What are you doing?" Buddy asked.

She giggled like a child. "Quiet. Let Daddy's little girl play with her toys."

Now, Buddy decided to relinquish his pride, and he turned his head towards the door and roared for help.

"Quiet – Mommy isn't allowed to hear," Trixybell told him, and to make sure of his silence she pushed the blade against his lips. "That's better," she said, as Buddy fell silent.

"We have to be quiet or Mommy will get mad."

Buddy tried to twist his head in an attempt to relieve the pain at his lips. Rather than freeing them, the blade sliced into the side of his mouth, widening his grimace.

"Now look what you've done!" she snapped angrily. "Mommy's gonna be real mad when she sees that."

"Dawn! Stop it. It's me, Buddy!" he said, and spat blood.

He watched as her head tilted to one side, and through her macabre mask, he witnessed her gain a brief moment of awareness. Her attention dissolved almost as quickly as it had appeared, however, leaving behind it, a blank and empty expression.

"Quiet now," she soothed. "It'll be alright if you're quiet. I won't have to hurt you."

Buddy clamped his bloodied lips together.

"Good," she said, tracing the blade across the dark skin of his stomach.

The tip continued onwards and headed towards his now deflated and shrivelled member. Trixybell giggled for a second time when she found his tiny penis poking out of a rug of curly hair.

"Doesn't Daddy want to play?" she asked him, a mechanical grin stretching her compressed lips.

Not sure of the correct response, he shook his head, but then seeing her immediate annoyance, he quickly stopped and nodded instead.

"Good," she said. "Now, where shall we begin?" The blade rose above his privates. "Here?"

He responded with an instant shake of his head.

"What about here?" she asked, moving the blade over his gut.

Another shake.

The knife moved even higher before eventually it stopped at his throat.

"Okay, what about here?"

Two teardrops ran down either side of Buddy's face. He shook his head in a silent plea.

"This is boring," she huffed. "You're not playing properly." She leaned over him and snapped, "If you're not gonna play, I can end this real quick!" The blade returned between his quivering thighs.

"Now let's start again. What about here?" she asked.

***

Josh watched as the last rays of sunshine found their way into his barricaded room. He checked the time. Only minutes of daylight remained. He moved away from the window and picked up the backpack. The light at his back blinked out. He hesitated at the door for a moment, and then quickly removed the chair. He placed his ear against the door and listened for any noises. None came. Opening the door slightly, he peered through the crack, half expecting a ghastly face and talons to be there, waiting for him.

The passageway was empty.

He stepped outside and gently pulled the door shut behind him. With the backpack over his good shoulder, he made his way towards the rear of the train. The squeal of brakes sounded as the carriage lurched slightly. The train had begun to slow.

Heading for the rear of the train, he found himself at the entrance to Anna's carriage. He froze, remaining on his side of the automatic doorway. The passageway beyond lay empty. Josh knew he should have waited at the other end of the train, but instead he found himself here. Why? Maybe in the hope Anna would appear at her door, in the safety of twilight, and beg for forgiveness. He stood and watched her compartment, in the belief that she would emerge at any second.

Then came a muffled scream. Josh catapulted off the wall, the backpack dropping from his shoulder as he rushed to the next carriage. He reached Anna's doorway in seconds, in time to hear another plea for mercy.

"STOP IT!" he cried, banging on her door.

But she did not. And again, he heard an urgent call. He stepped into the centre of the passageway ready to kick the door down, yet, after hearing another strangled cry for help, he realised the noise had come from the left, from Buddy Perkins' room.

"ANNA, STOP IT!" he yelled.

"… HELP…!"

Josh stepped back away from the door. He raised his foot and kicked out at the lock. He kicked out again, and again. The door flew open with a bang.

Entering the gloomy compartment, he spotted a dark figure straddled across the naked and bound salesman.

"GET OFF!" he ordered, and moved in.

The figure on top turned, forcing Josh to look upon the hideously scrunched face of Trixybell. For a second he thought he had interrupted some lurid sex game. However, as he turned to Buddy, he saw true terror written on the guy's face.

"She's insane!" Buddy stuttered through bloody lips. More blood oozed from numerous lesions, and the sheet underneath him had become a stained patchwork of glistening reds and stark whites.

"What the hell?" Josh mumbled.

Infuriated by this unwanted spectator, Trixybell released an insane howl before launching herself at him. She hit Josh hard and they both went down in a heap. He threw his hands up to protect himself from blood-soaked fingers. Nails scratched at his eyes in a blurred frenzy. Her attack was short-lived. He opened his eyes to find the crazy woman rearing over him with a crimson-stained blade held high.

"ANNA!" he yelled. "HELP ME!"

***

As if unexpectedly awakened, Anna felt the red mist instantly clear. She shook her head and chased away the remnants of the crimson fog. Jumping to her feet, she looked around to see if she could find the reason for her return to consciousness. She found only the expected. A slight frown creased her brow. Then, as she looked around the room, her eyes fixed upon the dark material that covered the window. Sunlight had retreated to be replaced now by the moon and stars.

The train slowed. Panic rose in her chest as she understood Josh would be disembarking at any moment. She reached the door in a millisecond. The door opened with a bang and she stepped into the narrow passageway. Instantly, she witnessed an extraordinary scene unfold before her.

"ANNA!"

She looked down at the tangled mess of bodies to find Josh at her feet.

"ANNA, HELP!" Josh pleaded.

Anna glimpsed the bloody knife waver dangerously over Josh,

and her instincts took over. She stepped inside the compartment and hit out at his assailant. The power of the blow sent Trixybell flying across the compartment, where she landed in a crumpled heap.

"Josh, what the hell?" Anna asked, bewildered.

She held her hand out. He hesitated for a moment, then grasped her hand and climbed to his feet.

"She's fucking insane," he cried.

"What's going on here?"

"I'm not sure. Look."

Anna saw the ripped, bloodied figure on the bed. "Oh… God."

She moved over to the mutilated figure. She cut the binds to his wrists with a simple swipe of her nails. Buddy's hands flopped down by the side of his head, a pool of blood splashed out, covering Anna's face in coppery droplets. She felt her body swoon with the bloodlust, and it took all of her willpower to force the hunger away.

"Josh, come on," Anna said, through gritted teeth.

"What are you doing?"

"He needs help – look at him."

Josh looked down at the salesman. Blood leaked everywhere from multiple cuts to his gut, legs and arms. Wearing a bloody mask, Buddy choked out a weak plea before he slipped into unconsciousness.

"What can we do?" Josh asked.

"Hold this," she told him, and pressed his hand against a wound that oozed blood. Josh held his hand against Buddy's flesh, feeling a mixture of hot blood and clammy skin.

"He's getting really cold."

"I know, just keep holding." She tore strips from the already stained sheet and quickly wrapped the wounds to Buddy's arms and legs.

"Christ, she must be one sick bitch," Josh remarked.

"Yeah – but at least the mystery is solved," Anna said, and ripped another length of cloth.

"What do you mean," Josh asked, moving his hand so Anna could tend to the injury.

"There's no time to explain right now. Help me get him to his feet."

Together, they pulled the overweight salesman off the soaked bed. Buddy's blood-slick skin caused him to slip from their fingers. They lost their grasp and he collapsed to the floor.

Now covered in blood, Anna sensed the return of the red mist. It crept over the edges of her vision like red smoke. She shook her head in an attempt to clear her mind but was unable to chase the haze completely away.

"Anna, what is it?" Josh asked.

"It's all this blood. I don't think I can hold it back much longer."

"Just a few more minutes."

They bent down to haul Buddy to his feet. Like three drunkards they staggered to the open doorway. As they struggled across the threshold, Buddy's head snapped up as he regained consciousness. He looked from side to side. Through numb lips, he said, "Say, Joe." His head twisted. "Say, Natasha."

"Easy there," Josh said, seeing the guy's eyes glaze over.

With the last of his strength, Buddy focused on the beautiful face of the woman at his side. "You're a real fox," he mumbled, then exhaustion pulled him down, and fatigue sucked him into darkness.

"Josh," Anna called.

She sensed the hunger return. Before he could respond, a piercing cry sounded from behind them. Josh felt a violent impact at his back. With Buddy Perkins still in his hands, he fell through the open doorway and into the narrow passageway.

He twisted onto his back to find Anna and Trixybell stood face to face. Josh understood instantly that Trixybell's madness was complete.

"Finish the bitch," he said.

"I heard that," Anna replied through jagged teeth. She stepped inside, reached behind her and slammed the door shut, sealing them in together.

Having lost one of her high heels, Trixybell kicked off her other shoe to stand barefoot. She held the blade in front of her, ready to spear her catch. Even in her madness, Trixybell understood that the vision before her was something more than just a figment of her damaged and twisted mind. She stepped away from this hideous rival. The blade flicked from side to side with a metallic flash of menace. Then a demented roar burst from Trixybell's compressed lips as she jabbed the blade forwards.

Anna jumped back. She cleared the immediate danger and sprang forwards to claw at one exposed side. Trixybell read the movement. She twisted her body and the attack went wide. Overextending herself, Anna had the brief glimpse of steel before pain ripped across her back. The blade sliced its way through flesh with ease, soft tissue parting in the wake of hard steel. Anna maintained her momentum and rolled over the bed, which made another sweep of the blade go wide. Still, the agony to her back brought tears to her eyes.

Trixybell launched herself across the bed. Half-blinded by tears, Anna thrust her hands out and caught the woman in mid-flight. Yet, weakened by the hunger, she was unable to hold her back. They fell to the floor in a tangled heap, with Anna caught underneath, their faces only inches apart.

Behind the thin membrane, Trixybell's eyes widened as she witnessed the true form of the beast. Rather than terror gripping her face, a wide, crooked smile split her lips. Through her misshapen veil, she released a bout of maniacal laughter. Her grip tightened around the knife. She struck down and the blade plunged towards Anna's throat.

With lightning speed, Anna threw a short punch against her assailant's face. She heard a crunch and the blade fell from bloody fingers, landing to one side and out of arm's reach. A second punch rocked Trixybell's head sideways and the nylon mask ripped open. Fragments of enamel scattered across the floor. Trixybell grinned now through broken, bloodied lips. She clambered over Anna in an attempt to retrieve the fallen weapon. Anna grabbed a handful of hair, dragging Trixybell away from the blade. She landed another powerful blow to the side of the demented woman's head, which caused more teeth to fly.

Trixybell, seethed within her own demented red mist, forgot about the blade, and instead clawed at Anna's eyes with her bare hands. Anna threw her arms over her face and managed to block the woman's frenzied attack. Sharp nails scraped deep cuts into the skin of her arms. The vicious attack lasted for only a few fleeting seconds before Anna sensed her adversary grow weak. She raised her legs under Trixybell and launched the lunatic across the compartment.

Climbing to her feet, Anna saw the woman stagger towards her. Trixybell threw herself across the space that separated them. The force of the attack knocked Anna backward. They hit the window and, in an explosion of shattered glass, they toppled sideways as both fell through the jagged hole.

Instinctively, Anna threw her hands out to find the edge of the framework, stopping her fall short. And, rather than toppling into the black void beyond, she hung half-in and half-out of the shattered window. A powerful draft dug frozen fingers underneath Anna's body. She felt as if the slipstream was about ready to prize her free and send her spinning to her death.

An unexpected pressure pushed against her chest. She found the crazy woman leering over her. Trixybell's torn mouth opened and, using what was left of her cracked and jagged teeth, she snapped at Anna's exposed throat. The fierce wind threw her attack wide and her broken teeth snapped around nothing but dark space.

Anna's arms bulged with effort, now straining against the additional weight. Clinging to the frame, she felt saw-like splinters cut into the palms of her hands. Her grip slipped and she fell further back. The wind whipped her long hair about her face. She caught a glimpse of something tall and skeletal. She squinted through the darkness. A signal pylon was heading directly towards her.

At about the same time, Trixybell spotted the tower as well. Her cut lips broke into a grotesque leer. She leaned further forwards until she had succeeded in pushing Anna's head into the pathway of the looming structure.

With her back pressed painfully against the frame and her hands holding nothing but the woman's flesh, Anna struggled to find any leverage. The signal tower raced towards her.

Unable to pull herself away from the structure, she looked at Trixybell's demented face.

"Here, let me help clear your head," Anna said.

Then, simultaneously, she released her grip on the woman's arms and relaxed her upper body. She fell further backwards, but, just before she toppled completely out of the window, she spread her legs wide and caught herself with her thighs. The tower hurtled towards her. She threw her arms outward before arching her back flat against the side of the carriage.

This release of pressure caused Trixybell to fall forwards. And, as the signal-pylon roared pass, it hit her, ripping her head from her shoulders. The pylon zoomed away, snagging an arm as it did, tearing it from the socket. Trixybell's decapitated body sprang back. Blood pumped from out of her carotid artery and jugular vein. Her mutilated body danced a short headless jig then collapsed onto the floor.

With her last ounce of strength, Anna pulled herself back inside the carriage. Now, finally giving in to the hunger that consumed her every fibre, she dropped over the body and began to feed.

***

After dragging the bloodied body of Buddy Perkins to the next carriage, Josh called upon the help of two passengers. Together, they hauled the salesman into the safety of another compartment. Sending one of the passengers for help, Josh stayed with Perkins briefly, but then, sensing their arrival at Grand Junction was imminent, he returned to Anna.

He found her amongst the bloody carnage in Perkins' compartment, and was sickened to discover her bent over the horrendously mutilated body of Trixybell in a feeding frenzy. He turned his back and bolted for the door. A vicelike grip held him fast. He stared at her blood-smeared face and tried to pull away, yet was unable to break from her grasp.

Anna pulled him back inside the ghastly room and dragged him to the window to show him the immediate threat of a police helicopter. Then, after quickly explaining the likelihood that a whole platoon of armed cops would be waiting for them at Grand Junction, she pulled him into the darkness beyond.

***

"Christ! Did you see that?" Balooga asked through the internal communications link.

The detective turned to the FBI agent and Fernandez's bleached face stared back.

"Please tell me that wasn't a woman," the agent said, clearly shaken.

"*WAS* a woman – poor bitch," Balooga told him. He shuddered at the sight and then turned towards the helicopter pilot. "How much further to the station?"

"About two minutes. We're coming up to Grand Junction Bridge now – look," the pilot said. The pilot dropped the nose of the helicopter and within seconds he had levelled the aircraft out alongside the train.

"What the fuck's going on in there?" Balooga asked, as he peered into the dark hole.

"What?" Fernandez asked, having just received static through his oversized headphones.

"I said… " – a squeal of static – "… in there?"

Fernandez shook his head to clear away the interference. Instead, he only succeeded in increasing the noise to an almost deafening pitch. He pulled his headphones off, and then quickly clamped his hands over his ears in an attempt to muffle out the thunder of the rotor-blades.

The fugitives appeared at the jagged hole. Balooga waved a hand to get Fernandez's attention. He pointed towards the carriage.

"Oh, shit," the agent said.

The detective slid further across the bench to press his face up against the side window. Unbelievably, he saw both Sawyer and the woman climb out through the broken window. "No fucking way," Balooga said, as they were about to jump. The ground under the train receded, replaced by a dark, churning river. In no time at all almost half the train had passed over the iron bridge. The two fugitives hung with their legs over the side of the carriage.

Balooga shouted to the pilot, "GET IN CLOSER."

Looking directly across at the two fugitives, Balooga got a quick glance into Sawyer's eyes. Unbelievably, he saw the young man smirk. Then, the grin disappeared as they pushed themselves away from the moving train and dropped into the abyss below. The detective watched as the two bodies dropped in silence.

"Christ," he breathed, as they disappeared underneath the dark water.

Fernandez turned towards the Chicago policeman. He shook his head and without a word expressed his understanding that nobody – no matter who, or what – could have survived that.

Chapter Thirty-Seven

Emilio Sanchez pulled the Lexus into the parking lot. He killed the engine and then made the short trip from the vehicle to the entrance of the morgue. Although in reality the trip lasted for only a few seconds, it seemed to take the detective an age to reach the entrance, as if his legs were wading through deep water. Struggling against this invisible current, he looked from left to right, keen eyes examining every hidden corner. He arrived at the lobby before checking behind. The lot was dark, deserted, *foreboding.* He entered the sombre building and, now familiar with the internal layout, he headed directly for the Medical Examiner's office.

Sanchez was extremely tense, his eyes roaming into every nook and cranny, and his ears strained to catch even the slightest of sounds.

Not long after dropping Balooga and the FBI agent at the airport, Sanchez had received an alarming phone call. What he had originally thought of as a crank call had now become a race against time. As he traversed the barren corridors he replayed the earlier conversation out in his head.

Sanchez – Hello?

Caller – Detective?

Sanchez – Yeah, who the hell is this?

Caller – Did you find the doctor?

Sanchez – Listen asshole, don't waste my time.

Caller – Well?

Sanchez – No, you prick – now who the hell are you?

Caller – Don't waste my time.

Sanchez – Where is she?

Caller – Look harder.

Sanchez – Where?

Caller – Use your little brain and think.

Sanchez – Shit, if this is some fuckin' game I'm not listening.

Caller – Oh, this is a game – but one where the loser stays lost.

Sanchez – What?

Caller – This is a game of three.

Sanchez – Three what?

Caller – Three possibilities.

Sanchez – What possibilities?

Caller – One – you get to the doctor first and she lives.

Sanchez – What?

Caller – Two – I get to the doctor first and she dies.

Sanchez – Listen asshole, I'm hanging up right now.

Caller – Or three – you fail to play and I kill you both.

Sanchez – Fuck you!

Caller – No, Detective, I've already got YOU fucked.

Sanchez – You're crazy.

Caller – I know.

Sanchez – Christ.

Caller – I'll give you one hour after sunset to find her.

Sanchez – What?

Caller – One hour. That's 8:30PM.

Sanchez – Or?

Caller – She dies.

Sanchez – I'm not playing your stupid game.

Caller – Okay, then you both die.

Sanchez – FUCK YOU!

Caller – Tick – tock – tick – tock.

Now, Sanchez reached the doctor's small office and found it empty. He entered. But found nothing to tell him of the doctor's whereabouts. He flipped his cell phone open with the intention of dialling the pathologist's number. His finger hovered over the first digit. Before he had time to punch it in, the cell emitted a series of bleeps. He raised the phone cautiously, as if it might bite him, and held it to his ear.

"Yeah?"

A familiar voice spoke to him, which caused his face to relax slightly.

"Hey, Chief, what is it?" Sanchez asked.

"What? You're where?" A pause. "Glenwood Springs?" A slight frown.

"Chief, speak up. I can't hear you." A huge look of surprise. "They did what?" A shake of his head.

"Still alive! You're kidding, right?" Raised eyebrows. "She's a what?" An invisible slap in the face. "Fuck me!" Return of the frown. "Chief, I don't think I heard the last bit right. Hello? Chief… "

With the cell held away from his ear, Sanchez gawked at it as if it was some bizarre prop found in one of David Cronemburg's weird and wonderful movies. Stunned, the detective lowered the cell to his side.

Instantly, the phone rang again.

"Chief?" Sanchez asked.

"Tick – tock," a voice said.

"Christ," Sanchez snapped, looking at his watch.

It was 8:27PM!

"You said an hour after dusk, which means I've still got three minutes left."

"I grow tired of our game. You've got one minute."

"What? Wait!"

"Fifty-eight seconds … Fifty-seven … Fifty-six …"

Sanchez hit END CALL and quickly punched in the pathologist's number. He pressed the cell to his ear, left the office and moved into the corridor. After a couple of precious seconds, he was rewarded with a ringing tone.

"C'mon, pick up," he said anxiously.

The ringing in his ear continued. Yet, as the minute ticked down, his urgent call went unanswered. He lowered the phone and spun around, looking for anything that might help with his search. Finding nothing, he held the phone back to his ear. The ringing continued and, realising it was going to stay that way, he hung up. And for just a brief second the ringing continued, although the connection at his side had been terminated. He hit REDIAL and waited. After a couple of seconds the distant ringing returned.

Sanchez exploded into action. He pushed his way through heavy plastic doors and found himself in the main examination room; all chrome tables and whitewashed walls. One side of the room was overrun by rows of square-shaped doorways. Inside were silent, cold occupants, their once individualism reduced to nothing more than a mere toe-tag.

He headed straight for the chambers, hearing the ringing increase as he went. Unable to pinpoint the exact location though, he began to randomly open doors. He dragged the gantries out, pulling at white sheets to reveal pallid and stiff corpses.

He threw open the last compartment. Instantly, the ringing magnified. He stood over the white shrouded outline and saw two dark spots of blood in exactly the right place for eyes. Holding his breath, and nerve, he pulled the bloodied cover back to reveal a bound and gagged body. He forced himself to look upon the woman's face and was totally shocked to find a pair of terrified eyes staring back at him.

"Doctor!" Sanchez gasped, surprised to be speaking to the living. He flipped his cell shut and the ringing abruptly ceased.

"Mmm-mm-mmmm," Stapleton mumbled.

"What?"

"Mmm-mm-mmmm!"

"Hold on," he told her. He reached down and pulled the gag away from her mouth.

"BEHIND YOU!" she screamed.

Sanchez spun around, his pistol out in front. The gun was yanked from his fingers, leaving him suddenly defenceless.

"Too late. Time's up!"

A pale face hovered above the detective, eyes burning with

both hate and hunger. A bony hand jabbed the weapon in Sanchez's direction. The detective took an instinctive step back. His hands rose in submission. The guy stepped closer.

"Wait a minute," Sanchez said.

"A minute is something you or I don't have," Jonus responded.

The detective looked into his eyes and knew instantly that they lacked any humility or compassion. Unable to hold the vehement gaze, he dropped his eyes back to the gun.

"Keys!" Jonus commanded.

"What?" Sanchez asked.

"For the car. Give me your keys."

"Wait. What for?"

Jonus stepped forward, aiming the revolver directly at Sanchez's head. "Now, I'll ask one more time," he said. "Give me the keys."

When the pale figure approached, Sanchez felt a stabbing sensation return to his mind. He saw memories flash before his eyes as if an invisible probe had begun to suck them from his head. For one terrifying second, he thought the probe was about to steal his entire soul, and leave him empty. However, as his recent conversation with Balooga played itself out, the probe quickly withdrew and, before he knew what had happened, he found himself holding out the keys to the Lexus.

Jonus snatched them up. "Good, bug. Now hurry or she's gonna bleed to death."

"What?" Sanchez asked, his mind a mishmash of incoherent thoughts.

The gun moved to the left fractionally before the muzzle exploded with a flash of fire. A deafening crack followed an instant later, followed by a scream of pain. Sanchez turned to find Doctor Stapleton writhing in agony. Blood poured profusely from a bullet hole to her leg.

"Christ! Are you crazy?" Sanchez asked, the mist suddenly clearing from his mind. He turned and found that Jonus had disappeared.

All that remained of his passing was the outline of his body, caught in the cloud of dispersing gun-smoke.

Chapter Thirty-Eight

With their shoulders hunched over, Balooga and Fernandez staggered away from the aircraft. The helicopter blades began to chop away at the darkness, before the skids gently rose, and with grace the aircraft took to the sky, disappearing into the black sky above.

The lawmen made their way back towards the bright lights of the late-night convenience store. A small bell at the top of the door rang out to acknowledge their return.

The large detective pulled the pilot's map from his jacket. He spread the map across the counter and looked up at Jack Mayfield. "Okay, where's the nearest town or inhabited area?" he asked.

The proprietor of the store turned his attention to the map. He traced the path of the Colorado River, seeing nothing but tree lines and mountain ranges. He shrugged his shoulders.

"I've already told you, there isn't any," he said.

"There must be something," Balooga pushed. "Please, look again."

"Wait a minute," Mayfield said. "Oh – yeah, there is the old skiing resort down near Dead Man's Pass."

"Where's that?"

Mayfield placed a thick, calloused digit over the map. "Here."

Balooga looked under the storekeeper's finger yet only found a series of indistinguishable lines and unfamiliar shapes. "So tell me, what's that?"

Mayfield lifted his finger away from the map. "It's the old Sunlight Skiing Resort."

"Which is?"

"Which is mostly a bunch of dilapidated huts and rundown skiing facilities. Used to be successful way back in the 70s but some big shot opened up 'The Sunshine Skiing Resort', which is less than ninety miles from here. It has steeper trails and open aspen groves to hike through – a real tourist attraction. Hell, our little complex didn't stand a chance. The resort closed within two seasons of Sunshine opening."

"So there's nothing there?"

"Nope."

"Shit," Balooga spat.

"Well, apart from one or two hunter's cabins," Mayfield added.

"Go on," Balooga pressed.

"Some of the townsfolk, they like to hunt around the base of the old complex, so they've kept one or two of the old shacks maintained – you know, in case of an emergency. Weather can change real quickly up there, not to mention the possibility of getting caught up in an avalanche."

"What do you think?" Balooga asked, turning towards the FBI agent.

"I think they're dead, Detective, that's what I think," Fernandez said, exasperated.

Still unable to accept or even entertain the lieutenant's insane idea that Anna Privalova was some sort of ghoul or bloodsucking night-stalker, Fernandez looked at Balooga and offered him a mournful shake of his head.

"It's over, Lieutenant. They're floating somewhere in the Colorado River. Let's stop wasting time and call in a diving team to drag the riverbed."

"You do whatever you've got to do. Me, I'm going there," Balooga said, and pointed at the map.

"This isn't your jurisdiction, remember?"

"Hell, if they're dead then what are you worried about? Let's just say I'm taking a short hike."

"You're crazy. It's freezing out there," Fernandez warned.

"Then I'd better buy some of these," Balooga told him. He looked around the store at its range of padded and insulated weather gear. "Okay, what do I need?" the detective asked Mayfield. The storekeeper moved to a rack of clothing. "One of these for sure," he said, lifting up a white padded jacket.

"How much is that?"

"Four-hundred-and-fifty bucks."

"What?" Balooga moaned.

"Hey, it'll last you a lifetime."

"Jesus! For that price, I hope I live a hell of a long time."

"Longer than you would without it," Mayfield told him.

"What else?"

For the next five or ten minutes, Mayfield led Balooga around the store, kitting him out in an array of padded and waterproof weather gear. They returned to the counter and the storekeeper began to till up the goods. Balooga moaned every time the till rang; and unable to watch the amount grow any further, he moved to the front of the store.

"This is crazy," Fernandez remarked, joining him.

The detective looked out into the dark, windy streets of Glenwood Springs. "Maybe, but this Privalova's real smart. I don't believe she'd have jumped if she thought it would kill her."

"But even if the fall didn't, the combination of frozen waters and wild rapids would."

"Perhaps, but until I know otherwise, I'm going to keep looking for them."

"And what if you do find them?"

"Then I'll bring them in."

"How? You have no weapons or manpower."

"I'll figure it out as I go along."

The till rang out for the last time. Balooga returned to the counter, leaving Sebastian Fernandez at the window.

"Okay, that'll be… "

"Wait – wait, don't tell me," Balooga interrupted, "just stick it all on this."

The storekeeper took the detective's credit card and ran the transaction through. Then, as he handed over the bill of sale, Mayfield heard a groan escape from between the detective's lips.

Unbuckling his belt, Balooga dropped his pants. He took up a pair of padded white pants and began to change. Within a couple of minutes he had pulled up the last of many zips. Now fully kitted out, he stood in the centre of the store like some miniature polar bear – ready for action. Balooga looked down at the map. "If I'm here," he said, and pointed to the centre of Lake Blue Mesa. "How do I get to there?" His finger moved over to Colorado's National Dinosaur Monument.

"Actually, you're here," Mayfield corrected, and pushed Balooga's finger across the map by three inches.

"Shit," Balooga said, now totally confused.

"You ain't too familiar with maps are you?" Mayfield observed.

"I'm from Chicago," Balooga retorted, as if that in itself was sufficient explanation.

"Here, let me," Fernandez said, back at Balooga's side. He took the map. "We're here, right?"

"Yeah," Mayfield agreed.

"And we need to get to there."

"Yeah."

"Then what's our best route?"

Chapter Thirty-Nine

The fire popped and spat. Anna took another log and tossed it in the midst of the raging flames. She waited until the log caught before turning away. Returning to the centre of the small cabin, she pulled the warm blanket tighter around her shoulders. She stopped at the table, next to Josh.

"You should move closer to the fire."

"I'm fine," he told her.

She saw his lips were still grey and that his body shook uncontrollably. Pulling away her own blanket, she wrapped it around his shoulders.

"Hey, what are you doing?" he asked.

"You need it more than I do," she said.

"No, wait," he argued, reaching out with blue fingers.

"Honey, leave it. I'm fine, honest," Anna insisted, placing her hand over his. "You're still freezing. Now trust me."

Josh tried to smile at her last words, but his numb face only managed to form a weak grimace.

After Josh had slipped into unconsciousness at the riverbank, he had not awakened again until he felt Anna pull at his damp clothes. He woke dressed only in his under-shorts and lying on the hard wooden floor of some uninhabited cabin. Anna was similarly dressed in only her underwear. He found their clothes hanging from a rope-line near the blazing fire.

"I thought you said it was gonna be boring?" Josh commented as he reached towards the open bar of chocolate on the table.

His blue fingers struggled with the confectionary. Anna reached over to break a piece off. She popped it into his mouth and then bent over as if to kiss him. Her lips brushed against his but felt a lack of response. She pulled away, her heart aching.

"Sorry. I'm still numb," Josh lied.

Embarrassed, hurt even, Anna tried to dismiss the kiss by asking, "Boring? What do you mean?"

"You said once we got on the train we'd keep it boring," Josh explained.

She thought he was referring to their violent encounter, so snapped, "You're a real shit, Josh Sawyer, do you know that?"

"What?" Josh asked, surprised by her reaction. "What do you mean?"

"I've already said I'm sorry," she replied, and nodded at his bandaged shoulder.

"No, wait. I didn't mean that. I meant the fire and Buddy Perkins and Trixybell." Anna turned away with shame after hearing the crazy woman's name. Josh realised his stupid mistake. "Shit, not you and Trixybell and her body, but – oh shit…"

He fell silent.

Anna returned to the fire and took up another log. She used it to poke at the ash, stoking the flames. With her back to him, she worked at the logs until the flames began to lap upwards with renewed energy. She turned her attention to their clothes and continued with her examination until she felt his hands at her sides.

"Anna," he said.

She turned to look at him, and he saw tears streaming down her face.

"Hey, stop that," Josh uttered, taking her in his arms.

"But I could have killed you," she cried.

"No you couldn't. Your body rejected my blood, remember?"

"But what if it had been too late?"

"Anna, listen to me. You can't think like that. It didn't happen that way, so let's just forget about it."

"How can you ever forgive me?" Anna asked through brown,

tear-filled eyes.

"Christ. If it hadn't been for you, I'd be dead four times over by now. If those three assholes in the alleyway had not killed me, then Trixybell surely would have. That's before we even get to the fire on the train or surviving the river."

With Anna's precisely timed drop, they had hit the water at its deepest. Although its sudden coldness almost stopped Josh's heart dead, he managed to hold on until Anna found him within the icy swill. She had wrapped her arms around him and protected him from the jagged rocks. As one, they rode the violent waters before Anna had pulled them both onto the riverbank. There, Josh had slipped into unconsciousness, until waking up inside this remote cabin.

"But if you hadn't met me, then none of that would have happened," she moaned now.

"Yeah, and you wouldn't have fled your apartment before Jonus arrived, so you'd probably be dead too. Anna, I don't understand why this is all happening, but for some reason we've been thrown together."

"I guess you're right."

"That's better," Josh said, as her tears began to dry.

"But I can still see that you're repulsed by me," she told him.

"No, that's wrong. That's so wrong," he said sincerely. He took her hands. "I admit I'm scared of you, but not repulsed. I understand when you did this," – a shrug of his injured shoulder – "you weren't exactly yourself, and I've already forgiven you. But this… feeding of yours, it's so difficult for me to accept."

"But that's who I am."

"I know, and I thought I could deal with it as long as you only took the lives of the wicked and evil."

"And I do," Anna responded, trying to convince him.

"Then explain why you thought Buddy Perkins was a killer."

She fell silent, pensive for a moment while trying to assemble her thoughts and feelings into words. She started with a question. "Remember how Jonus couldn't read your mind?"

"Yeah."

"Well, I've been thinking as to why."

"Go on."

"When you had your car crash, all those years ago, you had surgery for a blood clot, right?"

"Yeah, that's right," he agreed.

"So the part of the mind that Jonus taps into must be around the area of the brain where you had surgery, and because of the scar that was left he can't get through."

"Okay, that makes sense, but how does that explain Perkins?"

"Well it must work the same way for me. Trixybell must have been emotionally scarred, and that's why I couldn't read her true self."

"Then why did you think he was the killer?"

"Because somehow his soul must have picked up a residual warning and then, as he kissed my hand, he passed it through to me."

"And you couldn't tell the difference?"

"Maybe she was some sort of sociopath or even schizophrenic, and most of the time she could interact with the people around her and pass as normal."

"But eventually she'd slip back to her true self," Josh finished.

"Yeah," Anna agreed.

"Thank God," Josh said, relief spread across his bruised and battered face.

Anna sensed his relief was more than just a lifting of his concerns but also a purging of his spirit. "What is it?"

Josh gave a heavy sigh before explaining. "Anna, I'm not perfect, you know. I've done things I'm not particularly proud of and I thought when you attacked me somehow you'd sensed I was – you know – corrupt myself."

"Absolutely not," Anna told him firmly. "What happened had nothing to do with you. My own weaknesses sent me into a delirium. I didn't even know it was you, really. You have to remember, I've never allowed myself to become so overwhelmed by the hunger. It was just the combination of being injured and trapped that got the better of me, and it had absolutely nothing to do with you. Josh, you have a good heart, I promise."

"You're sure?"

"Yes, Josh, I'm sure. Listen, everybody does things they're ashamed of. But the people that are inherently good learn from their mistakes to become a better person. It's the people that can't see their wrongdoings, or worse enjoy them, that become twisted and immoral."

"Like Jonus and Trixybell?"

"Exactly like Jonus."

"But not Trixybell?"

"I don't know. Maybe in years to come someone like her can be cured. The mind is a complex thing, but eventually scientists and doctors will learn its secrets. But for now, I can take comfort in knowing that the people I… take can only bring pain and suffering to the world."

"So you think mankind could be cured of all his evils?" Josh asked.

"Not all. Some people are just evil in the true sense of the word, but I do believe one day medicine will cure most impurities."

"And then what will you do?" Josh asked, referring to her need for tainted blood.

"One of two things," she said, and her face became a mask of worry.

"I'm listening."

"One, I become like Jonus, or two, I get myself a fox outfit and sneak inside the chicken coop every night," she told him, and her face broke into a welcome smile.

"Hey, maybe we could live on a farm?" Josh joked.

"Yeah. Do you think I'd look good in galoshes?"

"You'd look good in anything," he smiled, and his eyes dropped over her bare skin.

"You too," she said, repaying the compliment.

"Me? You're joking, right?"

"No, I'm not joking," she replied, and forced her way inside his blanket. She kissed his lips for a long time. Then, with a provocative grin, she said, "And right now, I think you'd look really good in me.”

Chapter Forty

White shards of sleet struck noisily off the storefront. Powerful gusts scooped debris and litter off the deserted sidewalks. The airflow formed the trash into spinning funnels, and then sent the demented miniature tornadoes past the storefront and off into darkness.

"So once we're through Dead Man's Pass, it'll be plain sailing?" Agent Fernandez asked.

"Yeah, but at this time of year the mountains are deadly, and if you make anything louder than a squirrel fart then the whole mountain could come down on top of you," Mayfield warned.

"Then we'll just have to be real quiet," Balooga told him.

Dressed in similar white clothes, detective and agent now looked like a mother polar bear and her cub. As well as their insulated jackets and trousers, each had a small pack strapped to their backs. The packs contained an array of camping gear and other assorted objects.

"So how far is it to the pass?" Balooga asked.

"About three miles," Mayfield answered.

"Then we'd better start moving," the large detective said.

Balooga crossed the store to look out into the windswept streets. He pulled the thick collar of his jacket tightly around his neck. Then moved to the exit. He stepped out onto the dark and blustery sidewalk. Sleet battered against his face. The violent wind took hold, and the door behind him slammed shut. A couple of seconds passed before he heard the faint jingle of a bell. Then, Fernandez was at his side.

"This is crazy," he shouted over the gale.

"You don't have to do this, you know," Balooga said.

The FBI agent turned his back on the constant buffeting. "Yeah, I know, but you might need backup. And anyway, how could I pass up a chance at dressing like this?"

"Yeah, you look real dandy, Special Agent Pooh Bear."

"What time do you make it?" Fernandez asked.

Balooga pulled at his insulated cuffs. "Nine thirty-six."

"Okay, that gives us about ninety minutes to reach the pass and another thirty before we find the complex, so we should be there well before midnight."

"Why? What happens at midnight?" Balooga asked.

For the first time since meeting, the Agent's eyes twinkled with genuine mirth. "After midnight, we enter the witching hour."

"Christ… " Balooga cursed.

***

The passengers spewed out of the arrivals terminal and quickly headed for their luggage, eager to finish their trip and take shelter from the night's shrieking ghosts and chaotic spirits. After they collected their belongings, most of the passengers moved to the main foyer. There they were met by familiar flesh and blood, wrapped around the frames of excited and animatedly talking skeletons.

One particularly devilish ghoul strolled across the busy airport and, although most were not aware, the crowd around him unconsciously stepped away to allow this spectre to pass through untouched. Reaching the main entrance, the phantom tilted his bleached skull upwards to look upon a huge clock. He saw that it was only an hour until midnight and his pale face split into a humourless smile. Two bony hands rubbed together in enthusiastic delight.

Jonus emerged from the airport and felt nothing of the wind or stinging sleet. Joyful now, he strutted along the side of the freeway, heading towards a reunion that was only one-thousand years over due.

***

Balooga found himself trapped between two steep inclines.

"Where the hell are we?" he asked.

"Quiet…" Fernandez whispered. "Remember what Mayfield said about the snow?"

"Oh yeah. Shit," Balooga replied, and he looked about him as if he expected the white hills to come tumbling down around them.

"Give me the light," Fernandez said, as he unfolded a map.

Balooga reached inside his pocket to retrieve the small flashlight. "Here."

Fernandez took the flashlight and let it play over the crumpled and now sodden map.

"Christ! Where did all this sleet come from?" Balooga moaned.

"Here, help me with this," Fernandez ordered, as he struggled with the paper.

With his gloved hands, Balooga caught the wildly flapping corners and held them down. He watched as the flashlight moved in large circles around the map before eventually it found its way into the centre of the paper. He hunched his shoulders to ward off the bitter chill.

"Okay, I think we're here," Fernandez said, shining the light onto a smudged image.

"Yeah, right. So which way now?" Balooga asked.

The agent looked up into the darkness of a particularly steep incline. "That way, I think."

"Great, that's all we need," Balooga grumbled, deciding they were lost.

Fernandez folded the map over on itself. He pulled Balooga's arm, turning the big detective around, then flipped open the lieutenant's backpack and quickly tucked the map away. Tugging on a set of buckles, he secured the pack.

"Listen, just up there is Dead Man's Pass, so we're gonna be real quiet, okay?"

"Hell, you won't even know I'm here," Balooga reassured him.

"Right then, let's go," the agent said, and he began heading towards the incline.

Fernandez had taken only three steps when he heard a commotion from behind. He turned to find Balooga slip-sliding as he struggled to find his feet in the wet sludge.

"Christ," Fernandez sighed.

"Wooowaa," Balooga said, almost falling on his behind.

"Here, take my hand," Fernandez ordered.

Balooga reached out to grip his hand. Eventually, he managed to steady himself.

"Listen. If you're not up to this, we could go back," Fernandez remarked, as if reprimanding a child.

"I'm fine. Come on," Balooga said, and he took the lead.

"Shit," Fernandez muttered, watching the Chicago detective claw his way upwards. "They're gonna have to rename it Arsehole's Pass," he mumbled to himself.

"What?" Balooga asked, with a twist of his head.

"Nothing."

For the next half-hour or so, they struggled along as they battled against the combination of steep hills, torrential sleet, driving winds, the fear of falling snow, and worse, each other. Finally, they topped the summit and were rewarded with a huge panorama of open fields. Covered in thick snow the fields spread towards the colossal base of Sunlight Peak. Stretching up to the heavens, the summit of the mountain disappeared into the dark sky above. Now standing at a higher altitude, the agent and detective felt powdered snow fall onto exposed flesh. Laid out before them were brown smudges, which stained the white blanket of snow at irregular intervals. Most of the log cabins had been left to crumble or rot away. The moonlight reflected that one or two of them had been maintained however. One such structure drew the agent's attention.

Fernandez breathed out a plume of frozen air. "Look – over

there.”

Balooga followed the agent’s line of sight. A thin wisp of smoke came from the lowest structure. “What do you think?”

“Hell, it’s a bit too miserable for hunting,” the agent answered.

“I heard that,” Balooga agreed.

“So what’s our plan?”

“Let’s go and catch us two bad guys.”

Chapter Forty-One

Frank Mayfield shivered as he waited for the old pickup to warm up. He cranked the heater up, twisting the knob all the way into the red. The near worn-out fan spun noisily as it blew warm air into the Ford's cabin. He squinted through the river of sleet that washed over the windshield yet struggled to see further than a couple of feet. The pickup slowed to a crawl as he carefully made his way home.

Mayfield whistled a tuneless melody, looking forward to surprising his wife with his early return home. Pleased with the night's unexpectedly good business, he managed to push away the sombreness of the weather outside. The two lawmen had spent almost an entire month's takings. Now a wealthy man, Mayfield had decided to shut up shop and get home before this storm really took hold.

The pickup dropped into a ditch, but Mayfield effortlessly twisted the steering wheel to keep the vehicle on its intended path. Then, out of the darkness, an unexpected shape appeared, which caused him to throw the pickup sideways. The Ford missed the object by barely an inch, skidded in the sludge, and fell into a trench at the roadside. The abrupt stop jolted Mayfield in his seat. The seatbelt cut against his chest.

"Christ," he cursed.

He leaned back in his seat and looked through the rear-view mirror, but a torrent of sleet bent the outside world into a distorted and alien landscape. He pressed a button and his safety-belt sprang away, relieving the tightness to his chest. Turning fully in his seat, he found a blurry shadow heading towards the stricken vehicle. He switched the ignition off and killed the engine. The wipers stopped midway over the windshield. The only noise he heard now was the hollow drum of icy rain.

Rivulets of icy water streaked down the window, forcing Mayfield to look upon a distorted image. An inexplicable fear gripped his heart and he felt pain bite at his chest.

The face outside did not belong, not out here in this weather. Not with a smile, a smile devoid of any warmth at that. The guy was wearing simple summer clothes too! Mayfield had read about meth heads and burnouts jacked-up on angel dust, and recognised one here.

Mayfield cursed the detective for taking his gun; something he'd agreed to while the agent had been preoccupied. He then frantically searched the cabin for a substitute weapon. He found nothing more lethal than an ice-scraper and a packet of extra strong mints.

The ashen face appeared at the side window. "Need a push?"

Mayfield looked through the inch gap of the window at a pair of green eyes. He mumbled, "Yeah, she's stuck tight."

The face split in a wide, humourless smile. Spider-like fingers tapped on the thin barrier of glass. "Maybe I should give you a push?" Jonus suggested.

"What?" Mayfield asked, his heart working overtime.

"A push." The demented face looked back expectantly.

"Okay," Mayfield agreed, intent on getting the Ford clear and then getting the hell out of here. Alone.

The guy moved back and pushed against the rear of the pickup. Mayfield regained his senses. He turned the ignition and then shifted into gear, popping the clutch. He hit the gas pedal and threw the vehicle forwards. The wheels slipped in the sludge though, and the pickup slid backwards to remain embedded in the ditch.

"Shit," Mayfield said.

He hit the gas, rocking the pickup forwards, gaining sufficient momentum, but again the slippery surface halted his escape. He heard a hollow bang on the roof of the cabin and jumped in his seat. He watched in fear as the figure moved around the pickup.

"You get out and push and I'll drive," the pale face ordered.

Fuck you, pal, I ain't coming out there with you, Mayfield thought. Nonetheless, before he understood what he was doing, he heard the lock *pop* and found himself standing outside in the downpour.

"Good," Jonus said, dragging his soaked body inside the cabin. Two bony hands wrapped themselves around the steering wheel. Jonus twisted his sodden head to Mayfield. "Go and push at the rear."

"Okay," Mayfield answered, his bottom lip hanging slack. He stood soaking up the sleet for a moment before his confused brain sent him to the back of the pickup. Placing his slick hands onto the tail of the truck, he dug his feet into the mud. And, after readying himself, he threw his shoulder against the vehicle.

Jonus felt the pickup lurch forwards. He pressed on the gas and moved upwards by a couple of feet. The wheels began to slip, which made the engine rev crazily, and, after remaining at the rim for only a second or two, the vehicle slipped back into the ditch, held there by its tight, muddy grasp.

"AGAIN!" Jonus commanded.

Mayfield threw his entire weight against the Ford. He pushed with all his might. A bizarre thought crept its way inside his mind, and he knew then that his very survival depended on whether or not he could free the pickup. He roared with effort and heaved the vehicle towards the lip of the ditch. The pickup climbed the muddy bank, its twin headlights arcing upwards, cutting two shafts of light into the night sky.

Jonus saw the dark horizon appear over the hood of the pickup. The wheels beneath him finally took hold as they gripped the earth. He popped the gearshift in reverse. Then rammed his booted foot down onto the gas pedal. The pickup launched itself backwards into the ditch. Having gained sufficient speed and momentum, it began to climb the embankment. Mayfield was pulled under the wheels. And with his body providing better traction the pickup cleared the ditch before skidding to a halt at the roadside.

Jonus cranked down the side window and looked out towards the bloody and flattened mess of Frank Mayfield.

"Thanks for the ride, bug," he said.

He threw the pickup into gear and pulled the vehicle to the centre of the highway and in a blaze of taillights, the Ford headed back towards Glenwood Springs.

Chapter Forty-Two

In the centre of the small cabin, Anna stood dressed in a makeshift outfit, cut from the warm blankets they had used to make love on earlier. The blanket was wrapped around her waist and shoulders, and with her arms poking through torn holes the material looked like some crudely formed jacket.

"What do you think?" she asked, spinning full circle.

"Real sexy," Josh replied. He was dressed similarly to Anna, "Maybe you should start your own line of winter fashions."

"I think I might have something here," she said.

"I feel like some sort of medieval refugee," Josh moaned.

"I think they're cool," Anna said.

"Yeah, but for you it's probably like… nostalgic or something?" Josh commented, before scratching at his neck and arms. "This itches like hell," he added, as the coarse material irritated his skin.

"But they'll keep us warm."

"I still don't understand why we need to leave right now."

"Because it's not safe for us to stay."

"Who the hell's stupid enough to venture out in this? Josh asked, moving over to one of the windows. He peered out, seeing nothing but darkness and a blanket of heavy snow.

"You'd be surprised. I don't think Lieutenant Balooga is the kind of guy who gives up easily."

"But he thinks we're dead, right?" he asked.

"Maybe. I'm not sure," Anna admitted.

"That guy's becoming a real pain in the ass."

"Yeah, but in a few days we'll be out of the country and out of his and the FBI's jurisdiction."

"How? The credit card's gone along with the rest of our belongings, and we're in the middle of nowhere. And this is all the money we have," Josh said, pulling out a small handful of crumpled bills.

"Trust me."

"But what happened to LA?"

"Change of plan. Every safe house I've got in this country is now compromised, so we need to leave for a while," she explained.

"A while?"

"You know, a couple of decades. Maybe longer."

"What?" Josh blurted.

"Josh, it's not safe here anymore."

"But my father – and my studies?"

"They're gone. Forget about them," she told him.

"You're not fucking serious?"

"Absolutely."

"How can I forget about my father? He needs me."

"Not now he doesn't."

"What?"

"Josh, whatever life you had back in Chicago, it's gone. There's no going back."

"I've got to. He's old and I can't just leave him."

"Honey, you already have. I'm sorry, but there's no way we can ever go back. Maybe when things cool down we'll be able to send for him, but for now we need to concentrate on getting safe."

As the full impact of his situation hit him, Josh felt a deep ache spread through his stomach. His father's wrinkled face flashed to mind, causing a wave of choking emotion to wash over him. Fearful for the old man's welfare, he turned and looked out of the window.

Anna sensed his unease. "What's up?"

"I have to speak to him and explain what's going on," Josh answered.

"Josh, there's nothing around for miles. You said it yourself."

"There must be a phone line around somewhere."

"There isn't."

"Look, we have electricity, right?" he said. A single bare lamp hung from the wooden ceiling, the only indication that civilisation lay near.

"So?"

"So there might be a phone line in one of the other cabins."

"What other cabins?"

"Those," Josh said, pointing outside.

Anna joined him at the window. A short break in the snow revealed a spread of dark, desolate structures. "You're not serious?" she asked. "We've no time."

"I'll be just a minute," he said, and headed for the door.

"Josh, this is stupid. There won't be any phone lines. Why would there be?"

"Listen, I don't know where we are, but someone must use these cabins for something. So there might just be a phone somewhere."

"Can't it wait?"

"No."

"Why?"

"Because I might not get another chance."

"I don't understand."

"Anna, I don't know what's ahead of us, good or bad, but I do know Jonus is still out there somewhere, so I might not get another chance to speak to my father."

"Of course you will," Anna said.

"Can you promise me that?"

She opened her mouth and almost spoke, but, unable to lie, she finally admitted, "No, Josh, I can't promise anything."

"Listen. Stay here and wait. If I don't find a line within ten minutes I'll be right back," Josh told her. Without another word he opened the cabin door and slipped outside.

"Josh – wait!" Anna called, striding to the open doorway. She reached the door but the strength of the wind slammed it shut. "Shit," she breathed, and pulled it open. Outside, she saw driving snow and nothing else. Josh was already nowhere in sight.

***

The detective pointed through the snowstorm. "I thought I saw something."

"Where?"

Balooga waited until the snow broke and then, seeing the vague shape again, he said, "Look. Over there," and pointed in the distance.

Fernandez struggled to make out anything through this deluge. "I can't see a thing," he shouted over the wind.

"Never mind. Keep heading straight and you'll find the cabin," Balooga directed.

"What about you?"

"I'm going to check that out," he said, pointing towards the mystery figure.

"We'd better not split up."

"What's up, Agent Fernandez? Are you getting cold feet?"

"I just don't think it's a good idea. For one, you don't have a weapon."

"Really," Balooga responded. His gloved hand slipped inside the folds of his padded jacket. He surprised Fernandez by withdrawing a huge handgun.

"What the hell?" Fernandez mouthed, shocked. "Where did that come from?"

A broad grin split Balooga's face. "It's on loan from Frank Mayfield."

***

Josh slipped on the wooden steps and fell through the dark threshold. A musty, rotten smell filled his nostrils. He climbed to his feet. Then reached out to locate the light switch. The switch clicked on, rewarding Josh with a handful of corroded metal. Dropping the handful of rust, he quickly left the hut and moved on.

He tried to get his bearings now. Searching through the blizzard. Josh squinted to protect his eyes against the bitter chill. He decided he had had enough and turned full circle in an attempt to locate the lights of his cabin. He spotted a flicker of light in the distance. He ran his hand over his face to wipe away the icy flakes. In the distance the light blinked again.

Josh headed towards it.

***

Balooga slapped the head of the flashlight and brought the beam back to life. He pointed it into the white haze before continuing with his pursuit. Treading through the thick snow, he worked his way carefully up the hillside and in the direction of the mysterious silhouette. Within a couple of minutes he reached the outskirts of the old complex. He passed the first rundown shack and found it empty. The flashlight found the next cabin further up the mountainside. Balooga hunched his shoulders. He began to climb towards the dark structure.

***

Josh lost sight of the light for a second time. He stopped in his tracks to catch his breath. Confident he was at least heading in the right direction, he continued his descent, using the derelict cabins to navigate his way back to the safety of his hut.

Chiding himself for not listening to Anna in the first place, he spat out an obscenity. He felt the snow work its way underneath his clothes to numb his skin. He picked up his pace, bounding downward towards the base of the mountain. The white glow of their cabin cut its way through the storm.

He allowed himself a brief grin before homing in on the light.

He got within about thirty yards when a shadow stepped from the corner of a crooked hut. Unable to stop his progress, Josh collided with the object.

***

Anna crossed the cabin, leaving behind her a trail of dripping water. She reached the window and with one damp sleeve, she wiped away at a film of condensation. Outside, heavy snow fell to the earth in an incessant torrent.

Unable to find Josh, she had returned to the cabin in the hope that he had already returned. The cabin was empty. And, finding the floor dry, she quickly determined that he had not returned. Deciding it was best to stay here and wait for him, she concentrated on keeping the windows clear so the light from the single bulb could be seen from the outside.

She cleared the moisture away from the glass panels, then moved across the cabin and began to wipe clean another window. She caught a glimpse of someone's bent frame.

"Thank God," she said, relieved by his reappearance.

She stepped away from the window and headed for the doorway.

***

Josh rolled onto his back. For a second he watched the faint twinkle of stars above. He sat and found a huge handgun half buried before him. A brief frown creased his brow. How had the weapon gotten there? He took the firearm, and then sat with it in his lap. A moment of déjà vu passed – it wasn't the first time he'd found a gun. It was then he sensed someone else was concealed by the shadows.

"Wait!" a voice warned.

Josh instinctively pointed the gun at the speaker. "Who's there?"

"Christ, not again," Balooga moaned.

Josh climbed to his feet with the gun held out in front of him. When the shape revealed itself, he gasped at the unexpected sight of the Chicago detective.

"How the hell...?" he mumbled.

"Take it easy," Balooga said. "Let's just keep cool." The detective stepped out of the shadows. With his arms raised, he continued, "Look, kid, I'm unarmed. Why don't you point that piece somewhere else?"

"What?" Josh asked, still surprised by the detective's appearance.

"The gun," Balooga offered.

"Oh, yeah," Josh said, and he aimed the weapon towards the ground.

"Thanks," Balooga responded.

"How the hell did you find us?" Josh asked. Then he kicked himself for letting the word 'us' slip from his lips, knowing the detective would now be aware of Anna's close proximity.

"We just followed the river," Balooga explained, then he too chided himself for letting it slip that he was not alone either. For a second both men stood, sheepishly, embarrassed by their own stupidity.

Finally, Balooga lowered his arms. "Listen son, why don't we make our way back to that cabin of yours and sort this mess out?"

"I can't do that," Josh replied, taking a step away.

"Why not?" Balooga asked, following him.

"Hold it there, Detective," Josh warned. "I'll use this if I have to." He levelled the gun at Balooga.

"Okay, it's cool," Balooga said, halting.

They stood in silence for a moment. The snow fell around them in a pure white coating, bleaching away the scenery, turning the world into a colourless and barren panoramic landscape.

"I didn't mean from the train," Josh eventually said.

"What?"

"How you found us, before we jumped."

"Oh, that was simple." He paused for a second in the hope

that he hadn't antagonized the young man. Seeing he had not, he continued, "We found the name Carl Dua on your booking schedule and just followed the Star to Grand Junction."

"But how did you find out about the name?" Josh asked.

Balooga almost revealed the significance of the small piece of paper, but instead, he said, "Luck, I guess. You booked the name three times. It just stood out, that's all."

"Shit," Josh snapped. Then he realised the detective's explanation was a little sketchy. "Really? And what drew you to the name anyway?"

Thinking on his feet, Balooga replied, "Let's be honest, son, you ain't exactly travelling with Mother Teresa. I just figured out the name was an anagram of someone your friend reminded me of."

"Who?"

"Christ, kid, I thought you were smart," Balooga commented.

"Smart enough to be holding your gun," Josh countered. "And not for the first time either."

"Cute," Balooga said.

"Now tell me, who the hell is Carl Dua?"

Balooga opened his mouth. A pistol crack from further down the mountainside stopped him short.

***

Anna opened the door. "Josh, where the hell have you…?"

The question was choked short as a dark-skinned face looked back.

"Hold it right there," Fernandez said. The small handgun rose towards her head.

Although dressed in an assortment of winter clothes, Anna instantly identified this guy as FBI. She stepped back into the cabin with her hands raised and allowed him to enter. The agent stepped over the threshold. The second his foot cleared the doorway, she jumped forwards, slamming the door closed. She heard a sickening but satisfying crunch as bones shattered. The booted foot disappeared from the crack, followed by a short cry of pain. She pulled the door back and stepped onto the porch.

The agent's face had gone pale. His eyes turned to her, and Anna read a level of uncertainty in them. Then he seemed to come to some realisation, and his look of doubt quickly turned to fear. He brought the gun up. Her attention focused onto his gloved hand. One of his fingers bent around the trigger, tightly.

"Move and I'll shoot," Fernandez warned.

Before he could react, she lashed out to knock the gun from his hand. Yanked from his grip, his finger pulled against the trigger. The gun fired a single shot.

***

Balooga and Josh looked in the direction of the gunshot. Neither of them breathed, their chests tight with fear. The noise rushed up along the mountainside, reverberating as it went by them. They continued to trace its pathway upwards. Once the sound reached its zenith, beyond the mountain peak, the thinner air around the crest seemed to increase its amplitude. And for a few seconds the pistol-shot echoed noisily from one side of the valley to the next.

Josh turned to Balooga and whispered, "Anna."

"Fernandez," Balooga whispered back.

Both men looked towards the base of the complex. They stood motionless, their thoughts turned to their respective partners.

Fearful for Anna's safety, Josh took a step away from the detective and pushed his way through the powdered snow.

"Sawyer, where the hell are you going?" Balooga asked, taking a step closer to the young man.

The cabin nearest to them lurched sideways with an audible groan. Josh heard the noise and turned back to watch as the derelict structure shook and rocked about.

Josh turned his gaze upwards, beyond the cabin, and witnessed a huge wall of darkness descend upon them. For a second his blood turned colder than the snow around him. Then, with trembling lips, he muttered, "… Avalanche…"

"What?" Balooga asked.

Josh gripped the detective's padded sleeve. "AVALANCHE!" he shouted.

Balooga had a second to remain confused before he heard the deep rumble of hundreds of tons of snow.

"God Almighty," he moaned.

"COME ON!" Josh yelled.

He tugged at the detective's arm and managed to pull them both away from the advancing wall. Together now, they bounded down the mountainside. Not daring to look back, Josh waded his way through the snow with the detective at his side. The rumble behind him grew louder, and as he passed the derelict cabins, only a few seconds elapsed before he heard them crack and split as the moving wall smashed them to pieces.

"THIS WAY!"

Josh spotted Balooga cutting a path diagonally across the mountainside. Understanding at once that the detective was trying to outrun the more powerful centralised part of the avalanche, he changed direction and followed his lead.

He ran past another structure. This time he heard it disintegrate almost instantly. The wave of snow was suddenly at his back. His legs were thrown out from under him. He fell backwards to land heavily onto something that was both flat and solid. Throwing his arms out, he lost the gun, instead gripping onto the edges of a detached wooden door, holding on for dear life. He rode the crest of the solid wave like some insane surfer.

The door twisted sideways, and Josh found himself heading at great speed towards a large cabin. He shut his eyes and waited for the deadly impact. Instead of the expected bone-breaking crunch, he felt a slight bump as the door connected with a rock, which changed his direction. Rather than smashing against the large obstruction, he bounced and skidded past, escaping death by barely an inch.

***

Anna watched as the colossal wall of snow headed towards her. She stepped down from the porch into driving wind. Her heart pounded with fear. She sensed the change grip her body. With a gnarled hand, she pulled the agent to his feet.

"GET OFF!" Fernandez cried, witnessing her face change.

"SILENCE!" she snapped though jagged teeth.

The agent pulled his arm free, then stumbled over the steps and landed heavily on his back. It was only then that he noticed the ground below him trembled fiercely. He looked out into the night and spotted the advancing avalanche.

"Oh shit," he moaned.

The beast in front of him held out its arm. "C'mon. We need to move," it said.

Equally terrified by the vision standing before him, as he was by the one beyond, Fernandez rolled over and began to pull himself inside the cabin.

"You fool!" Anna snapped.

Ignoring her, the agent disappeared over the threshold.

"Idiot!" she called to him.

Then she sensed the danger was only seconds away. She sprang upwards, somersaulting backwards and landing on top of the cabin. From her vantage point, she watched as the huge wall of white powder rolled towards her. Then, unbelievably, she saw Josh riding the wave strapped to a wooden door. She almost laughed at the absurdity, but then she realised he was about to smash against the cabin.

"JOSH, JUMP!" she yelled to him.

Anna moved to the edge of the overhang. The first of the snow slammed up against the cabin. She launched herself into the air. She twisted in midair then reached out, as Josh passed beneath her, and pulled him from his ride. The wooden door shot from under him. It shattered against the side of the cabin with a mighty crack.

Falling into the churning snow both Josh and Anna were dragged down.

And the world around them disappeared.

Chapter Forty-Three

Balooga found himself stuck hip deep in a drift of frozen snow. Tugging at his legs, he managed to free them by a couple of inches only.

"Shit," he breathed.

Finding it difficult to move, due to the pack strapped tightly onto his back, he took a couple of minutes to undo the straps. Eventually, he shrugged out of the bothersome rucksack. Then, using his big, meaty hands as shovels, he began to dig the snow out from around his legs. After a couple of minutes, and, just before his hands froze solid, he pulled himself clear.

He crawled away from the small pit where his legs had been. Then slid along the surface on his stomach, until he felt the snow underneath him harden. Confident the packed snow would hold his weight now, he climbed to his knees and stood. He scanned around the bleak landscape. A pure, untarnished blanket of snow covered the entirety of the mountain base. He looked out but found nothing of the old skiing complex.

"Great. Just great," he grumbled.

He began to trudge down the mountainside, in the futile hope of finding either the agent or one of the two fugitives alive. He reached the bottom of the hill where the snow began to soften. His legs sank knee deep, which forced him to push his way slowly through the heavy mush.

The detective reached where he thought the centre of the complex should be. He stopped in his tracks and spun full circle, looking for any sign of life. Finding none, he leaned back and sat heavily into the snow.

A hand shot out from the snow in front of him.

Balooga jumped to his feet and watched as another hand appeared. In seconds, the hands had grown into arms. Balooga waded up to the flailing arms, and clawed away at the snow until he had revealed a dark mop of wet, tangled hair. A desperate inhalation of air sounded. Pulling at the arms, he helped drag the woman clear.

She lay at his side, shivering uncontrollably. After a few seconds, she managed to mumble, "Josh," and then point towards the hole.

The detective leaned over, looked inside the small void and found another rigid limb. He reached into the freezing maw and grabbed the arm, then yanked at the limp form. He struggled to free the body from the icy grip, his fingers slipping on clammy flesh. Suddenly the woman was at his side. Together they pulled Josh from the snow's frozen embrace.

"Is he breathing?" Anna asked.

Balooga saw a weak plume of breath escape from between blue lips. "Yeah, I think so." They pulled him away from the icy hole.

Balooga gazed at the woman. He looked upon her beautiful face but knew what he beheld was really some wicked devil.

"What of Fernandez?" he asked, holding his fear in check.

"Who?"

"The FBI agent."

"He was in the cabin," Anna explained.

"And where's that?" Balooga asked, but knew it could be anywhere, and that the agent must surely be lost.

"I don't know. You're probably sitting on it," she said.

His fear shifted to anger. "Real fucking funny."

"I'm not trying to be funny," she snapped back.

"Yeah? Well, it sounds like that to me."

"Hell, if you two assholes hadn't shown up then none of this would have happened!"

"Really? Well if you hadn't murdered half a dozen people within the last two days then we wouldn't be here!"

"I haven't murdered anyone, they all deserved to die!"

"Christ. You really are a monster!"

"Quiet!" someone hissed.

They both fell silent.

Josh pushed himself up onto one elbow. "What the hell are you trying to do? Bring the whole goddamn mountain down?"

"Hey, you're okay," Anna said, instantly forgetting the brief confrontation.

"Yeah, what happened?"

"Some idiot triggered an avalanche," she said, and looked at the detective reproachfully.

"Who?"

"I'm not sure, some FBI agent?" Anna said, turning to the detective.

"Sebastian Fernandez," Balooga announced. "And don't worry, he's probably dead too."

"What the hell are you talking about?" Josh asked, seeing the cop's hostility.

"Just someone else you can add to your list," Balooga spat.

"What list?" Josh asked through chattering teeth.

"The list of dead bodies you two seem intent on compiling."

"What's he on about?"

She glanced at Josh with eyes full of sadness. "Stupid idiot triggered the avalanche." Her shoulders dropped as she guessed the agent's fate. "I tried to help him but he wouldn't listen." She released a sigh as the burden of another lost soul descended upon her. "I'm sorry, Detective. There was nothing I could do."

"Yeah, I bet you are," he scorned, unconvinced by her sincerity.

"Listen, Detective, I take no pleasure in the loss of a good man."

"Cut the crap, I know exactly what you are," Balooga countered.

"Really? And what's that?"

Before Balooga could answer, Josh spoke. "Anna, wait a minute. You still can help him."

"How?" Anna asked.

Josh pulled himself up and took her hands. "Are you sure he's dead?"

Looking around at the whitewashed ground, Anna said, "He must be. Look, there's nothing left."

"Where was he when the snow hit?"

"Inside the cabin."

"So he may have gained some protection?"

"Josh, the cabin's gone."

"Yeah, I know. But he may not be," Josh said, excitement and hope forming his face into a mask of determination. He climbed to his feet and looked at the sea of blank snow.

"Honey, even if he did survive the impact, then you'll never find him."

"Not me – you," Josh said.

"What?"

He pulled Anna to her feet. "Listen, if he's alive then you can find him."

"How?"

"By feeling his emotions."

"Christ, this is bullshit," Balooga moaned.

"Silence," Anna commanded. She took a moment to scan around the bleak landscape.

"Okay, but where do we begin?" she asked.

"Right here," Josh suggested, pointing to his feet.

***

Air and cold. Too much of one and not enough of the other. These two factors would eventually lead to Sebastian Fernandez's demise. He lay in total darkness, the air around him thinning and the cold that gnawed at his skin growing. He tried to move his hand in an attempt to shift the mass that weighed heavily across his chest, but his arm remained pinned uselessly at his side. His shallow breathing increased as fear gripped his heart, which added to the already crushing pressure. Cocooned inside this icy tomb, the agent lay terrified and alone.

***

Anna stopped in her tracks, turned to her side and took a couple of steps away from Josh. She began to wade her way back in the direction from which she'd come, cutting a second trench through the snow. Josh stayed a couple paces behind her and followed in silence. Seated in his cold hollow, Balooga watched with curious interest.

Seeing Anna come to an abrupt halt, both men held their breath. However, after only a moment's pause, she continued towards the end of the boundary. She turned and started to cut a third channel.

Josh watched as Anna struggled to remain focused as she battled against the deluge of snow. "Anna, wait," he said, and moved to take the lead.

"Josh, you're too close," Anna warned, able to read his emotions.

"Wait a minute," he ordered.

In a combination of pumping legs and flailing arms, Josh began to clear a pathway for Anna to follow. He reached about ten feet in front of her before signalling for her to continue. Anna now moved along Josh's cleared pathway and inched her way over the powdered earth. She continued with her slow and methodical search until eventually she sensed something beneath her feet. Dropping to her knees, she thrust her hands into the snow. She closed her eyes, deep in concentration. She frowned.

"What is it?" Josh whispered.

"Shush!" she hissed towards him.

He fell quiet and watched.

Anna closed her eyes for a second time and concentrated on shutting out the sounds and smells of the night. After a few minutes, she succeeded in reducing the world around to silence.

Then she turned her full attention to the frozen earth. Her mind and soul drifted slowly downward as she began to search for the lost agent.

At first she felt only a vast emptiness radiate from under her numb fingertips. Then, just as she was about to reach the compact soil far below her, she sensed the rapid pounding of a heart. She focused on the distraught being, directing her concentration until all that consumed her consciousness was the rhythmic beat of life. For a brief second she thought she'd found the agent, but then the trapped being's terrified thoughts revealed a vision of unintelligible images, and she realised she'd found only the cold imprisonment of a buried animal.

"Damn!"

She allowed herself only the briefest of sorrow for the doomed animal before shifting her attention away. She took three further steps before dropping to her knees for a second time. A more powerful and recognizable fear emanated from below.

"Josh – here!" she called.

Josh rushed over to find Anna scooping away great handfuls of snow. He dropped down beside her and began to eagerly claw away at the compacted powder. He dug away with his good hand. Between them they rapidly cut out a deep hollow. Labouring beside her, he caught a glimpse of blurred talons. Rather than feeling either dread or revulsion, he felt only relief.

"Hurry, Josh. We're running out of time," Anna warned.

"Enough of this charade," Balooga spat, now joining them.

Josh ignored the detective, returned to the hole and continued to dig. Within minutes, he felt his strength begin to waver. Unable to dig away at the harder snow, he instead took position behind Anna, using the plaster cast on his arm to shovel away the excess.

Balooga stood and watched this crazed performance for a minute or so, and briefly thought they were actually digging out a fresh grave – perhaps his own – but then he caught the look of grim determination and panicked urgency on the woman's face. Instantly, he understood. He dropped down beside her and joined them.

"About time," Anna breathed.

Both Anna and Balooga clawed away at the snow as Josh worked the excess out over the rim, and eventually they dug deep enough to reach the remnants of a wooden structure.

"Wait," Anna called.

Both men stopped.

"Here, help me with this," she said, with a new urgency.

Balooga watched as her malformed hands wrapped themselves around a partially exposed wooden beam. He paused, fearful of the woman's abnormalities. However, realising they were close to Fernandez, he pushed his anxiety away and joined her by the timber.

"Okay. When I say go, we go – right?" Anna asked.

"Right," Balooga agreed.

He forced his own fingers down alongside the beam, then readied himself and waited for her command. He sensed her arms tense with effort and heard her suck in a lungful of air.

"NOW!" she ordered.

Together, they heaved at the wooden beam. Expecting them to work one end of the timber free, Balooga was surprised when he began to hear the wood splinter. He looked down between his hands and found cracks appearing along the surface of the timber. He almost stopped, shocked by the woman's strength, but, feeling the wood was about to give, he redoubled his efforts. The beam split in two to reveal a dark void beneath. Like rotten teeth the two halves of the beam protruded upwards, leaving an open wound between.

Anna squatted over the dark void. She scraped away more snow until she had formed a hole large enough for her to fit through.

"Anna – wait. I'll go," Josh volunteered.

"No way," Balooga objected. "You ain't leaving me up here with her."

"It's okay, Josh. You wouldn't be able to see anyway," Anna said.

"Okay, but be careful," Josh responded.

She offered him a brief smile before lowering herself into the darkness.

***

Anna dropped into the icy crevice. She found herself in the centre of a small cavity, formed by the remnants of the log cabin and a wall of compacted snow. Although she could make out one or two vague shapes or angles, the darkness that filled the hollow hid most of the contents. She closed her eyes, clearing her mind of the darkness that surrounded her. Within seconds she had focused upon the weak beat of a human heart.

Extending her arm in front of her, she used her hand like an insect's antenna to trace the surfaces around her. She moved as quickly as possible as she crawled further into the cavity. The makeshift ceiling sloped downward. Which forced her to crawl on her elbows and stomach. Eventually she reached the narrowest part of the hollow. Her hand felt flesh.

"Agent Fernandez, are you alright?"

"Who's there?" the agent replied weakly.

"I'm here to help."

"I can't breathe. There's no air."

"It's okay, just relax."

She heard a pitiful wheeze.

"No air…" Fernandez rasped.

Understanding the hole she had dug out would offer sufficient ventilation, Anna was temporarily confused by the agent's inability to draw breath. Then, as she traced her hand over his torso, she felt the solid outline of a wooden beam.

"Take it easy," she advised, "I'm going to have to shift some of this wreckage."

"I'm suffocating," the agent managed to say.

"No you're not. Just take short breaths, and relax."

Anna took hold of one of his hands and offered him a gentle reassurance. After a couple of minutes of continued labouring, the agent managed to gain control of his breathing.

"That's it. Good," Anna said. "I'm going to move something."

She took hold of the timber and heaved upwards. But was unable to gain sufficient leverage due to the tight slope of the ceiling.

"I'm gonna have to find a better position," she told the agent.

She shuffled her body away from him and twisted onto her back, then positioned her feet on either side of the wooden obstruction. Tensing her thighs, she thrust her legs upwards. The timber moved. She pushed further until she felt her legs lock. The beam moved away from the agent. Pinned by the weight, she said, "Fernandez, you're gonna have to crawl out."

"I don't think I can move," he moaned.

"Try," she ordered.

Fernandez pushed himself away from the frozen wall, flopping feebly onto his side. He lay motionless for a moment, pain rendering him immobile. The agony finally subsided enough for him to crawl out of the tight crevasse.

Anna felt the agent pass by her side. She relaxed her legs and let the wooden timber drop to the hard floor. She followed in the same direction as the agent. Together, they clambered towards the centre of the cavity, until they reached the small hole above them.

The agent released a sigh of relief at the sight of weak light.

"How do we get out?" he asked.

"I'm going to lift you up," Anna said.

Heaving him up towards the hole, she extended her arms until his head had cleared. She felt the weight of the agent freed from her grasp as he was roughly pulled from the hollow.

"Careful," Anna called. "He's injured."

She crouched down with the intention of springing towards the gap. An arm appeared through the small hole stopping her short. She stood to her full height, reached out and took the hand. With effortless strength, she was pulled from the icy womb.

Dropping to her knees, she took in a deep, cleansing breath.

She surprised herself by rubbing her hand across the surface of the snow, as if trying to wipe away an unwanted sensation. It was then that she noticed Balooga was off to her side, bent over a crumpled shape.

Josh!

Her eyes turned upward and witnessed a vision from ages past.

"Hello, Anna. It's been a while… "

Chapter Forty-Four

"Jonus… " Anna gasped.

The pale, emaciated face above her split into a triumphant leer. "Back from the dead," Jonus said, and his lips peeled away from his perfect teeth.

Anna reared back. She felt the dark valley walls close in around her and found herself struggling to draw breath. She looked over to Balooga. Josh hadn't moved an inch. She choked, "What have you done?"

Jonus saw her discomfort and he laughed heartily into the open night sky. "What, you're not pleased to see me?"

"No… " she moaned, thinking the worst had befallen Josh.

"Don't worry, I've let him live – for now," Jonus said.

She looked in the other direction and spotted the unconscious form of Fernandez, who was face down and partially covered by a layer of snow.

"But you being here – it's impossible," she finally managed to say.

"No, my child, this was inevitable, and I'm afraid inescapable," Jonus offered. With the pretence of sorrow, he added, "It is a shame it has come down to just you and me."

Anna faced her old adversary, confused and disorientated.

"But I killed you," she said, still trying to understand.

"No, my beautiful friend, you only … postponed my ascent into greatness and immortality."

Anna recovered from her initial shock. "I see the years have done nothing for your mind. You still rant like a lunatic."

A twinkle of madness flashed across his eyes in acknowledgment of her comment. Then, as his blood-red lips parted, he said, "Child, where we are headed only the insane and depraved will survive."

"Then you'll fit right in."

"Yes, I intend to. But first there is something I need."

Anna understood at once that he meant her heart. She took a step back, holding her arms protectively across her chest.

"Come, child, I will make it quick and painless."

"Stay back," she warned.

"My dear, it is time to relinquish the gift."

"It's not yours to have," Anna snapped back, with an added edge of spitefulness.

"You're wrong. It has always belonged to me. You've only been its keeper until the time came."

"What?"

Jonus looked upon her. "You still don't understand what this is all about?"

"All what?"

"You. Me. This. Everything."

"What have you become Jonus, a prophet?"

He tilted his bleached skull towards the stars, then closed his eyes and stood there for a moment, bathing in moonlight. Finally, he opened them to say, "I guess you deserve enlightenment before I take your soul."

"Educate me."

"Do you know what we are or how we came to be?"

Anna simply said, "I have always been – that's all."

Jonus offered her a slight shake of his head. "No, my dear, you have not. Your origins are the same as mine."

"So tell me."

"We were put upon this earth for a purpose and a great responsibility was bestowed upon us."

"Which was?"

"To serve."

"What?" Anna asked, stunned. "Me – serve? Ridiculous!"

"Fear not, our Master is no mortal man."

"I serve no one," Anna spat.

Anna's statement caused Jonus to release a great roar of laughter. "You fool! You have done nothing but serve."

"Enough of this. Speak the truth."

"The truth is, you and I have spent the last two thousand years amassing an army," Jonus explained.

"An army of what?"

"Of souls!"

"You're crazy."

"Maybe, but at least not blind," Jonus said. "Why do you think we must take the souls of these men to survive?"

Anna stood and tried to find an answer to his question, but eventually she could only respond with a question of her own.

"Why?"

"Because of our true purpose. Anna, we are the creatures of the one and only true god."

"The ramblings of a fool!"

"You are the fool, my dear. Only now, at the end, will you understand your true potential and objective. We have spent aeons helping our Master to prepare for the coming of the real Messiah."

"What?"

"The Dark King!" Jonus said, with uncharacteristic attachment.

***

Josh shook his head and tried to clear away the dull throbbing under his skull. He looked up and found the detective standing over him.

"What happened?"

"I don't know, some asshole appeared and you took a swipe at him," Balooga replied.

"Jonus!" Josh gasped. He grabbed Balooga's arm and pulled

himself up out of the snow.

"Easy, kid. You got tagged pretty hard," Balooga warned.

"I'm okay. We've got to help Anna."

"Wait. Who the hell is this guy?"

"He's the guy from her apartment, the one I told you about."

"What?"

"The guy who killed those two cops."

"Son-of-a-bitch," the detective snapped.

Balooga turned away from Josh and strode towards Anna and the figure that stood before her.

"Wait," Josh called. "Be careful!"

***

"The Dark King?" Anna repeated.

"Yes," Jonus confirmed, his eyes awash with divine madness. "Don't you see? We are *his* children."

"This is lunacy. You're talking like a weak-minded fool," Anna told him.

"No. I know this to be true. Can you not see? They," – he pointed towards the detective and Josh – "they are created in their frail and foolish God's image, as we are created in our strong and powerful Master's."

The two men drew near, and Anna raised a cautionary hand. They stopped, remaining at a safe distance, but within earshot. She turned her attention back to Jonus.

"This is lunacy. You actually believe we are the children of… the Beast?"

"Are we not strong and beautiful, but also created in the image of the Beast?" Jonus asked, referring to their true inner face.

"Maybe in some ways – yes."

"And was our Master not cast out of the heavens for recognising and embracing his strength and beauty?"

"Yes," she agreed. "But this is just coincidence."

"No," Jonus said. "I know this to be true, for I have witnessed the presence of our Master. When you left me to die, he appeared and offered his hand. And with his guidance, I regained my strength. Oh, if it wasn't for his love I would surely have descended into madness."

"Really?" Anna said, with a hint of mockery. "So you are his Chosen One?"

"Indeed!"

"Then who am I?" she asked.

Jonus stepped closer to raise a condemning finger. "You? You are a traitor!"

"What?"

"Yes, a traitor. You always did have an affiliation for these pathetic bugs. I knew you'd end up becoming one of them. Now you hide behind your conscience and a forged soul."

"I don't understand," Anna said.

"You and I are all that remains from an order of twelve," Jonus said.

"Twelve?"

"Yes, twelve disciples!"

"What?"

"Twelve disciples," Jonus repeated. "We were put upon this earth to prepare for the coming of the real Messiah."

"What the hell are you talking about?"

"Come, child, you know of whom I speak," Jonus said. "For the hour of fulfilment is near… "

"My God! You mean the Antichrist," she declared.

"Yes, my beautiful friend, the birth of the true King of Kings is almost upon us."

"Jonus, have you lost your mind?"

"No, I have only gained my purpose and reason for this world."

"Which is?"

"To protect our Master's son until he is of age," Jonus replied. "But first I need to prove my worthiness."

"How?"

"By taking your heart," he told her. He took a step closer, looming towards her like some beautiful but demented fallen angel.

"Wait!" Anna commanded. "You said I'd become a traitor. How?"

"It seems you strayed from the flock." Jonus's bleached face split into a contortion of false concern. "But don't worry – you still served our Master, even in your ignorance. For you have bestowed upon Him a great number of dark souls."

"You lie," Anna challenged.

"No, I speak the truth. For over a thousand years you have fed upon the wicked and immoral, and bestowed their power upon our Master. You see, he turned *your* weakness into *His* strength. You thought you were doing God's work – when all along you've only served your true purpose."

"No," Anna protested. "You lie."

"Oh, if only you'd embraced your true self and not surrounded yourself with these foolish men. You have become blinded by your own morality. I am amazed you have come this far. But even in your ignorance, your instinctive drive has accomplished part of the task."

"What task?"

"The task of reducing the order of twelve to just one. One powerful and mighty victor, who will lead the Master's infant son towards his rightful crown."

"You're crazy," Anna scoffed.

Jonus offered her a shake of his head. "No. Think what you have already done. You took the Viking King Ragnar's soul. Why?"

"Because of the gift of sunlight," Anna responded.

"And what good would a chaperon be if he cowered in the shadows of twilight?"

"What are you saying?"

"That only the strongest will be allowed to serve. You see, our Master is skilful. He understands weakness – weaknesses like that of Tomas, Peter and Judas Iscariot!"

"Disciples…" Anna said.

"Yes," Jonus agreed. "But all abandoned Christ. Oh, the irony.

God's own vanity was to become his son's eventual demise. Why surround Christ with twelve, when one would do?"

"You have lost your mind," Anna rebuffed, but somewhere deep inside her she felt the awakening of truth.

"Yes – open yourself to the reality," Jonus told her. "You cannot escape your destiny. This is what we were created for. You must serve our Master."

"No, my purpose must be something other than that of a foolish pawn."

The weight of this terrible fate consumed her thoughts, and she felt her limbs become weak. She took a step back and almost fell to her knees with despair.

"Anna, don't listen to him!"

She looked across the bleak and empty landscape and her eyes found Josh.

Josh stepped closer. "He's lying. This is a trick."

"Silence, bug!" Jonus commanded. "For you have already served your purpose and I will gladly send you to our Master."

"Enough of this bullshit," Josh snapped, and he moved to stand beside Anna.

Before he could reach her, Jonus spoke: "… It was allowed to give breath to the image of the beast, so that it could speak, and could cause all who would worship the image to be put to death. Moreover, it caused everyone, great and small, rich and poor, slave and free, to be branded with the mark on his right hand or forehead… "

"I don't understand. What is he saying? Josh asked.

Balooga stepped closer. "He's quoting from the Book of John."

"The what?" Josh asked.

"It's the Book of Revelations. He's telling you, you carry the mark of the Beast," Balooga explained.

Although Josh did not fully understand Balooga's or Jonus's comments, he began to grasp some of their intended meaning. A sudden chill of dread washed over him. He raised his right arm and looked upon the cracked cast. Then, with trembling fingers, he traced the outline of the stitches that marked his brow.

"Dear God," he murmured, "this can't be." He looked up and caught Anna's gaze. "Anna, is this true?"

She opened her mouth but words escaped her.

"Yes, bug, you have been nothing more than a stupid puppet, manipulated in order to aid my Master in his plan to rid himself of this wretched whore."

"No," Josh breathed, disbelievingly. "You're wrong."

Jonus released a heartless chuckle. "Even when the truth is revealed, you still doubt?"

"But why and for what purpose?" Anna finally asked. "You could have killed me at my apartment. Why engineer this whole charade?"

The pale face twisted itself into a gleeful leer. "Let's just say it was the final test. And I passed."

"Not yet," Balooga said, stepping closer. "You said… *'It was allowed to give breath to the image of the beast, so that it could speak, and could cause all who would worship the image to be put to death'…*"

"That's right, bug," Jonus acknowledged.

"So you're saying this kid bears the mark of the Beast. And in helping her, the true image of the Beast, to stay alive, then he also unwittingly helped to slay those who worship the image. Which means those who are evil, right?"

"The three street punks and Trixybell," Anna gasped.

"Anna, they were all bad. You said it yourself," Josh said, adding a deeper agony to Anna's heart. "You *have* only taken the wicked and immoral."

"Clever bugs are finally beginning to understand," Jonus said, with an exaggerated slow clap of his skeletal hands.

"So if they only kill evil to strengthen your Master, then who killed those two cops at her apartment?" Balooga asked.

"Why me," Jonus said, and his clapping quickly turned to enthusiastic applause.

"I already said it was him," Josh told the detective.

"I know you did, son. I just wanted to hear it from him."

Ignoring the two men, Jonus stepped up to Anna. "Now let's end this legacy and bring about the new era."

"You rush towards subservience and obedience with surprising conviction," she said, straightening.

Jonus stopped short and offered her a brief flash of white teeth. "No, Anna, I rush towards an eternity of fulfilment. Our Master's son will not be an infant forever. Once my work is done, I will bathe in the blood of the hunt. Just think! I'll be able to hunt endless prey, day or night, without fear of reprisal!"

"You must be dying with excitement," Anna mocked.

"Indeed," Jonus said. "Now it is time for you to join the rest of your brethren. For you are the last!"

Chapter Forty-Five

Jonus closed in on Anna. His body shuddered as it underwent an immediate transformation. His jaw buckled outwards into an open maw of sharp teeth. As his mouth swelled forward, it pulled elongated ears downwards and stretched them into crude points. The flesh of his nose shrivelled up towards his brow, which left two gaping nostrils in the centre of this hideous mask. He flexed powerful talons.

Anna stepped back, but resisted the change that threatened to descend upon her. Still confused by Jonus's revelations, she spoke in an attempt to buy herself more time.

"But this can't be. If we were once twelve, including Ragnar, then what of the other nine?"

"I have been busy these last one thousand years," Jonus began. "One by one, I have reduced the fold until all that stands between me and greatness is… *you*." The memories of his slain brethren eased their way inside his fevered mind, and Jonus's deformed face split into a mask of unbridled pleasure.

"How can you take pleasure in killing your own kind?" Anna asked, sickened by his satisfaction.

"Come, Anna. I am aware you took the powers of two."

"Two?"

"Enough of this. I know you took Ragnar and the bastard Vlad Tepes."

"Ragnar was *your* doing, and Tepes was a butcher of innocents. He had to die. Had I known what he was, I may have let him live. Even his atrocities would pale in comparison with those to come."

***

Balooga's mind began to work overtime. Some of what these two adversaries were saying had started to make sense. He pulled the small clear bag from his pocket and looked upon the single name found there.

Something worked its way inside his mind. Another name, and its meaning. Suddenly, he comprehended what great significance this name had.

"Carl Dua," he said, looking towards Anna.

Anna looked towards the detective. "What?"

"Think," Balooga said. "What it means."

She stood momentarily confused. Then understanding took over.

"Yes, of course," she said confidently. She turned her attention back towards Jonus then. "This legacy will only be fulfilled *if* we stand as one?"

"Yes," Jonus replied.

"So the Antichrist cannot be, unless one of us falls tonight?"

"Correct."

Anna's face split into a consuming but bitter smile. "Then come and claim your heritage."

She stood proud and then relinquished her soul to the change. Her normally beautiful features popped and cracked into a misshapen and shocking visage.

For a deafeningly quiet moment nothing moved, apart from one or two solitary snowdrops that found their way onto the canvas of snow. Finally, with a mighty bellow, Jonus shattered the silence as he launched himself towards her.

Feeling his rage and excitement, she sidestepped to her left and sent him sprawling behind her. Instantly, he sprang to his feet, lunged in, and clawed a series of gashes into her back. She screamed in anger. The agony of torn skin ripped its way into her flesh. Jonus saw her distress, so he attacked again in a blur of razor-sharp nails. One of his deadly claws struck towards her face. Anna caught sight of the pending assault. She arched her back further and watched the attack pass over her by a fraction of an inch. Springing back, she swiped her nails across his hideous face. Her offensive was fast, cutting a deep wound across his throat.

"Bitch!" Jonus spat, through a mouthful of hot blood.

"I see you're as slow and cumbersome as ever," Anna mocked.

He spat out a wad of red phlegm then grinned, revealing a row of blood-coated fangs. "Perhaps, but I have some new tricks."

They stood stationary, both waiting for an opening. Then Anna darted in and aimed for Jonus's exposed side. She raked her hand towards his ribs. A surprising heaviness wrapped itself around her arm. She watched as her arm froze in mid-space. For a second she thought the world around her had ground to a halt. Yet, she heard a clear and urgent warning, and the only thing to have stopped was, amazingly, herself.

"What is this...?" she breathed.

She blinked, for around her arm she witnessed a shimmering of translucent energy. Unable to move now, she stood frozen to the earth, outstretched like some ghoulish scarecrow.

Jonus hit her with a bone-crunching *thwack*, which knocked her head back and sent her senses reeling. The second his punch landed, she was released from her invisible constraints, and she fell backwards into the soft snow.

***

Josh saw that Anna had become disorientated and unable to defend herself. He clawed his way through the earth before lunging towards Jonus.

Jonus caught the assault from the corner of his eye. He flung his hand out, palm flat and, muttering incomprehensibly in some long-dead tongue, he constructed an unseen barrier between himself and his attacker.

323

Josh hit the invisible obstacle and came to an immediate stop. He fell instantly to the floor as if he had actually struck a brick wall. With the wind knocked from his lungs, he collapsed in a heap, desperately trying to suck in air.

Balooga witnessed this extraordinary event. "God Almighty…"

"I don't think He's listening tonight," Jonus offered.

He reached out with his cruel hand and yanked Anna to her feet. "How do you like my new tricks?" he asked.

"Real impressive," Anna managed to scoff, before another powerful blow sent her backwards.

Jonus's drenched hair flapped wildly around his ghastly face as he waded through the snow.

"This is fun," Anna remarked in mock bravado.

Jonus roared, infuriated by her audacity. He gripped a handful of her hair. Anna used his momentum against him. As she was roughly pulled to her feet, she folded her arm inwards and unleashed a blow to his head. Unable to stop her sudden attack, Jonus heard a sickening crunch as her elbow landed. The hard bone of Anna's arm hit him squarely in the face, reducing the soft flesh of his nose to a bloodied and painful pulp.

"Bidch!" Jonus snorted through his ruined nose.

"I like your new face better than your tricks," Anna said.

"Bidch!"

In a blind rage, Jonus threw himself at her. She caught him in mid-flight and in a tangled heap they fell into the snow.

Anna threw her arms over her face and managed to ward off Jonus's frantic attack. She forced her leg underneath his body and kicked him off, sending him flying. Jumping to her feet, she pursued him across the barren landscape. Then, unexpectedly, a large white shape blocked her path.

"Freeze!" Balooga warned.

During the commotion, he had managed to retrieve Fernandez's secondary firearm from the agent's ankle holster, and now stood pointing it at Jonus.

"You fool," Anna said, watching Balooga train the small gun on her foe.

"Don't worry, Sweetheart, this baby packs a punch," Balooga told her.

Jonus climbed to his feet and stepped in front of the lieutenant's outstretched arm. He moved closer until he was only three feet from the gun.

"Hold it right there," Balooga ordered.

In an exaggerated performance, Jonus raised his hands above his head. "Don't shoot." He froze with his arms in the air as if in submission. Then his jaws opened and a huge roar of laughter erupted from his mouth. "Do you think your puny toys can hurt me?" he snarled. "I'll kill you as easily as I did your two idiot friends."

Balooga clicked the hammer back before squeezing the trigger.

Jonus heard the sinews of Balooga's finger crack. Before the hammer hit the blasting-cap, he channelled his thoughts towards the muzzle. A silent flash of fire erupted from the barrel, followed by the deadly projectile. Jonus watched as the bullet whizzed towards him. The slug disintegrated in a shower of molten lead as it hit an invisible and impenetrable wall. With nowhere else to go the force created by the high velocity bullet reverberated back towards the detective's arm, taking the dissipating flames with it.

Balooga watched as flames rushed up his arm. He threw himself to the ground, plunging his burning arm into the snow, gasping at the mixture of agonising heat and intense cold.

***

Josh shook his head and regained his senses just in time to see Balooga's failed attack. He watched as the gun exploded in a flash of fire. Then, as the lieutenant dove to the ground, he saw the handgun spin through the air to disappear under a layer of snow. He climbed to his feet and bounded towards the fallen weapon.

He felt his leg slip through the snow below him, and finished half submerged in an icy embrace. Then, to his absolute horror, he felt the whole ground around him shudder with violent energy.

325

A mighty thunderclap exploded beneath him and the ground that held him fast disappeared, leaving a huge void of emptiness.

Chapter Forty-Six

Anna watched in horror as Josh vanished with the vast body of snow. She sprinted towards the chasm, avoiding a swipe from Jonus. She rolled underneath his attack and found herself at the edge of a newly formed abyss. Torn into the earth, the crevasse cut downwards in a deep and impenetrable darkness.

"Josh… No…"

"Anna…"

She spotted Josh hanging precariously from the wall, holding onto a piece of broken timber just four feet below her.

Josh clung onto the splintered beam that poked perilously from the icy wall. He hung on by one hand, his right arm dangling uselessly at his side. As he clutched at the timber, he felt himself pulled towards the dark bowels of the earth, and the darkness below him waited for his presence with impatient eagerness.

"Hold on," she called to him.

"I don't think I can."

"You've got to."

She crawled away from the chasm to quickly search around its edge. A short beam of wood protruded from the snow. She reached out to take it, but a hand snatched it away.

Jonus stood before her, holding the beam aloft. "Prepare to meet your Master," he said. Then, with tremendous might, he struck down at her head.

Anna saw the timber rush towards her but was unable to react quickly enough. It struck her across the side of the head.

A kaleidoscope of bright lights exploded in front of her eyes and her senses reeled. Blindly, she threw her arm up in an attempt to protect herself. She felt the bones of her arm snap. Her mouth opened and she released a scream of pain and anger. She tried to stand, but blow after blow kept her on her knees.

***

Balooga withdrew his hand from the snow to find it burnt and blistered. He pushed his pain aside, using his other hand to probe for the fallen weapon. He thrust his hand into the snow and raked his arm back and forth. Frantically searching, he heard a series of desperate screams. He paused and chanced a look up, to see Jonus beating the woman into submission.

Although he did not understand the full meaning of this conflict, he instinctively knew that it would become much worse if Jonus were to defeat her.

Knowing time was about to run out for the woman, he held his breath before closing his eyes. He offered up an urgent prayer and then thrust his fist towards the earth. A movement, like a snap of a cobra's head, halted the detective's hand. Wrapped around Balooga's wrist were the fingers belonging to a grey, unyielding hand.

"Fernandez… " Balooga mouthed, as he looked at the agent's ashen face.

A layer of pale, colourless flesh had replaced the FBI agent's normally dark skin. His lips were a deep blue and, as he opened them, a near inaudible sound tried to untangle itself from a plume of frosted breath.

"What?" Balooga asked, missing the agent's words.

Again, Fernandez spoke, but again Balooga missed his meaning. He leaned closer and lowered his ear to the agent's lips.

Scarcely able to draw breath, Sebastian Fernandez spoke: "… They shall walk with me in white, for so they deserve. He who is victorious shall thus be robed all in white; his name I will never strike off the roll of the living, for in the presence of my Father and his angels I will acknowledge him as mine… "

"What? I don't understand?" Balooga said.

Again, Fernandez managed to whisper his proclamation. With the last of his strength, he handed over the missing gun.

Balooga took the weapon. "Fernandez, what are you saying?"

The agent clutched at Balooga's sleeve. He laid his head back into the soft snow and closed his eyes. Before he passed out, he managed to whisper, "Have faith, Detective… Have faith… "

Balooga frowned in confusion. Then, as the agent's hand slipped away from his sleeve, he unexpectedly understood. He strode towards Jonus, stepping into range, and holding the gun out at arm's length. "Get away from her, you son-of-a-bitch," he ordered.

Jonus's bloodstained arm froze above his head. His ghastly face turned to the detective and he grunted with irritation.

"What now?"

Balooga stood with a newfound resolution; the moon crept out from around the peak of the mountain to cast a shard of light across the base of the valley. Furthermore, clad in his veneer of pure white clothing, the detective radiated a supreme and righteous glow.

"What is this?" Jonus asked, dazzled by the detective's brilliance.

"This is a message from two lost friends," the lieutenant said, before pulling the trigger.

The gun bucked in Balooga's hand.

Jonus threw his hand up in an attempt to block the deadly missile. However, instead of hitting the unseen barrier, the bullet travelled on. It passed beyond the incredible wall of energy before ripping a hole through his palm.

"Eat that," Balooga spat.

Stunned by the wound, Jonus peered through the ragged hole in his hand. Blinded now by the brilliant light that shone through the tattered wound, he clamped his eyelids shut, as if the glow was too much to bear. His hand dropped away. A rush of hot blood swelled into the back of his throat. He choked out a huge mouthful of crimson, then staggered back as his legs threatened to give. His torn hand rose to his mouth, and he spat out a small puddle of blood. The red liquid pooled in his palm for a second then it dripped through the bullet hole. Staining the snow at his feet. Reaching round to the back of his head, he probed with bloody fingers. To his horror, he discovered a huge hollow at the back of his neck.

"What have you done?" he rasped.

Then, as his eyelids fluttered with shock, he took another step back. His foot found the edge of the dark abyss and, with one final gurgling breath, he toppled over the edge.

Balooga stood motionless for a second. He heard the woman groan. He rushed over and knelt beside her. "Privalova, are you okay?"

She turned her head. "Josh. Help Josh," she breathed, pointing to the chasm.

Balooga scrambled over to the edge of the abyss and found Sawyer hanging from the icy wall.

"Help," Josh pleaded.

"Christ, kid. Hold on," Balooga advised.

"I'm slipping."

"Hold on," Balooga said. He thrust his blistered hand down. "Take it."

"I can't. Look," Josh responded, terror creeping into his throat. He forced Balooga's attention towards his plastered arm.

"Christ," Balooga cursed, as he looked upon a pale and fevered visage. Jonus hung from Josh's plastered arm, dangling like some hideous parasitic extension.

"I can't shake him," Josh groaned.

The pallid fiend was now trying to claw his way up the length of his arm.

"Privalova!" Balooga yelled.

Anna was at his side instantly.

"No," Anna gasped, seeing the vile figure. "Pull him up."

"I can't reach," Balooga replied.

She did a quick mental calculation. "Hold my legs!"

"What?"

"Hurry," she warned.

Lying on her front, she reached over the rim of the chasm and eased her way towards Josh and the piece of timber. Her hips passed over the edge. Before she fell further, a pair of strong hands fixed themselves to her thighs. Balooga held onto Anna's legs, pushing his own feet into the snow, anchoring them both at the lip of the crevice.

"Hold on Honey, I'm not gonna let you fall," Anna called.

With the extra weight of Jonus, Josh felt the dark emptiness of the abyss pull at him with greater enthusiasm. He desperately clung to the protruding beam, and his arm and shoulder screamed in agony. He clamped his eyes shut and focused the last of his energy on his rapidly failing fingers.

"Lower," Anna called to Balooga.

She felt herself drop by another foot or so. Her arm thrust out as she made a grab for him, but her fingers snatched around nothing but air.

Josh saw Anna's determined face. And, although the terror of falling had all but consumed him, he still felt a painful pang to his heart as he looked upon her battered and bruised face.

Enraged now, he shook his arm in an attempt to shake off the bastard that clung there. Pain erupted through his damaged shoulder, causing a sheen of cold sweat to pop out along the surface of his skin. His hand turned slick.

"I'm slipping."

"Hold steady," Anna said.

He regained his composure and maintained his hold, forcing his fingers to tighten.

Anna wriggled her hips and managed to gain another couple of inches. She reached out as far as she could, and felt the gnarled surface of the beam beneath her fingertips. She walked her fingers along it until she found Josh's clenched hand. "I've got you."

"Anna, hurry," Josh pleaded.

She tried to force her own fingers under his, but they were

fixed to the wood.

"Josh, you're going to have to let go."

He looked up. "No way."

She offered him a warm and gentle smile. "Trust me."

"Shit, I hate it when you say that," he told her. Then he held her gaze and said, "I love you."

"I love you too."

Fixed by each other's gaze for a moment, both were desperate to convey their feelings by thought alone. Finally, Josh offered her a slight nod of understanding. He took one last look at her beautiful face. Then closed his eyes.

"Fuck it."

He opened his hand and let go.

Anna watched as he began to fall. She reached out, but, instead of grabbing for him, she rammed her claws into the icy wall. Her nails dug into the frozen chasm and fixed themselves like miniature ice picks. Next, using her anchored arm, she pulled herself downwards along the surface and dropped deeper inside the abyss. She did all this within a millisecond. Her free hand thrust forward and she caught his wrist, halting his descent.

"I've got you," she said. Relief echoed throughout the chasm. She twisted her head and called to Balooga. "Pull us up!"

Josh watched as Anna disappeared over the lip. Before he knew it, he too cleared the abyss. He felt Anna snatch a handful of his jeans as he was roughly pulled over the edge by the seat of his pants. Clearing the lip, the weight of Jonus caused him to twist and slide so that he finished hanging face-first over the edge. He looked into Jonus's eyes and found something unexpected: fear.

"Please," Jonus said pitifully. He coughed and a globule of black drool leaked out onto his chin. "Please… help me," he begged.

Instinctively driven, Josh reached down with the intention of prizing Jonus free. Yet, as he looked into his desperate face, he knew he could not just coldheartedly send him to his death. Instead, he reached for the guy's hand.

"Josh – no," Anna said, now at his side.

"I can't just let him die," he told her.

"Why?"

"It's wrong."

"No, Josh, it's right. You've got to let him go."

"But wait. What about his blood. And daylight"

"Yes – yes!" Jonus said. "You need me."

"Wrong," Anna disagreed. She looked at Josh and broke into a merciless grin. "It doesn't matter. There is another!"

Stunned, Josh stared open-mouthed.

"What? No. Impossible!" Jonus cried.

Anna turned her attention back to her foe. "You always were an asshole. Vlad Tepes was nothing like us, he was a mere human!"

"No, he can't be," Jonus moaned.

Her face twisted itself into a mask of false compassion. "I'm afraid it's true. And now, my old friend, I must bid you farewell."

Anna reached over the edge and revealed an object that glittered with moonlight. She paused for a brief moment before plunging the metal implement into Josh's arm.

For a second, Josh misunderstood what she was doing. He watched as she thrust the sharp instrument into his arm and he almost cried for her to stop. Then, as she hacked away at the cracked plaster cast, he recognised the pair of scissors. Shocked by the appearance of the scissors for another second, Josh then remembered they were the same pair that he had hidden in his jeans pocket back on the train.

With single-minded determination, Anna slashed away at the tape and plaster. In seconds she had freed Josh from her adversary's vile grip.

Chapter Forty-Seven

Jonus appeared to remain frozen in space and time for a second before he snatched at Josh's unbound hand. However, the helping hand was quickly withdrawn and, instead of finding solace, he clutched at nothing but a dark emptiness. Like his heart, this dark emptiness held no mercy, pity, or understanding, and, offering no forgiveness, it instead sent him spinning into the abyss.

Josh and Anna watched in silence as Jonus disappeared into the deep chasm. His limp body bounced from one side of the abyss to the other, and it seemed like an eternity before his broken body was finally consumed by darkness. They felt neither pleasure nor happiness at his loss, but only a mixture of relief and sorrow.

Pushing themselves away from the edge, they joined Balooga. Together, they collapsed at the detective's side. For a while, all three fell silent, thoughtful.

Breaking the silence, Josh spoke first. "I don't understand. How did you know there was another?"

Anna pushed herself onto one elbow. She looked towards the detective. Too tired to speak, she offered him a slight nod, and the question was his.

Balooga acknowledged her request and then dug inside his pocket. He fished around inside his padded jacket for a while, eventually revealing a clear plastic bag. The small piece of burnt paper became visible.

"Because of this," he told them.

"What's that?" Josh asked.

Balooga paused for a moment. "I found it at her apartment," he finally replied.

Josh took the bag and read the single word written on the paper fragment.

"What's it mean?" he asked.

Balooga offered him a half-hearted laugh. "I can't believe you still don't see it."

"See what?"

"Christ, kid, where do you think the name Carl Dua comes from?"

Josh opened his mouth to tell the detective that he did not know. Before he spoke, though, the name printed on the paper released its secret.

"Carl Dua… It spells Dracula!" Josh exclaimed.

"Hurray," Balooga cried.

Pleased with this revelation, Josh lay with a ridiculous grin on his face. But almost as quickly as it had come, the grin slipped to a frown. He held the paper up. "But I still don't get it. What significance does this have?"

Anna found her voice. "Josh, do you know who Dracula was?"

"Yeah," he answered sheepishly.

"No, Josh, not the Hollywood version, but the *real* Dracula."

"Ah… No, not really," he replied.

"He was the prince of Romania who lived in the fifteenth century," Anna said. "He was also known as Vlad the Impaler, or by his more uncommon name, Vlad Tepes."

"And?"

"And he was only a man," she told him.

"But Jonus – he said this Vlad Tapes was like him."

"In spirit, maybe, but Jonus was an idiot. He didn't understand the true meaning of the word Dracula," Anna said.

"Which means?" Josh questioned.

"Which means, the son of Dracul," Balooga finished.

"Which means?" Josh repeated.

Balooga flicked his eyes heavenward. "If he was the son of

Dracul, then he must have been born, which means he must have been" – a slight pause – "a MAN."

"AMEN to that," Anna said.

"So there is another like him out there," Josh said, with an indication towards the dark abyss.

"If what Jonus has said is true, then unfortunately, yes," Anna responded.

They fell silent, absorbing the implications of this.

Balooga broke the silence. "What happens now?"

"That depends," Anna replied.

"On what?"

"On where *we* stand."

The detective became thoughtful. "If what I have seen tonight is any indication of what is to come, then we are headed towards dark times. Maybe it is not inevitable and can be undone, but all I know is that, if it does come down to a battle of good verses evil, then I do believe you are on the side of good."

Anna nodded in silent gratitude.

Balooga asked, "Remember when you asked me if I thought man was born inherently good?"

"Yes," Anna replied.

"Well, I still believe that he is. Just sometimes powers that are out of our control take over and the weak fall. But then there is the flip side to that."

"Go on," Anna said.

"I believe you and yours were created inherently bad, but somehow you became good. I only hope that if there is another like you out there, then he has become like you."

"It's possible," Anna agreed, but she did not totally believe it.

She stood and held out her hand. Josh took it and climbed to his feet. She looked into his eyes and at that moment she knew that, no matter what, he would stand beside her.

"Thank you," she told him.

"For what?" Josh asked.

"For what has passed and for what is to come," she said.

Josh laid his arm across her shoulders. He placed a gentle

kiss on her bloody cheek. She turned her face to his and offered him a deep, tender kiss. They embraced, both their souls finding shared warmth and comfort.

Standing in front of this extraordinary couple, Balooga felt surprisingly self-conscious and intrusive. The detective was eventually saved from their passionate embrace by a weak groan. He twisted to spot Sebastian Fernandez half buried under a blanket of snow.

"Jeez – Fernandez," he muttered, before dropping to the snow. He felt at the agent's throat and found a weak but steady pulse.

"Is he alright?" Anna asked, as she joined the detective.

"I'm not sure," Balooga replied.

She knelt beside the lieutenant and laid her hand on the agent's chest. "I think he's suffering from hypothermia," she said. "We need to get him to a hospital." She reached over with the intention of lifting him up, but Balooga caught her wrists, holding them tight.

"You have done enough," he insisted, "please, let me take him."

She felt his earlier feelings of hate and distrust dissipating, to be replaced now by respect and approval.

"If you need me, you know where to find me," he offered.

"Thank you, Detective."

He released her arms, and then quickly scooped Fernandez up. With ease, he threw the slight figure over his large shoulder.

"I guess this is goodbye."

"For now," Anna agreed.

The lieutenant turned to move away.

Josh called after him.

"What about this?" he asked, holding up the piece of paper.

Balooga stood thoughtful for a moment before saying, "That? I've never seen it before in my life."

"Oh, but isn't it evidence or something?" Josh asked.

"Nah – keep it. Call it a memento," Balooga told him, with an added wink. Then he made his way up the hillside, back towards Glenwood Springs.

Josh joined Anna. He took her hand and watched as the detective dwindled to a tiny white speck. Eventually, the speck blinked out.

"Do you think he's going to make it?" Josh asked.

"Who?"

"The agent."

"Somehow Josh, I think we're all going to make it."

"Amen to that," he said.

"C'mon, we must get away from here," she urged.

"But what about the gift of sunlight?"

Anna turned towards the abyss. "It's lost, for now."

"For now?"

"If Jonus is right and there is another, then they may hold the key to unlocking such a gift."

"So how do we find them?"

Anna paused for a moment. She tilted her head and listened to the night. Finally, she said, "Somehow Josh, I think they'll find us."

"Shit. Not again… " Josh said. "I think this is the beginning of something immense."

Anna released a soft chuckle. "Never a dull moment, hey?"

She leaned in and placed a kiss onto his cheek. Then she pulled away and quickly scanned their immediate surroundings.

"We'd better get going."

"Where?"

"Away from here," she said. "I don't know how Detective Balooga will explain what has happened here, but we can be sure the authorities will eventually come looking for us. They always do."

"Then I guess we should go."

"You're right," she agreed.

"Just one last thing," he said.

Josh stepped away from her and moved towards the edge of the abyss. Opening the plastic bag, he withdrew the small piece of burnt paper. He held his arm out and closed his eyes. He made a wish, or more correctly a deal, and then opened his hand to let the fragment drop. The piece of paper spun crazily around the chasm for a moment before the abyss finally accepted his offering. And, with a silent breath, it sucked the fragment into darkness.

He returned to her side. "Okay, can we please keep it boring, at least for a little while?"

Anna broke into a mischievous smile. "I guess we'll just have to wait and see what tomorrow brings."

Other titles by Paul Cave

For Everything A Reason – Joseph Ruebins is a natural-born fighter, a champion of his sport, yet no training could have prepared him for the events that were to follow at Madison Square Garden on the night of his ultimate fight. Ruebins had planned his retirement with precision and it wasn't supposed to be like this. Struck down by a sudden and debilitating stroke, Joseph finds himself in hospital; paralysed, fearful, and at the mercy of this cruel condition. Worse still, it quickly transpires that the sanctuary of the hospital is only temporary.

A killer is stalking these barren passageways. And, in a moment of brutality, Joseph's roommate is murdered in a vicious attack. Now an unwitting witness to this terrifying event, Joseph finds himself in mortal danger. Barely able to move or even communicate, he must summon every ounce of his strength in an attempt to outwit this cold-bloodied killer. Can this ex-champion of the world find a way, not only to survive, but also to protect his family – his life – his very existence..?

(978-0-956236-89-0 2QT Limited (Publishing) 2010)

Something of the Night –For years scientists had warned about the real possibility of a global strike from outer space: a global killer. Mathematicians had calculated that once in approximately every sixty million years the Earth has been hit by a meteorite of such proportions it drastically changes our climate, plunging the world into a decade of nuclear winters.

In a post-apocalyptic world in which the sun has been replaced by near-darkness, the few remaining survivors have been forced underground to protect themselves from the evil predators that roam the surface above.

Something else is out there, in the darkness, humanlike, but without a soul. Something that speaks intelligently, plans with cunning meticulousness and, just like its cousin, this new breed likes to hunt. Not the pitiful, scrawny livestock and wild animals that cling to life on the barren surface above. No, this new breed hunts for something far more rewarding . . . *US*

(978-1-908098-28-3 2QT Limited (Publishing) 2011)

www.ingramcontent.com/pod-product-compliance
Lightning Source LLC
Chambersburg PA
CBHW070427170726
48291CB00002B/392